VIRAGO
MODERN CLASSICS
462

ALEXANDRA KOLLONTAI (1872–1954), was one of the most famous women in Russian history. She was born in 1872 into an aristocratic liberal family. At the age of twenty she married Vladimir Kollontai, by whom she had one son. Her involvement in radical circles and her early preoccupation with women's emancipation created conflicts which caused her at the age of twenty six to leave her son and husband for a life of independent political action. She worked tirelessly for the revolution, and in 1917 was on the Central Committee of the Bolshevik party. One of the few to welcome Lenin from exile at the Finland Station, she became Commissar of Social Welfare – the only woman in Lenin's government.

Her political and personal life was always stormy: differences with Lenin forced her to leave the government in 1918: her two great loves, the revolutionaries Dybenko and Shlyapnikov, both died in the 1930s. Kollontai herself spent the last years of her life in a succession of diplomatic posts in Scandinavia and Mexico, virtually a political exile.

In her numerous books, pamphlets, and speeches Alexandra Kollontai passionately defended the ideals of the revolution, and developed innovatory theories on the role of women, convinced that real political change could only come with a transformation in sexual and family relationships. Her two works of fiction, *A Great Love* and *Love of Worker Bees* (reissued here by Virago) have as their central theme the conflicts women experience between love and work. Alexandra Kollontai died in Russia in 1954, unaware that her ideas were to gain her international recognition from a new generation.

Cathy Porter is also Kollontai's biographer (*Alexandra Kollontai: a biography*, Virago 1980).

Love of Worker Bees
and
A Great Love

Alexandra Kollontai

Translated and Introduced by
Cathy Porter

Afterword
by
Sheila Rowbotham

virago

VIRAGO

Published by Virago Press 1999
Reprinted 2011

Love of Worker Bees first published by Virago Press 1997
A Great Love first published by Virago Press 1981

Translation copyright © Cathy Porter 1999
Introduction copyright © Cathy Porter 1999

A CIP catalogue record for this book
is available from the British Library.

ISBN 978-1-86049-562-5

Typeset by Hewer Text Ltd, Edinburgh

Virago Press
An imprint of
Little, Brown Book Group
100 Victoria Embankment
London EC4Y 0DY

An Hachette UK Company
www.hachette.co.uk

www.virago.co.uk

Contents

Introduction

Alexandra Kollontai's views on sex, women and the family had a profound impact on the revolutionary movement in her native Russia. In her numerous writings on women, she envisaged a 'fundamental restructuring of the psyche' under communism, and looked forward to a time when men and women could come together freely in relationships based on 'mutual attraction, love and passion.' As the only woman in the revolutionary government formed after the Bolsheviks took power in October 1917, Kollontai was behind much of its early legislation to improve women's lives and liberate them from sexual prejudice and exploitation. Rediscovered in the west by the women's movement of the 1970s, she was the subject of biographies, books and articles, and translations of many of her works were published, including the six stories republished here today. Throughout all these writings she described the tensions women experienced between economics and biology, love and work, and these tensions guided her own lifelong search for synthesis.

She was born Alexandra Mikhailovna Domontovich in 1872, in the old tsarist capital of St Petersburg. Her father was a wealthy former general in the Tsar's army, a liberal, well-read man but a distant figure for most of her childhood. Her mother was the daughter of a Finnish wood-merchant, who escaped from a previous arranged marriage and brought to this love-match a son and two daughters. Energetic and resourceful, she spent much of her time running the family estates in St Petersburg and Finland where the family lived, and Alexandra grew up a solitary child, raiding her parents' library for political journals and novels.

At the age of sixteen she defied her parents' plans to bring her out into the St Petersburg marriage market, and two years later she defied them again by marrying her cousin Vladimir Kollontai, an elegant but impoverished former army captain. A year into the marriage, their son was born. Vladimir had recently become one of the reforming Tsar Alexander II's new factory inspectors. As he rose in the bureaucracy, Kollontai started privately referring to him as her 'tyrant', and writing short stories to keep her passions alive.

In 1896, the year she called the 'turning-point' of her life, she accompanied Vladimir to the Krengholm textile-mill outside the capital, and witnessed for the first time the appalling realities of working people's lives. Dismayed by Vladimir's assurances about the need for minor factory improvements, she sought out members of the Marxist Union of Struggle for the Working Class, formed the year before in St Petersburg to encourage workers to take industrial action, and 'led by a man named Lenin.'

1896 saw some of the Union's greatest propaganda successes, and in that year St Petersburg was convulsed by strikes. Kollontai's first eager studies of Marx had taught her something of the lives of women workers. Now she started visiting the capital's factories and textile-mills and met some of the women who were downing tools with the men and joining the strike-movement. Afterwards she wrote that it was these women who gave her the courage two years later to leave her husband and son and throw herself full-time into the revolution.

In 1922, in her *Autobiography of a Sexually Emancipated Woman*, she described this sad decision to leave her husband as prompted by 'the eternal defensive war against the encroachment of men on our individuality, a struggle revolving around the choice between work, or marriage and love.' The choice is an equally painful one for the women characters in each of these six stories, which all have as their starting-point the 'revolt against love's tyranny'.

Leaving her son in the care of her parents, she set off on her own to study Marxist economics in Zurich, where she discovered the revolutionary writings of Karl Liebknecht and Rosa Luxemburg. She returned to St Petersburg, moved in with her parents and son and rejoined the Social Democrats, then in the throes of the Bolshevik-Menshevik split. The more hardline politics of the Bolshevik underground tended to exclude women, especially those with children, and Kollontai allied herself with the Mensheviks. But like Olga Sergeevna in 'Three Generations', she found the split distasteful and was more interested in giving support to the factory women who were beginning to take part in the industrial negotiations which followed the strike wave of 1896, and who independently of the men were beginning to make their own demands for equal pay and maternity leave.

Like her mother, with her courageous challenge to the marriage conventions and her charity work amongst the peasants, many women of Kollontai's class were starting to speak out about the oppressed position of women in Russia, and were demanding access to the professions and the right to vote, be educated and marry the man of their choice. Kollontai believed such equalities would affect the interests only of privileged women unless the part women played in the economy was taken into account. The Marxist movement of which she was a part addressed itself to working women, and like Olga Sergeevna, and Natasha in 'A Great Love', she regarded women's liberation as inseparable from the liberation of the working class as a whole. It was women like these who created the powerful new women's movement which burst into militancy in Russia during the 1905 revolution, and which played its part in the February and October revolutions twelve years later.

On January 9 1905, a huge crowd of workers was hacked to death by soldiers outside the Winter Palace where they stood humbly petitioning Tsar Nicholas II for a constitutional government.

'Bloody Sunday' sparked off a wave of strikes, demonstrations and peasant uprisings throughout Russia. '1905 saw me on the streets,' Kollontai wrote. During that year she addressed demonstrations in St Petersburg's factories and textile-mills at which she urged workers to strike, then reported back to the party on what she found there. In the years that followed, she planned a conference for working women, set up a club for them in the capital, wrote articles and pamphlets on women's liberation and started work on her book *The Social Basis of the Women's Question*, in which she outlined a socialist approach to the women's movement.

1905 had thrown the family into revolution and had offered a glimpse of a more collective way of living, she wrote. But revolution couldn't hope automatically to loosen the threads that bound women to their subordinate roles; in order for these to be changed, women must be actively encouraged to discuss the problems they faced at work and in the family.

By 1908 Kollontai was wanted by the St Petersburg police. Leaving a group of factory-women to organise the conference there without her, she fled Russia and lived for the next nine years in exile. Basing herself in Germany, she joined the German socialist party and travelled around Europe and America campaigning for socialism and women's rights. She wrote about these years later in her book *Around Workers' Europe*.

Away from the struggle, she saw clearly how the politics of the revolutionary underground had inevitably split itself off from women and the family, and in doing so had split people's consciousness between 'selfish' emotions and the 'virtuous' life of the wider collective. Kollontai always insisted that the two were interdependent, and that social change could come only from a change in people's psyches.

Introduction

At this distance from Russia the connections between the two appeared even clearer, and her collection of stories *A Great Love*, (published in 1922 and subtitled 'Studies in the Psychology of Women') reflect many of her preoccupations during her years of exile. All the women characters here are intellectuals, isolated, somewhat rootless, prone to internalise. The heroine of 'Thirty-two Pages' travels on a train to meet her lover, and struggles with the competing claims of an unfinished dissertation. In 'Conversation Piece', a woman meets by chance at a railway-station the lover she has just left behind. Natasha, in 'A Great Love', finally summons up the courage to end a painful love affair with a fellow party-activist. But in all these stories, politics and the party are in the background and men are mere emotional shadows; it is women's personal experiences which are the starting-point, and women have the narrative voice.

'A Great Love' is the most autobiographical of these stories. At some point in 1909, Kollontai fell in love with an economist named Maslov who was living in exile in Germany then with his wife and children. Exhausted by the illicitness of the affair and by Maslov's attachment to a marriage which seemed to make both him and his wife so unhappy, Kollontai left for Paris. Here she met Lenin and his wife, Nadezhda Krupskaya, and discovered affinities between her own situation and Lenin's attachment to the passionate and beautiful French Bolshevik Inessa Armand, who was staying with the Lenins at the time.

Like Inessa Armand and Kollontai herself, Natasha in her fiction is a vital and generous woman who has broken with conventional marriage and wants to bring a radical new sexual politics into the class politics of the Russian underground. Whether or not 'A Great Love' was a *roman a clef*, Senya has much of Lenin's bounce and authority, even his cap and beard, and Natasha's 'great love' for him is inspired by shared work and a shared vision of revolution. But she finally tires of the menial political tasks he expects her to do for him, and the story ends as she steps onto the train that will take her back to the political underground and away from him for ever.

Kollontai broke with Maslov in 1913, and spent much of that year in London working at the British Museum on her book *Society and Motherhood*, published three years later. She returned to Berlin in 1914 amid the hysterical build-up to the First World War, and helped to organise a number of women's anti-war demonstrations there. Driven out of Germany by the police, she escaped to Switzerland and returned to Berlin the day war was declared. Once again she fled Germany, this time for Sweden. There she finally joined the Bolsheviks, the only group calling for an end to the war, and became part of the 'Northern Underground' which smuggled Bolshevik literature over the border to Russia. Amongst the things she wrote there was a letter to women workers in St Petersburg (now renamed Petrograd) urging them to organise anti-war Women's Day demonstrations, and her anti-war pamphlet 'Who Needs War?', which was translated into French, German and English and distributed to front-line soldiers in the trenches.

In February 1917, women in Petrograd celebrated Women's Day by taking to the streets in food riots and political strikes which soon spread to the entire city and turned into a general strike. On March 13, Tsar Nicholas finally abdicated.

Kollontai travelled back to Petrograd, and she was one of a small group of leading Bolsheviks who went to the Finland Station to meet Lenin and his entourage off the famous 'sealed train' that delivered them from exile. Over the next six months she wrote for the Bolshevik press, joined the new Petrograd Soviet, addressed meetings at factories and on street-corners, and was assigned the crucial task of bringing the Bolsheviks' anti-war message to sailors stationed on the battleships outside the capital. One of the sailors she met there was Pavel Dybenko, president of the Baltic Fleet Bolshevik central committee, and the two fell in love.

Introduction

All the stories here are about sex, in all its joyful and obsessional aspects, and the sexual charge of this revolution which turned people's relationships upside-down. Seventeen years her junior, Dybenko was from a peasant family, and the differences between them in age and class created a furore in Bolshevik circles from which Kollontai never really recovered. 'I wouldn't vouch for the reliability or endurance of women whose love affairs are intertwined with politics,' Lenin commented then in clear reference to her. In her pamphlet 'Sexual Relations and the Class Struggle', published the following year, Kollontai attacked the hypocrisy of this double standard, whereby 'a doctor can marry his cook, a professor can marry his young working-class student, but God help the woman writer or teacher who marries *her* cook or *her* young male student – especially if he is handsome.'

Throughout the summer of 1917 the sailors flocked to the Bolsheviks, and thousands of soldiers deserted their posts at the front line and joined them. On the night of October 25, Kollontai was at the clandestine Bolshevik central committee meeting which ordered soldiers to storm the Winter Palace. Next day a new Bolshevik government was installed, with Lenin at its head and Kollontai as its Commissar for Public Welfare.

Over the next three years the counter-revolutionary forces of the Whites, backed by the armies of fourteen Western powers, fought to topple Bolshevik power in Russia for fear that it would spread west. The government moved the capital to Moscow, and there Kollontai tried to tackle some of the enormous social problems facing the country as it was torn apart by civil war, foreign intervention and famine.

During the early months of revolution, the new government showed its determination to solve Russia's cultural, economic and administrative problems with a series of laws and decrees. As marriages collapsed under the strains of shared hardship, forced separations were setting men free to form new liaisons in

7

other towns, leaving their wives to work, support their children and fight for their rations. Kollontai helped to draft one of the first of the Bolsheviks' new laws, the revolutionary marriage law, which simplified divorce, banned the stigma of illegitimacy and recognised *de facto* marriage. But she knew that the chaotic state machinery would make the law worth no more than the paper it was written on unless women's problems at work were attended to, and that fundamental changes in family relationships would come only when women entered the skilled labour-force as the equals of men. This meant setting limits to women's working hours, giving them paid maternity leave and time off to breast-feed, and helping to socialise childcare and housework by establishing state creches and canteens in the factories. An even more urgent task facing her commisariat in 1917, however, was the reorganisation of Russia's children's homes to take in the thousands of orphaned and abandoned children who were roaming the country then, savage with hunger and frequently armed.

In November 1918 Kollontai and Inessa Armand organised a women's congress in the capital at which women could tell the party about some of the desperate material and psychological problems which beset them. Over a thousand red-kerchiefed women made the dangerous trek across war-torn Russia to the Kremlin and listened as Armand railed against pots and pans, and Kollontai outlined some of the ideas contained in her book *Communism And The Family*, in which she evoked the 'grim fortress' of marriage and her vision of a future in which people's loyalty would be to the collective rather than the nuclear family. She develops this theme in 'Vasilisa Malygina', 'Three Generations' and 'Sisters', published together as *Love of Worker Bees*, part of the series 'Revolution in Feelings and Morality'.

Olga Sergeevna relates the hardships many women faced after the revolution, returning exhausted from a sixteen-hour working day to cramped and uncomfortable collective living quarters.

But for many younger women, such as Vasilisa Malygina and Olga Sergeevna's daughter Zhenya, the universal labour-conscription imposed by the civil war, the squalid creches, the communal flats and canteens, were a rough and ready model for the communist society of the future. Daughters of Kollontai's generation, these are the 'new women' she portrayed elsewhere in her writings. Her description of Zhenya and her youthful promiscuity is handled very sensitively, and is contrasted with the attitudes of women like her mother who have downplayed personal emotions for the greater good of the party and have separated sexual liberation from the liberation written into its programme. But the story was considered very scandalous when it first appeared in Russia in 1923, and Kollontai was attacked for offering a 'model of petit-bourgeois debauchery' and depicting a post-war generation of young people incapable of lasting relationships.

Kollontai headed the new Women's Commission set up by the party shortly after the 1918 congress. The following spring she left Moscow by train on a six-month propaganda tour of the Southern Front, stopping off at towns and villages to urge the exhausted people to stay and fight the Whites. She returned to Moscow in the autumn of 1919. By then there were women's commissions in virtually every province of European Russia, and she became women's organiser in the countryside, travelling around Russia organising lectures, poster-displays and meetings. At these meetings women began at last to discuss the long-silent issues of prostitution, veneral disease and abortion, and Kollontai had a hand in the law passed in 1920 which made the Soviet republic the first country in the world to legalise abortion.

As the civil war came to an end, many women still felt they had reason to put their faith in party promises of equality. But this faith helped to conceal the many unprotected areas of their lives, and exposed them all too easily to insidious attitudes and policies of the past. In 1921 the party adopted its New Economic

Policy (NEP), which partially restored the market, and large numbers of unskilled workers, mainly urbanised peasants and women, were thrown out of their jobs. Peasants went back to their villages, many existing provisions for collectivised housework and childcare were dismantled, and women returned to the home. For the truly desperate, there were always the streets, and plenty of 'Nepmen' with money in their pockets and time to kill.

Throughout Kollontai's life in the revolution she saw the family clinging grimly to the old culture, fortifying itself against the chaos and emerging in the 1920s as a place of retreat. The three stories in *Love of Worker Bees* give flesh and blood to the ambiguities of this period of NEP, and give us a vivid picture of life in provincial Russia then.

When Vasilisa Malygina loses her job she lives with her 'Nepman' husband in his large chilly house, dressed in the clothes he buys for her, expected to manage his servants as he manages his workers and to provide a sanctuary for him from the harsh new business world outside. The narrator of 'Sisters' also loses her job, and shares many of Vasilisa's feelings of demoralisation as she waits alone in an empty house every evening for her husband to return from work. When he brings a prostitute home one night she overcomes her revulsion and speaks to her, and discovers how similar their lives are. 'Three Generations' gives a historical perspective to these problems, identifying the ways in which Zhenya, Olga Sergeevna and her mother put aside their differences to support each other.

The women in *Love of Worker Bees* are less educated and articulate than those in the other three stories. They are also less isolated, and all draw strength from one another, if necessary at the cost of breaking with lovers. As Vasilisa finally prepares to leave her husband she discovers that she is pregnant, and the story ends as she plans to set up a communal house in which to bring up her baby on her own.

Introduction

Many collective living experiments in 1920s Russia, like this one, took their inspiration from the civil war period. Kollontai shows women like Vasilisa and Zhenya emerging from these years as committed revolutionaries, determined not to give up the freedoms they have gained, and convinced that the new kinds of living arrangements can work.

In 1921 Kollontai joined the Workers' Opposition group, which urged more trade-union control over economic production. By then her opposition to NEP and her views on sex and women were increasingly alienating her from the party leadership. During the 10th party congress that year Lenin was ill and Stalin was acting party-secretary. The Workers' Opposition was banned and its members were expelled from the party, and this spelt the end of Kollontai's career as a revolutionary in Russia.

She applied to Stalin for a diplomatic post, and he sent her to Norway as a member of the Soviet Republic's first trade delegation there. Shortly after arriving in Oslo she ended her relationship with Dybenko, and it was as she came to terms with her personal and political isolation that she wrote these stories. When they were published in Moscow in 1923, they were greeted with a chorus of disapproval, and four years later Stalin had 'A Great Love' republished as a convenient weapon in his battle against Lenin's ailing widow.

Kollontai lived in diplomatic seclusion until her death in 1954. When her stories first appeared in Soviet Russia they suggested more complexity in people's feelings than was acceptable there at the time. Yet throughout her life, through three revolutions, two world wars, civil war and exile, she continued to believe in the possibilities within us, and against the world inhabited by her women characters she shows a better one they are in the process of making for themselves.

In her 1918 essay 'The New Woman', she wrote: 'The less we romanticise harsh reality and the more truthfully we present contempory women's psychology, her struggles, her migraines and her aspirations, the richer the material for the spiritual image of women we shall have to study.'

This truthfulness rings through each of the stories here, and their imaginative account of women's lives in the early years of this century still speak to us now at the end of it.

Love of Worker Bees

Vasilisa Malygina

1

Vasilisa Malygina was a working girl. Twenty-eight years old, she was a real city girl, thin and under-nourished looking with curly hair that had been cropped after a typhus attack. With her plain Russian blouse and her flat chest, you might from a distance have taken her for a boy.

She wasn't exactly pretty, but she did have the most wonderful perceptive brown eyes: just to look into those tender eyes of hers made people feel cheerful.

Vasilisa was a communist, and had joined the Bolsheviks when war had broken out. She loathed the war, and while everyone at the knitting workshop where she worked was busy making up garments to send to the front, frantically working overtime for Russia's victory, Vasilisa obstinately argued with them. War was a bloody business, she said, who needed it? It was nothing but a burden to people. And for the young soldiers going off like lambs to the slaughter, it was a tragedy.

Whenever she came across groups of soldiers in the street, marching in military formation, she would turn her back on them. How could they march along so jauntily, singing at the tops of their voices, going off to their deaths as though off on holiday! It wasn't as if they *had* to go, they could have refused. If they had just said we're not going off to be killed or to kill people like us, there wouldn't have been a war at all.

Vasilisa was well-read; her father was a typesetter and had taught her to read early. She loved Tolstoy, especially his folk-tales.

She was the only pacifist in the workshop, and would have lost her job if they hadn't needed workers so badly. As it was, the foreman just gave her a good talking to. Everyone knew about her views, and she was nicknamed the 'Tolstoyan'. All the other women at work tended to keep their distance from her, for hadn't she renounced her country and betrayed Russia? 'A lost soul!' they sighed whenever her name was mentioned.

It wasn't long before her reputation reached the ears of the local Bolshevik organizer, who sought her out. He realized that the girl was reliable, sure of her opinions and well suited to party work. So Vasilisa was drawn towards the Bolsheviks. Not at once of course, not by any means. At first she argued with the committee members, asking question after question, and forever storming out of meetings. But eventually she began to understand their position more clearly, and in the end it was she who suggested she start working properly for them. That was how Vasilisa became a Bolshevik.

She proved herself a passionate and assertive public speaker. She was never at a loss for words and could debate with Mensheviks and Socialist Revolutionaries alike. The other women at work were shy and tongue-tied, but not Vasilisa; she always spoke up when she had to, and she talked sense too. In no time she had gained the respect of her party comrades, who decided to adopt her as their candidate in the town council, or Duma, during Kerensky's Provisional Government.

This made the women workers very proud of her, and from then on whatever she said was law for them. She got on well with the more conservative women too. And even if she did shout at them they felt she knew best, for hadn't she been working in a factory ever since she was a young girl?

She felt if *she* didn't try and understand their needs, nobody would. However it wasn't so easy to make her party comrades see reason about these women. 'You should drop them,' they'd tell her. 'We've more important things to think about now.' This attitude would infuriate Vasilisa, who would lash out at her party friends, confront the party secretary, and demand that they listen to her. Why should women's matters be considered less important? Women had always been treated like that! It wasn't surprising they were so conservative! How could you hope to have a successful revolution without enlisting women? They were crucial. 'Winning over the women, that's half the battle,' was what Vasilisa always said.

She knew what she wanted, and she stuck by it. In 1918 she was a real Bolshevik fighter. Over the years many people lost heart, stayed at home, gave up. But she was always at work, making speeches, debating, organizing, getting things done – she was indefatigable. It was hard to imagine where she got the energy from, she was so pale and skinny. People always responded to those wonderful eyes of hers though, warm, brown and attentive.

One day a letter arrived for her at the little attic room where she lived. This was the letter she had been longing for, a letter from her darling husband and friend from whom she had been separated for so many lonely months. Not that there was anything to be done about it, what with the civil war and then the industrial front, for which the party had to mobilize all its members.

Vasilisa knew the revolution wasn't a game, and that everyone had to make sacrifices. That was why she had lived on her own all these months, away from her husband; that was her sacrifice to the revolution. When they were flung to opposite ends of Russia her women friends tried to console her, saying 'It'll be for the best, you'll see. This way he'll go on loving you longer, and you won't grow bored with him.' They might have been right, but she didn't care; she was wretched without him and missed him constantly.

True, she had very little time to herself and was busy from morning until late at night with her work for the party and the local soviet. One job piled on top of another, and vital and fascinating work it was too. But when the day was over and she returned to her little room – her garret, as they would have called it in her parents' village – a chill wind would freeze her heart and she longed for her husband. She would sit down to her tea, immersed in gloomy thoughts. Nobody needed her, she had no real friends, no proper goal to work for. Did other people care about her? Because if they did, she received precious little sign of it.

She had been particularly depressed recently because an important project of hers – her communal house – had just been wrecked, and now everyone was going around insulting and criticizing each other. Nobody seemed to realize how important it was to try and live collectively now; could it be they just weren't capable of it? The people in house had abused her, begrudging her her extra rations as a privileged worker. 'To hell with my rations!' she'd said. 'I'll manage without them!' Eventually her party comrades had calmed her down, but by then her head was spinning with exhaustion and frustration.

That was how her winter had passed. She would sit in her room at night, leaning her elbows on the table, nibbling on a fruit drop to save sugar, and thinking over the day's tribulations. She felt there was no hope for the revolution, nothing but 'endless' frustrations, backbiting and losing battles.

If only her Volodya had been there, she could have poured out her troubles to him and he would have embraced and caressed her. She remembered times when he'd said, 'What are you fretting about Vasya? Whenever I see you out there in front of other people you look such a tough little thing! "I'm not afraid of anything!" you say. But look at you now, huddled up like a ruffled sparrow under the eaves!' Then he would catch her up in his strong arms and carry her round the room, soothing her like a baby. The very thought made Vasya's heart ache with joy and love for her sweet handsome husband who loved her, who loved her so much . . .

Whenever her thoughts turned to him she felt even more dismal, and things would seem even bleaker in her lonely attic room. But as she cleared the tea things she reproached herself. What did she want out of life? Nothing but pleasure? Did she really want her Volodya constantly by her side, when she had work she loved and the respect of her friends? The revolution isn't a picnic, she would remind herself, everyone has to make sacrifices, aren't you asking rather a lot, Vasilisa Dementevna? Remember, it's everything for the collective now, everything for the revolution.

She tried to recall how the furore over the communal house had started. This house had nothing to do with her general work for the party and the soviet. She had long ago decided to set up a model house filled with a genuinely communist spirit. Not just some sort of dormitory where people lived their private lives and went their own ways – that kind of scheme invariably fostered resentment and bad feeling, for people who lived like that would think only of their own needs and wouldn't live collectively. It was something quite different that Vasilisa had in mind.

She had patiently set about organizing the house, one step at a time. What setbacks she had suffered! Twice the house had been taken away from her, but she had been ready to do battle with anyone, and had finally succeeded in getting her own way. So the house was set up with its communal kitchen, its laundry, its crêche and its dining-room. This dining-room was Vasilisa's pride and joy, and well it might be, with its curtains at the windows and its potted geraniums. There was a library too, which was used as a meeting room.

To begin with, everything went wonderfully. The women

living there would shower her with kisses, calling her their 'little treasure'. 'You're our guardian angel!' they'd say. 'We're so happy here, and it's all thanks to you!' But then imperceptibly things started to go wrong.

People began quibbling with the rules. There seemed no way to make people clean up after them, and there was constant bickering in the kitchen over the washing-up. The laundry was always being flooded and people had trouble pumping out the water. As one argument followed another and quarrelling and confusion reigned, Vasilisa became the target of everyone's resentment – as though she was the housekeeper and wasn't seeing to things properly! She had been reduced to imposing fines, which made them even more furious. Some had moved out, and more arguments and disagreements followed.

When this confusion was it its worst, a particularly malicious couple called the Feodoseevs decided to stir up trouble. They found fault with everything, they nagged, they harangued, first it was one thing, then another – there was no pleasing them! They had some authority in the house as they'd been among the first to move in, and consequently many people regarded them as in change and followed their example. But what they wanted and what was bothering them there was no way of knowing All Vasilisa knew was that they made her life hell, and each day they managed to provoke another unpleasant incident.

She finally broke down and sobbed, she was so tired and angry. But seeing that the whole thing might fall to pieces, she decided to make a new rule; everything was to be paid for cash down – water, electricity, rates, taxes, everything. She then wore herself out seeing to all these new arrangements, but nothing came of them. What could you do if noone had any money? The new economy was all very well, but you couldn't get far without money!

She was determined to go on fighting for her precious house though – she couldn't bear to see it collapse, and she wasn't the sort to let go of something once she committed herself to it. So she went to Moscow, spent days knocking on office doors and talking to the bosses, and managed to make out a good case for the house. Eventually they were so impressed by her account of it that she was given a subsidy for repairs, which meant she could claim a household allowance.

She returned home beaming with satisfaction to be confronted by the spiteful Feodoseevs. They seemed to suggest by their sullen malevolence that she had betrayed them in some way by pleading for the house. Then they started up a new line of attack, putting out scandalous rumours that she had been rigging the household accounts to put a bit by for herself. She could hardly bear to think of all the things they made her endure.

She badly needed a close friend with whom to talk things over, and had decided to write to Vladimir asking him to come. But he had written back explaining that he too had important work which he couldn't leave. He'd been promoted to a new job and had to straighten out the finances of the firm where he had previously been employed as a clerk. That winter had been one long uphill struggle for him too, and he couldn't tear himself away at this point; the firm depended on him.

So Vasilisa had to bear the whole squalid business on her own. And what hurt her most was that it was the workers, her friends and allies, who were the cause of everything. If they'd been bourgeois anti-communists she wouldn't have cared nearly so much!

Mercifully, however, the house committee supported her throughout. They didn't let her bring the case to court but decided the committee members themselves should sort it out for her. They concluded it was a clear case of slander, based on malice and ignorance. But just when they were about to evict the Feodoseevs, the couple had admitted their guilt, pleading for Vasilisa's forgiveness and assuring her how much they had always respected her. Vasilisa's victory brought her no joy, for she was worn out, worried sick, and at the end of her father.

After all that she had fallen ill, and although she went back to work almost immediately she felt as though something inside her had died. She no longer loved her house – she had suffered too much for it. It was as if her child had been sullied, and memories of her own childhood flooded back. She remembered her little brother Kolka showing her a sweet, and when she reached out for it he laughed spitefully and said, 'Look at me! I'm going to spoil your sweet for you!' Then he spit on it and give it to her, saying, 'Here you are, Vasilisa, you can eat your sweet now, it's delicious!'

And Vasilisa turned from him sobbing, 'Horrible boy! Why did you do that!'

That was how she felt about the house. She didn't want to be responsible for it any more. She would go on serving on the house committee, but she couldn't devote herself fully to it now – it could go to the dogs for all she cared! Towards the residents she felt nothing but coldness; hadn't they joined the Feodoseevs in attacking her? She began to keep her distance from people. Before, she'd always been so sympathetic to their problems, but after everything she'd been through she wanted nothing more than to be left in peace. She was very tired . . .

Now the long winter was over. The sun shone, the sparrows chirped under the eaves in the morning, and Vasilisa smiled as she remembered her darling Volodya calling her his ruffled sparrow. And with the spring, even though her anaemia was worse and her lungs troubled her, she felt the stirrings of new energy.

Through the window she could see the sky swirling with soft clouds, and the roof of the old ancestral mansion which now housed the Palace of Motherhood. In the garden the buds were beginning to swell and her heart was filled with spring. How cold it had been that winter! How alone she had felt with all her struggles and anxieties. Today was like a holiday.

Nothing in the world could go wrong today, for she had a letter from her lover, her darling Volodya! And what a letter too!

Please Vasya, don't torment me any more, I can't put up with much more of this. You keep promising to come and see me, then putting it off. If only you knew how unhappy you're making me! So my little fighter's been scrapping again, has she? There've been rumours about you even here. Some people say you've been in the newspapers! Now you've won your victory, surely you can spare the time to visit your Volodya, who loves you so much and longs to see you. You'll be amazed how grandly we're living now. I've got my own horse and cow, and there's always a car at my disposal. We have a servant too, so you won't have to worry about the housework and you'll be able to put your feet up. Spring is well and truly here, the apple-trees are covered in blossom. Do you realize we haven't spent one spring together! Our life together should be one long spring, shouldn't it, my darling!

I really need you now. I'm in a bit of trouble with the party committee. They've made some allegations against me, bringing up my anarchism again. I've told you about Savelyov. Well, the whole thing started because of him. Please. Vasya, you must help me clear it up. I'm sick and tired of these squabbles. They make life impossible! It'll be hard for them to criticize me, because I work well, but I need you all the same. I kiss your brown eyes. I shall always love you,

Your Volodya

Vasilisa sat lost in thought, staring out of the window at the sky and the clouds, smiling to herself as she thought about this wonderful letter. Volodya meant everything to her, and he loved her so much! His letter lay on her lap, and she stroked it as though it were his head. She forgot the sky, the roof, the clouds, and saw only her beautiful Volodya with his laughing eyes.

Her heart ached for him. How had she managed without him all winter? It was seven months since she had seen him. The fact that she hadn't been continually thinking about him made her feel wretched. She had so many worries and miseries of her own that winter, she simply hadn't had time. She'd managed to push her love for Volodya, her loneliness without him, into the recesses of her heart, and there her love had remained, sure and immutable. Now at last she had won her battles and rescued her precious brainchild, her communal house, from all those wretched troublemakers. Now she could think about her love again.

Remembering him now, she could almost sense his presence there beside her, and it was a sweet feeling. But she was also conscious of the burden this kind of love imposed. It had to be like this, for she was always anxious about what might happen to him. He had no sense of discipline – Vasilisa was forced to admit that people were right in criticizing his anarchic ways. He detested having to carry out party decisions, he had to have his own way. But when it came to work there were few people to match him, and as for business, he excelled at it.

Living apart, they had not got in the way of each other's work, and the arrangement suited them quite well. If there was work to be done she wanted to be able to give all her attention to it.

If Volodya was there she would want to be with him, then he'd neglect *his* work too. 'Work before everything,' he said, 'but there's our love too, and that's almost as important, isn't it Vasya?' And she agreed. She felt the same way, happy that they weren't just man and wife but comrades too.

Now he was begging her to come, as a friend might ask another, begging her to help him. She read the letter through once more – and slowly doubts started trickling into her mind. If this had anything to do with Savelyov it was bad news indeed, for Savelyov was a speculator and a thoroughly unscrupulous character. Really, Volodya should know better than to associate with a man like that! As a director, he should be completely above suspicion and have nothing to do with such shady types. He was always far too trusting. It was just like him to take pity on Savelyov and speak up for him.

But it was inexcusable to take pity on people like that – people people who helped themselves to public money should be punished for it. Volodya had a kind heart, but people couldn't be expected to realize that, and they would obviously interpret his 'friendship' with Savelyov quite differently. And Volodya had a lot of enemies; once he lost his temper there was no controlling him. What if there was a repetition of that incident three years ago, when they had brought a case against him? Vasilisa knew from painful experience how easy it was to ruin a person's reputation.

Now it was Volodya who was in trouble. She must go immediately, she must support him and make his accusers feel ashamed of themselves. She felt like leaving on the spot. What did she care about the house now? It was too late for her to rescue it properly anyway. Officially she'd won, but actually it was the Feodoseevs who'd come out on top.

She sighed, went to the window and looked down into the yard. She stood there a while, silently saying goodbye to the house with a grave expression on her face. Then her cheeks began to flush and she felt a sense of overwhelming happiness. 'Volodechka! Soon I'll be seeing my Volodya again! Oh my darling, I'm on my way!'

2

Vasilisa sat in her railway carriage; she had been travelling south for two days already, but another twenty-four hours lay ahead of her. It felt strange to be travelling equipped for the journey like a 'lady'. Volodya had sent her the money for the journey (it seemed he could afford anything these days), and had told her to buy a ticket for a sleeper. He had also sent her a length of material to make herself a nice dress; from now on, as the wife of a director, she would have to be 'properly dressed', he told her.

Vasilisa couldn't help laughing when she remembered how one of Volodya's colleagues had appeared at her door one day with the money and the material. He had unpacked it and gravely praised its quality, just like a salesman. Vasilisa had laughed and teased the fellow about it, but he obviously saw nothing to laugh about; the article, he solemnly informed her, was of the finest quality. After that she held her tongue, although she couldn't for the life of her understand these new executive types, nor how you were supposed to behave towards them.

When he left, Vasya stood turning over the material in her hands. She wasn't accustomed to giving much thought to clothes and fashions, but here was Volodya telling her she mustn't let him down! There was nothing for it, she'd have to get herself a smart dress, the kind of fashionable get-up women were wearing nowadays.

She had gone off to see her dressmaker friend and explained the situation to her. 'Please Grusha, make me something as up-to-date and fashionable as possible,' she begged, and Grusha had brought out some fashion magazines a friend had brought from Moscow the previous autumn. She'd been making dresses from them all winter, and people liked them.

Grusha spent a long time leafing through the magazines, and eventually spotted a dress. 'Look Vasya, this is just the thing for you! As you're so skinny, this will do wonders for you, it'll make your hips look wider and the front here is gathered so as to hide your small bosom. I'm going to make you a dress your husband will be proud of!'

'That's perfect, Grusha dear,' Vasilisa said. They bargained over the price, kissed each other goodbye, and Vasilisa left well pleased. It was just as well there were dressmakers around – she wouldn't have been able to make a dress to save her life! Volodya was different, he was an expert on women's fashions. When he was in America he had worked for various women's fashion stores and had picked up quite a bit of information on the subject. Nowadays such accomplishments were coming in useful, and the new 'red merchants' had to keep up with these things. Women's frippery was a commodity too!

Vasilisa was sitting on her own near the window of the sleeper. Her travelling companion was a raucous, heavily perfumed 'Nepwoman', decked out in rustling silk and jangling ear-rings. She was at that moment visiting the people in the next compartment, and she and her admirers could be heard shouting and laughing together.

With Vasilisa she been extremely aloof, pursing her lips primly as she said, 'Excuse me dear, you're sitting on my shawl, you'll crumple it.' Or 'Would you mind stepping out into the corridor for a moment dear, while I make myself up for the night?' This overperfumed woman behaved as though she owned the compartment, and was only tolerating Vasilisa out of the goodness of her heart. Vasilisa disliked being called 'dear', but she didn't want to get involved in an argument. She'd better try and get on with people now, she told herself, instead of arguing with them all the time!

Evening approached and spread long grey-blue shadows over the spring fields. The setting sun hung like a great red ball over the purple line of the distant forests. Rooks flew up from the fields and wheeled in the sky. Ahead stretched the telegraph wires, broken at intervals by poles.

This twilight induced in Vasilisa an unaccountable feeling of brooding melancholy, not sadness so much as a deep longing for something she couldn't name. In the last few days she had been feeling so recklessly cheerful, hastily winding up her work and making preparations for the journey. Everybody had been sorry to see her leave, and sad to think they might never see her again. Even the Feodoseev woman had come out to see her, kissing her and stammering her apologies. Vasilisa had found this deeply embarrassing; it wasn't hatred she felt for the woman so much as contempt – for her and her kind.

Then her friends had taken her to the station, and had even postponed a house meeting so as to see her off. The party committee was there too, as well as the children from the communal house, carrying some paper flowers they'd made for her, and Vasilisa suddenly realized she hadn't sacrificed her energy and her health for nothing; the seeds of communal living had been implanted in these people, and something was bound to come of it. As the train moved off and they stood waving their hats at her, the tears welled up in her eyes and she felt wretched to be leaving her dear friends behind.

But then the town moved out of sight, and soon copses and suburban villages flashed past the window and in no time the communal house had vanished from her mind, along with the joys and miseries of that winter, and her thoughts raced ahead, outstripping the train, in her eagerness to see her darling Volodya. She willed the train to hurry, to speed her loving heart to its destination . . .

So where had these melancholy thoughts sprung from? Her heart felt as though clamped with cold steel and tears came to her eyes. Maybe it was because a part of her life was slipping away, just like those stretches of fields outside the window with their spring growth of soft, amber-coloured grass. One field after another passed before her eyes, fields she would never see again . . . She cried a little, quietly and unobtrusively; then, wiping away the tears she immediately felt better, as though they had dissolved the icy knot of anxiety in her heart.

The lights went on in the compartment, the attendant drew the curtains, and the atmosphere became cosy and intimate. She was conscious again that two nights from now she would see Volodya, kiss him again – his voice sprang to life in her memory, his warm mouth, his strong arms. A sweet drowsy languor ran through her body. She began smiling to herself, and if it hadn't been for the Nepwoman fidgeting in front of the mirror she would have burst out singing for joy.

The Nepwoman left, slamming the door behind her. Stupid woman! Vasilisa closed her eyes and began thinking about Volodya again, going over episodes in their love affair. They'd been in love for five years now. Five years! It seemed as though they'd only met yesterday! She couldn't imagine a time when Volodya hadn't been her lover and friend. She settled down more comfortably in the corner seat, tucked her legs under her and closed her eyes. The carriage rocked gently, lulling her to sleep, but her thoughts ran on. She recalled how they had met for the first time.

It was at a meeting, just before that unforgettable October. What inspiring days they were. They'd been a mere handful of Bolsheviks, but to make up for it they worked doubly hard. The Mensheviks and the disruptive Socialist Revolutionaries had been in control at that time, persecuting the Bolsheviks, beating them up and calling them 'German spies' and 'traitors to their country' Yet every day the Bolsheviks increased in number.

Nobody ever knew what would happen next, but the Bolsheviks were determined on one thing – to achieve peace and oust the 'patriotic traitors' who wanted to continue the war. That much had been clear and that much they'd fought for, with energy and passion. Confident and uncompromising, their eyes shone with a determination which needed no words: we may die, they said, but give in, never! Nobody gave any thought to themselves – this wasn't the time for personal problems.

Much had been written about Vasilisa in the Socialist Revolutionary and Menshevik press – a lot of stupid lies which were part of their general attempt to discredit the Bolsheviks. Let them babble on until they were blue in the face, she thought at the time, it all served the Bolshevik purpose. People were coming more and more to believe the Bolsheviks were right.

'You might have some consideration for me,' her old mother had sobbed. 'Joining up with the Bolsheviks like that, you've disgraced your family and betrayed your country!'

To avoid domestic scenes like this, Vasilisa had moved in with a friend. There her mother's tears no longer affected her, and she had gradually broken away from her family. As though driven by some overwhelming force, she had become obsessed with her work for the Bolsheviks. Even if it destroyed her, she was determined to go on arguing, struggling, fighting.

The skirmishes became more explosive, the atmosphere increasingly charged. As news came through from Petrograd of the decisions of the congresses, of Trotsky's speeches and the summons to the Petrograd Soviet, a storm seemed inevitable It was then that she met Vladimir.

It was at a meeting held in a packed hall. People were standing on the window sills, sitting on the floor, in the gangways. It was almost impossible to breathe. Vasilisa couldn't now remember what the meeting about, but in her mind's eye she could still see the platform quite clearly. She remembered that it was the first time a Bolshevik had been elected president. The committee also consisted entirely of Bolsheviks and left Socialist Revolutionaries – and there had been one well-known anarchist from a co-operative; people always referred to him as 'the American'. That was Volodya

It was the first time she'd seen him, although she'd heard a lot about him. Some rhapsodized about him: 'What a man,' they said. 'He knows how to make people listen to him.' Other people criticized his brashness. But he had the support of the co-operative bakers and a group of industrial employees, and together they were a militant bunch, a force to be reckoned with.

The Bolsheviks had been delighted when Volodya outbid the Mensheviks, but angry when he opposed them. They couldn't make out where he stood. The secretary of the Bolshevik group disliked him. 'It's best to steer clear of allies like that. He's all over the place.'

But Stepan Alexeevich, one of the oldest and most respected Bolsheviks in town, laughed. 'Wait a while, don't rush him, he'll make an excellent Bolshevik in time. He's a go-ahead young fellow. Just let him work all those American ideas out of his system.'

Vasilisa hadn't paid much attention to all this. She couldn't be bothered to keep up with all these people who suddenly came into the limelight.

She arrived late and breathless at the meeting, where she was due to speak on the brick-building industry. Those days were one long meeting, and she was a popular speaker – people listened to her and liked her. They liked the fact that a woman was speaking publicly, and a working woman at that. She always spoke to the point and didn't mince words. She had developed her own original style of speaking, and the hall was always packed.

She went straight to the stage. Comrade Yurochkin (he was killed later at the Front) tugged her arm. 'We've won! The Bolsheviks have been voted on to the rostrum, along with the two left Socialist Revolutionaries and "the American", and he's as good as a Bolshevik. He's just about to speak now.'

Vasilisa glanced at 'the American', and for some reason felt surprised. So this was how an anarchist looked! She would have taken him for one of the gentry, with his starched collar and tie, his neatly combed and parted hair. He was handsome, with extraordinarily long eyelashes. When it was his turn to speak he stepped forward, putting his hand to his mouth as he cleared his throat.

'Just like the gentry,' Vasilisa decided, smiling for some reason.

His voice was pleasant and persuasive, and he spoke entertainingly and at length. He made everyone laugh, and when he finished she clapped and bravoed with the rest of the audience. As he returned to the table on the platform he inadvertently brushed against her and turned to apologize. She found herself blushing, and blushing made her even more embarrassed. How maddening! But the anarchist sat down at the table without noticing her, and carelessly leaning his elbow on the back of the chair, he lit a cigarette. The chairman leaned over, pointing to his cigarette and indicating that he should put it out. Vladimir shrugged and went on smoking, as if to say, your rules don't concern me. He inhaled twice, and when the president was preoccupied with another matter, he threw the cigarette on the floor.

Vasilisa remembered all this. She had pulled a face at him, but he had taken no notice. He only looked at her when her turn came to speak. That night she spoke particularly well, and although she was standing with her back to him she could sense he was looking at her. She deliberately over-praised the Bolsheviks and lashed out at the Mensheviks, the Socialist Revolutionaries and the anarchists – although at the time she didn't really know much about the anarchists. She only knew she wanted to rile 'the American' for his gentle-manly airs.

At that time she had long hair which she wore in a plait round her head. In the middle of her speech the plait slipped down on to her shoulder. As she spoke the became more and more excited, forgetting herself completely and not noticing the pins falling out of her hair. When the plait got in her way, she felt uncomfortable and tossed it back She didn't realize that the plait had bewitched Vladimir.

'I couldn't see you properly when I was listening to your speech, but when your plait fell on your shoulder I suddenly realized you weren't just a public speaker, you were Vasya the rebel – and a woman! And such a comical woman too, getting all flustered and putting a brave face on it, waving your arms and cursing the anarchists, while all the time your plait was coming undone and snakes of hair were rippling down your back like threads of gold. That's when I swore I'd get to know you properly.'

It was later that he told her this, after they'd become lovers.

When she finished her speech she hastily began plaiting up her hair again. Yurochkin picked up the pins for her.

'Thanks friend,' she said, feeling rather awkward with everyone looking at her.

She was afraid to look at 'the American' but she knew he'd noticed; he must think her ridiculous. This enraged her for some reason, and she felt furious with him. What did she care about the man?

The meeting was over; people got up to leave. Suddenly 'the American' was standing in front of her.

'Allow me to introduce myself,' he said, and told her his name and why he was there.

They shook hands, and he congratulated her on her speech. She blushed again, and they began talking and arguing, she supporting the Bolsheviks and he the anarchists. They moved out of the crowded hall onto the street where it was drizzling and windy. A cab was waiting for him from the co-operative, and he offered to take her home. She agreed and they got in. The cab was narrow and they sat in silence, huddled close together under its low roof.

Now Vasilisa and Vladimir stopped talking and arguing; they were calm and quiet. It didn't occur to either of them that they might be falling in love. The horse trotted along, its hooves splashing through the puddles, and they began to chat about trifles, about the rain, about next day's conference at the co-operative on the soap industry. They were both feeling extraordinarily happy.

When they finally arrived at Vasilisa's house and it was time to say goodbye, both knew they were sorry that the journey had passed so quickly, but neither of them said anything.

'I hope your feet didn't get wet?' Vladimir said solicitously.

'My feet?' she said, surprised and delighted.

It was the first time in her life that someone had worried about her like that. She began to laugh, showing her white teeth, and Vladimir longed to gather her into his arms and kiss her lips . . .

The wicket gate clicked as the watchman came out to let her into the building. 'Until tomorrow then!' shouted Vladimir. 'See you at the co-operative! Don't forget, will you! The meeting starts at two sharp. We do things the American way there!'

He tipped his hat and took his leave with a deep bow. Vasilisa turned at the gate and hesitated, as though waiting for someone. Then the gate slammed and she was alone in the darkened yard. Instantly the whole thing seemed like a mere escapade and she was overcome by feelings of anxiety and melancholy. Something made her feel wretched and angry, she painfully aware of how insignificant she was, how dispensable . . .

Vasya sat in the compartment, her woollen scarf tucked under her head as a pillow. She wasn't asleep, but she was dreaming, about her love. Like being in the cinema, reel after reel, image after image, happiness and misery, everything she'd lived through with Volodya came before her. These recollections were so pleasant that even the memory of past miseries were enjoyable. So things had sometimes been unhappy, but they were so much better now, she told herself, settling more comfortably into her seat. The train rocked on, soothing her, and she recalled the co-operative meeting.

It had been noisy and restless; the bakers were an assertive bunch. Vladimir was their chairman, the only person capable of restraining them, and although he had his work cut out, he always managed to control them. The veins on his forehead would swell from the strain. He didn't notice when Vasya came in and sat unobtrusively at the back, watching.

They passed a resolution of no confidence in the Provisional Government, demanding that the workers take the co-operative into their own hands, then they proceeded to elect their management board. All shareholders, members of the bourgeoisie and the Duma were disqualified and lost their deposits. Thenceforth the co-operative would not be one of the city co-operatives, but a group of bakers and industrial workers collaborating on a new project.

But the Mensheviks weren't going to sit and watch this happen, they'd sent their minions to the meeting to intervene. The meeting was just about to break up—it only remained for the managers to convene – when suddenly a Menshevik commissar, the chief authority in the city and one of Kerensky's henchmen, apeared at the door. He was followed by a group of Menshevik and Socialist Revolutionary leaders. When Vladimir spotted them, a sly look came into his eyes.

'Comrades, I declare the meeting closed,' he announced. 'It only remains for us to install the managers of the new revolutionary bakers' co-operative. Tomorrow there'll be a general meeting for the consideration of other business, but for the moment we can all go home.'

He spoke in calm, assured tones and the audience rose noisily to their feet.

'Hold on a minute, hold on, comrades,' called the commissar irritably. 'Don't close the meeting yet if you please.'

'You're too late I'm afraid, Mr Commissar, the meeting's already closed. If you wish to acquaint yourself with our resolutions please do so by all means; here they are. We were going to send a delegation to negotiate with you, but since you've come here in person so much the better. It's time you learnt that proper revolutionary conduct demands that officials should come to workers' organizations for their information.'

Vladimir stood there unperturbed, sorting out his papers, but his eyes under their thick lashes had a mischievous expression. The hall rang with cries of 'Hear hear! That's right!' and a lot of people were laughing. The commissar started to protest and went up to Vladimir, talking excitedly and nervously. But Vladimir wasn't at all put out, merely looked amused. He spoke in a loud, clear voice, and his answers to the commissar could be heard all over the hall. The audience guffawed and applauded Vladimir, crowing with pleasure when he invited the commissar to a party to celebrate the passing of the co-operative from the bourgeoisie into the hands of the bakers.

'Good for the American!' they shouted. 'He's a sharp one!'

The commissar eventually left, having achieved nothing, threatening to resort to force.

'You just try!' Vladimir snapped at him, his eyes flashing, and the hall resounded with his words.

'You just try, just try!' they all shouted. The atmosphere in the hall had become so menacing that the commissar and his Mensheviks were forced to slip out through the side door, but the noise in the hall persisted for a long time.

The meeting of the management board was postponed until that evening so people could get something to eat. They had been at the meeting since that morning and they were exhausted. Vasya was moving towards the exit with the others, when suddenly there was Vladimir, looking unruffled and smiling, quite unlike everyone else in his clean blue jacket. But today he no longer looked to Vasya like an aristocrat, today she felt he was one of them. He *must* be a Bolshevik! He'd been so brave, he would obviously stop at nothing. She could imagine him courageously facing bullets – even if he did wear a starched collar!

Vasya was seized with a sudden desire to place her hand trustingly in his large hand. Here was a man with whom she felt she could spend her life, happily and confidently. But what could she mean to someone like Vladimir? She saw herself through his eyes and sighed. He was so handsome, he'd seen such a lot, he'd been in America. What was she? Just a plain little thing, a simpleton who'd seen nothing beyond her own provincial town. How could he take her seriously? He hadn't even noticed her today!

His voice broke into her thoughts.

'Good day to you, Comrade Vasilisa! Well we got the gentleman commissar into a sweat, didn't we? That taught him a lesson; he won't be turning up here again. From now on we'll send them our resolutions just for their information!'

He was glowing with excitement over the affair, and Vasya found his mood infectious. They talked and laughed together happily, and if Vladimir hadn't been dragged away by his friends they would have stayed talking in the passage much longer, discussing the commissar and the resolutions that had been passed.

'There's nothing for it, I'm afraid I must go now, I shall have to leave you, comrade Vasilisa,' he said, and she heard the regret in his voice. She trembled with joy and raised her brown eyes to him. Vladimir immediately stopped what he was doing and looked into them as if looking into her heart. She felt as though he were drowning in her eyes.

'Stop hanging around there, Vladimir! You're holding us up and we're up to our eyes in work!'

'Coming!' he shouted to his friends, and squeezing Vasya's hand he hurried off. Vasya left too and wandered round the town not knowing where she was going, seeing nothing, neither people nor streets, only Vladimir. Nothing like this had ever happened to her before . . .

They began to meet more often. One frosty winter evening they were leaving a session of the soviet together. The sky was bright, and fresh white snow lay on the ground, the roofs and fences, and enveloped the trees in feathery flakes. The October days were over, and power was firmly in the hands of the soviets.

The Mensheviks and the right wing Socialist Revolutionaries had been ousted, though the internationalists remained as a problem. One group now dominated – the Bolsheviks. Their power was increasing steadily and the workers were behind them. Only the bourgeoisie, the priests and the officers opposed them now, and the soviets gave them no quarter. The waves of revolution hadn't subsided, and life wasn't yet back to normal. Red Guards patrolled the streets in the towns, and here and there was the occasional skirmish. But nevertheless it looked as though the hardest struggles might be over.

Vasilisa and Vladimir were talking about the days when they seized power in the town. It was Vladimir's bakers who had saved the day. They were tough and loyal and Vladimir was justifiably proud of them. Thanks to them he'd been elected to the soviet.

They were walking side by side through the quiet streets. Every so often a Red Guard would stop them and ask for the password. Vladimir, like them, was wearing a red armband and a fur hat, for he had joined the Red Guards. He'd been under fire too, Vasya had seen his sleeve with the bullet hole on the shoulder.

Though they were seeing a great deal of each other, there never seemed enough time for them to talk. Now, without having arranged it, they were leaving a meeting together. Immediately both of them felt at ease. They had so much to tell each other, like two old friends. And then all of a sudden, they would stop talking, sensing the strong bond between them.

They passed Vasya's house without even noticing, and before they knew it they were wandering through the outskirts of the town. Stopping in amazement, they began to laugh. Where on earth were they? They stood very still, gazing up at the sky and the blazing stars. How beautiful it was! At that moment they felt young and very happy.

Vasya said, 'In the country where I grew up we never had a

clock, so we learnt to tell the time by the stars. My father knew every star, and he always knew the right time.'

Then Vladimir began to tell her about his childhood. He came from a very large family of poor peasant stock who'd always had to scrape along. Vladimir longed to go to school, but the school was too far away, so he persuaded the priest's daughter to let him feed her geese, and in return she taught him to read and write. Vladimir's voice became more and more tender and wistful as he reminisced about the country, and the fields and copses near his parents' home. Just look at him! thought Vasya fondly, and from that moment he became even dearer to her.

He told her how he'd gone to America as a teenager, determined to make a place for himself there. After two years on a cargo ship, he'd worked as a docker, and was eventually blacklisted for joining a strike. He was forced to leave the state, and life had been tough. He went hungry, took any job that came his way. First he was a cleaner in a smart hotel – she should have seen all those flashy people! And as for the women, decked out in their tulle dresses, their diamonds and silk!

Then he worked for a while as a doorman at a fashion house. It paid well, but he was only hired because he was the right height and build and the braided uniform suited him. The job bored him stiff, and he could barely contain his rage at the sight of all the wealthy customers. He got a job as a chauffeur, driving a rich cotton merchant hundreds of miles across America in his limousine. But this too bored him – it was nothing but wage slavery, just like all his other jobs.

However, this businessman had encouraged him to work his way into the cotton business; he'd become a clerk and took courses in accountancy. Then in February 1917, revolution broke out in Russia and he dropped everything and want back.

But America had been a different world. He'd liked a lot of things about it. For instance, the businessman had stood up for him, even bailed him out when as a member of a proscribed

Alexandra Kollontai

organization he'd been sent to prison after a brush with the police. He had been impressed by such loyalty.

They walked on and on, along street after street, and Vasya listened to Vladimir talk. There was no stopping him! He wanted to tell her his entire life story. Once again they came to the gate of Vasya's house.

'Do you think I could come in and have some tea with you, Vasilisa?' asked Vladimir. 'My throat is dry, and I don't feel sleepy yet.'

Vasya hesitated: the friend with whom she lived was sure to be in bed. But it didn't matter. They would wake her up and all three have tea together – that would be even jollier. Why shouldn't she invite her 'American' in. She couldn't bear to leave him at this moment.

They went in, and Vladimir helped her put on the samovar. 'One should always give ladies a hand,' he said. 'That was one thing they took for granted in America.' They sat down to their tea, joking and teasing Vasilisa's friend whom they'd dragged out of bed and was sitting there blinking sleepily. Vasilisa was supremely happy.

Vladimir started to talk about America again, about all the beautiful women in silk stockings who arrived at the fashion house in their cars, while he held the door open for them in his braided uniform and feathered cocked hat. Once a woman had slipped him a note proposing an assignation, but he hadn't gone. He didn't like those females with their petty intrigues. Another woman had given him a rose. As Vasya listened to these stories she began to feel smaller and less attractive – all the joy drained from her heart. She frowned. 'So I suppose you were in love with all those beautiful women you met?' she asked in a toneless voice, and immediately felt furious with herself for voicing such a stupid question.

Vladimir looked closely at her and shook his head.

'All my life, Vasilisa Dementevna, I have been keeping my

heart and my love pure. The girl I fall in love with will have to be pure too. They were nothing but whores, those women, no better than streetwalkers.'

The joy had flooded back into her heart – and there it froze. So he was only going to fall in love with a virgin, was he? Well, she wasn't a virgin! First there'd been that brief love affair with Petya Razgulov who worked in the machine department. But then he'd been called away to the Front. There had been the party organizer, and they had even considered getting married. But he had to leave too, and when he stopped writing she eventually forgot him . . .

Did Vladimir really mean it when he said he could only love a virgin? Vasya looked at him intently, trying to follow what he was saying, but by now she was in such a state of panic that she could no longer make head or tail of anything.

He assumed he must be boring her with his stories, and abruptly broke off what he was saying and stood up. He took his leave of her hastily and rather coldly, and her eyes filled with tears. She longed to throw her arms around his neck, but did he really want her? She sobbed all that night, vowing that she avoid 'the American' from then on. What was the point of meeting him again, what could she mean to him?

But although Vasya might have intended to avoid 'the American', they were brought even more closely together soon afterwards. At a committee meeting to appoint a new mayor, a dispute arose; some people proposed Vladimir, but others wouldn't hear of him, in particular the secretary of the party who wouldn't be budged. The whole town was up in arms about 'the American', he said, riding about in his cab like a Tsarist local governor, doffing his hat in a lordly fashion at all and sundry. Ordinary people considered him a menace; he wouldn't accept party discipline, and there'd been more than one complaint about him recently for not observing party decrees in the co-operative.

Vasya defended Vladimir hotly at this meeting, though she certainly felt he was foolish to put on his swaggering airs. She was upset that they still referred to him as an anarchist. It was stupid to distrust him – as a worker he was more than a match for any Bolshevik! Stepan Alexeevich supported Vladimir too, and they put it to the vote. There were seven against him, six for – so that was that.

When Vladimir was told of the committee's decision, he flew into a rage and cursed the Bolsheviks. How could they distrust him when he'd worked heart and soul for the revolution? 'Constitutionalists! Centralists!' he yelled. 'You want your own police state!' He went on and on in this fashion, warning them about America, where people were ordered around and forbidden to do anything and the international movement was continually harassed. All this talk alarmed the committee even more, and they demanded that Vladimir submit to their decision.

But the feud continued and became increasingly bitter, with Vasya tormenting herself, defending Vladimir and arguing until she was hoarse. Then a new case was presented to the soviet: once again Vladimir's co-operative had failed to carry out a particular order.

Vladimir faced the soviet and kept repeating the same thing over and over again: 'I don't recognize these police measures! Each department must make its own rules! Discipline? I don't give a damn for your discipline! We didn't make the revolution, shed our blood, drive out the bourgeoisie just to go hang ourselves in a new noose! Who are all these commanders who've suddenly appeared out of the blue to order us around? Anyone would think *we* didn't know how to give orders!'

There had been fierce arguments, shouted threats. 'If you won't take orders we'll have to expel you from the soviet,' warned the chairman.

'You just try! shouted Vladimir, his eyes flashing. 'My bakers are fighters. If I summon them from the militia, who will you

42

have left to defend you? You'll be crushed under the heel of the bourgeoisie, because that's what you're heading for. This isn't a soviet, it's a branch of the Tsarist police force!'

This remark stabbed Vasya to the quick. Why did he have to say that? Vladimir stood his ground, white in the face, and continued to defend himself, while everyone around him grew more and more agitated.

'Arrest him!' they shouted. 'Expel him! Chuck him out, lazy good-for-nothing!'

It was Stepan Alexeevich who saved the situation. He suggested Vladimir go into another room so the soviet could discuss the affair without him there. Vladimir left, and Vasya with him.

She was angry with him for his idiotic diatribes; and when he'd proved himself by his dedication to the soviet too! But could someone really be judged on impulsive remarks? Why couldn't they judge him by his actions? Everyone knew how Vladimir defended the soviets; if it hadn't been for him, it was quite likely the soviets wouldn't have supported the Bolsheviks in October. It was he who had disarmed the officers, forced the mayor to flee the town and brought the mayor's supporters onto the streets, telling them, 'Well, get on with it then! You can shovel the snow off the road!'

Could they really expel him from the soviet merely for his irascible temper? Vasya was dreadfully upset as she went into the room behind the platform. Vladimir was sitting at the table plunged in gloom, his head propped on his arm. He glanced up at her, his eyes burning with resentment. He looked so distraught and anxious – suddenly Vasya saw him as a hurt child, small and vulnerable. She vowed to stop at nothing to protect him.

'So our constitutionalists have taken fright,' he began jauntily. 'Do you suppose it was my threats that scared them? But . . .'

He faltered. Vasya's expression was one of sympathy and reproach.

'You were wrong you know, Vladimir Ivanovich, and now you've only yourself to blame. Whatever possessed you to say all that? Don't you see, for them it can only mean one thing – that you're opposing the soviet?'

'And I shall continue to oppose it as long as it acts like the Tsarist police force,' insisted Vladimir obstinately.

'How can you say such things? You know you don't believe a word of it!'

Vasya moved closer to him; at this moment she felt very much older than him. She gazed at him affectionately and seriously. Vladimir looked into her eyes but said, nothing.

'Come on now, admit it, you lost your temper.'

Vladimir hung his head. 'The whole thing's a mess. They're furious with me.' Again he looked into Vasya's eyes like a child apologizing to his mother.

'There's nothing to be done, it's hopeless,' he said with a gesture of despair. Vasya's heart was filled with pain and tenderness for this man, who had become so dear to her. She put her hand on his head and stroked it gently.

'Please don't lose heart, Vladimir Ivanovich, you mustn't despair. That would never do for an anarchist! You must have faith in yourself and not allow people to insult you.'

She stood over him, stroking his head. He laid it trustingly on her breast.

'I've had a hard life you know, I've taken a lot of knocks, I thought in the revolution we'd all be able to work together like friends, but I suppose it's not going to be like that after all.'

'Everything will be all right,' Vasya said. 'We just have to learn to trust one another if we're going to work together.'

'No, everything won't be all right. Don't you see, I can't get on with people.'

'But you'll learn, I'm sure of it.'

Vasya lifted Vladimir's face to hers, gazing into his eyes as if to inspire him with her confidence. But his eyes were filled with anxiety and unhappiness. She leant over him and began to kiss his hair gently.

'You must try and put things right now. You must apologize, tell them you lost your temper and that they misunderstood you.'

'All right,' Vladimir agreed humbly, looking at her as though for support. Then moving suddenly towards her, he grasped her in his arms and pressed her violently to him, kissing her passionately.

Vasya ran back to the platform and went straight to Stepan Alexeevich. She had to save Vladimir Ivanovich.

The incident was finally settled, but hostility towards Vladimir lingered on and two camps began to emerge within the soviet. It looked as if the old days of friendly co-operation were over . . .

Riding along now in the dark train, Vasya longed to curb these memories, which kept crowding into her. She wanted to remember how their love affair had started. It had been shortly after the incident in the soviet. Vladimir had begun to walk her home regularly and they started seeking each out, and when they were on their own they began to be on informal 'ty' terms with each other.

On one occasion, when the girl sharing Vasya's flat was out, he had seized her in his arms. His kisses had been so passionate – even now she could remember those kisses. But she had struggled free of him and looked him straight in the eyes.

'No Volodya, please don't. I don't want us to deceive each other.'

He looked at her, shocked and bewildered.

'But why should I deceive you, Vasya? Don't you realize. I fell in love with you the moment I met you?'

'No, it's not that Volodya, it's something else. Yes, I do believe you but I . . . No stop, you see you told me once you'd only fall in love with a girl who was a virgin, and, well, I'm not a virgin, Volodya, I've had lovers . . .'

She was trembling as she spoke, terrified that she might lose new happiness.

But he interrupted her.

'Do you suppose I care about your old boyfriends? You belong to me now Vasya. As far as I'm concerned, you're the sweetest, purest person in the whole world. So you do love me, Vasya? You really love me? I can't believe you're mine, mine, and nobody else's! Now don't you dare even mention any of your old boyfriends to me again, do you hear? Don't tell me about them, I don't want to know! All I care about is that now you belong to me . . . !'

And so they became lovers.

It was dark now. The other woman was lying down and the compartment was pervaded with the flowery scent of her toilet-water. Vasilisa was lying on the upper berth, trying to sleep. But try as she might, sleep would not come; memories of her past with Volodya were too vivid. Somewhere at the back of her mind was the feeling that the past was over, the happiness of four years ago was just a memory. She couldn't imagine why she should feel this so acutely, when their lives still stretched ahead of them. She just felt, for some reason she couldn't grasp, that their love had changed – and that she herself had changed . . .

She lay brooding in the dark, her hands clasped behind her head. There hadn't been much time to think over the past three years. She now realized that she'd been so busy working all that time that there were a great many things she hadn't properly thought about, things she had somehow managed to push to the back of her mind; all Volodya's disagreements with the party for instance, his squabbles with the departments. In the very early days there was much less of that, and he'd been different. Of course there had been arguments, and he often crossed swords with the authorities, but Vasya was always able to make him see reason, for he trusted her judgement and would take her advice.

When the Whites launched their offensive against the, revolution and the town was threatened, Vladimir immediately set off for the Front. Vasya hadn't tried to prevent him going, just insisted that he join the party first. After much blustering and argument he had eventually joined. He became a Bolshevik, then left.

They didn't write to other much. He would pay her flying visits for a day or two, then they wouldn't see each other for weeks, even months, at a time. This was unavoidable, and they didn't even have time to miss each other too much.

Then out of the blue Vasilisa heard from the committee that Vladimir was up on a charge. She couldn't imagine what he had done. He was working in the provisions department, and had apparently been muddling his accounts; there was even a suspicion that he'd been pilfering.

Vasya was furious when she heard this. 'It's lies!' she said. 'I don't believe a word of it! Nothing but petty lies and slander!' Nevertheless it was obviously serious, and she rushed round dementedly making enquiries. He hadn't actually been arrested but he had been suspended from his job. She begged Stepan Alexeevich to give her a pass to take parcels to the Front, and three days later she set off. That had been her first visit to Volodya.

3

The journey had been beset with obstacles – delays and disconnected trains all the way. First she found she didn't have the paper documents, then the goods compartment was disconnected. She worried herself sick. What if his case had already come to court? It was then that Vasya realized how much she loved Vladimir, how precious he was to her. Everyone else believed that as an anarchist he was capable of acting despicably, but the more other people distrusted him, the more stubbornly she leapt to his defence. Nobody knew him like she did! He was such a gentle soul, as gentle as a woman – it

47

was only his manner that was rude and inflexible. Vasya knew that with kindness and affection he could be persuaded to behave himself. He was bitter, it was true; a worker's life was never a bed of roses!

When she eventually arrived she went straight to the army headquarters, and after a great deal of trouble had found out where Vladimir's quarters were. She had to drag herself through pouring rain to the other side of town, although luckily someone offered to show her the way and carry her parcels. She was tired, shivering with cold, but also overjoyed to find that they hadn't completed their investigations, and there was still no hard evidence against him. Opinion in the department seemed divided, and there were a lot of rumours and denunciations flying around.

Vasya had been greatly disturbed by their spiteful smirks when she announced herself as Vladimir's wife; they seemed to be concealing something from her. She was determined to investigate every detail of the case and see Comrade Toporkov, who had come from the party central committee and knew Vladimir's work record. How could they persecute him like this when there were all those Mensheviks and Socialist Revolutionaries, the real enemies, that they weren't bothering about! Why should an anarchist be treated worse than they were?

Vasilisa and her companions arrived at the little wooden house where Vladimir was quartered. The lights were on but the porch door was bolted. Her companion banged on the door. No reply. By now Vasya's stockings were soaked and she was anticipating not so much her joy at seeing Volodya as the relief of getting into a warm room and changing her dress and stockings. For five days she had been sitting in a heated goods van and had had almost no sleep.

'Let's knock on the window,' suggested her companion. Breaking a twig off a birch tree they rapped on the glass. The curtain jerked back, and Vasya caught a glimpse of Vladimir's head. He seemed to be in his nightshirt, peering out into the darkness. Then a woman's head bobbed up over his shoulder and disappeared from view. A sickening, agonizing sensation paralyzed Vasya.

Her companion shouted, 'Open up, comrade! I've brought your wife to see you!' The curtain was hastily drawn again, concealing Volodya and the woman from sight, and Vasya went back to the porch to wait for the door to be opened. What was taking him so long? She thought he'd never come.

Eventually the door was flung open and she found herself in Volodya's arms.

'You've come at last, my darling! Oh Vasya, my dearest friend!' he said, embracing and kissing her with tears of joy in his eyes.

'Take these parcels will you? What am I supposed to do with them?' Vasya's companion reminded her sullenly.

'Let's go into the house and have something to eat. My poor love, you must be so wet and cold,' Volodya said.

Inside it was bright and clean, with a bedroom and dining room – and there, sitting at a table, was a nurse with a white kerchief on her head and a red armband. She was extremely pretty and Vasilisa felt another stab of pain. Volodya introduced them to each other.

'This is nurse Varvara and this is my wife, Vasilisa Dementevna.' The two women shook hands and stared at each other, trying to read each other's thoughts. Vladimir bustled round.

'Come on Vasya, take off your coat. You're mistress here now. Look how well I live, better than your cubby-hole of a room, eh? Here, give me your coat. How wet it is – we'll have to hang it over the stove.'

The nurse remained where she was. 'Well Vladimir Ivanovich,' she said finally, 'we'll sort things out tomorrow. I wouldn't want to interfere in your family happiness now.'

She shook hands with Vasya and Vladimir and went out,

accompanied by the man who had come with Vasya. Then Vladimir picked Vasya up in his arms and carried her around the room, hugging and kissing her. He was obviously overjoyed to see her, and Vasya felt easier in her mind, ashamed of her previous suspicions. But between kisses she couldn't help blurting out, 'Who was that nurse?' throwing back her head as she did so in order to look Vladimir in the eyes.

'Her? Oh, she just came to see me about getting provisions for the hospital. We have to speed up deliveries, but there are delays everywhere. It's not my responsibility, but all the same they rely on me. The least thing, and they all come running to me.'

Then he began telling her about his case. He put her down and they went into the bedroom, and once again she was overcome by the same stabbing anxiety; the bed had been made hurriedly, the blankets hastily flung on top. She glanced at Vladimir, who was pacing around the room with one hand behind his back – a familiar habit of his which she loved – telling her about his case, how it had started and how it was progressing. Ignoring her own anxieties, Vasya listened to his account and felt mortified for him; it was obviously based on nothing but recriminations and envy. Her Volodya was honest, she knew he was!

She got some dry stockings out of her suitcase, but she had no shoes to change into. Noticing this, Vladimir exclaimed, 'Just look at the woman! She hasn't even got a spare pair of shoes! I know, I'll get you some nice leather and our cobbler will make my darling a pair of shoes. Let me take them off for you. Oh, how wet they are!'

He took off her shoes, threw her stockings onto the floor, and held Vasya's cold feet in his warm hands.

'Darling Volodka, you silly thing,' she said, laughing. She felt utterly happy. He loved her, and nothing else mattered!

They drank tea, chatting and discussing Vladimir's case. He was completely open with her and told her about all the times he'd been insolent, lost his temper, hadn't carried out instructions, wanted to have his own way, wouldn't take orders. He told her how he'd made the mistake of getting mixed up with various crooks in his job, but as for the charge of pilfering, surely Vasya couldn't believe him capable of such a thing? He stood in front of her, breathing rapidly, seething with rage.

'How could you even suspect such a thing, you of all people, Vasya . . . ?'

'It's not that Volodya, believe me. I'm just worried about the state of your accounts. They must be investigating them very carefully at the moment.'

'There's no need to worry about my accounts. The people who've cooked up this business won't find anything wrong with them. They're an open book. I didn't study accountancy for nothing, you know.'

Vasilisa felt relieved. She'd only have to see his comrades and negotiate with them, explaining the facts of the case.

'You're so clever, darling. Thank goodness you've come,' said Volodya. 'You know, I didn't dare hope you would. I know how busy you are. "She'll have no time for her husband," I thought to myself, no time for her Volodka!'

'But my sweetheart, if only you knew! I never have a moment's peace when I'm away from you. You're constantly on my mind, I worry in case anything bad has happened to you!'

'Vasya, you're my guardian angel,' he said very gravely, kissing her. Pensive and rather mournful for a moment, he said, 'I may not be worthy of you, but I love you more than anything in the world. You must believe me, I love you and only you, and nothing else is worth anything.'

Vasya was surprised how tense and uneasy he seemed, and didn't understand why.

It was time for bed. Vasya started straightening the bedclothes and threw back the blankets. Suddenly she stood stock still. There on the sheet was a spot of blood and a woman's blood-stained sanitary towel.

'Volodya! What's this?' she gasped. 'Tell me, Volodya!'

Vladimir hurled the towel to the floor.

'Damn that housekeeper! She must have been having a lie-in again without telling me. Look, she's stained the bed!' he jerked the sheet off the bed onto the floor.

'Vladimir!' Vasya cried, her wide eyes saying more than any words could express. Vladimir looked into them and was reduced to silence.

'Volodya! Please tell me what's going on!'

Volodya collapsed onto the bed, wringing his hands.

'Everything's ruined, completely ruined! But I swear to you, Vasya, you're the woman I love!'

'How *could* you! How *could* you do this to us?'

'Vasya, I'm a young man. I've been alone for months. They play up to me. But I hate them! The whole damn lot of them! Brazen whores, sluts!'

He stretched out his hands to her. Tears were pouring down his cheeks, dropping onto her hands.

'Vasya, please try to understand, otherwise I'm done for. My life is so hard. Please. Take pity on me.'

It was just like the episode long ago at the soviet. Leaning over him Vasya kissed his head, and once again her heart ached with love and pity for this man who was really such a child.

If she didn't understand and take pity on him, who would? He was surrounded by hostile people ready to hurl stones at him. He had hurt her feelings terribly, yet was that reason enough to leave him now of all times? How could she? He desperately needed her to protect him, like a mother, from life's blows. Her love wouldn't be worth much if she walked out on him because of one humiliation! Vasya's mind raced as she stood bending over him, stroking his hair.

Then, a knock at the door, a loud insistent knock which they both instantly understood. They embraced hurriedly, kissed passionately and went into the hall.

The preliminary investigations were over. It had been decided to arrest Vladimir. The ground began to sway under Vasya's feet, but he acted calmly, collecting his things, telling Vasya where to find the appropriate documents, whom to cite as witnesses, from whom to take evidence, and so on. Then they led him away . . .

Vasya would never in her whole life forget that night, although many years had passed since then. She had never experienced anything so devastating. Her heart was torn apart by those two great griefs – the ageless grief of the woman betrayed and the grief of a true friend and companion who has seen her loved one wronged. Grief for human malevolence, grief for injustice . . .

After Vladimir had been led off, Vasya rushed around the bedroom like a mad woman. All she could think about was that here, in this very room, on this very bed, Vladimir had kissed, caressed, made love to another woman! A beautiful woman with pouting lips and full breasts. Maybe he even loved this woman? Yes, maybe he'd lied to her to spare her feelings!

Vasilisa needed the truth! Why on this day of all days did they have to take her Vladimir away from her? She could have found out everything, if only he'd been there to answer her questions. If only he'd been there, he could have comforted her, rescued her from this morbid torment . . .

Then, as well as grief, she was seized with sudden rage against him. How dare he? He would never have slept with that woman if he loved *her*, and if he didn't love her why couldn't he say so and be done with it, instead of driving her mad with a lot of lies. She stormed around the room now in panic, saved only by a new thought which came to her with sudden painful clarity: what if his case was substantiated? What if they had arrested him for good reason? What if he really had been mixed up with those scoundrels, and was having to answer for it?

Her jealousy and anger disappeared, the nurse with the full

lips vanished from her mind, and now there was only a numbing anguished fear for Vladimir, a sickening, burning sense of shame for him. He had been publicly disgraced, arrested – and by his own comrades too! What was her own jealous outrage compared to this outrage against the man she loved? And a new grief seized her, for she felt that even in revolution there was no truth, no justice.

All weariness went, and she felt as though her body didn't belong to her. All that remained was a heart lacerated by the claws of her tormenting thoughts. She sat up all through that night, and by daybreak she had resolved to defend Vladimir, to save him from public disgrace. She would prove to the whole world that her husband was an honourable person, that he had been wronged, slandered, insulted.

Early that morning, a Red Army soldier arrived with a note from Vladimir.

'My sweet wife, my dearest beloved friend, Vasya, I don't care what happens to me now, nor to the case. It's one thought that's driving me mad – the thought of losing you. Vasya, you must please believe me! I can't live without you! If you don't love me any more, don't defend me. They can shoot me for all I care.

Yours, and only yours, Volodya. PS It's you I love, nobody else but you. You may not believe that, but I'd swear it even in the face of death.

A second postscript read: 'I've never held your past against you, so please try to understand me now and forgive me. I belong to you, Vasya, body and soul.'

Vasya read the note, then she re-read it and began to feel slightly easier in her mind. Of course, he was quite right! He'd never once blamed her for not being a virgin when they started living together. He was a man, what could you expect! How could he help it if some slut played up to him? She couldn't expect him to take a vow of chastity. She read the note one more time, kissed it, folded it neatly and put it away in her purse. Now it was time to get down to business and bail Volodya out.

In the days that followed, she dashed around in a frenzy of activity; at every step she confronted bureaucracy and apathy, and there were times when she felt like giving up. But she would rally, put a brave face on it and once more enter the fray. She didn't intend to be defeated by lies, or let a pack of informers and conspirators get the better of her Volodya.

Then she won a major victory. Comrade Torporkov himself was persuaded to take the matter up, and after reviewing the case thoroughly he proposed that it be dropped, since the charges weren't adequately substantiated. Instead two men called Sviridov and Malchenko were to be arrested.

The morning after this news, Vasya was confined to her bed with an attack of typhus. By evening she could no longer recognize anyone, even Volodya, who had just returned. Later she would recall her illness as a suffocating nightmare. Towards evening she opened her eyes, and looking around her she saw an unfamiliar room, with bottles of medicine on the table and a nurse in a kerchief sitting by her bed, an elderly, stern-looking woman. Vasya stared at her, distressed that she should have a nurse with her and enraged by the woman's white kerchief. She couldn't imagine what she was doing here.

'Are you thirsty?' the nurse asked, leaning over her and offering her a drink. Vasya drank thirstily, then lost consciousness again. In her comatose state she imagined Volodya was leaning over her, arranging her pillows. She half awoke.

Then once more she lost consciousness. And this time she dreamed – or was it real? – that two shadows glided into her room, no, not shadows but women, only they weren't real women . . . One was white, the other grey, and they whirled about the room in what seemed one moment like a dance, next moment like a test of strength. Vasya was aware that the figures represented Life and Death, and that they had come to fight over her. She was terrified. She wanted to cry out loud. But try as she might, she couldn't, for she had lost her voice, and this increased her terror. Her heart pounded as though about to burst . . .

Then, rat-a-tat! There was firing on the street! She managed to open her eyes. A night-light was burning, smoking faintly. It was the middle of the night, and she was all alone. She could hear the sound of mice scratching. They seemed to be scrabbling around under the floor boards, getting closer and closer to her bed. Vasya was seized with terror that they would hop on to the bed and run over her, and she wouldn't have the strength to get them off.

In a weak voice she called out: 'Volodya! Volodya!'

Immediately he was by her side, leaning over her, looking anxiously into her eyes. 'Vasya my love, what is it? What's wrong, my darling?'

'Volodya, is that you? Are you still alive? I'm not just imagining it?' She stretched out her weak arm to touch his head.

'I'm alive all right, sweetheart. I'm right here beside you. Now what are you crying about? What's happened to my Vasyuk? Did you have a nightmare? Are you feeling feverish?'

He kissed her hands tenderly, stroking her damp cropped head. 'No, it wasn't a dream, it's those mice scratching over there,' she said sheepishly with a weak smile.

'Mice!' laughed Volodya. 'Well, now my Vasya is a proper heroine! She's even afraid of mice! I told the nurse you weren't to be left on your own. I'm so relieved I got home when I did!'

Vasya wanted to ask him where he'd been, but was too exhausted to talk. Besides, the feeling of weakness was so pleasurable, so soothing; and best of all, she had her beloved Vladimir sitting there beside her. She grasped his hand weakly and clung to it.

'So you're alive,' she whispered, smiling.

'Of course I'm alive,' Volodya laughed, gently kissing her head.

Vasya opened her eyes.

'My hair! It's gone! Did they cut it off?'

'You mustn't worry about that. My Vasya looks like a boy now, that's what she always was really.'

Vasya smiled. She felt overwhelmed with happiness – happiness she hadn't felt since childhood. Then she dozed off. Volodya stayed with her, sitting beside her to make sure she slept undisturbed.

'Go to sleep now, Vasya,' he soothed her. 'There's no need for you to stay awake. When you're better you'll have time to look at me to your heart's content. If you don't sleep now you won't get better, and the doctor will blame me for being a bad nurse.'

'You won't leave me?'

'Why should I ever leave you? I'm going to sleep here beside you on the floor every night; I'll feel easier in my mind if I can see you. Tomorrow I'll be back at work.'

'Work? In the provisions department again?'

'Yes, everything's been sorted out, and those scoundrels have been arrested. My darling Vasyuk, what's to be done with you! You mustn't talk any more now, you must sleep, otherwise I'll go away immediately!'

She linked her weak fingers with his and closed her eyes obediently. Sleep came upon her sweetly, so gently, with Volodya there beside her, worrying and watching over her.

'Sweetheart,' she murmured.

'Go to sleep, little tomboy.'

'I *am* going to sleep, but I do love you. . .'

Volodya leaned over her and gently kissed her closed eyes. Vasya could have cried for happiness. If only she could die now! Never again would life grant her so much happiness.

Now, as she lay on her berth in the train, it terrified Vasilisa to recall these thoughts. Would life really never be so good again? What about now? Wouldn't she find the same joy and happiness? She was on her way to see her Volodechka. He'd sent for her, was waiting for her, and had even sent a colleague to make sure she came immediately. There'd been the money for the train ticket and the dress – that *must* mean he loved her. Vasya desperately wanted to believe that they could live together happily again, but somewhere in the depths of her heart there was this nagging doubt. Something had changed. Once again she lost herself in thoughts and memories of the past.

Their next separation had been totally unexpected. The battle front had shifted and Vladimir was summoned to leave. Vasya was still so weak from typhus she could barely move her legs. They parted affectionately, with no mention of the incident with the nurse. Vasya had come to realize that the woman really meant very little to Volodya, no more, as he put it, 'than a glass of vodka, something to drink and forget'.

And then, when she was strong enough, Vasya had returned home, to her old room, and had immediately gone back to work.

Everything at work was just as it had been, but something kept preying on Vasya's mind: she was plagued with doubts and anger about Volodya and that nurse with the pouting lips. Still, she loved Volodya deeply, and her illness and their shared anxieties seemed to have strengthened the bond between them. Previously they had been in love. Now that they united by unhappiness they were emotionally closer.

This love brought Vasya none of the blinding joy of her earlier love; it was deeper, perhaps stronger, but also overcast with shadows. But this was no time for love, these days of civil war and foreign invasion, negotiations and separations. Everyone was over-worked, and Vasilisa had to deal with the refugee problem. She was appointed to the housing committee of the soviet, and it was then she conceived her plan of setting up the communal house. It was to be run entirely on her lines, with help and funds from the soviet.

Love of Worker Bees

Vasya became utterly absorbed in this project. For many months it was the cornerstone of her life. Although memories of Volodya were constantly in her mind, she had no time to be miserable. Besides, he too was working. His affairs seemed to be going smoothly now, and she was confident that he was no longer throwing his weight around and was getting on better with the central administration and the bosses.

Then suddenly, out of the blue, there was Vladimir. He just walked into her room one day, utterly unexpectedly. Apparently he had been caught in cross-fire during a retreat and been wounded. It was nothing serious, but he needed rest and had been given sick-leave and told to go back to his wife, for 'board and lodging'.

Vasya was overjoyed, but she couldn't help feeling apprehensive. If only he could have come at some other time! She had put much energy into the past two months' work, and foresaw at least another month of hard work ahead. She had so much to do, so many commitments. There was a congress coming up soon, then there was the reorganization of the housing department and all her activities for the communal house – there was no end to her tasks. She was expected to be everywhere at once, and now Volodya had turned up wounded. Somehow she would have to take some time off work.

Though Vasya's joy at seeing him was clouded by these anxieties, Volodya was as happy as a child. He had brought with him the shoes he had promised her. 'Do try them', on, Vasya. I want to see how your tiny feet will look in them', he said excitedly.

She didn't want to hurt his feelings, though she was pressed for time – a meeting of the housing committee was due to start soon. She tried on the shoes, and suddenly she felt she was seeing her feet for the first time; it was quite true, she realized, they *were* tiny. She looked rapturously at him, dumb with gratitude.

'I'd pick you up, darling, but for my wretched arm,' he said happily. 'Oh, I love your small feet, and your brown eyes!'

He went on talking and joking, overjoyed to see her again, but Vasya was only half-listening; she should have been at the meeting long ago. She kept looking at the alarm-clock on the chest-of-drawers. The minutes were ticking by, people would be waiting for her. She began to feel angry; why should she keep them waiting like this? It was extremely bad manners for the president to be late.

It was evening when Vasya eventually returned from her meeting. She felt tired and distraught, for there had been a number of annoying incidents, but as she climbed the stairs to her garret her worries diminished.

Thank goodness Vladimir's here, she thought. I'll be able to tell him everything and ask him what he thinks.

But when she went into the room Vladimir was nowhere to be seen.

Where could he have gone? There were his hat and coat hanging on the peg. He must have gone out for a while. She began to tidy up the room and make tea on the oil stove. Still no Volodya. Where on earth could he have got to? She went out into the corridor, but he wasn't there. She went back to wait for him, growing more and more uneasy. Where *could* he be?

She went out once more into the corridor. And there was Vladimir coming out of the Feodoseevs' flat, taking his leave and laughing with them as if they were old friends. Why, for heaven's sake, had he taken it into his head to visit them? Surely she had told him they were up to no good?

'So you're here at last, Vasya,' he greeted her back in her room. 'I've been cooped up here all day, almost hanging myself with boredom. It was lucky I happened to meet Feodoseev, who dragged me off to his flat . . .'

'But you mustn't have anything to do with those people!' Vasya interrupted him. 'They're out to make trouble, you know that!'

'Well, do you expect me to stay closeted in your tiny room

dying of boredom? If you hadn't run away and left me alone all day, I wouldn't have had to visit the Feodoseevs . . .'

'But surely you can see how much work I have to do. I'd have been pleased to get away earlier, but I couldn't.'

'Of course, your work, quite so. But what about me, Vasya? What about the time you had typhus, and all those nights I sat up with you? I took off every minute I could to come and see how you were. *I'm* the sick one now Vasya, I'm still feverish . . .'

Vasya was hurt by the reproach in his voice; he was offended that she'd left him all day. But it couldn't be helped at the moment, with the conference coming up and all her work reorganizing the department.

'I can't help feeling you're not very pleased to see me, Vasya,' said Vladimir. 'I didn't think you'd act like this when we saw each other again.'

'How can you say that! Me, not pleased? But I . . . Oh, darling, my precious sweetheart!'

She flung her arms around his neck, almost knocking over the oil stove as she did so.

'There, there, my love,' he soothed her. 'It's just that I imagined you'd stopped loving me. I even wondered if you'd taken up with another man. You're so cold somehow, you seem indifferent to me, even your eyes are distant and unfriendly.'

'I'm just tired, Volodya. I don't have the energy to cope with everything.'

'Never mind, my little ruffian,' said Volodya, hugging and kissing her.

They lived together 'cooped up', as he put it, in her little garret room. At first everything went well, and however difficult Vasya found it to divide her time between work and husband, she did so cheerfully. Now there was someone to talk to about her new plans, someone to whom she could confess her failures. The only thing that bothered her was the housekeeping. At the Front, Vladimir had become accustomed to eating in style. Vasya's housekeeping, however, was absolutely minimal; she was quite happy with a frugal soviet-style meal, with tea and a lump of sugar. For the first few days they ate the provisions that Vladimir had brought with him.

'I got hold of some basics, flour, sugar and some sausage. I know you don't mind eating like a sparrow, and you never put food by', he said.

When Volodya's provisions came to an end he had to start eating soviet-style meals, which he detested.

'What's this millet mush you keep feeding me as if I were a hen?' he grumbled in disgust.

'But there's nothing else to be had! I'm living on my rations.'

'Nonsense! Why, the Feodoseevs don't get any more rations than you do, but yesterday they treated me to dinner, and a good dinner it was too, with fried potatoes, herrings, onions . . .'

'But Mrs Feodoseeva has time for cooking and shopping. I have to work so hard. I barely manage to get through all I have to do as it is.'

'Your problem is that you take on too much, and then look what happens. Why all this fuss about the communal house? The Feodoseevs were saying . . .'

'I know quite well what the Feodoseevs say, thank you,' said Vasya with mounting anger; it offended her greatly that Vladimir had anything to do with these people, her enemies. 'Look here, it isn't very loyal of you to listen to their criticisms of me.'

They began to quarrel and lost their tempers. Then they both felt annoyed with themselves and patched it up. But now Vasya began to worry even more that she wasn't looking after her husband properly. He had come to her sick and wounded, and now she could only give him soviet food to eat! He *was* more attentive to her needs; he'd brought her the shoes. Sometimes Vladimir refused to eat, and then she worried herself sick: After swallowing a few spoonfuls of gruel he would push his plate away, saying 'I'd rather go hungry than swallow these soviet shops of yours, I can't stomach it. Let's make tea and get someone to give us a bit of bread. I'll send you some flour from the Front later and you can repay them with that.'

It was obvious that they couldn't go on like this much longer; they would have to find some other way to cope. One day on her way to a meeting, she realized that thoughts about resolutions and policies were becoming jumbled up in her mind with preoccupations about millet gruel. What on earth could she give Volodya to eat? Given a little time she would be able to sort something out; she just needed time to think, to come up with some solution.

And then on her way to the meeting she met her cousin. Vasilisa was delighted to see her; she was the very person she needed. This cousin had a young daughter, Stesha, a lively young girl who had just left school and was living with her parents, helping her mother with the housework. Vasilisa arranged immediately for Stesha to come and do the housework during the day, and in return Vasilisa would give her cousin half her rations. She hurried off to her meeting much relieved. Tomorrow at least Volodya would get a proper meal.

Stesha proved to be a quick-witted girl who hit it off immediately with Volodya. Together they began to do the housework, bartering with items from their rations or getting things from the co-operative on the strength of one of Volodya's long-standing acquaintances. Vasya was content. But although Volodya no longer complained about his food, he continued to be resentful towards her.

'Your head's full of everything under the sun except me!' he said. 'It's as if I don't exist as far as you're concerned!'

This hurt Vasya deeply. She was already painfully torn between Volodya and her work, and it was especially unfortunate that he'd come at such a hectic period. She tried to explain this to him but he seemed not to understand.

'You've become cold, Vasya,' he frowned. 'Why, you've even forgotten how to make love.'

'I'm just tired, Volodya,' she said shamefacedly. 'I don't have the energy.

Volodya continued to sulk, and Vasya was forced to recognize that her behaviour towards him was not good enough. Her husband had come to see her after a long separation, and first thing in the morning she would rush off to work. When she came home in the evening she was barely able to put one foot in front of the other; she only just managed to sink on to the bed, let alone make love! Once a terrible thing had happened: she had fallen asleep while he was making love to her. He had taunted her about it the following morning.

'I ask you, where's the pleasure in making love to a dead body?' he joked, but he was obviously mortified. Vasya felt miserable and guilty. No wonder he thought she'd stopped loving him! But how was she to find the strength for everything?

One day, Vasya returned home earlier than usual to find Vladimir making supper on his own.

'What's going on?' she asked. 'Where's Stesha?'

'That Stesha of yours is a hussy. I've sent her packing, and if she dares show her face here again I shall throw her head first out of the window.'

'Why, what on earth has happened? What has she done?'

Just take my word for it, the girl's a slut. I wouldn't send her packing for nothing. It would only upset you if I told you what happened. She's a depraved little creature, I don't want things here tainted by her presence.'

It was not the time to ask questions. Stesha had obviously made Vladimir very angry. Most likely the girl had stolen something; it was quite common these days, and Vladimir valued his possessions. Even though he was generous and always shared with his friends, he still had a somewhat proprietorial instinct. If someone so much as borrowed something of his, he'd raise hell and find it hard to forgive them.

'So what are we going to do about the housekeeping now?' she asked.

'Oh, to hell with the housekeeping! I'll do the rounds of the food stalls and look up my old friends. I'll manage'.

Shortly after this, Stesha came to see Vasilisa at the housing department to ask for her rations.

'What happened between you and Vladimir Ivanovich, Stesha?' she asked the girl. 'What did you get up to?'

'*I* didn't get up to anything!' retorted Stesha, her eyes flashing, adjusting a comb in her hair. 'Your Vladimir Ivanovich grabs hold of me, so I give him a punch on the jaw, that's what! He was spitting blood for a long time afterwards. Teach him a lesson too!'

'Stop babbling, Stesha. Vladimir Ivanovich was having a little joke with you, that's all!' said Vasya, trying to speak calmly as her mind suddenly clouded over.

'Funny kind of joke, I say! He'd already thrown me on the bed; it's just as well I'm strong. Nobody's trying anything like that on *me*, I can tell you!'

Vasya tried to convince Stesha that it was all a game, and that she'd made Vladimir Ivanovich very angry with her. But Stesha set her mouth obstinately. What a load of rubbish! Anyway, what business was it of Vasya's? She would never set foot in their flat again, they could keep her rations!

Vasya was deeply depressed by the incident. She had no right to reproach Volodya, nor even to be hurt by his behaviour, for wasn't it all her fault? Hadn't she grown 'cold', and distressed her Volodechka? No wonder he thought she no longer loved him!

There was only one thing that really disturbed her, and that was that he had molested such a young girl. Stesha was just a baby. It was a good thing she had her wits about her and was fairly experienced, otherwise who knows what might have happened? Vasilisa was plagued by doubts. Should she tell Vladimir that she knew what had happened, or would it be better to say nothing? The problem was that she felt herself partly to blame.

It turned out that she had no chance to mention the subject to Vladimir, for their lives began to change. Vladimir started looking up old friends, members of the co-operative and former colleagues, and Vasya wouldn't see him for days on end. Volodya would still be asleep when she left the house in the morning, and when she came back during the day he would already have left. She returned in the evening to her empty garret, feeling irritable and dispirited, not knowing whether to go to sleep, or make some tea and wait up for him. So she would heat up some supper on the oil stove, sort out her papers for the following day, and listen for the sound of his footsteps in the corridor.

Finally, tired of waiting for him, she would put out the oil stove (she had to economize), and once again busy herself with her papers, looking through reports and sorting out petitions. Occasionally she heard hurried footsteps on the stairs, but no, it wasn't Vladimir. She'd eventually go to bed alone, miserable and cold, and quickly fall asleep. But even in her dreams she couldn't stop listening for him, waiting for her darling to come home.

Sometimes he would return in a happy cheerful mood, waking her up excitedly to hug her, and tell her all his stories, his news, his plans. Vasya would immediately feel comforted and happy, and forget all her anxieties about him. But there were times when he came home drunk, morose, maudlin, railing against himself and hurling abuse at Vasya. What sort of life was this, cooped up together in her miserable little garret with no pleasures, no real happiness, and a wife who wasn't a proper wife? It wasn't even as if they had any children . . .

Vasya found this jibe particularly unbearable. She didn't really want children, but she longed to be able to give him a child if that would make him happy. As it was, she found she couldn't get pregnant. Other women she knew commiserated

Love of Worker Bees

with her, for it was unimaginable that a woman could live without children. But Vasya was obviously not meant to be a mother.

After Vladimir's comment, Vasya went to see a doctor about her infertility. He had diagnosed anaemia. To cheer her up Vladimir decided to take her to the theatre. He bought the tickets, and she came home early at the agreed time. She found him dressed up in his best clothes, preening himself in front of the mirror, looking for all the world like a 'gentleman'. Vasya teased him, admiring her handsome husband.

'What about you?' he enquired anxiously. 'What are you going to wear? I hope you have a nice party dress to put on!'

Vasya laughed; party dress, indeed! It was all very well in America, they could afford to dress in style and wear a new get-up every day! She was just going to put on a clean blouse and her new shoes; that was the best she could do. Vladimir was frowning at her and looked angry. She began to feel nervous.

'Do you imagine that people in the theatre will only be looking at your feet? What about the rest of you, what do you think that looks like, draped in that sack?' he demanded.

'What are you so angry about, Volodya?'

'*I'm* not angry, it's you who'll be angry when you find yourself in the company of a lot of important people looking like that! Anyone would think we were living in a nunnery or a prison, the way you go on! No pleasures, no nice dresses, no proper home! You live in a rabbit-hutch, you drink water, eat slops, dress in rags . . . Why, even when I was unemployed in America I lived better than you do . . .!'

'But you know quite well that things can't be made perfect overnight Times are hard, Russia's suffering the most terrible devastation . . .'

'I wish you'd stop going on about the devastation! You'd do better to look to our new leaders instead! The old lot made a mess of things, and now the new ones have started to put things to right, people scream, "Do you want a return to the bourgeois life? Give us back the good old Bolshevik days!" You people don't know how to live, that's your trouble, that's why we'll always have chaos. I for one didn't make the revolution to live this kind of life!'

'But you don't believe we made the revolution just for our own benefit, do you?'

'Well, who did we make it for then?'

'For everybody.'

'Including the bourgeoisie, I suppose?'

'Oh, what nonsense you're talking! Obviously not! For the workers, for the proletarians . . .'

'So who are we then? Aren't we workers and proletarians?'

They continued to quarrel ferociously. Finally they left the house and walked down the street, splashing through the spring slush. Vladimir strode ahead in silence, Vasya struggling to keep up with him.

'Volodka dear, do please slow down a little, I'm out of breath,' she pleaded at last, and he began to walk more slowly, still refusing to talk.

At the theatre, Vladimir met his friends and spent the intervals with them, leaving Vasya on her own. She wished she hadn't wasted her evening in this way – it was no pleasure for her, and next day there would be twice as much work to do.

Soon after this, just before Vladimir was due to leave, the congress opened. He was keen to attend, although he wasn't a delegate. Many political questions were being debated at that time, and around these debates new factions were forming. Vladimir followed Vasya's line, enthusiastically joining her faction and throwing over all his old colleagues. They were inseparable, both at the congress and afterwards in the evenings. They spent all their free time at home drafting speeches, and a crowd of people from her faction would meet together in her room to draw up resolutions.

Vladimir found an old typewriter and happily accepted his role as 'girl typist'. It was so cheerful, everyone working together as friends, and with such genuine unity amongst them. Of course there would be furious arguments sometimes, when they all lost their tempers; then for no apparent reason, they would all burst out laughing. They loved these kinds of confrontations.

Stepan Alexeevich came too. He sat there stroking his grey beard, trimmed like an old merchant's, and keeping an affectionate eye on everyone. Vasilisa was constantly whispering in his ear. He had a high opinion of her, and had once said to a friend, 'She's got a good brain, that one.' Towards Vladimir, however, he acted rather coldly, and this troubled Vasya; she didn't know what to make of it. Vladimir didn't greatly like him either.

'He's sanctimonious, that Stepan Alexeevich of yours,' he complained. 'He reeks of incense. He's not a real fighter, just one of those behind-the-scenes operators!'

In the end Vasya's faction was defeated, but they managed to pick up more votes than expected, and that was enough of a victory for them.

Vladimir's sick-leave was due to expire before the end of the congress, and once more Vasya felt torn in two; on the one hand there was her husband needing her help to prepare for his journey back, and on the other there was the congress. But now she found this conflict exhilarating; she felt again that Vladimir was no longer simply her husband but also a comrade She was proud of him too, for he had been an invaluable help to their faction, and her friends didn't want him to leave either.

The day of his departure arrived.

'Goodbye, my Vasyuk,' he said. 'My little sparrow is going to stay under the eaves on her own. She'll have no one to moan to about her worries. But there'll be no one to get in the way of her work either!'

'Do you really imagine you get in the way of my work?' said Vasya, hugging him and kissing his neck.

'But it was you who said your husband took up so much of your time, and complained about the housework!'

'Please don't remind me of that! It's so much harder without you.'

She buried her head in his chest. 'You're not just my husband, you're my friend, that's why I love you so much.'

They kissed each other tenderly and said goodbye. But afterwards, hurrying back to the congress, Vasya suddenly thought to herself, 'However much I love being with him, I feel freer on my own. When I'm with Volodya. I have to think for two people, and work gets neglected.' Now she could immerse herself properly in her work. Work, and then rest. She hadn't slept properly when her husband was there.

'Have you seen your husband off?' Stepan Alexeevich asked her when she arrived back at the congress.

'Yes, he's gone.'

'It'll be easier for you now. You were overworking with him around.'

Vasya was amazed that Stepan Alexeevich should have understood this. She didn't reply, reluctant to admit such a thing, even to herself – it seemed an insult to Vladimir.

4

Vasilisa was up the moment it began to grow light. The train was due to arrive that morning and she must smarten herself up so her Volodya would be pleased with her appearance. Seven months without him, what an eternity! Vasilisa was as light-headed as the spring morning.

The Nepwoman was still in bed, yawning and stretching and peering at her face in her pocket mirror, but Vasya had already washed, carefully combed her hair and put on her new dress. Looking at herself in the train mirror she saw only her radiant eyes, lighting up her whole face. There seemed nothing wrong with her appearance. Surely this time Vladimir couldn't accuse her of going around in rags.

The train came to a halt at a wayside station, and Vasilisa looked out. Although it was still early morning the sun was already hot. In the north there had been only the faintest signs of spring, but here everything was bursting into flower.

The trees were covered with clusters of white flowers a little like lilac. They were unfamiliar to Vasya. Their leaves were similar to rowan but a softer colour and, they wafted a delicious sweet smell through the window.

'What kind of tree is that?' Vasya asked the conductor. 'We don't have them where I come from.'

'That's white acacia,' he answered. White acacia! How beautiful! The conductor picked some flowers and gave them to Vasya. They smelt wonderful, and Vasya suddenly felt so happy she wanted to cry. Everything around her seemed so interesting and beautiful, and most of all, she told herself, in only one hour she would see her darling Volodya again.

'Are we arriving soon?' Vasya badgered the conductor. It seemed the train would never move again, puffing away as if stuck for ever on this siding. Eventually it started; they passed a town, a cathedral, a barracks, then suburbs and finally they were at the station. Vasya peered excitedly through the open window. Where was he? Where was Volodya? The next thing she knew, he was rushing up to her from the other end of the carriage and she was in his arms.

'Volodka, Volodka, I can't believe it!' They kissed and embraced each other.

'Hand me your things and come and meet our secretary,' he said. 'Ivan Ivanovich, take these things, will you, and we'll go to my car. I've a couple of horses too now, Vasya, as well as my own cow, and I'd like to start breeding pigs. We've got lots of room, a whole farm in fact, just wait till you see it – you'll be able to live like a lady of the manor now. And my business is settling down nicely too; they've just reopened the department in Moscow . . .'

Vladimir talked on and on, eagerly telling her about his new life, his schemes, his ideas. Vasya sat there listening to him as they drove along, but though she found it fascinating, she was anxious to tell him a bit about herself, and to find out how he had managed without her, and whether he had missed her and been lonely.

They arrived at the house. Before her was an old-style private mansion with a garden; a young errand-boy in a braided cap hurried up to help them out of the car.

'Let's see how you like our home, Vasya,' said Vladimir. 'It's a bit better than your rabbit hutch under the eaves, eh?'

They went in. There was a carpeted staircase and a mirror in the anteroom. Vasya threw off her hat and coat and they went into the drawing room. There were sofas and carpets everywhere and a large clock in the dining room. There were still-life paintings in gilded frames on the walls and a stuffed bird hanging from a nail.

'So, do you like it?' Vladimir asked her, beaming expansively.

'Yes,' Vasya replied hesitantly, looking around her, not sure whether she liked it or not. It all seemed alien somehow, unfamiliar.

'And here's our bedroom!' announced Vladimir, flinging the door open. Two large windows overlooked the garden.

'Oh, look at the trees!' she said ecstatically. 'They're white acacias!' She hurried to the window, enchanted.

'Why don't you have a look at the room first? You'll have plenty of time to run around the garden. Not bad, is it, the way I've arranged it for you? Everything here I chose and arranged myself. Ever since I moved in I've been waiting for you to see it.'

'Oh, thank you, darling.' Vasya reached up to kiss him, but ignoring this he took her by the shoulders and turned her to face a large mirror in a wardrobe.

'Look, you'll find this terribly convenient when you get dressed. You can see yourself full length in the mirror. Below it are shelves for your hats and lingerie . . .'

'Really Volodya, what sort of hats and lingerie do you imagine I have! You must have found yourself a real "lady"!' Vasya laughed.

But Volodya went on unabashed. 'Look at the bed, will you? The coverlet's genuine silk. As a matter of fact I had some difficulty getting it, it didn't come with the house. And there's this pink lamp you can put on at night . . .'

Vladimir conducted Vasya round the whole house, pointing out every detail to her, delighting in it like a child – this little nest he had built for his wife. His obvious happiness made her smile too, but she felt ill at ease. She couldn't deny that the rooms were stylish and beautiful, but they felt alien to her. It was as if she had stepped into someone else's house; there were none of the things she actually needed, not even a table on which to put her books and papers. The only thing she really liked were the two windows overlooking the white acacias in the garden.

'Why don't you tidy yourself up a bit and have a wash, then we'll go and eat,' Vladimir said, going to the window to draw the blind.

'Oh please don't . . .' Vasya said. 'It's so lovely to look out at the garden.'

'I'm afraid we can't do that. The upholstery will fade if we don't draw the blinds during the day.' And so the blinds came down over the green garden, like heavy eyes and the grey featureless window seemed even more alien to Vasya. She washed her hands and began combing her hair in front of the mirror.

'What's that you've got on?' asked Volodya suddenly. 'Is that the dress you had made out of the material I sent you?'

'Yes, this is the material,' Vasya replied, eagerly waiting for him to compliment her.

73

'Well, come on now, show yourself off properly,' he said, turning her this way and that. But she saw from his face that he didn't like it.

'What on earth made you have these pleats at the hips? You've got such a slender figure, just right for the latest fashions. Where did you get this monstrosity from?'

Vasya stood there dumbfounded, blushing guiltily and blinking. 'Monstrosity? But Grusha said it was the latest fashion!'

'A fat lot your Grusha knows! All she's done is botched up a perfectly nice piece of material! You look like a priest's wife! You'd better throw the dress away and go back to your plain skirts, you look more yourself in them anyway. Like this you look like a peahen!'

Without appearing to notice Vasya's mortified face, he strode off into the dining room to speed up supper. Feverishly Vasya flung off Grusha's creation and hurriedly got herself into her old skirt and belted blouse. She felt wretched. Two miserable tears rolled down her cheeks onto her blouse. They dried at once, but an expression of cold resentment remained in her eyes.

Maria Semyonovna, the servant, a stout, middle-aged woman, introduced herself to Vasya during dinner. Vasya shook hands with her.

'That was quite unnecessary,' Vladimir said sharply, the moment Maria Semyonovna, had gone out of the room. 'Please remember in future that you are the mistress of the house, otherwise there'll be no end of bother and complaints.'

Vasya regarded her husband in blank amazement. 'I'm afraid I don't understand what you mean,' she said. Vladimir changed the subject, and started urging Vasya to eat. But she felt too wretched to think about food.

'You'll love the tablecloth I've bought, it's pure Morozov linen, with serviettes to match. I didn't order it to be laid because it's so expensive to have laundered.'

'Where did you get all these things from?' Vasya asked Vladimir rather sternly. 'I hope you haven't laid in great stocks of them!'

'What an idea!' he laughed. 'Do you know how much something like that costs nowadays? Millions of rubles! Do you imagine that on my director's salary I can buy a lot of luxuries like that? As a director I get these things with the house, and it was a good thing I arrived when I did, because I was able to get hold of all the fittings through various departments and on the strength of some contacts of mine. Of course they've put a stop to all that, you'd never get these things now. It's cash down or nothing these days! There are one or two things, of course, that I bought with my own money, the cupboard in the bedroom with the mirror, the silk quilt, the lamp in the drawing room . . .'

Vladimir enumerated all these objects with evident satisfaction, but Vasya's face became increasingly cold, her eyes occasionally expressing intense hostility.

'And how much have all these delightful luxuries cost you, may I ask?' Her voice trembled with restrained rage. Vladimir noticed nothing and continued to eat his cutlet and sauce, washing it down with beer.

'Well if you want it in round figures, not forgetting the discount I got for paying in cash, it comes out at around . . .' and with an impressive pause, designed to bring home to Vasya the gravity of the matter, he named a substantial sum of money. As he did so he raised his smiling eyes to her as if to say, Some husband, eh?

Vasya jumped up from the table and leaned over him, furious.

'Why, Vasya, what's the matter?' he cried in alarm.

'Tell me this minute where you got the money from! Tell me immediately, I want to know!'

'Come on. Vasya, calm down please! Do you imagine I came by it dishonestly? Maybe you just don't understand the value of money. If you just calm down and work out how much I earn you'll understand.' He then told her what his monthly salary was.

'Is your salary really that big? Even so, I don't see how as a communist you can spend it on this trash when you know how much poverty there is everywhere. People are starving, what about the unemployed? Have you forgotten about them too now you've become a director?'

Vasya questioned Vladimir mercilessly. 'Well Mr Director, answer me!' she said.

But Vladimir wouldn't budge. He reasoned with her, trying get her to change her mind. He even teased her, saying she had lived for so long like a sparrow she'd forgotten the value of money. There were plenty of people who earned far more than he did – and some of them really *did* flaunt their wealth.

But Vasya wouldn't be mollified. She had got the bit between her teeth, and wanted him to justify himself for not living like a proper communist.

Vladimir tried another tack. He explained the political aspects of his job. He told her what being a director entailed, and about the instructions he had received from the party Central Committee. He was absolutely insistent that the main priority was to ensure at all costs that business flourished and profits shot up. Before attacking him she should see for herself what he had accomplished in one year. He'd built up the business from nothing and had made it more profitable, so that it now compared well with any other government trust in the area.

Even if he did live like a 'civilized human being', as he put it, that didn't mean he had any less concern for every single one of his employees, down to the humblest loader. If she would only find out a bit more about it, she would stop nagging him like this. He hadn't expected it of her, his friend – it hadn't occurred to him that immediately she arrived she would side with his enemies. Work was hard enough as it was. Why should he wear himself out, only to have his wife attack him and put him on trial for the way he lived?

By now Vladimir was deeply offended. He had worked himself up into a rage, his eyes smouldered with anger and resentment. How *could* she distrust him? How could she pass judgement on him like this?

Vasya began to soften as she listened. Maybe he was right. After all, things had changed. The main thing was that his accounts were in order, business was flourishing, and the national wealth was increasing. There could be no disagreement with him on that.

'And what if I do get some possessions and set up a home for myself? I'm not going to live out my days in some communal house! Why should we be worse off than American workers? You should see how a lot of them live, with their pianos and Ford motor-cars and motor-cycles!'

Several times in the course of this conversation Maria Semyonovna peered into the room, anxious to serve the pancakes. She sighed. No sooner had they met than they started arguing! That was just how it used to be with the gentry, whom Maria Semyonouna had served before the revolution. They were no better, these communists, she thought irritably – letting the pancakes get cold like this!

Next day, Vladimir took Vasya on a tour of the factory, to the offices, the warehouses and the employees' living quarters. He took her into the accounting office, saying, 'Just look at our books now. You won't find anyone who keeps their accounts like this. You won't be able to accuse me of extravagance once you've seen how I've set things up here.' Then he asked the accountant to explain the principles of their book-keeping to Vasya. These were simple and precise, and had earned them special congratulations from the Central Committee, he said. Although Vasya couldn't follow it all, it was clear that a lot of hard work had gone into the business and that the people here loved their work. Volodya was obviously committed to the job.

He then showed her round the flats of the employees and made a special point of asking his colleagues' wives whether they were happy. He cast triumphant glances at Vasya as all of them came up with the same answer: 'Happy, I should say so! Considering the times we live in things couldn't be better, and it's all thanks to you, Vladimir Ivanovich, that we're living like this!'

'There you are, Vasya! And you were saying I'd become a spendthrift! Believe me, my first concern was to do everything I could for the workers. I exhausted myself for them at the beginning. Only later I thought about myself. You see how they live? It's the same for the workers as for the clerks, they're no worse off. I struggled hard for my workers, I couldn't have done more for them!'

'Well all right, you've done everything for them. But what have they done for themselves?'

'You really have the strangest ideas sometimes, Vasya! Don't you see, they and I work together! In the old days there was one rule for the director and another for the workers, but it's not like that here. You're an old stick-in-the-mud, Vasya. You'd better watch out, you'll get covered in moss!' He said this in a joking tone, but Vasya sensed how annoyed he was by her remarks.

He spent the whole day taking her round the various sections of the factory until Vasya was exhausted. Her temples throbbed, her back hurt, and she had a stabbing pain in her side. As soon as they got home, she thought, she would go to bed and have a nice sleep. Her head was still aching from the sound of carriage wheels.

However when they were returning to the house, Volodya announced that guests would soon be arriving for lunch and Vasya would have to receive them. The errand-boy let them in, and stood around awaiting orders. Vladimir took out a note-book, wrote a short message, and gave it to the boy.

'Run along then Vasya, I don't want any loitering. You're to give me the reply in person, understand?' Saying this, he turned to Vasilisa with an odd glance, guilty and watchful. 'Why are you gaping at me like that, Vasyuk?' he said, uncertainly.

'No reason,' she replied. 'So the errand-boy is also called Vasya too, is he?'

'Yes, that's right, oh, so that's it! You're upset that there are two Vasyas in my house! Really, what a woman you are! I believe you're jealous! There's nothing at all to worry about, you know there's only one Vasya in the world for me, you're the one I love.' He hugged her affectionately and kissed her, looking deep into her eyes. Then for the first time that day he started to caress her. Embracing, they went into the bedroom.

The guests soon arrived for lunch: Savelyov and Ivan Ivanovich, secretary of the board of directors. Savelyov was a tall, corpulent man, with carefully combed, thinning hair, wearing a ring on his index-finger. His intelligent eyes had a cunning look and it seemed to Vasya that the smile on his clean-shaven face had a certain irony about it, as if he an observer and didn't give a damn about anything just so long as he did all right out of it.

He greeted her, putting her hand to his lips. Vasya quickly withdrew it in confusion. 'I'm not used to that,' she said.

'As you wish,' he said, 'But I'm never averse to kissing a lady's hand, you know. It's an agreeable custom, and it certainly isn't going to make your husband jealous – not that he shouldn't be jealous, eh Vladimir Ivanovich? Come on, admit it!' He clapped Vladimir on the shoulder.

Vladimir laughed. 'Vasya's a model wife, I wouldn't dream of being jealous of her!'

'Well, she obviously doesn't take her husband as a model then!' Savelyov winked at Vladimir.

'I don't think I've given any cause . . .' Vladimir stammered.

But Savelyov interrupted him. 'That's all right. We all know you husbands! I was a husband myself once. Now I lead a bachelor life.'

Vasya didn't like Savelyov at all. But Volodya and he were discussing politics and business like old friends. Vasya would never have discussed politics with a speculator like that, or made jokes about the chairman of the executive committee. Volodya would have to be made to see reason on this, and put an end to the friendship.

They had wine with lunch which Ivan Ivanovich had brought along in a wicker flagon. Vasya listened to the discussion, trying to grasp the main points. Apparently the company was concerned about the hold-up of some large stocks which were due to rise in value but might arrive too late on the market. None of it had any significance for her, and she felt they were somehow evading the point Her throbbing head prevented her from listening properly anyway, and her eyes were beginning to hurt. She wished fervently that lunch would end.

At last they rose from the table, and Vladimir immediately ordered a car to take him to an important meeting on the transport problem.

'Really, Vladimir Ivanovich, how can you go off to a meeting tonight of all nights, when your wife has just arrived? Why don't you stay with her for a while? It's only proper, you know.' Smirking slightly, Savelyov shot a sidelong glance at Vladimir.

'Impossible, I'm afraid,' said Vladimir abruptly, cutting a cigar with absorbed attention. 'I'd have been only too delighted to stay at home this evening, but work presses'.

'But you know, there's work and there's work,' persisted Savelyov. And once again this detestable speculator seemed to wink at Vladimir, as though making fun of Vasya. 'I would have put off all my work today if I'd been you, to spend this first evening with my wife. After all, business isn't going to disappear.'

Vladimir didn't answer, and reached irritably for his cap. 'Let's be off then, Nikanor Platonovich.' They went out, and Savelyov and Ivan Ivanovich went too, leaving Vasya on her own in the huge empty house. She crossed the desolate cold rooms to the bedroom, where she stood for a while at the window, lost in thought. Then she lay down under the silk quilt, and immediately fell asleep.

She woke with a start. It was dark. Putting on the light, she saw it was quarter past twelve. Could she have been asleep that long? Past midnight, and still no Volodya. Getting out of bed, she splashed her face with cold water and went into the dining-room. The table was laid for supper and the light was on. All the other rooms were dark and deserted. Going into the kitchen, she found Maria Semyonovna clearing up.

'Isn't Vladimir Ivanovich back yet?' she asked.

'No, not yet,' she replied.

'Does he always come back from his meetings so late?'

'It varies.' Maria Semyonovna was in a surly mood.

'But do you always wait up for him like this? Don't you go to bed?'

'Vasya and me, we take it in turns. One night I'm on duty, next, it's his turn.'

'Will Vladimir be having supper?'

'He only has supper if he brings guests back, otherwise he goes straight to his room.'

Vasya stayed for a while, but Maria Semyonovna was too busy with her work to so much as glance at her. So she went back to the bedroom and flung open the window. It was a chilly spring night, with the sharp scent of acacias in the air. The frogs were croaking so loudly that at first she took them to be night birds. The sky was dark, scattered with a multitude of stars.

Looking out into the darkness, Vasya gradually grew calmer. Savelyov the speculator was forgotten now. Forgotten too were her pinpricks of resentment at Volodya's tactless behaviour towards her that day. Her heart was filled with one thought – she had come to see her darling, to help him understand the proper party line. No wonder you're in a mess if you've got mixed up with a lot of Nepmen, she would tell him. He wasn't to blame, and he obviously needed her advice, that was why he sent for her.

Vasya thought with pride of how Volodya had set up his business and what an exemplary worker he was. The day's events now appeared to her in a different light. Already she felt much more optimistic and clear-headed.

She was lost in thought and didn't hear the car drawing up outside, and Vladimir's footsteps crossing the carpets. She started at the sound of his voice.

'Why so deep in thought, Vasya?' he asked, with a look of tender anxiety.

'You're back at last, darling! I've been waiting an age for you to come!' She put her arms round his neck, and he caught her in his arms as he used to in the early days of their marriage. Vasya was beside herself with joy. He loved her, he loved as he had always done! How stupid she had been! Why had she been so irritable all day?

They sat down and drank tea, chatting away happily. Vasya told Volodya what she felt about Savelyov, arguing that it would be better for them not to be friends any more. Volodya didn't contradict her. He admitted that he had no more respect for the man than she did, but that he was an invaluable contact. He reminded Vasya that if it hadn't been for Savelyov, the business would never have been established in the first place. He had a number of long-standing connections, he had the trust of the merchants, and he was able to put Volodya in touch with them. In fact. Volodya had learnt an enormous amount from him. Although he was obviously a crook, and a bourgeois to boot, he was irreplaceable in business. That was why, when the local authorities 'in their wisdom' had arrested Savelyov, Volodya had stood up for him. In Moscow they had a high opinion of him in fact, and had given the local authorities a good ticking-off about the matter.

'But didn't you describe him to me in your letters as a swindler and a thief?' asked Vasya anxiously.

'Well now, how shall I put it? He's our agent, you see, so of course he has his own interests to take care of, but honestly he's no worse than any of the others. Besides, the others help themselves and don't work, whereas he works, and not because he has to, but because he's conscientious. He knows his job and loves it.'

All the same Vasya made Vladimir promise not to see so much of him in future. Work was one thing, but she saw no reason why he should be friends with him too. After finishing their tea they kissed and went into the bedroom. Vladimir held Vasya's head close to him, tenderly kissing her curls. 'This little head of yours is so precious to me,' he said thoughtfully. 'It couldn't ever become a stranger to me, could it? I'll never have a friend like you, Vasya. You're the only woman I love, my tough little Vasya.'

5

Next morning when Vasya awoke it was already late, and Vladimir had left for work. She must either have caught a cold on the journey or was sickening for something, for she had a stabbing pain in her side and a bad cough and fever. The weather was mild and sunny outside, but she wrapped herself in her shawl and stayed in bed. Maria Semyonovna came into the room, and stood by the door with her hands crossed on her large stomach, looking at Vasya and waiting for her to speak.

'Good morning to you, Maria Semyonovna, she said.

'Good morning,' the other responded tartly. 'What will you be ordering for lunch? Vladimir Ivanovich told me when he was leaving that you were to order lunch. There'll be guests, he said.'

Vasya was taken aback. She was used to plain soviet meals. Maria Semyonovna obviously realized that Vasya was at sea in these matters, and proposed some dishes herself. Vasya agreed to all her suggestions, only enquiring about prices. Everything seemed terribly expensive to her, but Maria Semyonovna merely pursed her lips. 'Well, you can't scrimp if you want to eat well. You need plenty of money for everything now the communists have done away with rationing.'

'But have you got the money?' Vasya asked anxiously.

'Well, there's a bit left from yesterday, but it won't tide us over today. The meat will be expensive, and we need more butter too.'

'Didn't Vladimir leave you any money?'

'He didn't leave me a kopeck, he just said "Go and see Vasilisa Dementevna and sort it out with her".' Maria Semyonovna stood there impassively, waiting for her money. She was obviously not going away until she got it. Vasya was at her wits' end. She had a little money of her own but she didn't want it frittered away on these housekeeping expenses or she'd be left with nothing for her own needs.

'I know,' Maria Semyonovna suggested, 'if you have a little money of your own you could give it to me to do the shopping, lend it to me on credit like, then ask Vladimir Ivanovich for it back later. He won't refuse you.'

Of course, Vasya thought with relief. That was the answer. Why hadn't she thought of it herself! Maria Semyonovna left satisfied, and Vasya went into the garden and wandered along the paths. But she was soon overcome by tiredness. She felt very unwell. She went back in, lay down on the bed and fell asleep over her book.

She tossed and turned in bed, her cheeks burning with fever, tormented by oppressive dreams. Once she woke up, looked around, and felt angry with herself for her lethargy. She should be in town, getting down to work. How absurd to come all this way to see Vladimir, only to fall ill! But she couldn't even manage to raise her head, and as soon as she closed her eyes again, her thoughts became troubled and confused. She dozed fitfully, unable to focus her thoughts.

The next thing she knew, Maria Semyonovna was standing over her again.

'Vasilisa Dementevna, Vladimir Ivanovich will be back for lunch any minute. You'd better get yourself dressed and I'll make the bed. He doesn't like it when the rooms are messy.'

'Can it be that late already?'

'It's five o'clock, and you've had nothing to eat. I was going to wake you but you were fast asleep. I know how tiring those long journeys are.'

'I don't know if it's the journey, but I seem to have caught a chill.'

'Well, you'd better put on your woollen dress, that'll keep you warm,' advised Maria Semyonovna. 'You don't need the shawl.'

'No, my dress won't do. My husband doesn't like it.'

'What do you mean, it won't do? There's nothing wrong with it, even though it has those pleats at the hips and the waist is in the wrong place. Look, that's where the waistline should be. I was a dressmaker once, so I do know a thing or two about fashion. Why don't you let me cut up the skirt for you, then we'll restyle the dress. By the time we've finished, Vladimir Ivanovich won't recognize it!'

'But will it be ready for him?' asked Vasya anxiously.

'No, of course not! You and I will do it together in our own time, bit by bit. In the meantime you can put on your black skirt and the jacket from the dress, and you'll look quite smart.'

Vasya stood endlessly in front of the mirror while Maria Semyonovna restyled everything, pricking her all over with pins as she made her alterations. Then she got hold of a lace collar from somewhere. The final effect was good – simple and smart. Vasya decided she liked it; she wondered what Vladimir would say.

She had only just got herself dressed when Vladimir arrived

with his guests, a colleague of his from the GPU* and his wife. The GPU man had a natty moustache, and was dressed in foppish yellow knee-high boots. Could this man really be a communist? Vasya was dumbfounded. She disliked him intensely. His wife was tarted up like a streetwalker in a diaphanous dress, with furs draped over her shoulder and rings sparkling on her fingers. Vladimir kissed her hand, and they exchanged pleasantries. Vasya couldn't make out a word of what they were saying – it seemed nothing but banal inanities. When they sat down at table, Vladimir leaned across towards his guests, and when he and the woman exchanged glances his eyes sparkled.

Vasya had been seated next to the GPU man. She knew he was in the party but she couldn't think of a word to say to him. Again, they drank wine for lunch, and Vladimir clinked glasses with the woman. She whispered something in his ear which made them both laugh; they made Vasya feel very uncomfortable.

The GPU man paid his wife no attention whatsoever, which Vasya found very odd and unpleasant. A facetious discussion started about fast-days, and the woman admitted that although she believed in God and went to confession she didn't observe the fasts. Again, Vasya was shocked. How could a GPU comrade be married to a 'believer'. She frowned angrily, and was seized with sudden fury at Vladimir. What sort of friends did he think these were?

Just as lunch was ending, Ivan Ivanovich arrived saying that Savelyov had booked a box at the theatre and had invited everyone to come.

'Shall we go, Vasya?' asked Vladimir.

'What, with Savelyov you mean?' She looked Vladimir in the eye, but he pretended not to understand. 'That's right, we'll make up a party with Nikanor Platonovich. A new operetta's opening tonight. They say its very entertaining, you'll enjoy yourself.'

'No, I can't go,' said Vasya.

* GPU: The Political Police Force

'But why not?'

'I don't feel at all well. I think I must have caught a chill on the journey.'

'You do look a bit under the weather,' said Vladimir, glancing at her. 'Your eyes are quite hollow. Here, give me your hand. Yes, it's terribly hot, of course you mustn't go. In that case I won't go either.'

'Why ever not? You go without me.' Then he guests joined in, entreating Vladimir to go to the theatre with them. At last he agreed. In the hall, in front of everybody, he embraced her, whispering in her ear, 'You look so pretty tonight, Vasya! Go to bed immediately, I'll be right back, I won't stay to the end.' He asked Maria Semyonovna keep an eye on her. Then they all left.

Vasya wandered about the rooms, once again overwhelmed by feelings of melancholy. This life was not to her liking at all. She couldn't have said precisely what was wrong with it, everything just seemed unfamiliar somehow. She felt alien here, superfluous. So what if Volodya loved her! He hardly took any interest in her. Just a hug and a kiss, and off he went!

She'd have understood if he had to go to a meeting or to work. But the theatre! Why had he gone to the theatre without her? Surely he had seen enough plays that winter! Vasya felt tormented by something she couldn't express, which sapped her strength and left her feeling miserable and uneasy.

I'll stay here one more week, she resolved. I'll see how Volodya's affairs develop, then I'll leave.

But as soon as she settled this in her mind another question presented itself. Where could she go? Back to the communal house? That was impossible, since her friend Grusha was living in her garret. Then there'd be the Feodoseevs all over again, the same old squabbles. She'd have to fight for the house, and no doubt she would quarrel with everybody in the process. She no longer had the energy for it, nor the confidence that she could cope with the situation.

She had nowhere to go, and the realization brought a gnawing anxiety. She began to feel cold; shivering, she tucked her hands into her sleeves. Back and forth she walked through the dark and empty rooms. She felt as if some calamity were lurking in this unfriendly house, lying in wait for her. But that was nonsense, she scolded herself, it was just a premonition, and communists didn't believe in premonition! But what was the meaning of this unendurable, blank despair?

When Vladimir came home early, as he had promised, Vasya was sitting up in bed reading. He sat down beside her and asked how she was. He looked serious and worn, as though he had just had some deeply sad experience.

'What's the matter, Volodya?' Vasya asked, surprised.

He buried his head in the pillow, and said in a pitiful voice.

'Oh, Vasya, I have such a hard life, you can't imagine how hard it is! You see only one side of it, but I don't think you really want to understand me properly. If only you knew how much I'd gone through this winter, you wouldn't criticize me, you'd pity me. I know your heart's in the right place, Vasya . . .'

Vasya stroked his head and tried to comfort him. She felt sorry for him, but couldn't help feeling a bit pleased too. At this moment she felt they were united by unhappiness. It was difficult to be a director, she comforted him, having to give orders to workers.

Volodya shook his head sadly. 'No, it's not that, Vasya. It's something else. There's something which plagues me and won't leave me in peace.'

'But what then? Are they planning to make trouble for you?'

Volodya didn't reply. It was as though he couldn't bring himself to tell her what was on his mind. Vasya hugged him.

'Please tell me, darling, what is it that keeps plaguing you like this?' She rested her head on his shoulder. Then suddenly she moved away, staring at him. 'You reek of perfume! Since when have you been wearing perfume?'

He drew back from her in confusion. 'Perfume? I suppose it was when the barber shaved me today. He uses perfume.'

He got up from the bed and began to concentrate intensely on his cigarette, inhaling very slowly. A few minutes later he went out of the room, saying he had some papers which urgently needed sorting through before tomorrow.

Vasya's cough did not improve. She still had a stabbing pain in her side and a fever, and although she made an effort whenever Vladimir was at home, he couldn't help noticing. Her coughing apparently prevented him from sleeping, and he made a bed for himself on the drawing-room sofa.

The days dragged on, empty and inactive. She was beset by petty domestic anxieties, for although Vladimir never gave her enough housekeeping money, he still demanded that everything be done 'in the proper style', as he put it. After Vasya had contributed her own money to the housekeeping, she found Volodya's veiled reproaches particularly disagreeable.

'But you can't already have spent all your money on the housekeeping! At this rate we'll never have enough to go round, what with you here and all the others to feed.' As if it was *she* who invited all these guests and ordered three-course meals for them!

However she couldn't really complain about Vladimir. He was solicitous, anxious about the state of her health. He called in the doctor, who diagnosed exhaustion and a slightly weak right lung, and told her to lie in the sun as much as possible and keep to a healthy diet. Vladimir urged her to follow the doctor's instructions and ordered Maria Semyonovna to look after her properly and see she ate at the proper times.

He even got hold of some cocoa for her and went off in his car to find her a folding chair in which she could sit in the sun. He was extremely attentive. But although he came to see her the moment he returned from the factory they didn't see much of each other, for he was very busy. Things were hectic at work, he was closely involved in the swings of the market, and all this made him preoccupied and exhausted.

One afternoon Vasya was lying in her folding chair on the lawn, basking like a lizard in the sun. She was already burnt as brown as a gypsy. She was thinking how strange it felt to be living like this, without work or worries. But it was a life without joy, more like a strange dream. She felt she might wake up at any moment and find herself in her real home, in the communal house. She remembered the housing department, her friends, Stepan Alexeevich, Grusha, even Mrs Feodoseeva. Those days had been more difficult, but so much happier!

She was waiting for Vladimir to return. He had promised to come home early, and today, as every day, she was determined that they should have a proper discussion about things and talk honestly. But day followed day, and there was never the opportunity to talk; either there were guests, or Vladimir had to work.

At least Savelyov no longer came. But there were other guests, uninteresting businessmen who lived in a different world from Vasya's. Their conversation revolved exclusively around loading and unloading, invoices and packaging, discounts and bonuses. Although Vasya recognized that these matters were vital to the economy of the Republic, and that things couldn't improve unless there was some sort of barter system, she found it very tedious to listen to them. If ever she mentioned party matters, some article by Bukharin, say, or a report in the newspapers about the German Communist party, they would stop for a moment, listen to her, then immediately go back to talking about freighting and loading, net weight and gross weight.

Vladimir never seemed to find these conversations tedious, and always brightened up when he was with his colleagues, arguing and consulting with them tirelessly. It was only when he was alone with Vasya that he became depressed, sighing, stroking her hand, and gazing at her with his great mournful eyes. It was as though he was imploring her to help him, apologizing to her for something, although she couldn't for the life of her imagine what could be tormenting him. After all, she hadn't heard a murmur against him recently.

What could be making Vladimir so wretched? Could it be that she was dying? This ridiculous thought immediately cheered Vasya up. That *must* mean he loved her! True, he didn't spend much time with her. But then she had to admit she hadn't made much fuss of him when he had come to stay with her. She had been out all day then, and had had no time for her husband! She wondered if her behaviour then had made him love her less now, and it worried her a great deal.

She lay there gazing at the tops of the trees against the bright blue sky, swaying gently, caressed by the breeze. The grass-hoppers were chirping in the grass, and from the end of the garden came the sound of birds, competing with each other in song. Vasya stood up and walked along the overgrown path, brushing against bushes of flowering lilac. What a heavenly smell! She picked a bunch of blossoms and a bee buzzing nearby settled on a flower and spread its wings.

'Brave little bee!' Vasya laughed. 'You're not afraid of a human being!'

Then all of a sudden she felt overwhelmed by a feeling of such pure joy that she caught her breath. Looking about her, the garden suddenly appeared to her in a magical light. The green grass, the luxuriant lilac bush, the little slime-covered pond with the frogs croaking out their messages – how beautiful it all was! How very beautiful! She feared to move, feared that this sudden, bright, winged joy might vanish as suddenly as it had come. She felt at that moment as though never in her life had she under-stood what it meant to be alive.

Suddenly she understood everything. To be alive was not a question of whether you were happy or unhappy, whether you worked or struggled. To be alive was to be like the birds carolling to each other in the boughs of the trees, the grasshoppers chirping in the grass, the bees circling over the lilas. *They* were alive! Why shouldn't she stay here for ever among the lilacs? Why shouldn't people live like God's creatures . . . ?

What was she thinking of? The very thought of God made her angry with herself. God indeed! What could have possessed her! It must be inactivity, this leisured life she was leading at Vladimir's expense. At this rate she would soon turn into a lady of leisure!

She walked quickly to the house, all desire to stay in the garden gone. But her mood of joy didn't leave her.

She was going into the bedroom to put the bunch of lilacs into a vase, when Vladimir's car drew up. He came straight in. 'They've started!' he announced. 'It's been a long time since I've had any trouble from them. Now the troublemakers have begun their infernal tricks all over again, only this time it's much worse. They've concocted some charge against me it seems, and I've been summoned before the Control Commission. We'll see who wins this time!' Vladimir was pacing around the room with one hand behind his back, a sure sign that he was upset.

'They've holding my anarchism against me and my lack of discipline, and the devil knows what else! I wear myself out, lick the business into shape, and instead of giving me a bit of help, all the people from the party committee can think of is how to put a spanner in the works! If they're going to start harassing me again, I'll just leave the party. I mean it! I'll leave without being pushed! They won't have to threaten to expel me, and that's final!'

It was obviously a genuine crisis. Vasya's heart sank. This must be the calamity she had been expecting. She tried to hide these feelings and to console Vladimir, but he was inconsolable.

'And what about your Stepan Alexeevich! He's a fine one, I must say! They ask him for a character reference, and would you believe it, he can think of nothing better to say about me than to praise my work. For the rest, he finds me "terribly self-satisfied" and "morally unreliable". I ask you! You'd think those people were priests, the way they go round judging people not for their work or their politics but for their "morals". I don't live "like a communist", apparently. Am I supposed to become a monk? Anyway, do these people behave any better in their private lives? You bet they don't! They won't be bringing charges against the head of the Agitation Department, even though he left his wife and three children and moved in with some girl he fancied! That kind of behaviour's acceptable, it seems! That's communist morality for you! Why is it only me who's expected to lie on a bed of nails? What business of theirs is my personal life?'

At this point in his tirade Vasya felt compelled to disagree with him. She felt the Control Commission was quite right to say that communists shouldn't take the bourgeoisie as their model, and that a communist, and a director at that, should set an example to everyone.

'But what the hell do you think I've done wrong?' Vladimir interrupted her. 'For God's sake, tell me in what way I'm not a good communist. Is it because I don't live in a pigsty? Or because I'm forced to be friendly with all kinds of riff-raff in the interests of my job? In that case, why don't you write out instructions as to who's to be admitted to the house, how many chairs we ought to have, how many pairs of trousers a communist should own . . .'

Vladimir was beside himself with rage as he tore into Vasya's critcisms. Vasya, on the other hand, was glad to have this chance to tell him at last about the doubts that had been lingering in her mind. She didn't know precisely what was wrong with the way he lived, she said, she just felt deep down that he neither lived nor behaved like a proper communist. He had everything he could possibly want, she didn't think business would suffer if the director's house had no mirrors or carpets! Nor did she think it was necessary to do deals over furnishings and gadgets with the Savelyovs of this world, and surely kissing pretty girls' hands wouldn't make the business prosper!

'So you're in on it too!' Vladimir shouted. 'I knew it! I could sense you came here to judge me, not as my friend. And now you're going along with my enemies. Well at least now I know you despise me as much as they do! Why don't you just say so to my face, instead of pretending you're on my side and nagging me all the time!'

Vladimir was white with rage and resentment. Vasya saw there was no point trying to contradict him in his present mood. She only hoped that he would take back what he said to her later.

'Vasya,' he continued, calmer now. 'I didn't expect this from you of all people. I never thought you would abandon me when I'm in such a mess. I've obviously misjudged everything. Ah, to hell with it. If everything's ruined, good luck to them, it's all the same to me.'

As he spoke, he gripped the table, tipping over the vase with the lilacs. The flowers scattered over the floor, and a bright stream of water trickled over the carpet.

'Now look what you've done!' Vasya cried. Waving his arm dismissively, Vladimir walked over to the window, where he stood for a while looking weary and disconsolate. Vasya couldn't help feeling deeply sorry for him, as she always did. His life was not an easy one, and she knew how hard it was nowadays to make the right choices about how to live.

'That's enough now, Volodya dear,' she said. 'You must try not to get depressed about it. It's early days, your case still has to be investigated. There are no criminal charges against you, it must just be your old problem, breaking the rules. Wait till I've seen the party committee and found out what it's all about. Who knows, maybe everything will come out all right in the end.'

She was standing beside him with one hand on his shoulder,

trying to look into his face, but he paid no attention. He remained sullen and engrossed in his thoughts. Vasya was alarmed by his behaviour. She felt they had suddenly become very remote from each other. She fell silent. The joy left her heart, leaving leaden and oppressive anxieties in its wake.

6

Next day Vasya trudged off to the party committee. The town was unfamiliar her, but in her distracted state she barely noticed her surroundings, intent only on getting there as quickly as possible. The more she had questioned Vladimir about his case, the more disturbed she had become. The charges against him, even if they were unfounded, were obviously very grave, and she couldn't imagine how the thing could be cleared up.

The party committee offices were housed in an old private mansion, with the red flag flying and the familiar symbol outside the door – just like the one at home Vasya suddenly felt more cheerful and realized how much she missed her old comrades; she could never regard those people who came to see Vladimir as real party people. She went in and asked the boy at the reception desk the way to the local chairman's office.

'You'll have to write down your name and business first. He may see you today, but you may have to wait till Thursday,' the boy replied. How Vasya loathed this bureaucracy! Still, there was nothing for it but to sit down at the table and fill out the form.

'Here, take this to the secretary,' said the boy, and the form was passed on to an errand-boy. Turning to Vasya, he said 'Up the stairs and turn right along the corridor to the door marked "Reception". You'll have to wait there.' He looked dreadfully bored. Then he suddenly brightened up as he caught sight of a young girl in a knee-length skirt and fashionable hat. 'Manka!' he shouted. 'Hey, Manka! What are you doing here?'

Manka fluttered her eyes at him, simpering, 'Just off to see some friends! Why shouldn't I pay a little visit to your committee offices?'

Vasya looked at the girl, trying to sum her up, and decided finally that she must be a prostitute. A familiar uneasy feeling came over her. In the old days a girl like that would never have dropped in so brazenly to see her friends at the party committee . . .

As Vasya walked down the long, brightly-lit corridor, men and women workers dashed past her. Everybody seemed to have work to get on with, and this made Vasya feel thoroughly idle. When she entered the reception room she was asked her surname by a secretary, a smooth-faced young man with a self-important air. Her name was checked against the register, kept by a hunchbacked girl.

'It won't be your turn for a while, as your business isn't urgent. You'll have to wait a bit,' she said Vasya sat down to wait with the others. Some workers with thin drawn faces and shabby jackets conferred with each other – some sort of delegation, most likely. There was a tall, well-dressed man in glasses reading a newspaper, an 'expert' by all appearances. An old working woman in a headscarf sat very still, sighing every so often as if praying for her sins to be forgiven. There was a healthy, exuberant Red Army soldier. Next to him sat an old peasant in a Russian coat, and next to him a priest in a cassock.

Just as Vasya was wondering what could have brought the priest there, the secretary announced 'Your turn, Father.' He let the priest into the chairman's office and then turned round to the others. 'He's a very clever man and could be useful to us,' he said.

From time to time girls with short hair and shabby skirts (communists evidently) would run in; efficient and preoccupied, they brought papers to be signed or questions to ask the secretary. After conferring with him briefly in whispers, they would run out again. A stylish, aristocratic-looking lady entered the room. Although she wasn't in the party, Vasya knew her to be the wife of a highly placed official. She demanded to see the chairman immediately, announcing that she had a letter from a member of the Central Committee, that she had come from Moscow and hadn't time to wait. At first the secretary was firm with her. Seeing the letter from the Central Committee, he wavered. But he couldn't go against the rules, he said. As this was a 'personal matter' would she kindly wait he turn in the queue?

The 'would-be lady', Vasya privately thought of her, was absolutely furious. She made it clear how much she despised the provinces. In Moscow she'd have been admitted at once! In Moscow everybody fought bureaucracy, but look at this place! Look at all those petty officials, with all the rules and regulations they thought up. She sat down with an offended air, carefully adjusting her sleeves.

Then a burly man burst into the room, with his cap on the back of his head and his overcoat unbuttoned, an overbearing man whom Vasya immediately put down as a Nepman.

'Comrade secretary, I ask you, what kind of a system do you have here?' he demanded. 'My time is extremely valuable, every minute counts, a shipment is coming in right now, and all you can do is hold me up with pettifogging red tape and make me fill out a lot of forms. Announce me this minute please. Kondrashev's the name!'

He had an air of fatuous complacency about him. You'd think he was Lenin himself, the way he behaves, thought Vasya, feeling all her old hatred of the bourgeoisie rising up. It was *this* man they should be arresting and putting in the dock, this arrogant fat face!

The secretary apologized, but he had his instructions. The Nepman paid no attention, and continued to insist imperiously that he should be admitted. In the end he got his way, and the secretary went into the office to announce him. Almost immediately he came back, looking flustered. 'The comrade chairman begs you to take a seat,' he said sheepishly. 'He's seeing two other people before you, both on urgent business.'

'What the hell is the meaning of these damned rules! Try and do business with these people and they do nothing but make a lot of idiotic demands, then threaten you and badmouth you as a saboteur! We all know who the *real* saboteurs are!'

So saying, he wiped the sweat from his forehead with a handkerchief and sat down fuming. The 'lady' eyed him approvingly. The 'expert' glanced censoriously at him from behind his newspaper. The workers remained engrossed in their business, apparently oblivious to this scene. Their turn came next.

Vasya found the wait tedious; going to the window she looked out onto the small garden where two young children were playing, chasing a dog.

'Pull Bobka's tail! He'll squeal but he won't bite! Come here, Bobka! Catch him, quick!' Their childish voices rang out.

At last Vasya's turn came and she went into the party chairman's office. Behind a large desk sat a small man with a goatee beard, and spectacles; his bones seemed to protrude from his thin shoulders. He glanced coldly at Vasya, and stretched out his hand to her without bothering to get up.

'Well, what can I do for you? Is it personal?' he asked in a neutral tone – she was just another petitioner after all.

'I've come to introduce myself to the committee,' she said. She had decided it would be as well not to bring up Volodya's case immediately, as it was obviously going to be anything but simple to talk about it. 'I arrived in town recently.'

'Yes, so I heard. Staying with us long, are you?'

'I have two months' leave, but as I've been ill I shall most likely stay on longer.'

'Are you resting, or will you be taking on some work?' he asked, not looking at Vasya as he spoke but continuing to sort through his papers as if to say, Why should I make small talk with you when I'm so busy.

'I can't take on anything permanent,' Vasya replied, 'but you could use me for agitational work.'

'We may be able to use you, yes. Next week we're starting a campaign around the transition to the local budget system. I hear you're an expert on the housing question?' He glanced at Vasya again briefly, then immersed himself once more in his papers.

'I worked for two years in the housing department,' she replied, 'and I organized a communal house.'

'Indeed! How very interesting! In that case you can show us how to make our communal houses pay.'

'I'm afraid I can't do that,' Vasya said, shaking her head. 'You see, as soon as we started becoming self-supporting the whole thing went to pieces. I think that communal houses should be more like schools, places for inspiring the communist spirit . . .'

'Look here, I really don't have time now for such matters,' he interrupted. 'But if you can give us some ideas on how to approach the thing – as well as a rough financial estimate – that would certainly help us reduce the state budget . . . So you think housing can be used as a method of educating people, do you? But we've schools for that, and universities too!'

The chairman laughed patronizingly from the heights of his wisdom. Vasya felt angry and rose abruptly to leave.

'I'll say goodbye then, comrade.'

'Yes, until we meet again,' he replied, regarding her more attentively. She returned his glance coldly, looking him straight in the eyes.

'If you'd like to work for the agitation department, all you have to do is go along and register. Why not drop in on the women's department too? They're always short of workers,' he suggested.

'Now that I'm here,' she said suddenly, 'I should like to ask you about Vladimir Ivanovich's case.' She looked at him severely as if saying, I know this business is all your doing!

'Yes, well, er, how shall I put it?' The chairman frowned, moving his cigarette to the corner of his twisted mouth and suddenly looking rather grave. 'Look here, I've heard about you, you're obviously a party comrade of an extremely high calibre. It wouldn't be proper for me to discuss Vladimir Ivanovich with you.'

'But what are your accusations against him? Vladimir Ivanovich can't have done anything criminal.'

'Well, I suppose it depends what you mean by criminal, doesn't it?' he replied. 'But I really can't go into the case with you. You'll have to make your own enquiries at the Control Commission. And now, my respects to you, goodbye for now.'

He nodded his head at her and buried himself once more in his papers. His message was obvious – don't bother me now, I've work to do.

Vasya left the chairman feeling angry and put out. Nobody would have been received like that in her home town, not even a non-party member! She had gone there to talk to her comrades and had been made to feel like a stranger! Vladimir was right when he said they had turned into petty officials, acting like pre-revolutionary governors. Vasya was walking along so deep in thought that she almost bumped into someone going the other way. There stood Mikhailo Pavlovich, an old friend, a worker in the machine department of the factory where Vasya had once worked.

'Well I never!' he exclaimed. 'I can't believe my eyes! Bless you, Vasilisa my dear!'

'Mikhailo Pavlovich, my dear friend!' They hugged and kissed.

'So you've come to stay with your husband, have you?'

'And what about you? What are you doing here?'

'I've come to purge the party! I'm a member of the Control Commission now. It's a full-time job – there's always a lot of shady business going on,' he said, laughing.

He had a red beard and a kindly face and was as enthusiastic as Vasya remembered him. They excitedly exchanged news and asked each other many questions.

Mikhailo Pavlovich insisted that Vasya should come to where he was lodging. He lived in a house which used to belong to the gentry, and he had the room next to the front door. It wasn't much to look at, just a bed with a basket beside it containing his belongings, two hard chairs and a table covered in newspapers, a few glasses and some tobacco. He had intended to move there temporarily, he said, but had ended up staying.

They recalled old friends and comrades, reminisced about their town, discussed which ventures had prospered and which had gone to the dogs. Then they touched on the subject of the NEP. The very term stuck in Mikhailo Pavlovich's throat, and he was none too keen on the chairman either.

'He's an upstart,' he said, 'With him it's all "me, me, me". Of course, he works hard, he's energetic and he's nobody's fool. But everything has to come from him. He wants to see his name in lights, to show everyone who's chairman. The workers don't like it one bit. They say the congress decided on more democracy, but instead what have we got? Even more bureaucracy and even more respect for rank! So much intrigue goes on behind the scenes nowadays, and that means a whole lot of new factions, and then work is held up and the authority of the party is undermined. The chairman's job ought to be to unite everybody. He's got to be impartial, like a father, but instead he harasses people.'

'Look, dear Mikhailo Pavlovich, how is the case against Vladimir going? What are the charges against him? Are they very serious? You can tell me as a friend, you know.'

Mikhailo Pavlovich stroked his beard. After thinking a moment he told Vasya that the case itself wasn't worth a kopek, and that if communists were going to be brought to trial for activities like Vladimir's almost every one of them would have to be indicted.

The whole thing started when Vladimir Ivanovich first arrived. He had immediately fallen out with the chairman for ordering him around, and Vladimir had refused to take orders. Vladimir had said 'Your rules don't concern me. That may be the party line, but I'm not subject to you. I shall deal only with the industrial authorities. Let them be the judges of my work.'

Reports of this conflict had finally reached Moscow. The Moscow party committee, while ostensibly supporting the chairman, took Vladimir under their protection and so nothing came of it. It was made to seem as if both of them were right!

But inevitably there were repercussions, and once again neither of them would budge an inch. After the slightest incident, both would independently send reports to Moscow.

Finally, a delegation had to be sent from Moscow to sort it out. Resolutions were drafted in the strongest possible terms and no sooner had they left than the fight started up again. It was then that the Control Commission was called in to investigate the matter. Mikhailo Pavlovich had attempted to settle things peacefully. The director was running his business on his own lines, he'd said. This was considered quite proper in industry, and the party central committee was satisfied with his work.

There were no direct charges against Vladimir, and Mikhailo Pavlovich thought it unlikely that any could be made to stick. He had told the Commission that he personally knew the 'anarchist American', and had lived in the same town as him back in 1917 when they had worked together closely. Even if he did live in fine style nowadays, even if his conduct was immoderate and his behaviour 'uncomradely' – well, who could claim to be innocent of such things these days?

But the chairman and various other members of the party commission were determined that the charges should get a serious hearing, and to use this case against the director to teach other people a lesson. They didn't want the party to go around condoning this sort of behaviour.

'But what are all these "activities" of his you keep referring to?' asked Vasya in bewilderment. 'I know he has a grand apartment, but it's not Vladimir's, it's what any director would get at the state's expense.'

'I'm afraid the case doesn't just concern his apartment. People are wondering where he got the money to set up two establishments,' Mikhailo Pavlovich replied.

'What do you mean, "two establishments"?' asked Vasya angrily. 'Do you suppose Vladimir Ivanovich has been supporting me as well? What an idea! If you really want to know, I've been putting my own money into the housekeeping! And that's only because Vladimir hasn't enough of his own. . . You see, it's only for the sake of his job that he has to give all these dinners and parties'.

Mikhailo Pavlovich listened to her with a pitying look, which made Vasya even angrier. Why *should* he pity her for standing up for her anarchist husband? She knew he hadn't approved when she had first started living with Vladimir.

'Well, what are you gaping at me for? Don't you believe me? How could you think for one moment that I'd rob him of his money like that?'

'But it's not you we're talking about, is it my dear?' he replied gently. 'The main problem is all these unsuitable friends of his . . .' He looked at her as though to see how she would react.

'Are you referring to Savelyov by any chance?' she asked.

'Well yes, there's Savelyov of course, and there are others too . . .'

'But Savelyov doesn't visit us any more. Vladimir promised not to have anything more to do with him – apart from business, that is. And as for the others, he's promised to see them strictly on business. There are people he doesn't like, who live in a completely different world to ours, but what's to be done. All these shareholders and technicians, they're all part of business . . .'

'Yes, quite so dear,' murmured Mikhailo Pavlovich abstractedly, stroking his beard.

Vasya went on to tell him about all the things she found so

difficult to come to terms with these days. People were different
now, and so was work. She often felt terribly confused as to what
was wrong and what was right, about how communists ought
and ought not to behave . . . She would have sat discussing all
these things with him for much longer if a friend hadn't come
round to take him to the Control Commission.

Before he left, Mikhail Pavlovich said he would introduce
Vasya to some 'regular comrades' from a factory, and he would
think hard about Vladimir's case. He warned Vasya, however,
that if Vladimir went on acting as he had been doing he would be
threatened with expulsion from the party.

Vladimir had obviously been waiting for her at the window, for
when she returned he met her on the porch.

'Back at last, Vasya my rebel! Where have you been fighting?
At the party committee? What did they have to say?'

As she told him he paced anxiously round the room, smoking.

'So, they're accusing me of living in two establishments, are
they? What a lot of hypocritical humbugs they are! It wouldn't
be any business of theirs if I lived in five establishments! What
does it matter so long as my accounts are in proper order, and I
don't steal the goods or take bribes?'

This talk of two establishments disturbed Vasya deeply. But
she was most emphatic about Savelyov. The thing would have to
stop here and now, and if ever he came to Vladimir's office he
must be sent packing the moment they had discussed their
business. Then she asked Vladimir about his workers. Was it
really true he was rude to them, and even shouted and cursed at
them? 'Nonsensical rumours! Rubbish!' he shouted. 'Of course
there are times when I shout at them and let them have it, and
with good reason too. It wouldn't do to get slack with some of
those fellows, especially the loaders – a lazy, irresponsible bunch
of men they are, I can tell you!'

Vasya didn't mention that the party was thinking of expelling him. Instead, she decided that she herself would make some changes at home. From now on there would be no more guests hanging around the place, they would eat more simply, and the horse Vladimir had bought would be sold. What use were horses anyway, if you had a car? At this Vladimir got very worked up, insisting what a fine horse it was, broken in to carry a lady's saddle too. It was hard to get hold of a horse like that nowadays, it was pure luck he had found it in the first place, and it hadn't been so expensive either. A horse meant capital these days!

'Capital! Really Volodya, are you going to set up in business as a capitalist then? You must give up these expensive habits of yours if you don't want to regret them later!'

'So you think they'll expel me from the party? What has the party come to, expelling people for their morals? Let them go ahead, I don't care! I'll just work for the state institutions!'

Vasya didn't try to contradict him. She merely insisted that from now on their life must change – they must live more modestly. Most important, he would have to break off contact with unsuitable friends. She promised to discuss things with Mikhailo Pavlovich again, and if need be go to Moscow and raise the matter with Torporkov, who had helped to get Vladimir acquitted on the previous charge.

Vladimir glanced at Vasya sitting on the window-sill, so pale and skinny with her huge mournful eyes and her thin face. Throwing his cigarette on the floor, he went over to her and kissed her, pressing her face close to his.

'Vasya sweetheart, don't leave me now, will you! Please support me, tell me what I should do. I know how wrong I've been, but it's you I've wronged, not them.' He put his head on her knees, like a child.

'But what have you done, Volodya?'

'Oh Vasya, don't you understand? Don't you realize yet?'

Alexandra Kollontai

'Well, if you mean you've betrayed yourself and your class, you needn't justify yourself to me!'

'Oh Vasya, Vasya!' he sighed, moving away from her. Then changing the subject abruptly he asked, 'Why isn't dinner ready yet? I'm famished. I haven't had anything to eat since morning.'

Soon after their first meeting, Mikhailo Pavlovich put Vasya in touch with a group of women mat makers, and she started going to the factory regularly to help them fight for better working conditions.

To be working with people again was a joy for her. It was like going home. She also met Mikhailo Pavlovich frequently and was soon on good terms with his friends, whose opinions she found she shared. These men, without actually forming an official group, were unanimous in attacking the chairman, and had no truck with the bosses either. There was one old worker they did respect – he hadn't lost touch with the people or started acting like a boss; they had elected him director of the steel-casting plant.

Vladimir's case was still unresolved, and according to Mikhailo Pavlovich some new evidence had come in – incriminating evidence, he warned Vasya. From now on Vladimir would have to be even more careful and avoid all dealings with Savelyov, who was apparently implicated in some extremely squalid deals. However vociferously the state institutions might protest, it was clear that the GPU wouldn't let this man get away with it for much longer.

Vasya was distraught with anxiety for Vladimir. It seemed so terribly unjust, especially at this time, when he was working flat out from morning to night. The minute he got home, he would sit down at his ledgers. He had received instructions from the party centre to radically reorganize the firm's book-keeping system. He called in a bank official to help him, and the two of them would often pore over the files until three in the morning. He

106

began to lose weight and sleep badly, which was hardly surprising considering the double load of problems he had to cope with.
And on top of this new and important work, he had to put up
with all the persecution and machinations. Vasya's heart bled for
him, and she felt nothing but tenderness for her poor victimized
husband.

They no longer entertained guests, and Savelyov's name was
never so much as mentioned. Apparently he had gone off
somewhere and good riddance too! Vladimir stopped going to
the theatre or visiting friends, and stayed at home every evening,
grim and preoccupied. Vasya racked her brains for ways to
distract him from his gloomy thoughts and help him reduce his
burden of work. It was really only at the mat-factory, when she
was involved with the women there, that she was able to put him
out of her mind.

These women had a hard life. Their wages were low, and as
there was never time to review their rates they were always owed
an increase. The union intervened on their behalf but it came to
nothing, and Vasya was furious at the mess they made of it. She
put pressure on the authorities and stood up for the women's
interests. She also helped to put the women's union on its feet so
they could bring a case before the arbitration committee. While
she was at the factory she would rushed around, oblivious to
everything else, completely forgetting the outside world until it
was time to go home.

She would walk back with Lisa Sorokina, the organizer, a very
bright girl with whom Vasya formed a close friendship. They
would talk as they walked along, outlining their plan of action
and discussing which of them should be chosen to put their case
to the arbitration committee. The time passed so quickly that
they often reached Vasya's house before she even noticed.

One day when she returned from a meeting, Vladimir came
out to meet her. He looked a changed man, beaming with that
special happy look of his. Hugging her, he said, 'Well Vasyuk,

congratulate me! I've just had a letter from Moscow and apparently they're appointing me to a new post – in other words I've been promoted! I'll be superintending a whole region from now on! I only have to stay on here another two months and wind everything up. What fools we'll make our Control Commission box. What will the chairman say now, I wonder!'

'I wouldn't rejoice too soon, if I were you,' Vasya warned, 'just in case the charges against you get in the way of your appointment.'

'Rubbish! The Control Commission definitely won't go making trouble for me now. They need me to work for them.' He was jubilant as a child. 'Well, little rebel,' he said, fondling her, 'I've got something for you to celebrate, a little present.' He led her into the bedroom. Laid out on the bed was a length of blue silk, and beside it some lawn.

'Look, this silk will make a lovely dress for you darling. you could do with smartening yourself up a bit, this grey-blue colour really suits you. And here's this lawn for some shirts'

'Shirts! But Volodka dear, what are you thinking of!' exclaimed Vasya, laughing. 'Material like this for shirts?'

'This is the finest ladies' lawn,' he insisted. 'I know it's used for underwear, but I wish you didn't have to wear those terrible hair shirts of yours – they remind me of balloons.'

'But surely it could be made into something better than just shirts? And the silk, well of course it's lovely, but you shouldn't have got it. Was it for cash? How could you spend your money on a thing like that?' She shook her head. Volodya's presents gave her no pleasure; his extravagence made her feel uncomfortable, but she hated hurting his feelings.

'Don't you like it then?' asked Volodya.

'It's beautiful material, it really is. But surely Volodya, you must see it's not my style.'

'But how about when we go to the theatre?'

'So that's how a director's wife is supposed to get herself up for the theatre!' The mere thought of herself dressed up in the blue silk made her laugh. 'Thank you darling, all the same, for being so kind and taking so much trouble.' Standing on tiptoe she hugged and kissed him passionately.

'You haven't forgotten how to kiss then, Vasya. I thought you didn't love your poor husband any more, turning me out of the bedroom and never coming to give me even a little kiss!'

'But Volodya, you know neither of us have time – you've had so much on your mind.'

'So you still love me?'

'How could I ever stop loving you!'

'Do you want me to remind you how we used to make love?' he asked, and they both laughed, as though they had met again after a long separation.

Vasya was just setting off for the factory next day when she remembered Bukharin's *ABC of Communism*, which she had meant to take with her. It was on Volodya's bookshelf and she hurried back into his study to collect it. As she was opening the glass door of the cupboard, a packet fell off the shelf and the wrapping came undone. Stooping to pick it up, her heart contracted. There was a piece of blue silk identical to the one he had given her, and the same lawn too, covered with bands of open lace work.

Dimly thoughts began to stir in her mind. 'He lives in two establishments.' Could there be some truth in it? The very idea was too terrifying to contemplate. A wave of jealous suspicion swept over her. 'He lives in two establishments . . .' He had certainly been unpredictable recently, one moment acting like a stranger and barely recognizing her, the next being excessively affectionate towards her as though he felt guilty about something.

She began to recall how always smelt of perfume after he had been to the theatre, how he preened himself in front of the mirror when he was going out for the evening. She remembered the nurse with the pouting lips, the blood stain on the sheet . . .

Everything clouded over, her hands felt numb, and an indescribable pain gripped her heart. How could Volodya deceive her, his dearest friend! Her adored husband and companion, making love to another woman behind her back, when she was right here beside him! If they weren't living together it might have been different, for she would never expect a man to be permanently faithful to her. But now, when she was offering him all her love, all her tenderness, everything, how could he do such a thing?

Perhaps he no longer loved her? She couldn't even entertain such a thought, and began to clutch wildly at straws of comfort. If he no longer loved her, why would he treat her so affectionately and considerately? And why would he have called for her to come to him in the first place? It was impossible – they were friends and lovers who had gone through so much together they had become as one. Was it true? Was it yet another calamity? She could not, would not, believe it.

And yet . . . why did he spend so little time at home? Why was he always so wretched? Why wasn't he delighted to see her any more? Why did he seize any pretext, such as her cough, to sleep on his own? Thinking about these suspicions, she wanted to cry out, but she was too appalled by them to be able to take in their full meaning. It's all lies, she told herself, lies! He loves me, he must love me! He made love to me only yesterday. Maybe the material belongs to someone else, maybe he had to deliver it to someone . . . Why had she jumped to the conclusion that this was his parcel? His name wasn't even on it. She must have invented the whole thing.

Now she began to feel ashamed of distrusting him. She was like an old woman, keeping tabs on her husband. But despite her attempts to reassure herself, the serpent gnawed away, and try as she would, it wouldn't leave her alone. There *must* be a simple explanation. When Vladimir got back she would ask him about everything, they would talk it over together, she would give him the chance to explain, she would find out the truth. Picking up her book, she went off to the factory. She was late as it was.

After work she hurried home, anxious not to be late for dinner. At the factory she had been at peace, but the minute she found herself alone on the street her jealousy began to stir again. Two separate establishments, two pieces of silk, two pieces of lawn . . .

How did Vladimir know they made underwear from it, if he hadn't learnt it from streetwalkers and ladies with money to burn?

And what was that he said about her blouses? Hair shirts that reminded him of balloons. Did he really dislike her blouses? In the old days he had loved her in them. In the old days he would never have gone out like that, leaving her alone when she had just arrived. And if he had really been going to a meeting, as he said, why had he primped himself in front of the mirror, and why did he reek of perfume afterwards? Why did he no longer look at her with that old, special joy?

She would demand an explanation: who had he got the material for, why had he concealed it on his bookshelf, why hadn't he left it lying on the table? If he tried to evade her questions or lie to her, she would never forgive him. She ran up the steps to the porch and hurriedly rang the bell. The car was parked outside – Vladimir was already back.

He would have to explain himself the moment she saw him. If he had been deceiving and humiliating her the way a husband humiliates a wife he no longer loves . . . the very thought made her boil with agitation and rage. Why was it taking so long for the door to open!

At last the bolt rattled and Maria Semyonovna opened the door.

'We've guests from Moscow,' she announced. 'Six people, six mouths to feed. What a business!'

111

Vasya couldn't imagine who these guests might be. She heard them chatting away in the drawing-room. Vladimir was there playing host, and introduced them to his wife. The guests turned out to be men from the syndicate who had brought the plans for the new work schedule. Vasya was immediately eager to hear about the latest news from Moscow and the recent political developments which were on everybody's mind.

But then she saw Maria Semyonovna standing in the doorway, beckoning furtively to her. She badly needed some help in the kitchen; Vasya the errand-boy had been sent out to get wine, Ivan Ivanovich had gone off to fetch appetizers, while poor Maria Semyonovna was rushed off her feet trying to attend to the roast in the kitchen, and laying the table at the same time. Vladimir had given orders that everything was to be done in style and the table laid formally. Vasya would have to help. They bustled round. Ivan Ivanovich returned – just as well, as they needed an extra hand. All this time, Vasya was too busy to think about the blue silk. She wanted to be sure she didn't let Volodya down; now he was a director, he couldn't afford to lose face in front of the men from the syndicate. Soon the other Vasya ran in with the wine, and Ivan Ivanovich uncorked the bottles.

The table was eventually ready, decked out as for an Easter banquet, with appetizers, wine, flowers, the Morozov napkins and the best silver knives. They called in the guests, and Vladimir cast an anxious eye over everything. Then he seemed to relax.

But surely he could have given Vasya just a brief glance of gratitude for working so hard to please him? Her anxieties reawakened, she felt utterly dismal and rejected. She made small talk with the guests, but all the time the blue material was on her mind. Who could it be for? She began to look at Volodya with new eyes – he might have been a stranger, for only a stranger could have lied to her like this and allowed the serpent to bury itself in her heart.

Vasya was kept busy all evening. She sent the errand-boy for and extra pillows to make the guests comfortable for the night, and all the time she was arranging their beds in the study she kept looking at the cursed bookshelf. The blue material was still there and she was still no wiser as to who it was for. She was exhausted.

She gave the guests their tea, but all they could talk about was grades of merchandise, methods of packaging, specifications, estimates. This was the world of business again. All these men were former merchants, including the two communists among them who were already experienced traders and had become real 'red merchants'. Vladimir blossomed in their company. He talked proudly of his business, which had far outstripped the others and was increasing its profits every month. The merchants evidently had great respect for him, and listened attentively to everything he had to say, completely disregarding the opinions of the other bosses.

At any other time Vasya would have been happy for Vladimir, but today she couldn't have cared less. There he was, talking away about business, business, with never a thought for her. Couldn't he see how exhausted she was, how tortured by jealousy?

She couldn't help wondering whether, if he was dishonest with her, he mightn't be dishonest in business too. Maybe the party committee had been right to press charges. Oh, what were these syndicalists talking about now? They hadn't stopped talking all day. If only they would leave her alone with Vladimir, so she could ask him about the material . . .

Vasya began to get ready for bed. Vladimir was going to be sleeping with her that night as the guests had taken up the other rooms. She was waiting for him, listening for his footsteps. He had said good night to the guests and was giving Ivan Ivanovich his orders for the next day. When she heard him approach the door, her heart began to thump and her knees gave way so that she had to sit down on the bed. She was going to ask him the moment he came in.

But Vladimir was too full of himself to give her the chance. He wanted her advice on how they should reorganize the bureaucracy so as to strengthen the position of the communists and keep the bourgeois syndicalists under party control.

'Do advise me, Vasya,' he begged her. 'You're the expert on these matters. Think about it, will you? Tomorrow I'm going to examine the new charter with them, but I'd like you to read it through beforehand and give it your undivided attention. The bourgeoisie are doing their damnedest to get their pot-bellies into the government and attack workers' power, but they haven't a hope, no fear! We'll get them by the short hairs. It's just a problem of organizing the bureaucracy so it can't move an inch without the party and the *real* communists.'

'But how can you say that, when you're not even following party regulations?' Vasya demanded. 'Many's the time you said it would be no great catastrophe to be expelled from the party, you could survive without it!'

'Never mind what I said in a temper,' Vladimir grinned at her, 'you know me better than that. How could I live without the party? You really think I could break with it?' He began pulling off his boots, thinking aloud. 'As soon as this stupid case is behind me Vasya, you and I will start living together properly. You'll see what an exemplary communist I become once I'm transferred to this new district! No more confronting the chairman; in fact I'll soon be in the party pantheon!'

He was happy, his eyes alight, not at all his recent bad-tempered self. 'Let's go to sleep now,' he said. He was just about to switch off the lamp when Vasya stopped him.

'No, please, wait a minute, I . . . There's something I want to ask you . . .' she stammered, propping herself up on her elbow so she could see his face better. Her heart was beating violently and her voice sounded strange. Vladimir was immediately on his guard.

'Well get on with it, what do you want to ask me?' he said, not looking at Vasya and staring at the wall.

'I want to know why you've got that material in your bookcase, that silk and lawn?'

'What silk? Oh, I suppose you mean the patterns.'

'No, I don't mean the patterns! It's a whole length of material, the same as you gave me, and I want to know who it's for! Tell me, who is it for?' She watched Vladimir's face closely.

'Well, do you really want to know? D'you mean you haven't guessed?'

'No.'

'Well you see, it's like this: Ivan Ivanovich asked me to get a coupon for the material to give his fiancée. He's always plaguing me to do things. Whatever I have, he has to have too, he apes me in everything.' He explained this simply and unhurriedly.

Vasya blushed with shame. 'Ivan Ivanovich? For his fiancée? Oh, and I thought . . .'

'What did you think?' laughed Vladimir, turning to look at her.

'Oh, Volodya darling!' Vasya said, kissing him, feeling deeply ashamed of herself. How *could* she have harboured such thoughts against him, suspected her friend like that?

'So tell me what you thought? You're quite a little detective, aren't you, a regular interrogator!' He hugged Vasya, but a trace of anxiety lurked in his eyes.

'Now let's get some sleep, shall we? No more kissing now. Tomorrow we have to entertain our guests and we'll never get through our business. I must get up early.'

He switched off the lamp. Vasya felt terribly relieved and was just falling asleep when the serpent stung again. Suddenly she felt wide awake.

What did he call her a detective for? That must mean there *was* some reason to spy on him. Vladimir was already sound asleep, but she lay there awake, shivering and staring into the darkness.

Did she believe him or not? On and on through the sleepless night the question nagged her tired brain. No answer came.

After the men from the syndicate had left, Vladimir had more work than ever, reorganizing the business – as if he hadn't got enough worries already. But there were compensations.

One day Mikhailo Pavlovich invited Vasya to his room to tell her that a special decree had come from the party centre. Apparently there were now no direct charges against Vladimir, and more importantly, no more rumours about his insubordination and 'irregular behaviour'; the case had been dropped and she could now rest easy about it. Vasya breathed a sigh of relief – she almost succumbed to old habit and said thank God. Mikhailo Pavlovich was pleased about the outcome too, more for Vasya's sake, since he was very fond of her and felt sorry for her.

Then Vasya suffered a great blow. When the women workers' case came before the arbitration committee, it was decided in favour of the management. The women were irate and there was talk of strike action. The Mensheviks, working under the guise of non-aligned, non-party members, also began to agitate for a strike and fuelled the women's fury. Vasya had a bad cough and a high fever, but despite this she spent days at the factory, arguing furiously with the management and demanding concessions, while at the same the trying to make the women see reason.

She was so absorbed in her work that she forgot about the blue silk. Then suddenly she was jolted into remembering, and somehow from that moment the serpent couldn't be dislodged.

It all started with the dog. One day the errand-boy brought a white poodle to the house, with a ribbon tied between its ears.

'Whose is that dog?' Vasya demanded. 'Where does it come from? Why have you brought it here?'

The boy replied that Vladimir had given orders for the poodle to stay in the house for the time being. It belonged to Savelyov, he said, and when Savelyov went away the poodle pined for him.

Vladimir's sudden concern for the dog amazed Vasya. Surely he couldn't have done it simply to please Savelyov? All her old hatred of Savelyov returned; she was furious that Vladimir had continued his friendship with this worthless man. When Vladimir came home the poodle was all over him, as though welcoming its master. Vladimir petted it and talked to it.

'Where does this dog come from, Volodya?' asked Vasya. 'Does it belong to Savelyov?'

'Indeed not,' he replied. 'It belongs to Ivan Ivanovich's fiancée. She's gone away, and Ivan Ivanovich has asked us to have it here in the meantime.'

'But the errand boy said it was Savelyov's.'

'Well, he's got it wrong. It's true the dog was staying in Savelyov's house the last few days. Vasya had to take it from there. I suppose he thought it was Savelyov's.'

The explanation seemed simple enough, but it didn't ring true. Once again Vasya didn't know whether to believe him or not. When Ivan Ivanovich arrived, she tackled him about the dog, and he related all the details at great length: his fiancée had asked him to look after it but he had no room for it – he didn't even have a house. So then he had sent it to Savelyov's, but there was only one servant and she often went out, locking the poodle in on its own . . . and so on, and so on. Whatever the truth of the story might be, Vasya took an instant dislike to the animal.

Shortly after this episode, Vladimir went away for a few days to a conference of the syndicate. Vasya thought she would be miserable without him, but in fact she suddenly felt freed from the dead weight of anxiety she carried around when she was with him. She stopped feeling her unspoken resentment at the way he ignored her existence. Without him things began to go better, for when he was there her foolish feminine heart craved signs of his affection, even though she realized he was preoccupied and his head was full of other things. Alone, there was no waiting, no listening, no struggling against feelings of resentment.

She invited her factory friends, Lisa Sorokina and Mikhailo Pavlovich, over to dinner. She loved entertaining people like this. After the meal they discussed party politics, walked in the garden and sang songs. Everyone enjoyed themselves, especially Vasya; how different from making polite conversation in the drawing-room with men like Savelyov or the syndicalists! Time flew by.

Vladimir returned one morning on an early train to find her drinking tea. She jumped up to greet him, but without kissing her, he merely took her hand and pressed it to his lips for a long time. When he looked up she saw his eyes were filled with tears.

'What's wrong, Volodya?' she asked with a sinking heart. 'Have there been more problems?'

'No, Vasya, nothing like that. Life's hard, that's all . . . I'm sick and tired.' He sat down at the table and rested his head on his hands, the tears pouring down his cheeks.

'Do tell me what's upsetting you, Volodya. Tell me sweetheart, it will make things easier.'

'Will it really, Vasyuk?' he asked her mournfully. 'I've thought such a lot about it, I've racked my brains – you can't imagine how much thinking I've done, Vasya. I don't believe talking about it would make it easier. I can't see any solution.'

These odd garbled hints made Vasya's heart miss a beat.

'Volodya, you must stop torturing me like this. What are you talking about? Tell me the truth, I beg you. I can't stand it any longer, I'm worn out with worry. I never have any peace of mind . . .' As she spoke she began gasping for breath, then started to cough.

'There, you've started coughing. How can I talk to you now?' There was reproach and sorrow in his voice. As she continued to cough he frowned and lit a cigarette. 'Why not drink some tea? Maybe that'll stop it.'

'I'll take one of my lozenges,' she said. Her coughing fit subsided and she poured Vladimir some tea.

He began, in his usual matter-of-fact manner, to tell her about problems at work. He had been informed of them by Ivan Ivanovich as soon as he'd got off the train. The loaders were causing a lot of disruption, demanding more wages for overtime and reducing their output. Because of this, the syndicate was suffering heavy losses, and now the loaders were threatening to strike if they weren't paid immediately. Vladimir thought there might even be saboteurs amongst them, inciting them: you couldn't keep watch on all of them. A fine state of affairs! He only had to go away for a few days and this blew up in his absence! What were the other bosses doing? Apparently they didn't want to stir up more trouble. So now there would be long drawn-out talks, giving extra ammunition to the chairman . . .

'Is that what made you say life was hard, and there was no solution? All because of the loaders?' asked Vasya suddenly.

'Yes, of course. What did you think I meant?' Vladimir puffed his cigarette and slowly stirred his tea, then went on talking about the problem and how best to settle it without scandal and publicity.

But Vasya was only half listening. The old suspicions tugged at her heart. Would he *really* have cried just because of problems with his loaders? That wasn't like Vladimir. There must be something else on his mind – such as the blue silk . . .

She wasn't going to give way to her feelings of jealousy now. Vladimir must be very tired. His dealings with the Control Commission had worn him down to the point where the merest trifle was liable to upset him.

Yet Vasya longed for reassurance. She wanted desperately to believe that Vladimir's worries were only business worries.

7

Vasya finally won her case at the factory. She persuaded the management to grant concessions, and afterwards the jubilant women carried her in triumph on their shoulders. Vasya realized that but for the chairman their case would never have been won, for she had talked a great deal to him and had come to appreciate him as an uncompromising fellow who refused to humour the managers.

She hurried home after this victory. Nearing the house, she saw the yard filled with loaders. They were arguing loudly amongst themselves. 'Higher pay!' some of the more vociferous were shouting. 'Otherwise we'll down tools and stop work! Let the bosses and clerks do the loading!'

Slipping unnoticed into the crowd, she listened to what they were saying and began to ask questions. They talked noisily, explaining their grievances to her: they were underpaid and got no overtime, and the accounts hadn't been kept properly. The men surrounded her, threatening the management and demanding that she take up their case and explain matters to her husband.

She listened to everything they had to say and continued to question them. Their complaints were familiar, their demands were reasonable. The men were beside themselves, furious with the bosses and clerks for the easy lives they lived at the expense of the loaders, who couldn't even afford food or clothes for their children.

Vasya realized they needed help to make their case heard. They would have to put pressure on management through their union; they wouldn't get far without proper organization and clear plans. The leaders came to an agreement with her. They decided to formulate their demands, and then if management didn't concede to them, they would go straight to the arbitration committee. She became passionately absorbed in the business, oblivious to her position as director's wife. She had no choice – she *had* to advise these friends who were so lacking in experience and leadership.

She invited the leaders into the house so they could put their demands on paper. As they passed through the reception rooms on the way to the bedroom, the men cast furtive glances at the director's furniture. It was only then that Vasya realized how irregular it was for her to have let them in. But it was too late now. The men sat down at her table and began drawing up their demands.

It was quiet outside. The loaders had broken up into small groups, waiting, chatting and smoking. Suddenly they started murmuring – the director's car drew up and Vladimir stepped out.

'What's going on here?' Vasya heard him shout angrily. 'So you've taken it into your heads to hold meetings here, have you? Are you going to threaten me with your grievances? Well, I don't intend to discuss them with you here, understand? This is my private house. You'll have to go to the manager's office. If it's about pay, go and complain to your union, it's nothing to do with management. They've enough problems as it is. If you intend to strike, that's your affair. If your union agrees, then by all means organize a strike. But now get out of here! I refuse to listen and that's final. We'll discuss it at the office.'

Slamming the front door behind him, he went into the house and marched straight to the bedroom. Opening the door he saw Vasya there, sitting at the table talking to the loaders. He froze.

'What the hell's going on! How did you men get in? How dare you break into my house without my permission? Clear off! Get out this minute!'

'But, Vladimir Ivanovich,' protested the loaders, 'we didn't come in on our own . . . Your wife here . . .'

'Clear off I said, otherwise . . .' Vladimir was white with rage, and looked as though he could barely restrain himself from going for them. But as they were moving towards the door, Vasya intervened.

'Are you out of your mind, Vladimir? How *dare* you? *I* invited them in! Comrades, please wait, don't leave!'

121

She ran to stop them, but Vladimir caught her and gripped her elbow so hard she cried out.

'So you invited them in, did you?' He said. Who asked you to interfere in my affairs, I'd like to know? You don't have to answer to the syndicate. Run off to your mat-factory if you like organizing strikes so much, you little busybody!'

'So you're trying to get rid of me, are you! I suppose if I'm on good terms with my friends here I don't protect your interests as director and I lower your bonuses!'

'Vile hypocrite!' he shouted at her.

Vasya felt as though he had lashed her with a whip. Vile? Her, vile? They confronted each other with hatred, like sworn enemies. An unutterable sadness filled her heart, a feeling of black anxiety that seemed to spell the end of all her happiness.

The minute the loaders had left, Vladimir went off to the manager's office, leaving Vasya sprawled across the bed, her face buried in the silk quilt, soaking it with her tears. But crying would never dissolve this grief. For Vladimir she was something vile; they had become strangers, hostile, enemies at war.

The days that followed were grey and joyless. Vladimir stayed at home much of the time, but there seemed little point in this now they were so estranged. They spoke to each other only when they had to, and both went their separate ways. When Vasya fell ill again it was Ivan Ivanovich who sent for the doctor, who told her to get more rest. Vladimir and Ivan Ivanovich were wholly preoccupied with their work for the accounts department. They would sit up until late at night in the study and emerge only to eat, taciturn and bad-tempered.

Lisa Sorokina came round to see Vasya, bringing her news from the factory and messages of love and sympathy from all the women there. But Vasya was too unhappy about her quarrel with Vladimir to care about her illness. She knew that neither of them could ever forget their confrontation over the loaders, neither in their hearts would ever forgive the other.

Vasya considered going back to her home town. She felt homesick, but she had no home. She couldn't stay with her parents, they would just moan about their lives and curse the Bolsheviks. There was nowhere for her to go. She wrote to Grusha asking her to find a room for her, and to Stepan Alexeevich begging him to find her some party work in a factory: she was determined to leave as soon as she heard from them. What was the point of her staying if nobody needed her? Vladimir would be perfectly able to survive without her.

The days dragged on, melancholy and interminable.

By now it was midsummer and in the garden the cherries had ripened and the plums were turning dark blue. Delicate white lilies were in bloom, swaying on tall slender stems. But none of these things gave Vasya any pleasure as she wandered about the garden. She remembered how happy she had been that spring when she lay outside in her folding chair, and she felt even more wretched. She had felt like an entirely different person then, innocent and trusting. She had lost something she couldn't understand or put a name to; she only knew that she had lost it for ever.

Occasionally Vladimir would come to the study window, anxiously peering at her as she paced listlessly around the garden. He would stand there frowning for a while, – then disappear back to his business with Ivan Ivanovich. Vasya would sigh with disappointment. She always hoped he would come out into the garden to see her, but he didn't. He had no time for her; his business was more important than her unhappiness.

One morning Vasya was awakened by a rustling sound and she saw Vladimir looking through his cupboard for something.

'What are you doing up at this hour of the morning, Volodya?'

'I'm just going to meet a consignment of goods off the train,' he replied.

'On your own?' she asked.

'Yes, I have to do the stock-taking,' he said. As she looked at him struggling to put on a new tie in front of the mirror all her old affection for him flooded back.

'Come here Volodya, let me help you with it,' she said, and he went over to her obediently and sat on the bed while she knotted his tie. They looked at one another and embraced silently.

'Oh my love, Vasyuk darling, it's so painful to be strangers. It can't go on like this, can it?' he asked sadly, and drew her curly head towards him.

'Do you imagine it isn't painful for me too? Life's not worth living like this.'

'Why have we fallen out, Vasya?'

'I don't know, something terrible has come between us . . . !'

'No, Vasya!' he interrupted her. 'Nothing can ever come between us. I belong to you.'

'So you still love me?'

'Silly thing!' he said, kissing her. 'Let's put an end to our quarrel now! It's so stupid and it makes us both so unhappy. I couldn't endure the thought of losing you Vasya, you know I couldn't live without you. Suppose we stop bickering from now on?'

'All right, but only if you stop ordering me around!'

'And only if *you* stop setting the loaders against me!' They both laughed.

'Go back to sleep now, Vasya. You'll get sick again today if you don't sleep properly. I'll be back in an hour or two.' He tucked her up, kissed her eyes and went out of the room, leaving Vasya feeling so relieved and happy that she fell at once into a deep and blissful sleep. All her old happiness had returned, all her fears gone.

Vladimir didn't return directly from the unloading, but telephoned to say he had to go to the office and would be back for lunch. Vasya was feeling a lot better that day but decided not to go to the factory. Instead she helped Maria Semyonovna with the housework, and the two of them gave the house a thorough clean.

Just before lunch the telephone rang and Vasya went to answer it.

'Hello, is Vladimir Ivanovich back?' asked a female voice.

'No, not yet. Who's speaking?'

'I'm calling from the office.'

'Then why are you calling him at home? He should be at the office himself at the moment.'

'No, he's not at the office, he's already left. Sorry to have troubled you,' said the woman.

Vasya knew that voice! She knew it and disliked it. She remembered that this woman had rung several times when she first arrived. Then the calls had stopped.

Vasya immediately went to ask Ivan Ivanovich who it was making all these calls to Vladimir from the office – during working hours too. Ivan Ivanovich said it must be one of the secretaries. Why should one of the secretaries call him? Once more the familiar doubts overwhelmed her and the serpent stirred.

Vladimir brought back two colleagues for lunch. They could talk of nothing but the morning's deliveries, though Vladimir did find the time to ask Vasya how she was feeling and whether she had been out in the sun as the doctor ordered.

'No, I wasn't sunbathing,' said Vasya icily. Then almost before she realized it she blurted out, 'That lady phoned again, you know, the one who's always calling you from the office.'

'A lady? Who could that be, I wonder?' said Vladimir, wide-eyed with astonishment. 'From the office, you say? It must be Shelgunova – a lady indeed! She's a respectable housewife with children, I'll have you know! You've seen her, Vasya, that fat woman with the warty face.' He spoke easily, but Vasya's anxieties were not so easily allayed. It rang false to her.

After lunch the two managers took their leave, and Vasya happily contemplated the prospect of spending the rest of the day with Vladimir. If he was with her she would find the consolation which their conversation this morning had promised. But no sooner had he seen the managers off than the telephone rang jarringly from the study. Vladimir answered it hurriedly.

'Yes, yes, it's me,' he said curtly . . .

'But I told you not to call me . . .'

'Yes of course, if family circumstances permit . . .'

'No, not on any account, I forbid it once and for all . . . All right, all right,' he yielded. 'But only very briefly, mind. Goodbye.'

Vasya stood in the next room, listening. Who could he be talking to? Who was he promising to see 'very briefly'? Who could he 'forbid' like that?

Vladimir came out of the study and went into the bedroom, ignoring Vasya and walking straight past her. She followed him. He was standing in front of the mirror, combing his hair.

'Who were you talking to on the telephone, Volodya?' she asked.

'Savelyov,' he answered.

'So he's back, is he?'

'Yes, he came back this morning.'

'Did you meet him?'

'Would you mind telling me what this is about, an interrogation? You know perfectly well that the deliveries came this morning.' He spoke irritably.

'So you're going to see him? Did you promise to go?'

'Yes, I'm going to see him.'

Neither spoke. Vasya's heart was pounding as though it would burst, but she no longer cared about anything. The agony was unendurable. She went up to Volodya, taking his hand and saying, 'Volodya, please, I'm begging you, don't go! Don't start everything all over again.'

'All what over again, what are you talking about?' he asked.

'You know quite well who I'm talking about that seedy

racketeer. I've got it on good authority that the main charge against you is your unsuitable friendships . . .'

'Oh so you're starting that up again, are you? Parroting what the party bosses keep screaming at me? Do you want to wear me down, all of you? Break my will so you can tie me to your apron strings?' Vladimir snatched his hand furiously from hers.

'Stop Vladimir, stop! What do you mean – I don't want to tie you to my apron strings! Be reasonable! It's you we're talking about, not me. You mustn't dig your own grave in this way. You've enough enemies as it is, you don't have to start up your friendship with Savelyov again!'

'What's Savelyov got to do with it?'

'But isn't it Savelyov you're going to see?' Vasya looked at him, faltering.

'Yes, of course. But so what? It's just a business visit, can't you understand? I can't get out of it now.'

'I don't believe you!' she said vehemently. 'I'm sure you can put it off until tomorrow. Just phone the office and tell them . . .'

'Oh Vasya, what a baby you are!' he said, relenting a little. 'All right, if you really want to know, the fact is, Savelyov wasn't calling on business. We settled our business at the office. It's just that there's small party of close friends at his house and he was inviting me round for a hand of cards. I haven't set foot out of the house for almost a month now, I'm stuck here working all the time. You must allow me some free time occasionally, Vasya. I'm still young, I want to live a little. You can't expect me to live like a hermit.'

'Yes I do understand that, Volodya,' said Vasya dejectedly. 'Of course you're right, dear. I don't want to stop you having a good time. But I beg you not to start up again with Savelyov – he's a crook and a menace and you know it. You don't even respect him. What does he mean to you anyway? The word will get out that Vladimir Ivanovich is friends with Savelyov again, and then what will you do? Volodya darling, I implore you not to go there today. You can phone him and refuse . . .'

'This is ridiculous!' he snapped. 'If the chairman wants to spend his time bringing court cases based on people's friendships then he's more of a garbage-heap than a chairman if you ask me. And you, Vasya, you're blowing the whole thing out of proportion!'

'But what about *me*? What if I don't want you to go there, Volodya? I know he doesn't like me, I'm sure he invited you just to spite me. I heard you telling him you couldn't come because of "family circumstances", and you both laughed. Oh, Volodya,' she said desperately, 'it makes me so unhappy when you laugh at me like that, and especially with someone like Savelyov . . . You know I'd never forbid you to go.'

'But that's exactly what you're doing now!'

'If that's what you think, why don't you go then! Just go and see him, but remember one thing', she said, her eyes flashing. 'Remember there's a limit to what I can stand. I've helped you out of trouble, I've suffered for you, I've defended you, and I've had enough. Go, if that's what you want to do, but I know what I shall do . . .' Her voice broke.

'Look here, I'm fed up with these hysterical outbursts of yours!' he said, losing his temper at last. 'What's got into you? What do you want of me?'

'Oh, Volodya,' she began to cry, 'I've hardly ever asked you for anything, but now I'm imploring you to stay, for your sake and mine!'

'Oh my God! Females! All the same! Every damned one of you! I've had enough!' He pushed past Vasya and went quickly into the hall, banging the front door as he went out. The car engine started up.

Vasya howled like an animal in pain.

8

'Lisa, I need your help. Can you put me up? I've left him for good.' Vasya's voice was breaking but her eyes were dry. Her misery went too deep for tears.

'So you've left him! About time too! We were all amazed you stuck it for so long.'

'It's unbearable, we've become strangers, Lisa,' said Vasya.

'Well, I'd be surprised if you weren't. What did you see in him in the first place?'

Vasya said nothing. Then she started explaining how she felt. She still couldn't believe what had happened, she only knew she couldn't forgive him that final insult. The first time she had been prepared to forgive him. But now she felt as though he had trampled on her dead body, and she couldn't understand the reason. Surely it wasn't simply so he could go off for a game of cards with a scoundrel like Savelyov and his cronies?

For all Vladimir cared she could die of unhappiness, just as long as he was having a good time. Was that love? How could her friend and comrade, a communist too, behave like that? Vasya rambled on. Lisa found it hard to picture what had happened between them, let alone how Savelyov came into it.

'But don't you see Lisa, it's Savelyov who's the cause of it all. Vladimir was going to see him . . .'

'You don't really believe he was going to see Savelyov, do you?' Lisa interrupted

'Well, who else could it be? Do you suppose it wasn't Savelyov then?'

'It's not a question of "supposing"!' expostulated Lisa. 'My God, the whole town knows about it, it's only you who are blind to what's happening! Either that, or you deliberately refuse to see . . .'

'See what, Lisa? Tell me!'

'The fact that your dear Vladimir has got a girlfriend!'

'A girlfriend!' Vasya couldn't take this in immediately. She stared at Lisa wide-eyed, not with fear or grief but with amazement. 'Did you say a girlfriend? But who is she?'

'She's not one of us, she's not a worker. She's a secretary.'

'So you know her?'

'Well, I've seen her – the whole town knows her.'

'How?'

'Because of the way she flaunts her fancy clothes, that's why our friends are so angry with your Vladimir. Did it never occur to you, after all that Mikhailo Pavlovich told you about those friends of his? Look at you! You're not usually an idiot, but you've behaved like a proper idiot in this business!'

But it was something else that bothered Vasya at that moment. 'Does he love her?'

'Well, you never know. I suppose he must if he's been carrying on with her all these months. Everyone thought when you came he'd break it off, but not a bit of it! He still goes on visiting her in her flat, in his fancy motor-car.'

'So she has her own flat?'

'Oh yes, and it's smarter than your house, too!' said Lisa.

So this was what they meant by two establishments! Now Vasya understood everything. Except one thing. Why had Volodya lied to her and tortured her like that?

'But what did you expect? Did you expect him to bring his woman to see you? Or ask your permission to go and see her? It was up to *you* to see what was happening, but you didn't because you were a fool, and now you've only yourself to blame!'

'Please, Lisa. You don't need to keep reminding me I've been a fool! That's not the important thing. What's important is whether he loves her or whether it's, you know, just one of those things.'

'What do you mean, one of those things? He must love her. He spends all his money on her, he gives her expensive presents . . .'

'You think so? I'm not sure. You see . . .'

'You don't really think he still loves you, do you? Vasya my dear, you must stop deceiving yourself, it'll only make it more painful. Obviously he cares for you because you're his wife and a dear friend too. But as for loving you, believe me, Vasya, he stopped loving you long ago.'

'I don't believe you!' Vasya shook her head.

Annoyed by what she saw as Vasya's foolishness, Lisa began to describe Volodya's girlfriend to her in deliberately flattering terms. She was incredibly beautiful, incredibly well dressed. She always wore silk and was surrounded by admirers vying for her favours, among whom was Savelyov, a close friend of hers. They spent wild evenings together, and rumour had it that Vladimir went halves with Savelyov over her keep. Vasya found the idea of Vladimir being part of that world unbearably painful. Could he really love this tart? She couldn't believe it. Whatever people said, she didn't believe it! It didn't make sense.

'Well, if you don't want to believe it, that's your business!' retorted Lisa. 'But ask anyone you like, and they'll all tell you the same thing. She used to be a clerk, Savelyov's personal secretary, then she started to "visit" the directors and God knows who else, for money. There are rumours that Ivan Ivanovich and some of the managers visit her. But however much of a whore she may be, she doesn't have a prostitute's ticket – she can thank the Soviet government for abolishing them!'

'But Vladimir could never love a woman like that!' Vasya protested.

'What makes you think that? Men are capable of loving women exactly like that, especially men like your Vladimir. As far as he's concerned, the more depraved they are the more he likes them. . .'

'Stop it Lisa! How dare you say that! You don't know him! What gives you the right to judge him?'

'But why do you defend him when he humiliates you in front of the whole town? It's a different story as far as she's concerned, believe me! He'd stand by her through thick and thin!'

'What do you mean, humiliates me? You've making it up! Anyway, what business is it of mine how Vladimir behaves? I'm not responsible for him! You don't understand Lisa, it's not *that* I care about . . .'

'Yes I know, you care that he's stopped loving you.'

'No, it's not that either really, although of course that's terribly painful. The main thing is that I know what I feel but somehow I can't express it any more. I don't know how it's happened. We used to be so very close, before Vladimir started concealing things and lying to me. Then he started being afraid of me. Me of all people – it seems impossible! Did he imagine I'd stand in the way of his love affair? Surely he couldn't have thought that. I can't make any sense of it. He can't really love that woman so much . . .'

'Well, she's certainly spread enough scandal about it,' said Lisa with a gesture of impatience. 'There's no way of making you see sense, Vasya. You're obviously still besotted with your Volodka. "Beat me, trample on me, I don't mind, I'm just your meek and humble wife." That may be all right for you but it wouldn't be for me. I'd pay him back for everything he'd done to me!'

Vasya refrained from arguing, but the more mercilessly Lisa condemned Vladimir, the more adamantly she defended him. She wanted to convince Lisa that she didn't blame him for having a girlfriend and for loving another woman, but for concealing it all from her, as he would from a complete stranger. Nor was he treating her just as a stranger either, but as a person he couldn't trust, as if he feared that as his wife she would insist on her conjugal rights!

'That's exactly what you should do!' shouted Lisa. 'You *must* do it! How dare he degrade you like that! You must leave him. He's not good enough for you Vasya, he's not worth your little finger!'

Vasya argued with her hotly. It was always the same. However much she might criticize Vladimir herself, whenever anyone else attacked him she rushed to his defence and was furious that people should misunderstand him. *She* was the only person who understood her 'American'. It was only when she mentioned the word 'American' that she began to cry. Memories of the Vladimir she had loved, the man who had led the co-operative and defended the soviets, flooded back, and she was overcome with misery. She clung to Lisa, sobbing. Thoughts of Vladimir the director disappeared. All she felt was an unbearable nostalgia for the Vladimir she had fallen in love with.

'It's so terrible, Lisenka, I can't help it!'

'I know my darling, my precious. Do you know, the same thing happened to me last year, and it's given me the strength to face anything. It will pass dearest, it really will pass.'

Lisa stroked Vasya's head and comforted her friend as best she could. Then she put her in her own bed, and made up a bed for herself on some chairs. She had had an exhausting day and was soon sound asleep.

But Vasya couldn't sleep. She tossed and turned, sitting up, lying down again, racked by anxieties and chaotic thoughts which tormented her and tore her apart . . . There was that terrible night when she had seen the blood stain in the bed and they came to arrest Vladimir. But it was no longer jealousy which obsessed her now, but the idea that Vladimir had distrusted her – she could forgive him anything but that. The heart has its own laws, but she couldn't for the life of her grasp why he had so little faith in her that he couldn't tell her he loved another woman.

It was so simple! He had been living on his own for months, and had started an affair. After all, he was a passionate man. She remembered Stesha. She supposed he must have slept with her once, and that was that. But this woman probably wouldn't let him go so easily. Lisa said she was putting pressure on him – so she couldn't really love him, she must be taking advantage of him. Vasya knew how clever that kind of woman could be. She was obviously not going to let go of someone like Vladimir, however much he might want to break it off.

She remembered again how miserable he had been recently, and how unpredictable – affectionate and then suddenly distant towards her for no apparent reason. Now she realized how tormented he must have been. What torture it must have been for him to live with someone he loved when this woman was sharpening her claws behind his back!

Vasya remembered all those times when Vladimir seemed on the point of asking her forgiveness for something, then suddenly stopped short. Like the morning when the trouble with the loaders started. She had felt apprehensive at the time, and then she had started coughing and Vladimir had changed the subject. Was this because he took pity on her? And if so, did that mean he loved her?

Then Vasya recalled the pieces of blue silk, identical for both his women, and realized there was no reason to suppose he loved her. He was merely saying, 'Here, this is for you, because you're my wife even though you're repellent to me! I bought my beautiful mistress a present but I didn't forget you! Take your silk and shut up!'

Damn him! Damn him! Vasya clenched her fists, overcome with a desire to strike him. The coils of jealousy engulfed her, and she felt suffocated by misery.

She could find no peace of mind. Had he really gone to Savelyov's yesterday? But then she remembered – Savelyov was irrelevant, he was merely Vladimir's alibi, a 'cover' so no one would be any the wiser about what was going on. If Savelyov had been the cause of everything, she would never have forgiven Vladimir. 'I don't care whether you forgive me or not, I'm going to get my own way. Go on, die of grief, I'm off to enjoy myself. I wouldn't sacrifice a kopek for you, because you're repellent to me . . .' If he had really trampled on her feelings yesterday just for that gang of racketeers and their idiotic card games she would never have forgiven him.

It was yesterday's events which had made her so unhappy, and had made her leave him. If she had known then that he had a girlfriend and was going through the agonies of being in love, she might have controlled her rage. She would have cried certainly, and would have been terribly distressed, but she would have understood.

She might have understood about his girlfriend, but would she have forgiven him? She had forgiven him about Stesha, who was a friend after all. Would she have grown to like the white poodle, to put the damned blue silk out of her mind? But now wasn't the time to be thinking about such things. The only thing that mattered was whether they could live together as friends, concealing nothing from each other. At one time they had gone hand in hand together into battle, now they were going their separate ways. What remained to hold them together? Their hearts? But what if Vladimir took his heart away from her, what was left then? Nothing. There was no reconciliation possible, nothing but misery. Nobody in the world had ever known such misery.

The next morning Lisa had just left for work when Maria Semyonovna came in, her head covered in a lace kerchief. It was a hot summer's day, and she was out of breath and very red in the face.

'Good day to you, Vasilisa Dementevna,' she said. 'I've brought a letter from your husband. He told me to take a cab and get here as quickly as I could, but where can you find a cab nowadays? I'm out of breath!'

It was a government envelope – Vasya tore it open with fingers that were so numb she could hardly make them obey her. She began to read . . .

'Vasya! What has happened? What are you doing to me? Why do you torture me? Do you want this scandal to spread through the whole district and give my enemies more ammunition against me? Do you want to destroy me? You said you were my friend. How can you side with my enemies like this? You're tearing me apart! I can't live like this any longer. If you don't love me any more then tell me honestly, but don't attack me behind my back. You know I love only you – people may gossip about me, but it's nothing but a silly affair. Listen to me! I wasn't at Savelyov's yesterday, but I swear I didn't betray you where I was, for wherever I am, my heart will always be with you. It's unbearable, Vasya, I beg you to have pity on me and come home so I can look into your sweet eyes and tell you everything, the whole truth. If you're a true friend to me I know you'll come. If you don't, then it's goodbye. Believe me when I say I won't be able to live without you.

Your heartbroken Volodya.'

Vasya read the letter twice and her heart was filled with such a sweet joy that one tears rushed to her eyes. 'Silly affair', he said. 'I love only you!' Then suddenly she was filled with rage. As if *she* had 'torn him apart', indeed! So *she* was expected to take pity on him.

And would he take pity on her, and stop tearing *her* apart? Her tears dried and she set her pale lips. 'So he's unhappy! He thinks he's unhappy, when he's just spent the night in another woman's arms and given her blue silk . . .'

All pity for him disappeared. Yesterday she had begged him desperately to stay, beseeching him with her words, her eyes, but he had pushed her away, shouted those typical male insults and gone off!

And now he was writing 'I love only you!' What rubbish! He didn't love her at all! And if he did, a fine sort of love it was, nothing but insults and scenes and anxiety. She could do without that kind of love! And why had he written 'Goodbye,

believe me when I say I won't be able to live without you . . .'
What did he mean by that? Why, it meant absolutely nothing, it
was an empty threat, calculated to arouse her pity and make her
come running to him like a fool. Vasya read his letter a third
time.

Maria Semyonovna sat there, placid and indifferent, wiping the
sweat from her face and fanning herself with her handkerchief.

'Vladimir Ivanovich returned the moment you left,' she said.
'He asked where you were and I said "How should I know?" Then
he went into his study and sat down to his papers. After a bit he
telephoned Ivan Ivanovich and asked him to come over, and they
sat in his study for a while. Around midnight he came into the
kitchen and asked me whether you'd come back yet, and when I
said no he went out again. Well, when he'd seen Ivan Ivanovich
off he went into the bedroom. He must have seen your note I
suppose, because I could hear him sobbing, destroying himself
with grief he was, like a baby. He was pacing around all night,
and wouldn't drink his tea this morning. "I don't want anything," he said, "just fetch Vasilisa Dementevna for me. Go
round to all her friends and don't you dare show your face in this
house until you find her." '

These words made Vasya's heart ache, but now her old
feelings of tenderness for Vladimir merely irritated her and
filled her with hopelessness. So he'd spent the night alone,
waiting for her, longing for her, sobbing for her, and then he'd
called for her. She longed to be with him and was tortured by
jealousy. It was obvious that the bond between them wasn't
irrevocably broken and they still cared deeply for each other. But
why prolong the agony? Why should she go back merely to
explain and understand, and go through the same thing with
him all over again?

'So what did Vladimir Ivanovich do when you left me room?
Did he go to the office?' she asked Maria Semyonovna.

'When I left him? Well, he phoned his girlfriend at once, most likely to tell her how miserable he was, or how happy he was, you never know with men do you? As long as there's no scandal, they don't care . . .'

So he'd phoned his girl friend that very morning! After writing his letter to Vasya! Maybe Lisa was right, and he only wanted to keep Vasya to avoid scandal. If she hadn't been his wife he would have let her go. He had called for her now just so he could lord it over her again. This time she'd had enough! She must control her foolish heart, for she wasn't going to him, she wasn't walking into his trap. She felt faint.

'Tell Vladimir, will you, that there's no reply for him, that's all. Now please go as quickly as you can!'

'I can't go any quicker than my legs will carry me, can I?' grumbled Maria Semyonovna. 'Besides, you're acting much too hastily. I'd give it more thought, Vasilisa Dementevna, if I were you. Of course he's wronged you, and you're his wife, but you've wronged him too, you know. You should never have left your young husband on his own for months an end. And you know what a wonderful husband Vladimir Ivanovich is to you – he always takes good care of you. Didn't he get you cocoa when you were sick? Didn't he tell me to buy you fresh eggs? He takes better care of you than you do of yourself, he'd never refuse you anything. As for the other women, which man isn't guilty of something on the side, I'd like to know? You're his wife, you're the one he respects. The other one, well he just gives her money and presents, that's all there is to it!'

Maria Semyonovna would never understand. She wouldn't understand that if Vladimir was no longer Vasya's true friend, if she could no longer trust him and there was no closeness between them, they couldn't go on living together.

'Why don't you wait till this evening, Vasilisa Dementevna? I can go home now and tell your husband you're thinking things over and you'll send him an answer this evening. That would be much more sensible. Otherwise I'll have to tell him you decided all in a rush, just spat the words out and told me to be off. When you're upset like this, you can make mistakes you live to regret, and then you'll be sorry.'

'No Maria Semyonovna please don't try to make me change my mind. I mean what I said, I'm not going to go back to him ever again. It's all over.' Vasya lips trembled and large tears fell down her thin cheeks.

'Well, it's up to you. I've given you my advice, but it's your decision.'

Maria Semyonova left, and Vasya longed to howl like an animal, a long anguished howl that the whole street would hear. It was all over and she wasn't going back. Goodbye Volodya, goodbye my darling! She stretched out her thin arms to hum longing for him with all her heart, the tears pouring down her cheeks, while cold reason kept telling her, 'Stop, that's enough. You're not going back to him. It's over, it's the end.' She cried for a long time, then burying her head in Lisa's pillow she fell asleep exhausted.

She was woken abruptly by a loud hooting, and heard a car draw up outside the window. Who could it be? She leapt up. Maybe Vladimir had come to see her! Trembling with hope and joy she ran to the shutters and flung them open. But it was Vasya the errand-boy standing at the door.

'There's been a terrible disaster, Vasilisa Dementevna!' he said breathlessly. 'Vladimir Ivanovich has gone and poisoned him-self!'

'What! What did you say!' Vasya rushed towards him, seizing him by the hand. 'Is he dead?'

'No, not yet. He's still alive, but he's raving terribly and in awful pain. He's calling for you, they sent me to fetch you in the car!'

Vasya rushed to the car just as she was, without putting on her coat. Her teeth were chattering and she was shivering. She had killed her beloved! She had destroyed him, failed him, let him down when he called for her, called from the depths of his heart! Vasya's eyes were large, stupefied, not so much with grief as with something she was as powerless to control as death itself.

Vasya the errand-boy didn't notice her expression and began a brisk account of everything that had happened. He was thrilled by the drama. Apparently Vladimir had left for the office that morning, stayed there an hour, then returned home and gone into his study. The boy was sweeping the yard outside and saw him go to the cupboard with the chemical phials used for testing colours. Later the boy went into the hall and heard a terrible moaning. He went into the study and found Vladimir Ivanovich lying on the couch. His eyes were rolled upwards, his mouth was open and there was foam on his lips. He looked as though he was dead.

Then there was chaos. The boy ran out to get the doctor, who was just sitting down to his dinner. 'A man's dying, you'll have plenty of time to eat your dinner later!' the boy shouted before rushing to the chemist. Ivan Ivanovich come to the house. Everyone was rushing all over the place – there was total confusion.

Vasya tried to listen as the boy chattered on, but she couldn't concentrate. She felt at that moment as though she had ceased to exist. Now only Volodya and his suffering were real. She felt her identity merge with his. If Volodya did survive, her life too would be over, and there would stretch before her only the void, emptier than the grave.

9

Vasya went into the hall just as Ivan Ivanovich was seeing one of the doctors out. She stopped him. 'Is he alive?'

We're doing all we can of course, but we can't say anything definite until morning,' he said.

She tiptoed towards the bedroom. The groans grew louder as

she approached, and in her agonized state she felt as though she were Vladimir and the groans were hers.

Everything was unusually untidy in the bedroom. The carpet had been rolled up, the bed had been shifted – but where was Volodya? Then she saw a large white object on the couch. His face was grey, his eyes closed. The groaning stopped. Oh no! Surely he wasn't dead!

'Volodya! Volodya!' she gasped.

Another doctor turned on her with an angry look. 'Shh, I beg you, no hysterics please!' He was bending over Vladimir, assisted by a nurse in a white cap. They looked serious and severe and refused to allow Vasya near him. Volodya opened his eyes and drew several rapid breaths. He was alive!

'Doctor,' Vasya whispered, 'please tell me the truth. Is there any hope?'

'As long as the heart continues to function there is always hope,' snapped the doctor.

What did that mean, she wondered, 'as long as the heart continues to function'? What if it didn't? But she daren't question the doctor again. He and the nurse were now lifting Vladimir's head and pouring something into his mouth. He started to groan again, spasmodic, animal groans, and as Vasya listened in her numbed, blank state, she felt she could endure no more.

It grew dark and the night-light was put on in the bedroom. More doctors arrived, and after conferring together they sent the errand-boy off to the health-department to get a permit for some special medicine. Vasya was still not allowed to sit by Vladimir and now he stopped calling for her. One moment he seemed to drift into a coma, the next he would start groaning again, excruciating groans. It seemed to Vasya as though with each groan the life was going out of his body, as though his spirit was fighting with his body, his body refusing to release the spirit. She felt useless, getting under the doctors' feet, unable to do anything to help.

141

Then a thought struck her with a terrible force. Rumours about this must already be circulating. People would be saying, 'Just fancy, a communist trying to kill himself! I wonder what he did it for!' And then the whole story would come out. She must think of some plausible explanation immediately.

She thought fast – he had eaten some poisonous mushrooms! Yes, he'd eaten them at lunch, and now he was at death's door! She remembered staying with her grandmother in the country where this had happened. A tailor had come from town to stay with his brother and had picked some poisonous mushrooms; he'd cooked them, eaten them and died.

Vasya made a series of telephone calls. First she called Mikhailo Pavlovich, hinting that when she saw him she would explain things in more detail, but she just wanted to tell him about this terrible disaster; Vladimir Ivanovich had eaten poisonous mushrooms and was close to death. Then she called the chairman, and a few other friends. After that, she alerted Ivan Ivanovich to the story, asking him to explain it to the managers and clerks.

Vasilisa spent a long time rehearsing Maria Semyonovna and Vasya the errand-boy in what to say. The errand-boy was shrewd and knowing. He sniffed disdainfully and shrugged his shoulders, but finally agreed to the explanation. What a fuss! Still, what did it matter to him? Let it be mushrooms for all he cared!

Maria Semyonovna, however, crossed her hands on her stomach, pursed her lips and refused to go along with it. She was hurt. 'How can you poison yourself like that with mushrooms!' she objected. 'Now everyone will say, "What's the cook been up to?" '

But Vasya insisted, telling her that everyone else had already been given this explanation for the illness.

'As you wish. But it's stupid. Anything but mushrooms! Who in their right mind would cook him poisonous mushrooms!'

Love of Worker Bees

Vasya left the kitchen. Maria Semyonovna remained flustered and stirred the food angrily. 'They've created scandal after scandal, confusion after confusion, and now they want *me* to take the blame! They've made a hash of things that even the devil himself wouldn't touch, and now, God save us, it's me who has to clear it up for them! Maria Semyonovna's the culprit, they'll say. As if I didn't know a poisonous mushroom from a good one. As if I'd ever put such a thing on his plate! Twenty years I've been at the stove. I'm no ordinary cook or a kitchen-maid doing a cooking job, I've a whole drawer full of recommendations. General Gololubov's late wife was ever such an important lady, but she never called me anything but Maria Semyonovna! Then there were the Pokatilovs, million-aires they were, they gave me a gold watch and chain of Christmas, on account of my sauces. And now I come here and it's "Maria Semyonovna put poison mushrooms in the director's food!" I never thought I'd live to be insulted like this, when I've served him and done my best for him. I've always been sorry for that Vasilisa too, and more than once I held my tongue about her husband's sweetheart . . . And this is all I get by way of gratitude! It's downright scandalous! And they call themselves communists too!'

'What's getting you so steamed up, Maria Semyonovna?' interrupted the errand-boy in a blasé tone, stirring the soup with gusto. 'As if it mattered what we have to tell folks! They'll never keep it quiet anyway, you won't take the blame. It's just to avoid scandal they invented that about the mushrooms. Any-way, I like it! A regular mix-up and no mistake, just like the cinema! It's a real comedy!'

'Well you might find it a comedy, stupid boy, a man is in there dying and all you can say is what a comedy is! What's going to become of us all? Nobody has any respect for life now, the slightest thing and they shoot a man down, bang like that! You don't even care about your own life. Mark my words, it's all because you've abandoned the Lord!'

'Now don't start going on about God,' said Vasya impatiently.

143

'I may not be a communist, but at least I don't believe in God.

'And a very bad thing too, young man. Anyway, why are you lounging around wagging that foolish tongue of yours instead of getting on with your work? You can help me clear the plates. Oh those devilish doctors! Look at all those plates they've used! They keep asking for tea and refreshments but it won't make any difference, they still can't do anything. It will be as God ordains. I said as much to that hussy who waits on Vladimir Ivanovich's sweetheart. I'd just started to serve the doctor's dinner when she slips in through the back entrance, swishing her skirts and rustling her lawn apron. She had a bow like a white butterfly tied round her head. "My mistress sent me to ask about the state of Vladimir Ivanovich's health" she says. So I say, "As for his health, he may at any moment surrender his soul to the Lord, since the Lord punishes each and every one of us for our sins. And you can tell that mistress of yours that she'd better go to church and repent. For by heaven, it's her and no one else who's been the ruin of him!" '

Maria Semyonovna might be taciturn with Vasilisa, but with anyone else who would listen there was no stopping her.

In the days that followed, the house was crowded with Vladimir's colleagues who dropped in to visit him, and with doctors who held lengthy consultations. Lisa came and sat up night after night with Vasya to prevent her brooding about Volodya. Lisa felt she was to blame for having turned Vasya against him, and this was unbearable to her.

'It wasn't you, Lisa,' Vasya reassured her. 'It was me. It was only when I faced the idea of him dying that I realized there was nobody in the world who was more precious to me! How could I possibly live without him now, when I was the cause of all this . . . ?'

Next morning it was very quiet in the house, and Vasya was sitting alone at Vladimir's bedside, resting her head on his arm.

She was wondering what would happen if he died, leaving her nothing to live for? What would the revolution or the party matter then? The party needed people who had no crime on their conscience, but for her there would always be the knowledge that she had killed Vladimir. And for nothing but female jealousy!

Of course, if Volodya had been secretly involved in fraudulent deals with Savelyov and his cronies, undermining the country, then she would have been vindicated, but as it was she had driven her friend to attempt suicide because of another woman.

And what a friend he had proved too! She had thought he no longer loved her! How could she have thought this when he had gone to the terrible extreme of trying to kill himself for her? He must feel life without her had no joy to offer him. And despite her unhappiness, this realization made her want to cry tears not of bitterness but of gentle repentance.

She looked at Volodya and whispered tenderly, 'Will you ever forgive me, darling? Will you ever forgive me for what I did to you, my precious?'

Vladimir stirred, tossing his head restlessly. 'Water, water,' he murmured.

'Here you are my love, drink this.' She raised his head carefully from the pillow as the nurse had shown her, and helped him drink. He opened his eyes and looked at her without appearing to see her.

'Are you feeling a little better, Volodechka?' Vasya asked, leaning over him solicitously.

He didn't reply, just blinked his eyes. Then in a weak voice he asked, 'Is Ivan Ivanovich here?'

'No, he's gone home. Why, do you need him?' He nodded.

'Telephone him and ask him over,' he said.

'But the doctor said you weren't to work,' she said gently. An expression of impatience and suffering crossed his face.

'Please don't nag me now. Just call him . . .'. He closed his eyes again.

Vasya's heart missed a beat. Why had he said 'don't nag me now'? So he hadn't forgiven her for causing his suffering. She called Ivan Ivanovich, and when he arrived Vladimir asked her to leave the room as he wished to be alone with him. She went out into the garden.

The sun no longer caressed her as it had that spring. It was so hot that it scorched her head, shoulders and arms. A bush of crimson roses had burst into blossom and the dahlias were in flower. The garden was rampantly overgrown, honeysuckle intertwined with lilac and laced with ivy. In this heat the sky was the colour of molten silver. Vasya began to pace along the scorched paths. Vladimir would never forgive her. If only she had come to him that morning when he called for her, none of this would have happened. Now she had lost him for ever. She had lost not only her husband and lover, but her dearest friend. He would never trust her again, never again seek her support . . .

Vasya leaned against the acacia tree – the same tree which in spring had blossomed so profusely, and closed her eyes. If only she had poisoned herself. If only she were dead . . .

Then she heard Ivan Ivanovich shouting, 'Vasilisa Dementevna! Vladimir Ivanovich is calling for you!' He started up the car and Vasya wondered where he could be going – maybe to take a message to Vladimir's girlfriend. Not that Vasya cared any more, for it was all over.

The summer sun was unbearably hot. Inside, the blinds had been drawn and Vladimir was dozing. Vasya knelt at the head of his bed and kept away the flies. 'Let him sleep and rest,' she thought. 'He's suffered enough.'

Maria Semyonovna had gone off shopping and the errand-boy was also out somewhere; Vasya and Vladimir were alone in the house. She was glad to be alone with him like this, for she felt for the first time as though he belonged to her and to nobody else. As she looked at him lying there so helpless and weak she longed for him to understand, to see into her heart and sense how passionately she loved him. How chilling it was always to be craving his affection, when he was so taciturn and sullen with her, when he never even noticed her. She only had to arrange his pillows not quite to his liking for him to say irritably, 'You're as bad as the nurse! Why can't you arrange them properly!' Of course, that sort of thing was to be expected from an invalid, but she still wished he wouldn't be like that with her.

Was it possible he would never forgive her, that this cold, estranged existence of theirs would drag on and on. She looked at Vladimir's sweet familiar face with those wonderful eyelashes which she had fallen in love with the moment she first saw him. He had fallen in love with her plait, but her plait was gone! It was like something out of a fairy take. She had bewitched her lover with her plait and when the plait was cut off her lover had left her . . .

How they had loved each other in 1917! And afterwards too: she remembered that night during the White attack when they had both gone out to arrest the conspirators. 'They may kill me. Vasya,' he said, 'but you must promise not to let that stop you doing what you have to do. There'll be plenty of time for crying later.'

'And the same goes for you too, Volodya' she replied. 'Let's both swear to each other that we'll go on whatever happens.'

They clasped hands and gazed into each other's eyes, then set about their business. It was a frosty night, and the footsteps of their detachment crunched in the hard snow.

At the memory of past happiness, tears of nostalgia poured down her cheeks. So far she hadn't cried once over this catastrophe, she had tried desperately to put a brave face on it and forget her own feelings, but now she was crying for the old days.

'Why Vasya, Vasya, whatever's the matter?' Volodya raised his head from the pillow and looked at her – not with the cold eyes of a stranger, but with his old affectionate look, compassionate and sad. 'Tell me what's the matter Vasyuk, why are you crying, my poor little one?' He laid his hand tenderly on her curly head.

'Volodya darling, my precious Volodya, will you ever forgive me?'

'Silly Vasya, what have I to forgive you for? Please stop crying and we'll talk about it. Sit here, closer to me, that's right. It's so hard for us if we don't talk, isn't it, Vasya?'

'But I'm afraid you'll upset yourself, my darling. Suppose we leave it till later?'

'No, we won't be able to say what we want to say to each other later. It will relieve my mind to talk about it. I was in agony Vasya, that's why I tried to kill myself. Even now I have the will to live again, I still can't see a way out of it.'

'But surely we can find a way together, Volodya, we can't have become such strangers that we can't do it together!'

'So you know everything, Vasya?'

She nodded. 'Yes, I know all about it.'

'And you understand why I've been so depressed and anxious. You kept carping at me about all sorts of ridiculous things, nagging me about Savelyov . . .'

'Yes Volodya, I know.'

'There was another thing you were wrong about too. You thought I loved her, but I never loved her. It's you I love Vasya, my guardian angel, my dearest and most faithful friend. She was something different, call it infatuation if you like, anything but love. And you were jealous of her, you were suspicious and spied on me.'

'But I never did that, Volodya!' remonstrated Vasya.

'What do you mean? Don't you remember the incident with the material? Don't you remember badgering me about why I smelt of perfume or where Savelyov was living? You wanted evidence for your suspicions.'

'Yes, but I didn't spy on you Volodya, it's not true. I was being driven mad by my fears. And I did try to drive them out of my head because I didn't want to lose my trust in you.'

'Well, your fears aside, you were jealous all the same, admit it. You never said so outright, you just made life unbearable by harassing me. What more is there to say? We were both to blame.'

Neither said anything for a while. Then in a wretched voice Vasya asked, 'Volodya, is our life together always going to be like this?'

'I don't know Vasya, I don't know what to do about it. I'm at the end of my tether.'

There was another long silence.

'Volodya, don't you think you might be happier with her?' Vasya asked at last, cautiously, amazed that it caused her so little pain.

'Oh Vasya, Vasya! Why don't you trust me? I wanted to kill myself when I thought I'd lost you! Isn't that proof enough that it's you I love?' His voice, his eyes were filled with reproach, and Vasya's heart began to tremble for joy and her brown eyes shone with sudden happiness. 'Volodya darling, my husband!' Pressing herself against his body, she put her arms around his neck and sought his lips.

'No Vasya, not now, calm yourself! You see how weak I am, I can't kiss you yet.' He smiled and stroked her hair, but his expression was one of deep sadness. It seemed there was no way through the barrier that separated them, no way through the impenetrable thicket of estrangement.

10

Vladimir eventually went back to work. The morning after he had left the house for the office, Vasya couldn't help feeling happy to be free again. She hurried off to the party committee.

From there she was going on to the mat-factory, where Lisa needed her help in preparing for a trade union conference.

Vasya was smiling as she hurried to the committee. She felt as though suddenly released from a cage, and all was well with the world. It had been a long time since she had seen her friends, and they had missed her. She was much valued by them, for she was efficient and responsive to the problems of others, and she never made a fuss.

They put her to work annotating texts, preparing material and speeches. The time flew by. Before she knew it, it was eight o'clock. Vladimir must be getting tired of waiting for her and she was worried that without her there he wouldn't eat what the doctor had ordered.

She walked back with Lisa, and they discussed the news from Moscow that a friend had brought back. There were many things going on in the party at that time which perplexed them, and Lisa disagreed with the new line. She sided with the men from the factory who were putting up their own candidates for the forthcoming party congress; this was clearly going to involve another battle with the chairman . . .

Vasya felt envious of Lisa, for although she went to the factory she was never able to take any real part in anything; she was beginning to feel like a fellow-traveller.

'Well, that's because you've turned into a director's wife,' Lisa retorted. 'You'd get involved again soon enough if you lived on your own.'

Vasya sighed. She didn't need Lisa to remind her of this, but it wasn't the time to be thinking of such things. As soon as Vladimir was better she would leave him and go back home.

'Oh, no you won't,' said Lisa. 'You'll never leave him! You're tied hand and foot to your Vladimir Ivanovich. You're nothing but a meek and humble little wife!'

Vasya said nothing. What could she say? She knew Lisa was right, but after everything that had happened, she could hardly complain. Volodya was alive and out of pain, that was all she cared about now.

When she got home he wasn't there. 'Where is Vladimir Ivanovich?' she asked Maria Semyonovna. 'Isn't he home yet?'

'Yes, he came in at three and waited for you. He waited and waited, then as you didn't come he had lunch with Ivan Ivanovich, and now they've both gone off in the car,' said Maria Semyonovna. 'Oh, and there's a note for you on the table.'

Vasya grabbed the note and read:

Dearest Vasya,

We agreed that from now on we'd have no more secrets and you said you'd always understand. It's absolutely essential that I go to her tonight. I'll tell you the reasons later, and I know you'll understand. Please remember what we agreed together and don't be upset.

Love, Volodya.

Her hands slumped to her side. Not again! Nothing had changed! But why had she imagined it would? She had known all along that Ivan Ivanovich's role was to flit between Volodya and the woman, to act as their go-between, and Volodya was honourably doing as she had asked, and telling her the truth. So why did the old agony rise up again, why was she overcome with anger again, as though he were deceiving her?

Maria Semyonovna was laying the table. 'Are you going to eat or not?' she asked, glancing disapprovingly at Vasya. 'I hope you're not up to your old tricks again. I don't know, first it's one of you not eating, then it's the other, and never a thought about all the cooking! And then it's more quarrels and tears. You'll end up driving each other into the grave! You can do as you please, Vasilisa Dementevna, and be as angry with me as you like, but I'm going to tell you the truth. You're no wife to Vladimir Ivanovich! Just look at you, eating your heart out over his letter and then crying just because he's gone to his mistress! What I say is you've brought it on yourself. Why, the man's just up from his death bed – he poisoned himself because of you! And the moment he's out of the door, off you run! Of course, if you had a job to go to that would be another matter, because you'd have to go to work. But no, all you do is hang around those meetings of yours, trying to talk sense into a lot of stupid women. If you ask me, you should start putting your own house in order before you go off teaching other folk, because I can tell you I'm ashamed to be a servant of yours! This is no home, it's a slum!' So saying, Maria Semyonovna disappeared into the kitchen, slamming the door angrily behind her.

She reappeared a few minutes later in a more benevolent mood, carrying an omelette and a glass of cocoa for Vasya.

'There now Vasilisa Dementevna dear, have something to eat and stop tiring your brain with all that thinking.'

Sitting down beside Vasya at the table, she began to reminisce about a similar occurrence in the house of General Gololubov's late wife, involving the French governess. After it was over, the General had been reconciled with his wife and had lived on excellent terms with her until her death.

Vasya was only half listening as Maria Semyonovna rambled on. She didn't interrupt. During Vladimir's illness the two had become allies. Maria Semyonovna had been sorry for Vasya, and Vasya shared Maria Semyonovna's irritation with the doctors, the specialists, Vladimir's colleagues – all of them bourgeois to a man!

So Vasya was obliged to listen to Maria Semyonovna's interminable anecdotes about the Pokatilovs, who were million-aires, and about how the General's late wife had doted on her . . . Despite her bad temper, Maria Semyonovna was a good soul. But Vasya longed to be left alone, to think and make sense of things.

'Thank you so much for the meal, Maria Semyonovna;' she said at last. 'I really must go and sort out my papers.'

'Is that all you're eating then? I wouldn't have cooked so much if I'd known. You'll do yourself in, Vasilisa Dementevna, you really will. It won't do at all. If you want to know what I think, Vladimir Ivanovich's girlfriend isn't worth a kopek. She's not worth your little finger!'

That was exactly what Lisa had said. 'Why, what makes you think that, Maria Semyonovna?' Vasya asked. 'Everybody says how lovely she is.'

'What have looks to do with it? All powdered and painted she is, like a clown! She's only got one thing on her mind, clothes, and how to squeeze as much as she can out of men.'

'Do you know her then? Have you seen her?'

'Oh, you can't help knowing her! Many's the night she spent here before you came. Little baggage! Gives herself airs too, you have to heat up water for her in the night. It's "Give me this, fetch me that!" She acts the lady, says she was born into the gentry. It's a lie! The gentry weren't like that, they were always polite and said please and thank you to the servants. That hussy does nothing but order people around, "Give me this, take that" . . .'

'What's her name?' Vasya interrupted.

'Her name's Nina Konstantinovna. She's got some fancy surname too which I can't remember, but everyone in town just calls her Nina Konstantinovna.'

'I should like to see her, just once,' mused Vasya, turning Volodya's letter over in her hands.

'Well, that can be arranged easily enough!' said Maria Semyonovna 'She takes a walk in the park every day when there's music at the bandstand. We can go tomorrow, and you'll be able to see our princess for yourself. There used to be plenty of women like that gadding about the streets of Moscow, I can tell you!'

'So she goes to hear the music, does she? Well suppose we do go then, Maria Semyonovna. I might feel easier in my mind once I've had a look at her.'

Maria Semyonovna shook her head dubiously, but there was no stopping Vasya now, and she was curious to see a confrontation between the two rivals.

Vasya left the room and paced around the dark house. Darkness was more consoling to her anxious mind. Everything had seemed fine that morning. Volodya had been better and had gone back to work. Vasya had started work again and had decided she was definitely going home, for she was determined no longer to be the 'director's wife'. She felt much easier in her mind since she and Vladimir had spoken honestly to each other.

Yet here she was again, feeling all the old pangs of uncertainty. How could she be obsessed by jealousy when Vladimir had kept his side of the agreement and had told her the truth as a friend? Why was she so wretched? It must be her fault for wanting too much. She should never have assumed so blithely that Vladimir would come back to her and break with the other woman. Her misery revolved round this, and whatever she told herself, she realized she had been hoping desperately that he would do just that.

It all came back to the same thing. Once again Vladimir was spending the evening with the other woman, leaving Vasya alone in the house. Had he no feelings for her? She no longer understood anything. She had no idea whether he loved her, his friend, or the other woman, his beautiful mistress. He might say he loved Vasya, but his actions contradicted this, and her misgivings were becoming intolerably oppressive.

It would be better to accept that he no longer loved her, and just leave. But how *could* she leave him? She might realize too late that once again she had been mistaken. He might even try to kill himself again . . . It was out of the question to leave him now. Besides, it would be very hard to be apart from him in her present anxious state. It would be easier to cope with the situation if she was with him. All she knew was that she still loved him, and that if she didn't, she wouldn't be suffering so terribly.

Yet however much she loved him, she seemed to understand him less and less. It was as if they were walking through a forest along two paths which diverged more and more the deeper they went in. However much she loved him, she still found herself condemning him.

Why had he become involved with a woman like that in the first place? It would have been less shameful if she was one of them, a comrade and a communist, but this woman seemed like a real old-style mistress. Even Volodya had admitted that she was 'different', a pampered lady. According to him, she had no sympathy for the Bolsheviks or the communists, and yearned for a return to the 'old times'.

Apparently she had once lived in luxury. Her family had had seventeen servants and she had her own horse, broken in to carry a lady's saddle. When the revolution came, her father had joined the Whites. Her mother had died at this time and her brother became a White officer and was killed in action. Left on her own, she looked for work and as she knew several foreign languages she was able to get a job as a secretary at the manager's office. That was where she and Volodya had met.

She had fallen in love with him and started writing to him. Vasya wasn't there at the time, Volodya was desperately lonely and they embarked on a love affair. News of it soon spread around the office and people began to look askance at Nina Konstantinovna. She couldn't bear it, and eventually left her job. It was then that Savelyov had taken her on as his secretary . . .

Vasya paced up and down the room as she remembered her conversation with Vladimir about her.

'Just his secretary?' She had asked before she could stop herself. Her impulse to irritate him was as strong as her desire to find out about the woman.

'Where did you pick up that vile piece of gossip!' shouted

Vladimir, his face red with rage. 'Aren't you ashamed of yourself, repeating such filth! I thought better of you! I never imagined you'd start acting like some old woman, dragging someone into the gutter. How could you say such a thing!'

He then explained that Savelyov had become a sort of guardian to Nina Konstantinovna. He been a family friend, and when she lost her family he had taken care of her, given her advice and money. It was he who had got her the job at the manager's office, and when she left he once more came to her rescue. She had nowhere to live and nowhere to go, and she couldn't possibly move in with Vladimir. When Savelyov had proposed that she move into his house she refused, saying she would rather go on the streets. Eventually Savelyov had found a self-contained flat where he could set up his office and he suggested Nina Konstantinovna live there. He was merely acting as her guardian, in her best interests.

It infuriated Vasya to hear Volodya refer so lovingly to the woman, and she couldn't prevent herself from saying, 'and I bet he makes passes at her too!' She never realized Volodya could be so gullible. Vasya didn't trust the woman an inch – *everybody* said she was a whore.

Vladimir once more lost his temper. 'Lies! Lies and gossip!' he yelled. 'What makes you so eager to wallow in scandalmongering? If you want to know the truth about her, ask *me*! Nina Konstantinovna has eyes for nobody but me. I'm the one she loves! She's a lovely woman Savelyov isn't the only man to make passes at her. What of it! There's Makletsov, you know, the man from the Foreign Trade Department – he's offered her diamonds and every luxury money can buy, but Nina just shows him the door. Of course I'm not saying Savelyov's indifferent to her, and his love for her may not be purely paternal, but Nina's repelled by him, physically I mean. I assure you there could never be anything between those two, it's inconceivable. I know Nina too well. . .'

It was obviously himself he was trying to convince, Vasya realized this only too well, but what was even more distressing was that Savelyov should be embroiled in everything Volodya did. She obviously had good reason to dislike the man, and it was with good reason too that the Control Commission had warned Vladimir to keep away from him.

'Anyway,' she said, 'whether or not Savelyov is involved is neither here nor there. What matters is that there's a lot of gossip going round, and the general opinion is that you and he go halves in keeping this girl friend of yours?'

'Well, you can spit in the eye of anyone who dares suggest such a thing!' said Vladimir. 'I wouldn't expect you to understand this Vasya, but my main misery is that when I first slept with Nina she was a virgin, nobody else had touched her . . .'

This statement pierced Vasya's heart like a needle. She recalled the night in 1917 when they were drinking tea in Vasya's room, and he said 'I shall only give my heart to a woman who is still a virgin'. Then she remembered him stroking her hair after they'd made love, saying 'There's no purer person in the world than you, my Vasya.'

'A virgin! What rubbish!' she snapped irritably. 'What are you babbling about, Vladimir? Do you really mean to say people's purity lies in their virginity? You sound like a dyed-in-the-wool conservative!' She was furious now.

'But Vasya, you must realize it's not me who thinks like that, it's her. For her, it's the most terrible misfortune to have slept with me without being married first! Now she regards herself as a "fallen woman", and it breaks her heart. Can't you grasp that, Vasya? You can't imagine the agony she suffers. She doesn't think like us proletarians, you see. According to her, the first man to sleep with her should be the one to marry her.'

'Why on earth didn't you tell me this in the first place then? What's to stop you marrying her? I wouldn't want to stand in your way!'

'Oh Vasya, Vasya, an intelligent person like you, but just a peasant when it comes to love! How could I marry her, Vasya? We're utterly incompatible! We're completely unalike in every way! I don't really love her, I feel nothing but pity for her. How could I marry her, tell me that?'

Nothing but pity! Did he really mean that? Vasya began to tremble with happiness, she wanted desperately to believe him.

'But why do you go on seeing her if there's no love or understanding between you, and it brings you both so much unhappiness?' she asked.

'Do you think I could just abandon her, Vasya? Things aren't so simple. I have to consider what will become of her if I leave her. Who knows, she might allow Savelyov to keep her, or become a prostitute.'

'Why does she have to be kept? Why can't she go out and find herself a job?'

'Easier said than done these days! You try finding a job with people being made redundant all over the place! I don't know what kind of a job she could do anyway. It would never do for Nina to get an ordinary factory job.'

Vasya longed to shout, Why not an ordinary factory job? What's so special about her? But she had to consider Vladimir's feelings, for he was still far from well and the doctor had warned her not to excite him. The conversation had been upsetting enough for him as it was.

But now, as she kept her lonely vigil in the dark house, Vasya keenly regretted that she hadn't shouted out the truth and told Vladimir what she thought of the woman's tricks.

She didn't believe Nina Konstantinovna's repeated assurances that she loved Vladimir. She was obviously leading him on so as to get the most out of two men. It wasn't because she was a whore that Vasya detested her, but because she was unscrupulous. Whores could be a lot better than society ladies. There was curly haired Zinka, for one – she had been shot by the Whites, and as she lay dying she shouted 'Long live the Soviet government! Long live the Revolution!' She'd been a prostitute all right, but as soon as revolution broke out she seemed to take on a new lease of life. She started working for the political police with passionate enthusiasm, taking on the most perilous and punitive assignments.

Now if Vladimir had fallen in love with a woman like that, Vasya would have understood! But Nina was a lady, a bourgeois, a class enemy, a ruthless woman who was leading Vladimir on to suit her own purposes. What could be her hold on him? The strength of her position obviously lay in his pity for her. 'I'm so weak and helpless and I was a virgin . . . !' Yes, thought Vasya, you've been a virgin since you left a white mark behind you with that spotless virginity of yours! Why, surely all that 'virginity' must have gone to those men who've been giving you presents for it! Yet Vladimir actually believes you and feels sorry for you! Vasya was beside herself with rage at the woman . . .

Maria Semyonovna's querulous voice broke into her thoughts. 'Vasilisa Dementevna! Holy Mother of God! Are you going to pace up and down like that much longer? You'd do better to save your strength my dear, you'll need it for all those meetings of yours! Now be a good girl, go to sleep and stop waiting up for that husband of yours. There's no reason why you should let him in your room if he's been with another woman; I can make up a bed for him in the drawing-room.'

Vasya hugged her and felt even more miserable. It seemed everyone felt sorry for her except the man she loved, her husband and supposedly her best friend. He was sorry only for that cunning creature who clung to him like a snake . . .

Vasya lay in bed, her eyes wide open, oppressed by a great weight of misery which kept sleep away. It seemed that a long time passed before Vladimir strode in and turned on the light. 'Vasyuk, are you asleep?' he said.

'No, I'm not asleep.'

'So you're angry with me, he Vasyuk?' Sitting on the bed, he tried to kiss her, but she turned her face away.

'Ah, so you *are* angry. Just as I thought. What about our agreement? I told you everything, because you begged me to, and now it seems I'd have done better to lie.' Vasya didn't reply. 'Look, it would never do for us to start all those arguments and recriminations again, would it? What are you so angry about? Is it because I visited Nina? Can't you understand, Vasya? All this time you and I have been together, she's been alone! Don't you realize she's been worrying herself sick about me too? She's suffered too, you know.'

Vasya felt like crying out, 'I don't give a damn if she has!' but she bit her lip and said nothing, her heart pounding.

'You needn't imagine anything happened between us tonight, Vasyuk,' he went on. 'I wasn't alone with her. Savelyov was there, and Ivan Ivanovich came soon afterwards. We had to sort things out. Do you know why I went to see her today? It was to say goodbye to her for good . . . What are you gawping at me for? Don't you believe me? Ask Ivan Ivanovich, he'll tell you. I told him to come and help with the unpleasant job of moving Nina Konstantinovna out and clearing her apartment.'

'So where's she going?' asked Vasya dully.

'To Moscow. Savelyov's going with her. He has some relatives there who Nina can stay with while she looks for a job. It'll be easier for everybody this way.'

Vasya said nothing, but her expression was one of utter incredulity. Why this sudden change? What could have happened? He couldn't have discovered all of a sudden that he didn't love the woman.

'Let's not start talking about love,' he said hastily. 'That's not the point at the moment. The point is, Nina realized things couldn't go on this way. In fact it was her decision to go to Moscow. It's been on her mind for some time. That morning when you ran away from your Volodka, she phoned me and said she couldn't live like this any longer, that I must choose between you, otherwise she'd leave for Moscow.'

'Oh, I see. So that was why you poisoned yourself! One of us had already gone and the other was threatening to go if you didn't marry her! Oh, what a fool, what a dumb fool I've been! Now I understand everything! It was because you were afraid of losing her! I thought it was because of *me* that you tried to kill yourself!' Vasya broke out into hysterical laughter.

'You're distorting everything, Vasya! How can you be so cruel! My old Vasyuk was never like this' Vladimir said sadly, getting up from the bed. 'We're obviously getting nowhere, and I did so want to clear everything up so there wouldn't be any more secrets between us. It seems the more open we try to be, the worse things become. You're like a different person, spiteful and unkind.'

'Oh no, Volodya, no, wait a moment! Don't go, please!' Vasya's voice was breaking, for she felt in despair. 'Let's talk about it if we must. So why are you sending her to Moscow, when it's her you love and not me! You'd have stayed with me today if it was me you loved, but it's her you care about, it's her you pity!'

'Vasya, Vasya, you're being unfair! If only you knew how much Nina has suffered, she's only young, just a child really. She has no friends and everyone slings mud at her, and all for what, Vasya? Just because she had the misfortune to fall in love with me! You're different, Vasya. You've got the party, and you've got your friends. She has nobody but me. I'm her only protector, her only support.' Vladimir was pacing round the room, one hand behind his back.

Then he told Vasya about the time Nina had become pregnant by him. All his dreams had come true! A child! His child! What joy, and what misery!

'Well, where is the child then?' Vasya was dumbfounded.

'Do you imagine that Nina could have had it, with all the scandal, and your unhappiness? We wanted to spare you. It nearly broke her heart of course – it almost killed her to make the decision. But for your sake, Vasya, we decided between us that she would have an abortion.'

For *her* sake? He'd come to this arrangement with a completely unknown woman, he and this unknown woman had decided between them to 'spare' Vasya, as though she were some kind of enemy, not someone to be trusted? It was this Nina woman, not Vasya, he had gone to in his unhappiness. He *must* be closer to Nina; Nina, not Vasya, was obviously his friend and lover.

'It was on the day you arrived that I discovered Nina was pregnant,' he said. 'Now do you realize why I was so unhappy, Vasya?' She nodded in silence. Vladimir said that to avoid gossip, Nina had left for another town where Savelyov had made the necessary arrangements. The operation hadn't been a complete success and there were complications; Vladimir had had to visit her there.

'Was that the time when the loaders first went on strike?' she asked.

'Yes, about then I suppose.'

'I see.' So that was why he had cried when he was sitting at the table, because of Nina, nothing to do with the loaders at all!

'And tell me, did she come back that morning when Savelyov arrived?' Vasya continued.

'Yes.'

'Yes, I thought so.'

Neither of them said anything. Cruel words hovered in the air. If they spoke them they would be sorry but then it would be too late, their love would be damaged, mutilated like a face disfigured by smallpox. No consolation, no joy . . .

'Vasya!' Vladimir broke into the oppressive silence. 'Why do we put ourselves through this? Who's to blame? I swear I was only trying to do everything I could to spare your feelings.'

'If you'd trusted me as a friend, you wouldn't have needed to spare my feelings,' she said.

Vladimir sat down beside her and took her hand. 'But Vasya, I know you're my friend – don't you see it makes it all the more difficult.' He put his head on her shoulder as he had in the old days, and she stroked his head with a mixture of grief and joy. Despite everything he was still here beside her, maybe he even loved her.

'Volodya,' she began cautiously, 'do you think it might have been better if I'd left, not her?'

'Oh Vasya, please don't start that again, don't plague me like this. Support me, don't let me do the wrong thing again. I've opened my heart to you as a friend and told you everything. Now stop talking about leaving me.'

'But I'm only thinking of you, Volodya. If you really loved her . . .'

'What's love got to do with it, Vasya! Love is one thing, but I can't understand why you think Nina and I could have anything in common. She's not a comrade, she could never be a true friend like you are. I'm just sorry for her, and worried about what will happen to her if I walk out on her and break it off for good. I still feel responsible for the woman, can't you understand? She was a virgin!'

'Oh Volodya, that's ridiculous! How on earth can you consider yourself responsible for her? She isn't a child, she knew what she was doing. Anyway, who cares about their precious virginity any more nowadays?'

'Well that's how the proletariat thinks of course, but Nina's not like that. For her it's a terrible thing to have on her conscience . . .'

'Exactly. That's why I said I should be the one to leave, then you can go ahead and marry her!'

'Please Vasya, not again! Stop testing my feelings for you. Anyway, it's too late now, everything's been settled. Nina

Konstantinovna is leaving for Moscow on Thursday, and that will be the end of it. We'll be able to forget the whole thing and start again.' He said this so calmly that Vasya almost believed him. 'Vasya darling, just be patient for a few more days and meanwhile please don't let's exhaust ourselves. When she leaves, you and I can live as we always used to. I wouldn't be surprised if things were even better now, after all we've been through together.' He embraced her and kissed her eyes.

'I'd like to sleep with you tonight Vasya, may I? I'm so tired, my head is spinning.' He lay down beside her, rested his head on her shoulder and fell asleep.

But Vasya could not sleep. If he really loved her he would have sensed what she was feeling and made some gesture of affection towards her. And as she looked at his familiar head, she realized how alien were the thoughts inside it. His lovely lashes concealed expressions of such tenderness, but she knew his tenderness was not for her. His lips, his kisses, aroused another woman's passion. She pushed his head off her shoulder – he was a stranger to her!

'Why are you teasing your Volya-Sunny?' Vladimir murmured sleepily. Whoever called him by that name? It certainly wasn't her! Even in his sleep he couldn't distinguish between this other woman and herself!

She looked furiously at her sleeping husband – her husband? Her dear friend? The man she had loved in the days when they fought together for the revolution. Now he was an utter stranger. Vasya felt cold and alone, mocked and tormented by the serpent of jealousy.

11

It was an enervatingly hot summer. The relentless sky had sent no rain to wash the dusty trees or water the wilting grass. The park was dusty and withered. The band was playing, but few people were around. Some children were romping near the bandstand and groups of Red Army soldiers were sitting about or promenading with women on their arms. On a bench in the shade a surpliced priest sat leaning on his crozier, deep in thought.

Beside him sat a nanny with a toddler. Vasya and Maria sat down next to them. It was an inconspicuous place from which they would be able to see everything and wait for Nina Konstantinovna to appear.

'I hope we see our princess today,' said Maria Semyonovna. 'She generally comes here when the band plays, to show off her new outfit. The ladies come here specially to see the latest fashion. They know that whatever it is, Nina Konstantinova will be wearing it.' Vasya listened absentmindedly. She longed to see what Nina Konstantinova looked like, but she had a terrible feeling that when she saw her she would become distraught.

'Look!' she clutched Maria Semyonovna. 'That woman in pink, the one sitting on that bench to the right of the bandstand, is that her?'

'What can you be thinking of! That's not Nina Konstantinovna! You'll pick her out at once! Like a mannequin she is, dressed up to the nines!'

They sat there watching, but still Nina didn't appear. Then just as they were on the point of giving up and going home, Nina Konstantinova suddenly appeared from the other end of the park with Savelyov and two young men. She paused beside the bandstand, chatting to them, oblivious to the way everyone was gaping at her. So here she was at last! She wore a thin white dress which enveloped her body in soft folds and clearly exposed her breasts, and long sand-coloured gloves. A matching hat tilted over her eyes so Vasya couldn't see her face properly. All she could see were her lips, bright crimson as though smeared with blood.

'Why, look at her lips! They're like blood!' she exclaimed.

'That's lipstick,' Maria Semenovna explained sagely. 'You should see her eyes too, all smudged with soot! I'd like to get a cloth and scrub all that mess off her face, *then* we'd see what she really looked like! Hah! Even I'd be a beauty for you if they primped me up like that!'

Nina Konstantinova was leaning on a white lace parasol kicking it with the heel of her white slipper. She laughed and tossed her head, and the two young men laughed with her. Savelyov stood aside all this time, tracing patterns in the sand with his cane, looking bored.

'I can't see her face with that hat on!' protested Vasya.

'Well, why don't we walk past them?' suggested Maria Se-myonovna. 'Then you can get a proper look at our princess. I wouldn't look too closely if I were you, there's not much to look at. When I was in the service of General Gololubov's late wife I saw plenty of real ladies and beauties, I can tell you. She's no match for them!'

But Vasya was filled with morbid curiosity. She had to understand what made Volodya love a woman like this. As they were getting up to walk towards her, Nina shook hands with the young men and said goodbye, loudly enough for Vasya to catch the words: 'See you again soon in Moscow, then!' She turned towards the park gate, followed by Savelyov.

'Shall we catch them up, Vasilisa Dementevna?' whispered Maria Semyonovna. 'No, better not. It's different for her highness, but people know you, there'd be gossip!'

Vasya slowed down without taking her eyes off Nina

She was tall and stately and swung her shoulders as she walked, but as she got further from the bandstand her head began to droop and Vasya thought she was crying. Savelyov leaned over and began to remonstrate with her, but she shook her head. Then she raised a yellow gloved hand to her face to wipe away a tear. So she was crying! She must have come here to say her farewell to the music!

What if she did love Volodya after all, and wasn't merely taking advantage of him. These thoughts increased Vasya's uneasiness, for even now that she'd seen Nina Konstantinova she didn't feel any happier. Her jealousy had left her, now it was something different, a sort of compassion for the woman was dimly surfacing in her mind. Why was Nina crying? Why had she come to hear the music? Was she saying goodbye once and for all to past happiness? Vasya was annoyed with herself for allowing these feelings to prey on her mind. As if she didn't have enough worries. A fine state of affairs, breaking her heart because the woman was leaving her Volodya!

Shortly after the episode in the park Nina Konstantinova left for Moscow. Two weeks passed. Vasya felt all she had to do was to start enjoying life again. Nina had gone and Vladimir was all hers. Now she knew she was more important to him, and Nina really had been just a passing affair. She began to smile and laugh more, and her cough improved. She attended the party committee regularly and Vladimir absorbed himself in work, reorganizing the business on the lines laid down by the syndicate. As soon as he had wound up this affairs, he and Vasya would be able to leave for Moscow and then Vladimir would be transferred to a new district. At the moment he seemed happy to immerse himself in his work, and everything appeared to be going well. . .

And yet the old happiness they had known before was gone. There seemed nothing they could do about it. Vladimir wasn't exactly unkind, but he found it hard to control his temper, and would fly into sudden rages with Vasya. Once it was because she returned late for lunch from the party committee, and he shouted at her for keeping the guests waiting. Did she expect them to sit down and eat before their hostess arrived? Another time he lost his temper because his collars were dirty. At this Vasya lost her temper too. Why should she be responsible for them, she demanded? He could take care of himself, or ask Maria Semyo-novna to do them! This row left them on bad terms. And all because of some stupid collars!

One day Vasya came home in the pouring rain. She had left her fur hat at the party committee room to save it from getting wet, and had tied a handkerchief round her head. Vladimir frowned when he saw her. 'What a fright!' he said. 'Just look at yourself! Your shoes are worn at the heels, your skirt's spattered with mud, and that handkerchief on your head makes you look like a peasant woman! You're a frump!'

Vasya retorted furiously, 'Well, we can't all deck ourselves out like mannequins, can we? I'm not batting my eyes at Savelyov!' Vladimir shot her a furious glance and although he said nothing, Vasya felt he wanted to strike her and was barely managing to restrain himself.

Things weren't working out as they should have done. They wanted so much to be friends again, but the least thing would make them lose their tempers. And then Vladimir was always having fantasies about his new job and how they would set up house and arrange their domestic affairs, all of which Vasya found very tedious. What was the point of having your own house? Where was the pleasure in it? It would have been quite different if it was a communal house, but Vladimir disagreed violently with her on this and attacked her 'conservatism'.

Then Vasya would talk to him about how in her Marxist study group they were debating whether history was created by economics alone or by ideology too. She became terribly excited as she struggled to explain everything they had been discussing. But he found it boring. It was nothing but a diversion for him. The real thing was how to make business more profitable . . . And then another argument would start.

Gradually they found they had less and less to talk about or do when they were alone together. Sometimes they would telephone Ivan Ivanovich and ask him to come over, for they felt more at ease in his company. Vasya was still waiting for a letter from her home town, but the days came and went, and she heard nothing, either from Grusha or from Stepan Alexeevich. What could they be doing? She would never have admitted it, but she longed for them to ask her to come back, although she still wasn't sure whether she would go or not.

Then at last a letter came, a registered letter from Stepan Alexeevich. It was brief and to the point: he wanted Vasya to take over a new work scheme laid down by the Central Committee, in a group of textile factories. These factories were just outside town and she would be able to live there. He awaited her reply.

Vasya's heart beat faster at the prospect of going back to her friends. What sort of life was it here, without a proper job or real happiness, only constant anxieties? She felt tied hand and foot – like the jackdaw her brother Kolka had caught in the forest when they were children. He had tied its wings with thread to stop it flying away, and it would strut around the floor, opening its beak wide, looking at the windows with its intelligent black eyes, and trying to flap its wings. After a few desperate attempts, flapping and cawing, it would pick its way across the floor, resigned never to fly again.

If Vasya's wings had been tied by the joys of love, that would have been different. But it was her wretched fears which held her back, her anxiety lest something should happen to Vladimir again, her sense of gratitude to him for staying with her and sending his mistress packing. The threads that bound her to him were fine but they were fast, and tied so artfully that even Vasya herself had never noticed before how they trapped her.

'Vasilisa Dementevna!' Maria Senyonovna's voice broke into her thoughts. 'We're out of beer! We should tell Vladimir Ivanovich to make sure they send some round from the brewery. What if guests arrive unexpectedly for dinner! I'll have to dash round and rustle some up I suppose!' She looked at Vasya closely, one of her disapproving looks. 'Just look at you, Vasilisa Dementevna! You do nothing but sulk all day! What is it now, might I ask? God be praised. I say, the mannequin's gone to Moscow and you've got your Vladimir Ivanovich to yourself. Does he so much as stir one step from the door, unless it's to go to work? No, he does not. So why are you always such a misery? Husbands don't like that. They like their wives to be cheerful and brighten up the home so when they get back from work they can forget their worries. They need some peace to look forward to at the end of the day!'

Vasya smiled as she listened to these well-worn views. Who knows, maybe Maria Semyonovna was right! Maybe she should try to pull herself together and become the old Vasya again, like she was in 1918. They worked hard in those days, yet they still managed to have fun. How would it be if she went to see Vladimir in his office this minute! She would surprise him, arrive unannounced, and tell him about the job. She would laugh as she told him she couldn't possibly part from her Volodya, and that she was going to refuse. Then he would realize how much she loved her darling and he would be overjoyed, hugging her and kissing her eyes!

He'll call me his own little Vasya like he used to, she thought excitedly as she picked out a white blouse to wear and tied a dark blue scarf around her neck. She carefully put on her hat in front of the mirror and arranged her curls. Today she was going to make herself pretty for Volodya, today she was taking him a special present – her letter to Stepan Alexeevich refusing his offer of work! Today she had decided to go with Volodya to the new district, and to find work there.

Arriving at the office, she went straight to the director's room. It was empty. Vladimir was at a meeting. Vasya sat down to wait, glancing through some Moscow newspapers, smiling to herself. She was going to show him how grateful she was for everything – for loving her more than anyone else and sending his mistress away!

Love of Worker Bees

The mail arrived and was put on the director's table. They were mostly business letters. Vasya began to sort through them in case there was anything for her. Suddenly her heart started pounding and she caught her breath. An oblong pink envelope addressed with tiny elegant handwriting – it could only be from Nina Konstantinovna!

So it wasn't over. All the old deceptions were continuing. She felt as though she were falling, the room spun before her eyes. She must have staggered forward, for next thing she knew she had knocked an ashtray off the table and broken it. That oblong pink envelope seemed to control her destiny. In a flash the letter was in her pocket. This would be the end of the lies.

Just then, Vladimir entered the room with some managers. 'Hello there, Vasya,' he said in surprise. 'What are you doing here? Have you come on business, or is it a social call?'

'There's no more beer in the house, we have to order some more from the brewery,' she replied flatly.

'Look at you! Turning into a proper little housewife, aren't you? I won't be recognizing my old Vasya soon!' he laughed happily.

Laugh on she thought, you don't know how I hate the chains you put on my freedom! I'll break them and expose every one of your lies!

'Is that all you came about, Vasya? You have to leave now, do you?'

Vasya nodded dumbly; she was shaking so much she was barely able to control herself.

Unable to wait until she got home, she went to the park and sat down on a bench. Frantically tearing open the pink envelope, she began to read.

My darling Sunny-Volya, my sweetheart, my tormenter, my master. One more day and no word from you. This is the third day now. Have you forgotten about me? Have you stopped loving your Egyptian monkey, your naughty Nina? I don't believe it! Yet I can't help being afraid when you're with her, and I'm all alone.

I'm afraid because I know how she orders you around, and how she influences you. She'll try and convince you our love is a 'sin against communism', that we should 'abstain' in true communist fashion, deny ourselves everything that gives us pleasure, and only love each other on Saturdays. I'm afraid of her, because I know her power over you. But my God, I'm not taking you away from her – I'm asking so little of you! She's recognized by the whole world as your wife, you're with her all the time for ever and ever, while all I ask is a few hòurs of your time bécause I love you so much. Please take pity on me, for if you don't, nobody else will, nobody in the world!

I wake up in the night, terrified that you've stopped loving me and are about to leave me, terrified at what would happen to me then . . . I'm too terrified even to think about it. You know how Nikanor Platonovich watches me like a spider, and however much he plays the papa, you and I know what he's after! He'd be overjoyed if you left me, because then I'd be completely alone, helpless and defenceless against him! He'd be delighted! There are days when I hate him so much I'd rather go on the streets, anything just so I don't have to be at his mercy all the time!

Volya my darling Volya, I love you insanely. Do you think this nightmare will end some day, and you'll come and rescue your Ninka? Won't you take pity on your monkey? Don't you ever think about me? You are so cruel to me, so unkind. I imagine you kissing that other woman – it's her you love, I know it! It breaks my heart! I want you so much, my passionate insatiable Volodya! Don't you long to kiss me and hold me in your arms? I can't bear it – I want to put my soft arms around you, my breasts ache for you to caress them. I can't endure much more of this Volya. I can't live without you. Why did you send me away to Moscow?

This can't go on. When you move to the new district you must find me a little house with a garden, where you'll be able to visit me when it grows dark, and I'll show you there's nothing in the whole world better or more important than a love like ours.

When will you come to Moscow? Will *she* be coming with you? Why can't you take a week off and we'll be together! Just think of it – a whole week to ourselves!

Nikanor Platonovich tells me that in the new district you're going to have a sweet detached house with a dining-room in gothic style. He says there's no lamp, and I've already found a heavenly chandelier for it. It's on the expensive side, but absolutely exquisite. I know you'll love it.

I've babbled on enough. This letter's going to be so long you won't have anywhere to hide it!

I may joke, but I feel like crying. Will you ever understand how wretched I am? Oh, why won't life allow us to be happy together? But don't worry, you're the boss, I'll stop grumbling. I think I'm a bit wiser now after everything I've suffered. You must do as you think best. I'll do anything you say, but one thing I won't let you take away from me – your kisses, your love and your pity for your poor, lonely confused little Nina.

Moscow, Ostozhenka Street 18, Apartment 7 (not 17 as you wrote last time – it was only by luck that I got your letter!)

I belong to you, from my lips to my toes,

Your own Nina.

There was a PS in the margin. 'Just think, I'm so happy, I found that powder I was looking for, L'Origan Coty!'

Vasya read Nina's letter slowly, lingering over each word, reading not only with her eyes but with her whole heart. When she finally finished, she put it on her knees and gazed at the dry dusty grass at her feet where a bee was buzzing angrily. It flew amongst the blades, darting off irritably then returning to rummage in the same patch of grass.

In the spring, when the lilac was in flower, the bees had been buzzing so cheerfully. But this one was bad-tempered, as if the summer had deceived it. Suddenly Vasya realized that her thoughts were on the bee, not the letter. She felt no particular unhappiness, just a sensation of utter indifference.

Gradually the serpent set to work again; Nina's words had stung her. 'Smooth arms, soft lips . . .' The serpent's vile tongue lashed her heart with the words, and she struggled against the pain. Surely there must be some corner of her heart which wasn't filled with poison!

Slowly, painstakingly, she folded the letter and put it back in its envelope. She got up, went past the bandstand and walked towards the gate. There was no music playing today, no people, no music. Now Vasya finally knew who it was that Volodya loved.

She went through the wicket-gate of the dusty park, out onto the street rumbling with traffic. For her, the park had become a graveyard, for she had just been to a funeral – the funeral of her happiness.

12

When Vasya finally got home she found Vladimir back earlier than usual. He was cheerful and full of good news; the long-awaited letter had come from the Central Committee confirming his new appointment. He had to leave for Moscow immediately.

'Moscow?' said Vasya. 'I see. Well, I'm going away too, but not to Moscow. I'm going back to my home town.' She spoke with apparent calm, but her feelings were in chaos as she thought of Nina's oblong pink envelope in her pocket. But Volodya didn't seem to notice Vasya's drawn face, or the sparks of anger in her eyes. He obviously had no idea what she was planning. She went into the bedroom to pack her suitcase.

'Are you going to visit your family then? Excellent! We can

Love of Worker Bees

meet in Moscow, unless you'd rather go straight to the new place.' Hope had momentarily flooded her heart, her last hope – that he would protest and prevent her from going. Now that hope was shattered.

'I'm not going with you at all. I've been asked to go back home to work, and I'll be staying there, not temporarily, for good. I've had enough. I've been suffocating in this cage of yours for too long, I'm tired of playing the director's wife. You must find yourself a wife who appreciates this life . . .'

The words nearly choked her, but she went on talking, falling over her words in her haste to get everything out. She wouldn't be deceived in this way any more. She was glad it was finally over. All the time she was surrounded by those bourgeois syndicate men she had been longing to get back to her work, and had endured it only for Vladimir's sake. She was sad she was no longer necessary to him, that their love and friendship were over, but she could no longer simply be his wife, his hostess and his cover, just so he could say 'I live with a communist, and I keep another woman in a secret house for my pleasure'.

How cleverly they'd arranged everything, Vladimir and Nina! There was only one thing they'd forgotten, and that was whether Vasya was prepared to agree to such a disgusting arrangement. Vasya's eyes were green with rage and she started to gasp for words.

Vladimir shook his head angrily. 'Vasya, I can't believe you mean all this. I don't recognize you in this mood! Why can't you understand – if I've concealed anything from you it's only been to protect you!'

'Thanks a lot, I don't need your protection – I'm strong enough to take the truth. Do you imagine your love for me is the only thing in my life? You can put your love for me right back where you found it, because it's been nothing but torment for me. I want to leave you just as soon as I can, and get out of here. I don't want to know what you do with yourself after that. Fall in love with whoever you want, sleep with them, lie to people, deceive them, become a big director, be a traitor to communism, it's all the same to me!'

'But Vasya, Vasya, what about our friendship? And your promise to understand everything?'

'Our friendship? What of it? Where has it gone? Where is it, tell me that! I don't believe anything you say any more, Vladimir, you've killed my confidence in you. Did you imagine I'd have stopped you if you came to me and said "Vasya, it's terrible I know, but something very sad has happened – I've fallen in love with someone else"? Did you think I'd have blamed you, or stood in the way of your happiness? No Vladimir, you forgot that I wasn't just your wife but your friend. That's why I'm so hurt, can't you understand that? That's why I shall never forgive you, as long as I live . . .' The tears began to run down her cheeks, and brushing them off with her sleeve she turned away from Vladimir.

'I had such confidence in our love, but you trampled on it. How can two people go on living together when one of them no longer has trust in the other? No, this has to be the end, our life together is over . . .'

Her heart was aching and she shook with emotion as she turned away from him again and sat down on the bed, crumpling the silk eiderdown in her hands, her eyes full of tears. He sat down beside her and grasped her shoulders.

'Vasya, how can you say you've become a stranger to me, that you don't love me any more? How can it be true? Why would you be so upset if you no longer loved me? Have you tried to consider my feelings? Don't you believe I still love you? Please try to understand me. I do love Nina, yes, but it's completely different. My love for you is deeper, it's much more real. Without you I'm nothing, I have nowhere to go. Whatever I tried to do without you I'd always be wondering what you'd say about it. You're my guiding star! I need you, Vasya!'

Love of Worker Bees

'You only think about yourself, don't you?' said Vasya sadly
... What about me? This life is stifling me, Vladimir! I can
accept the fact that you have a mistress. What I can't accept is
that we're no longer friends.'

'Do you think I don't feel the same? Tell me how it happened! I
don't understand anything any more. We miss each other when
we're apart, but when we're together we irritate each other. You
tell me it wasn't like this in the past, but we never spent much
time together before, did we? We never had a settled family life –
we were always too busy working, we could only pay each other
brief visits. Why don't we try living like that again? Would you
like that? We could both do what we wanted, and as soon as we
got bored with each other we could separate. Then my Vasya
would be her tough little self again, the Vasya I love so much,
and we wouldn't have to lie to each other any more. We can't
just break it off Vasya, it would be too painful to separate
completely. Please be kind to me, Vasya!' He laid his head on her
knees, burying his face in her lap. Neither of them spoke.

In the quietness, both began to feel the warm sensation of
desire, and little sparks of their old passion, so long buried under
the ashes of insults and suspicion, began slowly to kindle.

'Vasya darling!' Vladimir's strong arms embraced her and
drew her to him, overwhelming her with kisses. Vasya gave
herself to this sweet forgotten passion. At this moment she knew
he loved her undividedly, he loved her as he had always loved
her. Now Volodya was betraying his Nina not only with his body
but with his mind and his feelings, and this knowledge brought
Vasya a kind of ruthless pleasure quite new to her. It felt painful
but good: let him betray Nina like this!

Strange morbid days followed. The spark of their passion,
smouldering so long like an extinguished bonfire, was fanned by
a gust of autumn wind. It flamed up wildly and spread, licking
their charred wounds and seeking out the corners in their hearts
which hadn't been scarred by its flame.

Vladimir was passionate; Vasya surrendered tenderly. It was as though they had fallen in love again. They assured each other they could never live apart, and at night they would cling together, terrified of losing each other. Vladimir would kiss Vasya's eyes and she would stroke his dear face. They had never loved so passionately, but now there was a sweet nostalgia and bitter happiness about it: both knew that finding each other again was their way of burying their love and happiness.

One moment Vasya would be smiling and joking, the next she would collapse into tears. And while Vladimir caressed her and they looked into each other's eyes, she could read in his an expression of the utmost sadness. They seemed to be wordlessly saying goodbye to her. And so as not to have to see them and his tears, to kill the unbearable sadness, she would put her thin arms around his neck and seek his lips. He would press her to his heart and fondle her, seeking her body insatiably until she was beside herself with ecstasy and they both fell asleep in exhaustion.

Strange morbid days, suffocating and dark . . . No real happiness now, none of the winged joy born of love.

13

So they agreed that Vasya would go and work in her home town for the time being, and when Vladimir had settled into the new town they would meet. Where they were to meet wasn't clear, the question of separation was not mentioned. On the surface everything seemed simple, clear, reasonable and above all honest. The one thing Vasya didn't tell him was that she had stolen Nina's letter; she has hidden it away and was keeping it. She felt she still needed it.

However, she did insist that Vladimir send Nina a telegram to say he would be arriving in Moscow alone. She couldn't have explained why she did this when it cost her so much, it was just something she had to do. Vladimir stalled for a while, looking suspicious and apprehensive, but he finally agreed, and afterwards he was even more affectionate and passionate towards her.

Vasya no longer cared. It seemed right that they drink the last remaining drops of their happiness together, for they combined the intoxication of passion with the sweet grief of separation. She became brisk and cheerful – it was a long time since Volodya had seen her like that.

'I feel as if I've cast off a skin that didn't fit me. I wasn't much good as a director's wife, was I? You need a different kind of wife! I'm no good for you, I'll never make a Nepwoman!' Vasya joked.

'I don't know who you are any more,' admitted Volodya. 'All I know is that you're my old tough Vasya, and I wouldn't give you up even if five party committees needed you! In time maybe, yes, but at the moment there's no reason why we should separate.'

Vasya laughed. So be it. Why shouldn't they meet for short visits, not as husband and wife, but as free agents and friends? Vladimir agreed this would make things easier between them, but he still insisted that he couldn't exist without her beside him. 'I have so few friends in the world Vasya, especially at the moment when everything's going to the dogs and everybody's out for what they can get. You and I are true friends, aren't we Vasya?'

They could talk now as if the barriers between them had been broken down, and the old obsessions seemed to leave Vasya. But then just as she was feeling at peace, feelings of jealousy would suddenly stir. Vladimir would sometimes become very distant for no apparent reason, and would talk about Nina. It was evident that he thought about her a great deal.

She was so well educated, she could chatter away in French with a Frenchman, in German with a German, she had been to an institute . . .

'If she's so well educated, why can't she find work then? Or is she used to living off other people? She's a parasite through and through – that's what a mistress is for, I suppose.' Vasya realized she shouldn't talk like this, but she wanted to take out some of her pain on Volodya.

'Vasya, why do you say things like that? It's so unkind. It's another Vasilisa Dementevna talking, not the Vasya I admire.'

But hurt and ashamed though she felt, she couldn't stop herself goading him again and again until he finally lost his temper and she would realize what she was doing. 'Darling, please try not to be angry with me, forgive me for being so unkind. You know how much I love you; if I didn't, the whole thing wouldn't torment me so much!'

Then they would reach out to each other and drown everything in suffocating kisses, the intoxication of their love-making. No need to think or suffer. Forget everything, cheat the harsh and unbearable truth . . .

Some days later, having said her farewells to the people on the party committee, Vasya went home to pack. She had to see to everything, collect boxes and suitcases, baste and straw in which to wrap things. She asked Maria Semyonovna how to pack so it wouldn't get broken or damaged on the journey to the director's new home.

'Why are you making such a fuss?' Maria Semyonovna fretted. 'I don't know why you're taking the trouble now you've made up your mind to go back to your own town. Mark my words, the minute you've gone, his girlfriend will come through the door to take your place. Why should you take all this trouble and work yourself to death for her benefit!'

But her words made no impression on Vasya. She no longer felt she was helping Volodya as his wife. If she'd been his wife she wouldn't have done it, she would have attacked him for his bourgeois ways. Now he was going his way and she was going hers there was no reason not to help him, just as one friend would help another. She no longer bore him any grudge; if he wanted to trail all this junk behind him and overload the public transport system with his boxes of crockery and suitcases full of silk clothes, that was his affair. She wouldn't have landed herself with all this luggage, but why shouldn't she help him with the packing now that it no longer mattered to her?

Volodya was amazed. There was no need for her suddenly to be such a conscientious housewife, he said, when there was Ivan Ivanovich and the managers to do it. And anyway, who would arrange all these things in his new house, if she didn't come soon?

'What use is Nina Konstantinovna, then? Or doesn't she like to dirty her lovely white hands? Perhaps she's too much of a lady for that. All she has to do is to see that everything is done to her liking, make sure her meals are served on silver salvers, and enjoy the fruits of other people's hard work and money . . .'

Immediately she was furious with herself for hurting Volodya, and couldn't imagine what had got into her. Volodya looked at her reproachfully, and she flung her arms round him.

'Oh darling, I hate myself for being so cruel to you; it's only because I love you so much. Don't be angry with me darling, it was only a joke!' And she buried her face in his jacket, stifling the tears that welled up in her throat. She did still love him! She loved him dreadfully, suffered for him, was terrified of losing him, living without him.

'My poor sweetheart,' he soothed her. 'Dear little Vasyuk, I know you so well, that's why I love you and shall never be able to tear myself away from you. For me there's no other Vasya in the whole world. I'll never have a friend like you . . .' Once again that bitter heady passion enveloped them and they stifled their pain in embraces.

'Leave a corner in your heart for your old anarchist lover, won't you?'

'If you'll remember your tough Vasyuk – and our past happiness'.

Strange and intoxicating, those last days together, suffocating and dark.

14

Vasya knocked on the door of her garret where Grusha now lived. They had told her downstairs that she was back from work, but the door was locked. Where could she be? Could she be asleep? Then turning round she saw her hurrying along the corridor, carrying a teapot and some hot water.

'Grusha!'

'Vasilisa, my precious! When did you arrive? Well I never, fancy seeing you!' Grusha put the teapot on the floor and the two friends hugged each other. 'Come in, make yourself at home, remember it's your garret, it's all thanks to you I'm living here. Let me unlock the door. There've been a lot of robberies in this house, you know, I have to lock up even when I fetch water. Mr Furazhin had his autumn coat stolen the other day, straight off the hook where it was hanging, and it was almost new too. We alerted the whole house and called in the militia, but they couldn't find anything. Well Vasya, you're back in your old home, why not take off your coat and have a wash after your journey? I was just going to make some tea. Would you like a bite to eat? There are eggs, bread, apples . . .'

Home? Grusha – said this was her 'home'. Would Vasya ever have a home? Looking round her, she saw the same familiar garret, but it was no longer Vasya's. There was a treddle sewing-machine and a dressmaker's dummy in the corner, scraps of material scattered around, patterns and pieces of thread on the floor. The walls were bare; gone were the pictures of Marx and Lenin and the group of communards which she had put up when they celebrated the anniversary of the revolution. Now there was just a faded red paper fan and beside it a tattered postcard depicting an Easter egg and an archaic inscription in gold letters: Christ is Risen! There was an icon in the corner too.

Grusha wasn't in the party. She believed in God and observed the fast-days, even though she supported the soviets and was friendly with a number of communists. She had had a fiancé who fought with the Whites, and she didn't know whether he was alive or not. If he had been killed, it could only have been by the Red Army, and that was why Grusha didn't want to become a communist; she wanted to treasure the memory of her fiancé. 'He'd curse me from the other world if I joined you,' was what she said.

At first Vasya hadn't been able to understand how Grusha could love a White soldier, but now she knew differently, now she knew that feelings had laws of their own. She and Vladimir had gone their separate ways, but their love was still alive, and it gave her no peace of mind.

Grusha was overjoyed to see Vasya, and kept plying her with questions. Why hadn't she put on weight, with all that money her husband had? She'd come back looking as scraggy as when she left, even skinnier!

Vasya could say nothing. She had somehow imagined that when she saw Grusha again she would hug her and sob out all her troubles to her, but now that Grusha was there, reticence overcame her and she couldn't find the right words. How could she begin to describe what she was going through?

People in the building soon heard about Vasya's arrival. The old tenants were happy she had come back, the new ones were curious to see what she looked like. The housing committee representative glowered; he hoped she wasn't going to go ferreting around in his administrative affairs again.

But it was the children from the children's club who were the first to come running into Grusha's room, and straight away the eldest one approached Vasya with a complaint; apparently under the NEP the children's club had been closed, and the authorities said it couldn't be re-purchased from the State, since according to them the premises were needed for something else. Where were the schoolchildren to prepare their lessons now? Their botanical collections had been removed, and their library distributed amongst other clubs or sold.

Vasya couldn't imagine how this could have happened, and immediately set to work to sort it out. She would have to go this very day to the housing department. The NEP was all very well, but how dare they lay a finger on something the workers themselves had organized through their own efforts! 'I'm going to fight this,' she said. 'Don't worry children, I shall defend your rights. I'm not going to let them get away with this, even if it means going to Moscow!'

The older children laughed. They had known Vasya would defend them, and here she was, going off to fight for them! She had always been known as a fighter, and it was true!

After this the older residents came to greet her, each of them eagerly telling her their problems and stories. She listened carefully as she always did, questioning them closely, giving advice and comfort. Before long, there was such a crowd of people in the garret that there was hardly room to breathe.

'Listen friends, couldn't you wait a bit!' implored Grusha. 'You haven't even let her have a bite to eat after her journey, the poor thing's worn out. You might think of all those nights she's been travelling, instead of plaguing her with your demands!'

'No, Grusha,' Vasya said, 'please don't stop them, I'm not a bit tired. Now what were you telling me, Timofey Tomofeyevich? Oh yes, about your taxes. I don't understand, it's not as if you're a landlord or a director . . .' As she said this Volodya came into her mind, and for a moment she felt the old pain again. But it was immediately submerged by other people's worries; she had no time to think.

One by one her old friends left, and Vasya tidied herself up to go to the party committee. She was anxious to get moving and didn't notice how tired she was. As she buttoned her blouse she listened to Grusha's news: so-and-so was married, so-and-so had left the party, so-and-so was elected to the soviet . . .

Suddenly Mrs Feodeseeva's voice resounded through the corridor. 'Where's our little darling, our precious guardian angel, Vasilisa Dementevna?' Before she knew it, the woman had flung herself at her, hugging her and drooling over her, soaking her with tears. 'I've been waiting so long for you to come back, my angel. You're my only hope now. I said to myself, as soon as our guardian angel's back she'll sort things out. Once she's back he won't dare insult his lawful wife like this, the wretch, he'll be ashamed to turn this building into a cesspool – him and that slut of his. Our Vasya will take pity on me, struggling alone with my poor little ones. She'll bring him to justice, then he'll have to do what the party says. You're my last hope, my pet.'

Vasya was usually quick to grasp other people's problems, but now she was at a loss to know what Mrs Feodoseeva was talking about. She had changed beyond recognition. Before, she been a strong, large-bosomed woman, now she looked old, yellow and haggard.

She proceeded to tell Vasya her story. Apparently Feodoseev had embarked on an affair with an 'unbaptized little Jewess' named Dora and had left his wife for her. He was disgracing her throughout the entire neighbourhood, shamelessly renouncing his own children and spending all his money on his girl friend. ' "Take me in", he says to her. "My family can die in a ditch for all I care, don't leave me, pockmarked wretch that I am!" What can Dora see in him, the little fool!' spat Mrs Feodoseeva.

He's not even a proper man! Ugh! Rat-faced little shrimp! Eight years I put up with him and kissed his poxy face for the sake of the children. "However ugly you are, Vasilevich", I told myself, "it's fate that bound us together and the church wedded us, so I'll have to put up with you." I always found him revolting, crawling over me with his kisses, but I endured it and never so much as looked at another man. I thought at least he'd be grateful – to think I wasted my youth on that pockmarked shrimp! And now see what happens! As soon as I lose my looks he starts chasing after little girls. Now he's hooked up with his Jewess and is making an exhibition of himself throughout the neighbourhood . . .'

Mrs Feodoseeva was sobbing, and as Vasya listened her heart flooded with emotion. Her own grief was reflected in Mrs Feodoseeva's; it was infinitely depressing to experience her old feelings of outrage in this way.

She suddenly felt weary and drained of energy. She no longer had any desire to go to the party committee, all she wanted was to bury her head in a pillow and hide her face. But Mrs Feodoseeva went on sobbing, kissing her shoulders, imploring her 'wise Vasilisa' to make her husband see sense and defend the interests of her children by threatening him with a party trial.

But as soon as Vasya arrived at the party committee, she forgot about everything else. Only the party mattered. She argued with them and made enquiries about the children's library. It was so absorbing that her spirits soared, and later her friends walked her home. They had so much to discuss, and she felt so happy and full of energy that she flew up the stairs to her little garret. It was only then she realized how tired she was.

While Grusha was bustling around making supper, Vasya lay on the bed and at once fell into a deep sleep. Looking at her lying there, Grusha didn't know whether to wake her or not; Vasya looked so worn out that she decided to let her sleep on. She undressed her like a child, took off her shoes, and covered her with a blanket. Then she draped a shawl round the lamp and sat down to make buttonholes.

Suddenly there was a knock at the door. Who the devil could it be? Grusha wondered, angry at being disturbed. She opened the door, and there stood Feodoseeva's husband.

'What do you want?' she asked him.

'I've come to see Vasilisa Dementevna. Is she in?'

'Have you taken leave of your senses! Here's someone just arrived from long journey, worn out after all those sleepless nights, and all people can do is besiege her like a pack of starving dogs after a bone! Vasilisa Dementevna is asleep!'

Grusha stood at the door haranguing poor Feodoseev, who insisted on being let in. Grusha refused, and he finally agreed to come back the next day. She slammed the door in his face. Dirty little creep! What about his lawful wife and his three children, while Dora flaunted that big belly of hers! Let him clear up the mess himself! Grusha disapproved of Feodoseev and had no sympathy for Dora taking up with a married man, as if there weren't enough single men around! Grusha had never been able to forget her fiancé, and now she was 'keeping herself pure'. She applied this strict moral code to everyone.

15

When Vasya woke she felt clear-headed and much calmer. The autumn sun danced through the window and tinged the sewing-machine with gold. Grusha was heating a flat-iron on the oil-stove, preparing to put the finishing touches to a dress.

'Who's the dress for?' Vasya asked.

'For the secretary of the executive committee, it's her name day,' Grusha replied.

'Do people still celebrate their name days then?'

'I should say they do! And more splendidly than under the gentry too! You should see the huge tables full of food, wine, vodka!' Grusha's iron hissed and she had to stop talking.

Vasya snuggled down into the familiar narrow bed. She had slept with Volodya on this bed. How had there been room! Lately even in a large bed they had felt cramped and got in each other's way. It had been different in the old days.

Her heart was filled with a melancholy which threatened her peace of mind. But gradually she felt calm and reconciled again, like a garden after a storm. Maybe the worst torment was over.

Grusha suddenly remembered Feodoseev.

'Let him come in then,' said Vasya. But she felt reluctant, and annoyed that she had to get involved with the Feodoseevs again. Why should it be those mischief-makers of all people who had suffered the same misfortune as she had? She asked Grusha about Dora.

'Don't you remember her?' Grusha asked in surprise. 'She's that dark, pretty girl who did a tambourine dance at the Komsomol celebration.'

Vasya remembered liking her. She was on the Higher Education Commission, and was working with the tanners. She was clever, still very young, and she sang well. Poor Mrs Feodoseeva! What a contrast!

Grusha didn't agree with Vasya about Dora at all. 'You have to follow the rules,' she said. 'If the communists tolerate husbands behaving like that, every man would be free to leave his wife and children and run off with younger girls.' She had heard that the party was preparing a case against Dora.

'That must be Mrs Feodoseeva's doing then,' said Vasya, coming to Dora's defence. 'What a repulsive woman she is! There's no law on earth to compel a man to go on living with a wife he doesn't love! You can't make Feodoseev sleep with his wife by force of law. She's a trouble-maker, she loathes him anyway!' Vasya got very worked up, and gave vent to her feelings about Mrs Feodoseeva.

But as she argued about Mrs Feodoseeva she was thinking of Vladimir, and as she defended Dora she was seeing a white lace parasol and Nina's red lips . . .

Grusha was amazed that Vasya should be so caught up in the Feodoseevs's affairs. 'You'd think they were your closest friends!' she said. 'To think of the way you used to complain to me about them, and the problems they caused you! It's your business, but I advise you not to get mixed up in this scandal. Two dogs can fight between themselves, let them sort it out between them . . .'

But Vasya insisted that if they got up some charge against Dora, she would defend her. Did Mrs Feodoseeva in all honesty imagine that being his legal wife gave her such rights? Because if she did she was wrong. There were other rights too, and no laws could ever apply to the rulings of the heart. There was no human being strong enough to go against them, everyone had their own needs.

Grusha was ironing the hem of the secretary's dress. She glanced up and peered at Vasya, as if trying to read her thoughts. Vasya frowned. Why was Grusha looking at her like that? Wasn't she right? What rules did Grusha want to see imposed on the heart?

'Who can say?' said Grusha. 'Of course people's feelings are what count, you're not human without feelings. But just now when I was looking at you, Vasya, I saw how you were suffering, and how full of resentment you were. And when you were standing up for Feodoseev. I could have sworn you were thinking of your husband and trying to find excuses for him. That's the only way I can explain it.'

Vasya looked down without replying, and Grusha asked no more questions. She took the dress off the ironing-board, shook it and pulled out the loose threads. It was ready.

'Have you finished?' Vasya enquired, her thoughts far away.

'Yes, that's it now.'

'Well Grusha, I'd better be off to the party committee. If Mr Feodoseev comes, tell him to wait will you?'

'All right,' sighed Grusha.

A new, active phase in Vasya's life began. Before she left for her job at the textile-factory she had to consult Stepan Alexeevich, study her instructions and spend several evenings at sessions with skilled workers. Time flew and she was too busy to think about her feelings. Then there were the Feodoseevs' problems to sort out, and Dora too. In the end, they all three come to her with their worries and she couldn't get rid of them.

Feodoseev told her his side of the story. He had got to know Dora Abramovna through the higher education department. He was singing in a choir, and Dora Abramovna took a liking to his bass voice and suggested he take music lessons; she was a trained musician herself. She introduced him to the department, and things developed from there.

When his wife got wind of the affair, all hell was let loose. Feodoseev was furious with her for her scandal-mongering and for setting Dora Abramovna's friends against her. She was spreading lies that Dora was fleecing him for money, and was living off Feodoseev's earnings. In fact it was the other way round. Dora wouldn't take anything off him, and what was more, she was genuinely concerned about his family and would willingly have given them her last kopek. She'd always been interested in children, and it was she who had got places for the younger ones in a kindergarten, and got exercise-books and textbooks for the elder child who was at school. And she did all this in such a way that his wife would never know about it.

It was Dora who fitted Feodoseev out with a tie and shirt for concerts – but out of spite people were putting the whole thing in a different light. Feodoseev's heart bled for Dora. It didn't matter about his reputation, she was the one he was concerned about. What if she had difficulties with the party because of him? It was his wife's fault for standing in their way.

All the time Feodoseev was talking, Vasya was thinking about Vladimir and Nina. This was how they must have tortured themselves as they looked for solutions to their situation. They must have been angry with Vasya in exactly this way for standing between them and their happiness. Feodoseeva should get out of the way. She should stop clinging to the past, preventing present happiness. It was useless anyway, for happiness has its own momentum.

But then, Vasya thought, who was she to talk? Wasn't she still standing in the way, clinging to past happiness? Feodoseev obviously adored Dora. He only had to mention her name and he became a gentler person. Vladimir too changed whenever he mentioned Nina's name.

'Dora Abramovna has a heart of gold,' he was saying. 'Everyone in the union thinks highly of her. The non-party members can't believe the party's bringing a case against her. Some of them are positively pleased about it. They say she can come over to their side, they'll stick by her loyally.'

No sooner had Feodoseev gone than Mrs Feodoseeva waylaid Vasya, kissing her, ingratiating herself and entreating her to take her side. Vasya disliked the woman intensely and shook her away; from that moment on Feodoseeva inveighed against the entire household, pouring abuse indiscriminately on the three of them, Dora, her husband and Vasya.

Vasya arranged to meet Dora at the party committee. They found themselves a secluded corner in a room full of typists typing away. The clatter made it easy for them to talk without being overheard.

Dora was wrapped in a shawl to conceal her pregnant stomach. It was she who started talking, not about herself but about Feodoseev.

She was very concerned about him, she said, she valued him and thought highly of his talent. He had a remarkable voice, as good as Shalyapin's, it just needed training. That was partly why Dora was pressing him to leave his family and marry her. Then he could throw in his job at the cobbler's workshop and concentrate on his singing.

But although Dora lavished praise on Feodoseev, she also complained about his indecisiveness. When he was with her, he was prepared to do anything. No sooner was it settled that he would leave his wife and get a divorce than he'd get home and it would all go by the board. He just couldn't face it, and they would have to start all over again. Dora had been struggling like this for months, and still he hadn't moved an inch.

A feeling of unease came over Vasya as she listened to Dora. Nina must have talked like that about Vladimir!

For Dora, the conventions of marriage and divorce were irrelevant, 'a lot of mumbo-jumbo'. She was all for free unions, but Mrs Feodoseeva would never leave them in peace unless they registered at the Commisariat. So Dora got herself pregnant to force Feodoseev to get a divorce. She wasn't afraid of becoming a mother, and could manage perfectly well without a husband if she had to.

Had Nina done that too, Vasya wondered? Had she got pregnant to force Vladimir to get a divorce?

As Dora went on talking and pleading for Vasya's sympathy, Vasya became immersed in her own thoughts. Dora saw only the good in Feodoseev. That must be how Nina loved Vladimir. Vasya was incapable of loving like that. She knew and loved Vladimir's bad sides too. Loving him meant suffering for the bad things about him, wanting to help him change; maybe this was what had hurt Volodya so much.

'Why does his wife have to cling to him like that?' Dora asked angrily. 'Did they ever love one another? If so it must have been a long time ago, because they have nothing in common now. Does she know him and appreciate him? Does she understand his needs?'

We were just the same thought Vasya. It was like that between me and Vladimir, him not knowing what I wanted, and me not knowing what he was thinking. That was why our lives went their separate ways.

'He's a complete stranger to Mrs Feodoseeva, they're different in every way. Their tastes are different, their aspirations are different. She's only clinging to him because he's her husband. She doesn't need him as a person, she doesn't need him at all!' said Dora.

And asking herself these same questions, Vasya realized clearly that she didn't need Vladimir as he was now.

'What kind of love is it anyway?' persisted Dora. 'They can't agree on anything, there's nothing but quarreling, they both go their own ways, with no friendship or trust between them.'

Yes, yes, agreed Vasya silently. No friendship or trust!

'Feodoseev and I understand each other without having to speak – our minds work the same way', said Dora.

That must be how Vladimir and Nina loved one another! There were so many things Vasya was only slowly beginning to understand, so many new feelings . . .

Although Vasya had much urgent party work to do before she left for her new job, she didn't neglect the Feodoseevs, and bustled around trying to speed up their divorce, getting Feodoseev reconciled with his friends, exonerating Dora in the eyes of the party. For some reason she couldn't have defined, she felt this to be very important.

Vasya was hurrying home from the party committee. She was to leave for the textile-factory the next day, and her mind was filled with how she would reorganize the work there, carry out the party's instructions, and make contact with the non-party members too. Now the non-party members' attitudes were often so similar to the communists', they could be relied on. She trusted them to examine the facts for themselves and question everything, for these people didn't take anything on trust. She would allocate them their jobs before she worried about their political views.

As Vasya's mind went over these questions, she forget her old grief. She was no longer conscious of having lost her husband

and friend, nor could she even recall very clearly the events of the summer, when she had been the director's wife. Hurrying along she realized she had eaten nothing since that morning, but the thought of food made her want to vomit and her head started spinning. What day was it? Could she be ill, or could she be . . . ? There was an unformulated question in her mind. Wasn't this the third month she bad missed a period? She ought to go and see her doctor friend, Maria Andreevna, who lived in a nearby street. They had worked together once, organizing crêches for communal houses. Maria Andreevna would be able to examine Vasya and tell her whether she was too sick to leave.

Vasya turned into the street, went up to a white door and rang the bell. Maria Andreevna came to the door, delighted to see her.

'What have you come to see me about? Is it on business or do you want advice?'

Vasya was overcome with embarrassment and blushed. Maria Andreevna gave her a sharp look, then took her by the arm.

'Come, let's go into my surgery and I'll examine you,' she said. She questioned Vasya about her appetite, her periods and her dizziness, but it was if she knew the answers in advance. Then she examined her. Vasya didn't enjoy this at all, and felt very awkward; she had never been examined by a woman doctor before. When she was made to lie on the examination couch she was panic-stricken.

After it was over and she was putting on her clothes again, her hands trembled so much she was barely able to do up her buttons. Maria Andreevna stood by the sink in her white coat, carefully washing her hands in soap and water. 'Well, Vasilisa my dear,' she said, breaking the silence. 'I don't know whether to congratulate you or console you, but there's no doubt about it, you're pregnant.'

'Pregnant?' gasped Vasya. Then involuntarily the thought of a baby brought a smile to her lips.

'So what do you intend to do?' continued the doctor briskly, drying her hands on an embroidered towel. 'Are you going back to your husband?'

'My husband? Oh no!' Vasya shook her head vehemently. 'No, I'll never go back to him, we've separated for good.'

'So you've separated, have you? Well, it wasn't a very good time for it to happen, was it? How do you think you'll cope, my dear? Maybe things can be put right between you, eh? How are you going to manage on your own with a child? You're not strong either.'

'But I won't be alone,' Vasya interrupted her. 'Tomorrow I'm leaving for the textile factory. There's a good cell of workers there, most of them women, between us we'll arrange a crêche. I meant to ask you, how did you manage to re-purchase your crêche from the state? Would you give me some advice?'

So they began to discuss crêches, and subsidies, and dues and the salaries of professional workers . . . Vasya quite forgot about her news, and it was only as they were saying goodbye that Maria Andreevna reminded her.

'Now Vasya, you won't overwork, will you? Remember you're not strong, I can't help worrying about you.'

She gave Vasya lots of advice, telling her the 'do's' and 'don'ts', which Vasya carefully memorized.

She walked back along the street, smiling. A baby! How wonderful! She'd be a model mother! After all, it should be possible to bring up a child in true communist fashion. There was no reason for women to set up with husbands and families if it merely tied them to the cooking and domestic chores. They would get a crêche going, and re-purchase a children's hostel. It would be a demonstration of childrearing to everyone. And as she began to think about it, Vladimir vanished from her thoughts as though he had no connection with the baby . . .

When Vasya got home she started packing. Suddenly she came across a box containing Volodya's old letters and a photograph of him. On top of it was the oblong pink envelope,

Nina Konstantinova's letter. She looked at it, and turned it over. She knew it would only stir up old and painful associations and she would feel chilled by Volodya's lies and deceits, and her own jealousy. Nevertheless she took the letter and sat down near the window to read it once more. The light was already fading.

Unfolding the familiar piece of paper, she began to read, line by line. She felt no melancholy now. The serpent had lost its venom, and her heart was at peace. Wholly unexpectedly, a feeling of compassion stirred. She wept for Nina Konstantinova, for the outraged misery and pain of this poor woman. She remembered how Nina had wiped away her tears with the tips of her fingers as she left the bandstand. Why should she have to suffer like that? What anguish she must have endured! She had been pregnant too, and had had to get rid of her child. Vasya went to the table, piled Grusha's dressmaking patterns to one side, set some ink in front of her and started writing.

Dear Nina Konstantinovna,

I don't know who you are. I only saw you once, and frankly I didn't take a great liking to you. But when you left the bandstand and started to cry, I felt I understood how unhappy you were and felt sorry for you. I've just read again your letter to Vladimir Ivanovich, which I'm returning to you as I was wrong to steal it from him. But I think it's done its job, so please don't be too angry with me.

I've thought about your letter, and now I've re-read it I realize I don't feel angry with you any more. I realize how much you must have suffered on my account. I've said this to Vladimir and now I'll say it to you; let's stop playing cat-and-mouse with each other.

You must marry Vladimir Ivanovich and become his lawful wife. You're more suited to each other, I'm sure, than we were. I can't be his wife any longer because our tastes have changed. We're different now, quite separate. I

196

don't understand what he thinks any more, and he doesn't understand me. Our life together was miserable – it would have been like that even without you. We separated not because you took Vladimir away from me, but because his heart no longer had any love in it for me.

I shall live now as I lived before I was with Vladimir. He's all you have in the world, you've nothing else to live for, it's always like that when two people really love each other. Vladimir Ivanovich and I had a common-law marriage, so there'll be no need for a divorce. I don't resent you, and if I'd known before how deeply you loved each other I would have done this long ago. Tell Vladimir Ivanovich I'm not angry with him and I'll be his friend as I have always been. If you ever need me, I shall be very happy to help you in any way. I used to feel deep hatred for you, but now I think I understand things I feel sorry about all the tears you must have wept, all your suffering and worring.

As one sister to another, I want you to be happy. Give my regards to Vladimir, and tell him from me to look after his young wife! I'll give you my new address in case you need it.

If you write to me, I shall reply. We're not enemies, you and I. We never meant to cause each other pain.

I wish you happiness.

Yours, Vasilisa Malygina.

She wrote the address neatly, put both letters into an envelope, licked it and stuck it down.

It was only then that she finally grasped that this was the end. No more pain, no more tormenting serpent, no more of the old gnawing nostalgia. No more Volodya 'the American'. Now he was just plain Vladimir Ivanovich. When she thought about Vladimir she saw Nina, and when she thought about Nina she saw Vladimir there beside her. They had become one person for her, inseparable and indivisible. As one person, they could bring her no more unhappiness.

The old passion was spent, burnt to ashes, and she felt at peace with herself. Her mind was calm and clear after the storm.

16

She remained standing at the window, admiring the sunset. The sky was stormy, overcast with purple gold-edged clouds. Crows wheeled overhead, cawing as they looked for a place to roost, and the air smelt of dead leaves, mushrooms and damp autumn earth. It was a sweet, childhood smell, far from the stale enervating air of Vladimir's house. She breathed deeply, eagerly drinking it in. Leaning out of the window, she caught sight of Grusha in the yard below, taking her washing off the line for the night. 'Hey, Grusha!' called. 'Come up quickly! I've some good news to tell you!'

'I'm just coming!' replied Grusha. When she came in, she threw the washing on to the bed. 'What's the news then? Have you got a letter? Is that it?'

'I didn't get a letter, I just sent one, and guess who to.'

'Vladimir Ivanovich', said Grusha.

'Wrong! Not him but his girl friend, or rather his future wife, Nina Konstantinovna.'

'What did you do that for?' asked Grusha, puzzled.

'Well you see, Grusha,' Vasya explained, 'I read the letter Nina wrote to Vladimir, and I began to feel sorry for her. She's suffered so much because of me. She got rid of her baby, she ate her heart out. Such pointless suffering! We aren't rivals or enemies. If she'd taken Vladimir away from me without loving him, just to get his money, of course I wouldn't have forgiven her, I'd have hated her. But now I know about her, why should I hate her? She loves him deeply, far more than I do; that gives her the right to marry him. Without Vladimir she has nothing to live for – that's what she wrote. "Without you I'm lost." Do I need Vladimir that way? I've thought about it all so much Grusha, and I've realized it's not him I'm sad about. It would be different if Volodya the American were to come back, but he doesn't exist for me now. Why should I go on torturing poor Nina, and coming between them? I don't really want to share my life with a director anyway.'

'I agree, a director's not for you,' said Grusha firmly. 'It's bad the way so many bosses lose touch with people and become directors. But we don't have to be sad about it, Vasilisa. Look how many of the old comrades are still with us! And you should see the non-party members too! I tell you, you'll find more real proletarian communists amongst them than in the party now!'

'Yes, it's true. But what about that bunch who traded in their class loyalities for lamps and silk eiderdowns! We don't talk the same language! That's why I've been asking myself why I should harass Nina and cling to Vladimir when he's neither properly married to me nor really free of me. What good does it do me? It's time to end it, without recriminations. We've all suffered enough as it is. It was something I couldn't grasp when I'd just left him. I kept waiting and hoping for something, I didn't know what. I thought if Vladimir left me for another woman I'd die without him. I was in a daze when I got here. I couldn't see what to do. But as soon as I got back to work on the party committee there were other people's problems to worry about and the pain gradually went. Now, believe it or not, I honestly don't feel jealous or unhappy any longer. I feel quite calm.

'Well, praise the Lord!' said Grusha, hastily crossing herself and glancing at the icon in the corner. 'It wasn't for nothing I've been praying all these nights on my knees to the blessed virgin. I begged her to pity a woman in distress and heal our poor Vasilisa!'

Vasya smiled. 'You're awful, Grusha! Do you still believe in those icons of yours? But you're right. I'm healed now. These past months I've been going around in such a state I forgot who I was, I forgot the party, everything was a fog. But now I'm better. Life is good and everything seems new and exciting. No more Vladimir now, just the party. I remember this was how I felt after I'd had typhus and was starting to get better.'

'I only hope you don't fall ill again when that husband of yours starts writing you remorseful letters,' said Grusha.

'No, Grusha,' Vasya shook her head pensively. 'That's not going to happen. I feel as if I've been through a personal revolution. All the grief and reproaches have gone. We were all three fighting each other in a cursed magic circle, and all trying to get out of it. We hated each other and would have gone on hating each other if we hadn't managed to escape. It was when I began to understand how Nina was feeling that I saw my way out. I had nothing to forgive her for – I was sorry for her, as if she was my sister. Both of us women went through the same things. She suffered no less than I did, through no fault of hers, because our lives had become so pointless. As soon as I began to sympathize with her I felt much better, Grusha.'

'Well, I'm not surprised,' said Grusha. 'That means you definitely don't love him any more, because love always brings unhappiness. As soon as love allows you a glimpse of happiness, grief slips into its shadow. So when there's no more grief left, it can only mean love is over!'

'That can't be true, Grusha, you must be wrong,' Vasya shook her head. 'I haven't stopped loving Vladimir, he's still very dear to me, it's just that my love for him has changed. There's no more of the old resentment and hatred. I'm glad we once loved each other and were happy together. Why should I be angry with him? Whose fault is it if he doesn't love me any more, I'm glad about the past; Vladimir and Nina are like a dear brother and sister to me now. Believe me Grusha, I mean it! We've been happy, now it's their turn. Everyone has a right to happiness as long as it doesn't involve lies and deceit.'

'That's all very true, what you say about deceiving, but it's beyond me how you can think of Nina as a sister! You're becoming a philosopher, Vasilisa! You'd better not overdo the philosophizing, or you'll overdo your communism too! Of course its best to forgive Vladimir for Nina, out of heart out of mind. But there's no need to *love* them! Keep your love and sympathy for the working people – they need you now. They're losing confidence, they need courage and hope, not party dogma. Believe me Vasilisa, I always know what's happening. I may not be in the party, but I see everything that's going on, I understand communism just as well as you do.'

'Of course Grusha, you're one of us, everyone knows that. But how can you go on believing in your icons? Now don't be cross with me, stop frowning like that! I take it back! I don't want us to argue, because today is a special day! I feel reckless, I feel happy! And you'll never guess what finally cured me!'

'I can't imagine!'

'The Feodoseevs!'

'How amazing! Well, in that case I wish them and I'll forgive that vile Mrs Feodoseeva all her sins!'

They both laughed. 'But I still haven't told you the main news, Grusha,' Vasya went on. 'I've been to the doctor and I'm having a baby!'

'Pregnant!' Grusha clapped her hands excitedly, then spoke more gravely. 'But Vasya, how could you let your husband touch you? You can't bring up a child without a father! Or will you have an abortion, like everyone's doing these days.'

'Why should I have an abortion? I'm perfectly capable of bringing up a child myself. What do I need a husband for? It's all fairy-stories about fathers! Look at Mrs Feodoseeva, she's got three to look after now Feodoseev has gone off with Dora!'

'But how are you going to raise a child on your own?'

'What do you mean, on my own? Everything will be perfect, we'll set up a crêche. In fact, I thought of asking you to help us run it. I know how you love children. And soon there'll be a new baby, for all of us!'

'A communist baby!'

'Precisely so!' They both laughed.

'I must get on with my packing now, Grusha. The train's leaving early tomorrow morning. Tomorrow I'll be starting work and organizing my life. Stepan Alexeevich has given me his blessing. I'm so happy to be starting work again Grusha, you just can't imagine how happy I feel!'

She caught Grusha's hands and they whirled around the room like a couple of children, almost knocking over the tailor's dummy, and laughing so loudly that people in the yard below could hear them. 'We must live, Grusha!' shouted Vasya.

Live and work, work and fight, live and love life, like the bees in the lilac, like the birds at the bottom of the garden, like the crickets in the grass!

Three Generations

One morning in the office, among a pile of business and personal letters, I came across a thick envelope which caught my attention. Deciding that it must be an article, I opened it immediately. It turned out to be a letter, several pages long. I looked for the signature and was surprised to see that it was from Olga Veselovskaya.

I knew comrade Olga Sergeevna Veselovskaya to be an extremely responsible worker, who had an administrative job in one of the major sections of soviet industry. She was not the least bit interested in working with women, so I couldn't imagine why she should be writing me this long letter. I glanced at the envelope, and it was then that I saw the large inscription written in red pencil: 'Strictly Personal'.

For the women who write to me, 'Personal' generally indicates some family crisis. Could the same Olga Sergeevna be caught up in some personal drama? It seemed impossible. There was urgent business awaiting my attention so I couldn't read it immediately, but the letter and the image of Olga Sergeevna kept coming into my mind.

I remembered my business meetings with her. Her dry, re-strained manner and her extraordinary, renowned 'unwomanly' efficiency. I recalled her husband, Rybakov, a good man who had once been a worker. He had a pleasant open face and was generally liked, but was less highly thought of than his wife. He worked under her in the same department, and was younger than she was. They were both conscientious people, and whenever I had seen them together their relationship seemed exceptionally harmonious.

I remembered him saying once, 'Why are you still arguing? Didn't you hear Olga Sergeevna's opinion on the subject?' For him she obviously represented the highest authority. Then I remembered how Olga Sergeevna's face had changed, losing its somewhat remote expression and becoming suddenly human, when they told her at a conference once that her husband had been taken ill. He was not a healthy man. It was possible that her letter had something to do with his illness, but surely she wouldn't have written at such length about that.

I was still working in my office when evening approached, and it was only then that I got around to reading the letter. It began:

I am in a quandary. In all the forty-three years of my life I have never been in such a ridiculous position. I simply don't know where to turn.

You know me only as a worker, you know my reputation for being rather pedantic and heavy-handed. So it may be hard for you to imagine that I, at my age, am going through a 'female' crisis. And very commonplace crisis too, all the more galling and painful for being of such music-hall banality.

But I feel the banality is only in its superficial aspects, not its essence, and that the whole thing is a direct result of the conflict between our everyday life and our political ideas in Russia at present; along with everything that is splendid, there is much that is petty and mean, oppressive and rotten.

At times it sickens me to have to face the things I'm writing to you about, and the idea that they are not isolated occurrences fills me with feelings of disgust. But at other times I feel that I am wrong, and that part of me is talking like someone from the old days. Maybe my daughter Zhenya and my husband are right when they say I still have strong bourgeois prejudices, that I'm distorting the picture.

Please help me to get to the bottom of it. I don't know who is right, them or me. If I am wrong, and am merely expressing attitudes instilled in me by my upbringing, then help me to understand things in the light of the new morality.

The letter broke off at this point, and Olga Sergeevna continued her narrative on the next page, in steadier handwriting.

I would like to come to the point immediately, to tell you the essence of my emotional crisis, but if I recount only the facts without telling you anything of my previous life you might get a false picture of things. You might see only the superficial events, without realizing that they are not the real cause of my suffering, which is far more profound and complicated. The facts I can understand, but as for the motives behind them . . .

In short, I'm going to ask you to bear with me and read my letter all the way through. Please remember that I am writing to you as a friend who is looking to you for support.

There were a few blots on the letter, which resumed on the next page.

Do you remember my mother? She was alive until recently. To the end was running her mobile library in the province of N. She worked there for the Department of Popular Education. But I don't need to describe my mother to you, you knew her personally.

Yes, I had known Maria Stepanovna Olshevich and remembered her well. A typical humanitarian of the 90s, a publisher of popular scientific works, a translator and tireless worker for popular enlightenment, she carried much authority with the liberals of the day, and even the underground activists respected her in their way. She had in fact given a great deal of financial assistance to the underground, and her circle of acquaintances was large and varied.

Politically she had been closer to the Populists, but she had never taken an active part in politics. Her passion was for books, libraries and the enlightenment of the peasantry and impoverished city-dwellers. All the local organizations, soviet, professional and party, had come to her funeral a few months ago.

A tall woman, slim and erect, with a lovely tilt to her head and a fine expressive face, she had always inspired a deferential respect, even fear. She had a dry, clear voice, and spoke briefly and to the point, a cigarette constantly in her mouth. She dressed simply and never followed fashion; but she had the beautiful, well-cared-for hands of a lady, and on her fourth finger she wore a thick gold ring set with a dark ruby.

Olga Sergeevna continued:

But what you may not have known is that when my mother was young she too had an emotional crisis. After it was over she developed a rigid moral code in matters of love, and deep down she condemned anyone who did not adhere to this code – she even despised them. My mother was a good person, and progressive in her attitudes, but in matters that concerned sexual morality she was severe and pitiless.

The disagreements between my mother and myself were not based on political differences, as you might suppose, but specifically on our differing interpretations of the 'necessary' and the 'possible' as far as my personal crises were concerned.

My mother had married a soldier for love, against her parents' wishes. She lived the provincial life of a regimental officer's lady, and, according to her she was happy with this life for a while. She had two sons, was regarded as a model wife and mother, and her husband idolized her.

But gradually she began to feel oppressed by this passive and prosperous life. You know what an inexhaustible source of energy my mother was. She had received a good education for those days, she had read a lot, been abroad and corresponded with Tolstoy. I'm sure you can imagine that a regimental commander could not satisfy her needs.

Fate willed her to meet the *zemstvo* doctor, Sergei Ivanovich Veselovsky. Sergei Ivanovich, my father, was a character out of Chekhov, with the same vague idealism. He was a man constantly aspiring to something, to the unknown, with a fondness for eating and good living, greatly perplexed when faced with evil and injustice. He was handsome and healthy, read the same books as my mother, talked with emotion about life in the countryside, grieved for the 'unenlightened peasantry', and had platonic dreams of establishing libraries, schools and enlightenment throughout Russia.

It all turned out as one might have expected. One hot summer evening when the regimental commander was away on army manoeuvres, my mother found herself in the arms of my future father. A book, *Mobile Libraries in New Zealand*, lay unread beside them in the grass.

My father was apparently reluctant to regard the poetic idyll of that summer evening as warranting any radical change in his life. He valued his freedom, moreover he had at the time a housekeeper, a young peasant widow . . .

But my mother, as I said, had her own rules on sexual morality, and she told me later that she never tried to resist her love for my father, since for her love had more rights than had conjugal obligations. Love for her was something great and sacred, she was incapable of toying with emotions and would have considered it ignoble. In Sergei Ivanovich she found, to use her words, everything that her heart, soul and mind were seeking – a man she loved passionately, a person she respected, and a friend with whom she could embark hand in hand on the great task of enlightenment.

It only remained for her to annul her union with the colonel. She remained impervious to the prospect of scandal; she knew clearly that she wanted to build a new life, and, more importantly, one she had freely chosen. She asked Sergei Ivanovich to meet her one morning; they met in the lime grove, where, to the chirruping of crickets, she read him her brief resolute letter to her husband – a letter which concealed nothing and asked him for a divorce.

Sergei Ivanovich was taken aback by this. He had not anticipated such swift, action. I think he mumbled something to the effect that my mother should guard her reputation, and even spoke of her maternal obligations to her sons. But my mother, although flabbergasted by his words, was inexorable, and as at that time she was enchantingly pretty and my father was still in amorous mood, the conversation ended in more kisses, which strengthened my mother's resolve to bring everything into the open immediately.

But it didn't prove easy. The poor colonel, who was passionately in love with my mother, was demented with grief and anger. One moment he would hurl reproaches at his wife, threatening to kill her, himself and the scoundrel of a doctor; the next moment he would lapse into penitent mood and implore her to stay, if only as mother and housekeeper.

My mother felt very sorry for him, but her love for her hero with the compatible soul was more powerful than her pity, and, convinced that no argument would prevail on her husband, she collected her things, her money and her papers, kissed her sons, and left the colonel without so much as a word of farewell.

For a long time the province could task of nothing but this scandal. The liberals sided with my mother and regarded the act of leaving her soldier husband for a *zemstvo* doctor as some kind of protest against the Tsarist regime. Someone even dedicated some verses to her in the local newspaper, someone else proposed a toast at a *zemstvo* dinner to the heroic women who cross the threshold of conventional marriage to join those toiling for the welfare of the people . . .

Mother began to live openly with Sergei Ivanovich, and immediately set about realizing her cherished scheme about which my Chekhovian hero of a father also waxed lyrical – of establishing a mobile library. The scheme demanded an enormous amount of effort and energy, for these were the 1880's, the savage years of reaction after Alexander II was assassinated. But with characteristic persistence my mother confronted *zemstvo* leaders and local governors, travelled to St Petersburg, made contacts, argued her case and stood her ground. Just when the scheme was close to realization, my mother was arrested, along with poor perplexed Sergei Ivanovich, and they were sent into exile – not a very remote place. It was there that I was born.

My mother lost none of her old fighting spirit in exile, where she formed a self-education circle, taught, and laid the basis for libraries.

My father languished, put on weight and went to seed. But on their return from exile he found he had gained himself a reputation as a revolutionary, and he fell in with the more active *zemstvo* members. Mother meanwhile busied herself with renewed enthusiasm in spreading enlightenment throughout the district, and for a while my parents' life seems to have followed a well-defined and untroubled path.

But then an unpleasant incident happened; my mother caught her balding but still attractive husband making a totally unambiguous proposition to the farm girl, Arisha. Father tried to make excuses, but it proved more serious than he had anticipated for Arisha was pregnant.

Without lengthy discussions, my mother packed her things, and taking me with her, moved to the district capital, leaving my father a business-like letter without reproaches or recriminations.

She insisted, among other things, that he provide for Arisha's child, and that he curb his consumption of alcohol, of which he was becoming increasingly fond.

All these details I learnt much later from my mother, who obviously hoped that by being frank about herself she could persuade me onto the path of duty.

I well remember Mother's enormous self-control in bearing her grief at that time. Not once did I see her in tears, even though according to her she never stopped loving Sergei Ivanovich, and was faithful to him for the rest of her life. In the district capital she set about organizing a publishing house which brought out popular scientific books and which bore her name. I was with her constantly. From my earliest childhood I was part of her circle of people involved in revolutionary ideas and activities, and as an adolescent I was already reading the underground press and was familiar with 'illegals' and 'illegal' activities. We lived very modestly, even ascetically. Our home was always dominated by an atmosphere of work, with ideas and plans constantly hovering in the air. I was just fifteen when I was first arrested, something which made my mother very proud.

But it was then that our ideological paths began to diverge. I joined the Marxists while she remained a Populist. Working in the ranks of the revolutionary movement, I got to know a subsequently prominent member of the Marxist Union of Struggle. He was older than I, and politically experienced. Under his influence I became a Marxist, and later a Bolshevik.

We became sexually involved, although we refused on principle to get married. My mother tut-tutted at first, saying I was much too young, that I should have waited, that I must have my father's character, which did not augur well for constancy in love. But eventually she became reconciled with the situation, and we moved in with her and continued our work. However as the man I was living with was an 'illegal', we all ended up being arrested. Mother was defended by her friends, but I went into exile with my 'husband'.

I'm afraid you must be bored with this preamble, but without it you won't be able to make sense of my present dilemma. Remember, I'm the daughter and pupil of Maria Stepanovna!

And no amount of logic will obliterate the things you absorb in childhood and assimilate in youth. So please have patience and go on reading my letter, for I'm coming now to the crisis of the second generation!

I managed to escape from exile, although my 'husband' had to stay behind. I found my way to St Petersburg, where to cover my tracks some friends found me a position as a governess in the house of a prosperous engineer called M.

The house was furnished lavishly – they lived in style. People who came to the house were interested in politics in the same way as they were interested in the Arts theatre or the deadent paintings of Vrubel. For them, politics was merely an entertaining subject for drawing room conversation, although in his student days M had been a Marxist.

I was unfamiliar with this world, and found it remote and alien. It was during my first evening there that I confronted my host (on the question of Bernsteinism, as far as I can remember) with a passionate enthusiasm that was wholly inappropriate to the atmosphere of the drawing room. I then spent a sleepless night tormented and infuriated by my own lack of restraint.

I was particularly incensed for some reason by M's ironically tender glances at me. There was something about the man that irritated me the moment I set eyes on him. But although he struck me as unsympathetic and unprincipled, I wanted passionately to convince him that we Marxists were right; I wanted to make him change his mind.

His wife was a fragile doll of a woman, dressed up in lace and furs, who somehow managed to produce five sturdy children. She followed her husband everywhere, watching him with adoring eyes, laughingly assuring people that despite the rules, the longer she lived with him the more in love with him she was.

I was exasperated by this atmosphere of cosiness, this ostentatious family happiness. M's consideration for his pretty wife, and his perpetual anxieties about her health drove me to fury, and I would deliberately make spiteful and insulting remarks about prosperous liberals, smug petit-bourgeois lives and philistine crassness. I would talk about life in exile, and reduce the nervous Lydia Andreevna, M's wife, to hysterical tears.

'Why did you do that?' M would reproach me afterwards, with a look of sad, tender reproof.

I sometimes fancied I hated them both so much I might drop some sort of careless remark, so the police would raid their house and disrupt their blissful serenity. But I could not move out of the house, for it was not only a refuge for me but a convenient secret meeting-place. Whenever I mentioned to my comrades the idea of moving, they would get angry, and couldn't understand my reasons.

'Why have anything to do with them if you feel like that?' they would say. 'You should keep out of their way.'

But that was inconceivable. Although I was aware how much I loathed M's handsome self-satisfied figure, his slightly guttural voice and careless gait, I would be on edge if I did not see him for a day or two. I was mortified that I should be so superfluous, such a stranger in their home, and his slightest negligence towards me caused me acute misery.

But every time we met we would quarrel, arguing until we were hoarse, shouting and cursing each other. An observer might have supposed we hated each other. But then sometimes in the middle of these arguments our eyes would meet, and these glances had their own special vocabulary which I was afraid to understand . . .

On one occasion, when party business kept me out of town longer than anticipated, I did not return until late at night. M opened the door to me.

'So you've come back at last!' he said. 'I'd lost all hope that you would.' And before I knew it I found myself in his arms, overwhelmed by his kisses.

It was strange. Yet I wasn't at all surprised, and had long been expecting it to happen.

At dawn I went back to my room and he spent the rest of the night in his study, where he always slept whenever he had to work late.

The following evening there were guests, and we began arguing again, passionately, implacably. Once again it seemed we were enemies. But when the guests had left, M proposed that I take a ride with him to the islands (it was spring, and a white St Petersburg night). His wife insisted laughingly that I go with him – it struck her as amusing, she would never have deigned to be jealous of me.

My life gradually became very complicated. It was a difficult time for the party, and I was up to my eyes in work and political anxieties. Like a coward, I kept putting off the moment when I would have to bring matters to a head with M. I excused myself by saying I had no time, and, waited for the imminent departure of M's wife to the south with the children. And do you know, however unlikely at might seem, it was at this time that I began to think especially lovingly of my friend and husband in exile, and took active steps to get him released.

If you had asked me whom I loved then, I would unhesitatingly have replied my husband, my friend. But if that had been conditional on leaving M, I would sooner have died. M was a stranger to me, and yet oddly similar too. I hated the way he looked at me, I hated his habits and his lifestyle, but as a person I loved him desperately, for all his weaknesses and imperfections, for all those qualities which were so opposed to everything I valued and loved in people. Our love brought neither of us happiness, yet neither of us could contemplate parting.

I was amazed, and still am, by what it was that attracted me to M. Even in those days I wasn't pretty, I had no idea how to dress and no desire to either; I was austere and 'unfeminine'. Yet I knew that M loved me in a way he had never loved his pretty and adoring wife.

We spent the summer alone in the house together, a strange and agonizing summer, full of conflicting emotions for both of us. Neither of us had a moment's happiness, yet neither was afraid to reveal to the other how unhappy we were, and in some strange way this brought us closer together.

Then as autumn approached I discovered that I was pregnant. Maybe I should have terminated the pregnancy, but neither of us could entertain the idea. I left for my mother's . . .

Olga Sergeevna's letter broke off at this point. It had obviously been written at different times. It continued, in shaky pencilled handwriting, on an office form.

Immediately I arrived at my mother's, I told her everything. I told her of my misery, my duplicity and the feelings which, in their different ways, were tormenting me and M as well: of his love both for me and for his wife.

When Mother had heard me out she sat for a long time in her bedroom in silence, lost in thought and puffing on a cigarette.

Next morning, she came into my room, and sitting down on the bed, announced firmly: 'It's quite clear that you love M. The first thing you must do is to write to Konstantin!' (That was my husband).

'But what am I going to write to him?'

'What an absurd question! Why, that you're in love with someone else of course. You can't leave him with illusions about the situation, any thought of sparing his feelings would be misplaced – it would only create more misery later on.'

'But I don't want to spare his feelings. I love Konstantin, I've never stopped loving him.'

'How could you have fallen in love with another man if you hadn't stopped loving him?' asked my mother, perplexed. 'You're talking nonsense!'

'It's not nonsense at all! That's what's causing all this misery.'

I attempted to explain to Mother once again the two emotions which I felt simultaneously – my deep love for Konstantin, my emotional rapport with him, and my wild attraction for M, whom as a person I could neither love nor respect. But she simply didn't understand.

'Well, if it's only physical attraction you feel for M, and

it's Konstantin you love and respect, then you'd better pull yourself together and leave M.'

'But that's the problem, Mother. It's not just physical attraction I feel for M, it's love too, a different kind of love. If someone told me M was in danger, I'd give my life to save him. If I was told to die for Konstantin, I'd refuse. Yet it's Konstantin I love and need emotionally – without him my life would be cold and empty. I don't love and respect M in that way.'

'What rubbish!' said my mother angrily. But she was becoming confused, first demanding that I write immediately to Konstantin and break with him, then telling me to leave M. I felt for the first time in my life that I had made a mistake in going to her for support. Our chief disagreement lay in her insistence that I break with one or other of them, whereas I instinctively wanted to keep both Konstantin and M. This decision seemed to me more correct and more humane, more appropriate to the underlying truth of the situation.

The outcome was that I wrote to Konstantin telling him everything, not only the facts of the situation, but my anxieties as well, my doubts and divided feelings. At first I got only a brief reply from him, in which he said he would have to assimilate things and come to terms with them before he could reply properly. But even these few lines were filled with a warmth that immediately told me that Konstantin, unlike my mother, would understand.

And indeed Konstantin did finally understand. Far away from me in his place of exile, he lived through all my anxieties, my conflicting emotions, and came to accept me as I was. He resigned himself to the inevitable and asserted his claim only to that part of me which still reached out to him and could not live without him. As far as I was concerned, the matter had been partially resolved.

But my mother was still waiting for some decision to be made. She found it galling that I should receive letters from M (in her name!) as well as letters from Konstantin, and that both made me happy.

It was at this point that she began to tell me about her own 'crisis of the heart', to try and force me to make a decision. She was distressed by what she saw as my cowardice and lack of will-power.

'In every other way you're so strong, so persistent and fearless. I can't understand why love should make you so cowardly. I wonder if you inherited it from your father?' Mother mused aloud. She could not accept that a decision had already been made – everything had been brought into the open and we were all trying to accept each other as we were.

'So what about M's wife? Are you going to tell her everything too, and make her "accept" the situation?'

'No, she doesn't come into this, we can't tell her anything. You see, M has never been emotionally close to her. He loved her, and still does, his love for me has robbed her of nothing.'

At this, Mother lost her temper and told me we were vulgar philistines, that these four-way marriages might well flourish in ultra-decadent Paris, but that sooner or later I was going to have to choose.

In the spring my baby was born, a little girl. M came to stay with us and those few weeks in Mother's house were the happiest of my life. It was strange the way that Mother and M immediately established a much warmer relationship than had ever existed between her and Konstantin. By the time M left, Mother had decided that the choice was obvious: I must live with the father of my child.

But strangely enough, the more Mother took M's side, the more I became aware of how lonely I was without

Konstantin. It was as if Mother and M were in one camp, and Konstantin and I were in the other. I suppose that ideologically this was the case: my mother, the humanitarian and Populist, on the same side as the representative of the liberal bourgeoisie; Konstantin and I in the camp of the proletariat.

Then another arrest and another period of exile postponed the whole issue. My little girl lived with her grandmother and I continued to write to M and Konstantin, until eventually Konstantin and I had the good fortune to meet in exile.

To my mother's horror we started living with each other again. We did so without dramas or scenes of forgiveness. We lived with each other naturally and happily, two people who were emotionally at one. It was then that my mother begain in her heart to despise me, writing me letters filled with reproaches, sadness and the most profound resentment, taking M's side, saying that I was destroying the man I loved out of a sense of mere compassion.

M delivered several ultimatums to me and then abruptly broke off all relations, and I remained with Konstantin.

The springtime of liberalism came around, with banquets held under the benevolent eye of Svyatopolk-Mirsky. We returned from exile, and fate once more brought me to St Petersburg. A meeting with M was inevitable, and I will not conceal from you the fact that I desired and actively sought a meeting.

When we did meet, it was as though we had never parted. Everything started again, all the agony, all the joy, all the doubts, our feelings of mutual isolation and the power of our mutual attraction.

But I feared the power of our feelings all the more now that M, carried away by this renewed outburst of passion, was prepared to leave his wife, insisting that we make

public our liaison and get married. More than ever I felt
how emotionally alien we were from each other. The
political struggle was flaring up and the parties were more
sharply divided than ever, clearly defining their positions.
What had been a merely theoretical argument three years
ago now became a vital platform for action. M had not
even progressed as far as a liberationist position. We were
literally speaking different languages.

I despised myself every time we met, and pined desperately when we were apart. M hated my work, despised the
Bolsheviks and longed to possess me 'for ever and always'.
I loathed the petit-bourgeois in him, attacked him for his
liberalism, but lacked the strength to tear him from my
heart. There was something strangely maternal about my
feelings for him at that time – I was sorry for him, I felt he
was untrue to himself, that I had to help him understand
himself. How could I abandon him at the political
crossroads . . . ?

This agony went on for several months, until unexpectedly Konstantin arrived. This time my confession caused
him great pain, and his feelings of jealousy were only too
evident. Nevertheless, we started living together, as
'friends'. This was more than M could endure, and he flew
into a rage, refusing to believe we weren't sleeping together, demanding that I leave Konstantin, and all but
leaving his wife himself. In short, every day brought some
new painful incident.

Eventually something absurd occurred. M burst into our
flat, yelling obscenities at Konstantin and demanding that I
leave with him there and then, otherwise everything would
be over between us.

I didn't go. We parted as enemies. Konstantin and I had a
terribly difficult time after that; he saw I was unhappy
because of his jealousy, but he was unable to help me. For

the first and only time in my life (although at this very moment I'm experiencing something similar) I could not devote myself to work. Everything was submerged by unhappiness.

At this point my mother arrived, summoned by M's despairing letters. She came with my daughter, and with her own uncompromising demand that I stop prevaricating and come to a decision.

'But I made up my mind long ago, Mother,' I protested.

'Well, in that case stop living with him.' (she meant Konstantin). 'You say you're no longer his wife and I believe you, but why the pretence? Why are you torturing M like this?

'No Mother, you're wrong, I'm going to stay with Konstantin.'

But she closed her ears to this. She knew from M's letters about the events of the past months. I had written to her too, describing my hesitations and anxieties.

'You love M,' she repeated stubbornly, 'and love has its own laws. You're cluttering them up with a lot of intellectual logic. You mustn't break your heart, you must be courageous in love and break down all obstacles, even your political differences. You can make a Marxist out of M. He loves you so much he'd do anything for you, besides, you're much stronger than he is.'

But Mother's advice only had the opposite effect on me, and I felt even more acutely that I mustn't join my life with M's, for I knew it would mean spiritual bankruptcy. Mother arranged a meeting with M and tried to reconcile us in the presence of our child, but with all the hypocrisy and misery it came to nothing. The historic year of 1905 came. Events swept us up inexorably, and private lives retreated into insignificance. My petty griefs were submerged in the ocean of historical events as the revolution raged about us. I left for south Russia, Konstantin went abroad and Mother hurried off to her estate in the provinces. M stayed on to lead one of the liberal 'unions'.

We worked and hoped, we fretted and argued. We struggled. And then the reaction set in, leaving us with still less time to think about ourselves.

In the autumn of 1908, I met M again by chance, in a god-forsaken little factory town. The post-1905 reaction had intensified and the revolution was crushed. M had put aside his temporary radicalism of 1905. He had risen in the world of industrial finance and become an important figure, whose arrival in any town would be noted in the provincial newspapers.

I knew he was in the same town. The knowledge troubled me, as it used to in the old days, and prevented me from getting on with my work. I avoided him and didn't want another meeting with him.

But then the police got on to me. My friends warned that I should get away immediately and find some safe refuge, if only until morning, not so much for myself as for the documents I had on me, which I didn't want to destroy. A cunning idea occurred to me. Why not go to M's place? I would be in no danger in the factory flat where he was staying as a guest of honour.

And so I went to him. A footman announced my arrival (I used my old surname), and M came out. He looked genuinely pleased to see me. But when we were alone and I told him my reason for coming, he was visibly shaken. His look changed to one of hostility and lost all trace of his old affection for me. As we stood looking at each other like strangers, both of us must have been wondering how it was that we had once loved each other so passionately, suffered so intensely, nearly died without each other. I felt this was some distant relative of M's standing before me, not M himself. His appearance bore a remote resemblance to the man I had loved, but in general he appeared to me as a totally uninteresting stranger.

I regretted having come, but I decided to go through with it for the sake of the documents, however much my bourgeois self cursed and shrank from the task. He could be useful to me, and the shock might make him lose a bit of weight! He for his part courteously gave me to understand how inconvenient my presence there was for him, while I pretended not to understand what he was talking about and invoked the rights of our old friendship.

So he was left with no alternative but to let me stay the night. My God, I can imagine how badly M slept that night! I slept excellently, however, unaffected by the knowledge that sleeping (or more likely not sleeping) two rooms from mine was the man whose footsteps, whose laughter, whose fleeting glances had in the past induced a burning wave of passion in me, whose presence I could sense from the other end of the house.

It was that night that I finally realized our love was over. All that was left was emptiness and our little girl, about whom M had not even asked. Next day we took leave of each other coldly, without expressing any desire to see each other again. The past was buried and forgotten.

But the curious thing was that shortly afterwards I met Konstantin, whom I had not seen for a very long time. We had been working in different parts of Russia. And do you know, I felt extraordinarily remote from him too, and began to regard him in a new light. It was as though everything we had experienced in those hectic years of the revolution had left its mark, and had obliterated all trace of our familiar selves. We disagreed in our interpretation of events, our approach to the tasks of the moment, we differed in our vision of the future.

Konstantin had a difficult time, and had fallen out with the party. There had been troubles of a semi-personal, semi-political nature, which had left marks of bitterness and pessimism. He no longer argued with his old passionate faith in the revolution, and he was convinced that for many years to come there would be a period of stagnation. With an anger coloured by his own feelings of personal resentment, he pointed out all our mistakes. He had adopted a position of cautious watchfulness, and his words and gestures were those of a man grown weary in battle, who without admitting it to himself was unconsciously withdrawing from the political movement to find himself a calm refuge.

I, on the other hand, was filled with renewed energy, for unlike him I had been stirred and inspired by the revolution. I felt I had matured emotionally and grown stronger, and that now I would truly be able to work to the limits of my ability. Though Konstantin and I were affectionate when we met, and we planned to work together once more, it was not long before I realized how fundamentally estranged we had become. When the opportunity presented itself to me to go abroad (illegally of course), I resolved to pursue my chemistry studies, which had been interrupted by party work.

I never met Konstantin again, and he gradually moved away from us altogether. When war broke out he didn't oppose it, and worked as a teacher in a secondary school. He actively sabotaged the soviets, and as far as I know he died taking part in one of the White Guard conspiracies.

M managed to leave the country in time to avoid the 'punishing hand of the proletariat'. But for me both these men had long been dead by then, and their fates no longer concerned me.

But you must be wondering as you read my unconscionably long autobiography where the crisis is in all this. These are past experiences, long buried in oblivion. What exactly is the problem?

I felt that if you were to understand my present unhappiness you should know a little about what sort of person I am. My story should show you, if nothing else, that my female instincts are no less strong than anyone else's, and that I have some understanding of the complexities of the human heart. But for all my tolerance, I am utterly unable to deal with the situation which has now arisen with my daughter.

As I mentioned before, I occasionally console myself with the thought that just as my mother, Maria Stepanovna, was unable to understand me, so I do not understand my Zhenya. But the whole business strikes me as so fundamentally tawdry that I just sink into lethargy. Please help me make sense of it, be critical of me if necessary. The problem may simply be that I am behind the times, and the new style of our lives has bred a new psychology which is unfamiliar to me.

I cannot write any more today. If you don't mind, I think I'll come and see you. Now that you know something of my past, I shall more easily be able to describe the problem simply and concisely. Will you ring me and let me know when you'll be on your own? Late evenings are best for me. I shall await your call. Comradely greetings to you,

From Olga Sergeevna

A few days later. Olga Sergeevna came to see me at the appointed time, late in the evening. I noticed immediately how drawn she looked and the troubled expression in her eyes. But it was with a new interest that I looked at this modestly dressed woman with the neatly arranged hair and the quiet, self-possessed manner. There was an undeniable charm about her, the charm of a fully integrated personality. Nevertheless, looking at her as we discussed recent political matters, I found it hard to reconcile the image of this highly placed worker and industrial organizer with the woman who had written me.'

'Now let's talk about my problem, shall we,' said Olga Sergeevna, interrupting herself in that dry clear voice of hers which reminded me of her mother's compelling tone. 'The problem is my daughter, Zhenya. I'd like you to have a word with her. It may be there's something I don't understand, and this is just the usual clash between the generations.

'But may be it something else; maybe Zhenya has been corrupted by the abnormal conditions of her upbringing. Even as a little girl she was being carted from one place to another, with her grandmother, with me, with friends. Over the past few years she's lived in a factory, been fully involved in factory life. She went to work at the Front, took part in the recent production drive. Naturally she's experienced things which in the past girls of her age would only have heard about. Perhaps this is as it should be, and one has to face it, but on the other hand . . .

'Oh if only you knew how confused I've been these last weeks – I don't know what's right and what's wrong! It used to make me happy that Zhenya was so unprejudiced and that she faced up to life so boldly; she could get herself out of any sort of difficulty, she wasn't intellectually equivocal, she was honest to the point of naïvety, it often seemed to me, and now suddenly . . .

'Briefly the facts are these. You know that when I was studying abroad I met Comrade Ryabkov whom I nursed back to health in Davos. Since that time we have lived as man and wife. Of course, I'm older than he is, and you might say he was my pupil, but in all these seven years together we've been very happy. When we returned together in 1917 we both helped support the power of the soviets.

'You know what a sunny disposition Comrade Ryabkov has – he's a true proletarian by temperament and a totally uncompromising person by nature. I don't need to tell you what kind of a worker he is either, everybody knows about that. I thought there was no cloud in our relationship and that everything was happy and simple between us.

'Last year when we settled in Moscow I decided Zhenya should live with us. She's a party worker as you know, although she's only twenty. She's a tireless, passionate girl – like her grandmother. And she has a good reputation in her district.

'You know our housing allocation; one room for three people. We're cramped, but that's unavoidable in present circumstances. Besides we're very rarely at home, especially me, I'm frequently out of town visiting factories. When after such a long separation Zhenya moved in with us, she immediately became close to us. Things were exceptionally friendly. I didn't feel like her mother. Just being with her made me feel young. Her energy, her laughter, and her youthful self-confidence were infectious.

'Comrade Rybakov got on with her splendidly too, and I was delighted, as I had feared that they wouldn't take to each other. But Zhenya and Andrei became excellent comrades, and I would send them off together to the theatre, or to meetings and conferences. We lived together harmoniously, and what pleased me most of all was that Andrei became so much more cheerful and fell ill less often.

'Everything was fine until . . . until something happened which changed everything . . .'

Olga Sergeevna broke off suddenly, as if she found it too painful to continue. I waited, while she looked over my shoulder out of the window.

'Well Olga Sergeevna,' I said at last, 'I suspect that what happened is distressing but inevitable – Zhenya and comrade Rybakov slept together. Come on, what's so dreadful and sordid about that? You must try to understand.'

'Oh, but it's not that! It's not that at all!' Olga Sergeevna interrupted me hastily. 'No, it's just that afterwards I felt I could suddenly see into their minds . . .'

'And what did you see there?'

'Oh, it was a kind of heartlessness which I found incomprehensible, a calm confidence about their rights – there was something cold and rational about it, a kind of cynicism. You see, there's no love involved, no passion or regrets, nor any desire to end the situation either. It's as if everything is as it should be, and it's only me who doesn't understand.

'Sometimes their behaviour strikes me as contemptible moral laxity and promiscuity, but then I'm assailed by doubts and wonder if I'm just behind the times. After all, my mother didn't understand my emotional crisis. So that's why I'm asking you to help me to make sense of things.'

Olga Sergeevna then told me that her daughter had come to see her at work and had asked her for a ten-minute interview since, as she said, 'there's no other way of getting hold of you, Mother.'

Very calmly, and without preamble, she had informed her mother that she had all the symptoms of pregnancy. Olga Sergeevna was aghast, and exclaimed 'But by whom?'

'I don't know,' Zhenya replied. Her mother had concluded that she did not want to tell her, but the news devastated her.

Zhenya asked her mother's advice on how to arrange an abortion (the new law legalising abortion had just come into effect), and which papers to take to which department. She didn't want a baby, she didn't have time.

Olga Sergeevna hadn't told her husband of Zhenya's news, as she regarded it as Zhenya's personal affair, she could always tell him herself it she wanted to. But there was something, some unconscious anxiety about the whole thing, which preyed on her. Doubts began to stir, and details of their life together started taking on a different light.

Olga Sergeevna despised herself for these thoughts and tried to drive them from her mind, but they persisted and prevented her from getting on with her work. And they persisted so obstinately that one evening in the middle of a conference she pretended to be unwell, went home – and found her daughter and her husband in each other's arms.

'You know, it wasn't so much that which shocked me, it was what happened afterwards. Andrei grabbed his hat and walked out, and when I blurted out to Zhenya "But why did you tell me you didn't know who the father was?" she replied quite calmly: "I'll repeat what I said then – I don't know who it is. It might be Andrei, it might be the other one." '

"What do you mean, the other one?"

"Well, these past few months I've been involved with another man, nobody you know."

'Can you understand how flabbergasted I was at this? Zhenya then told me that even when she was taking parcels to the Front she was having sexual relationships. But the thing I found most shocking was that she declared quite openly that she did not love anyone and she never had.'

"But why did you sleep with men then? Is it because you're really so attracted to them physically? You're still so young, it's not normal at your age!"

"How can I put it, Mother? For a long time I was physically attracted to men, as you probably understand it anyway. That was until I met this other man, the one I've been with these past months, although it's all over now. But I liked the men I slept with, and they liked me. That way it's simple, and it doesn't tie you to anything. I can't understand what you're so upset about, Mother. It would be different if I was prostituting myself or being raped. But this is something I do of my own free will. We stay together as long as we get on with each other, and when we no longer do, we part company and nobody gets hurt. Of course, I'm going to lose two or three weeks' work because of the abortion, which is a pity. But that's my own fault. Next time I'll take proper precautions." '

When Olga Sergeevna asked her how, after everything she'd said, she could have two relationships at the same time, and why she should want to since she did not love them, Zhenya replied that it had been a coincidence. The other man had attracted her emotionally, but treated her like a baby and refused to take her seriously, which infuriated her. It was this that had led her to take up with Andrei, whom she felt to be a kindred spirit, loved as a friend, and with whom she always felt happy and comfortable.

'And do they know about each other?' Olga Sergeevna had asked her.

'Yes, of course. I don't see that I have anything to conceal from them. They don't have to sleep with me if they don't like it. I have my own life, Andrei doesn't mind,' she had replied. 'Oh, the other man got angry about it and started to give ultimatums, but he came round in the end. Anyway, I've left him now. I lost interest in him, he was so crude, I really don't like that sort of person.'

Olga Sergeevna then tried to point out how unacceptable this frivolous attitude to sexual relationships was – frivolous about life, and about people in general.

But Zhenya argued back, saying 'Look Mother, you say my behaviour is shabby, that you shouldn't sleep with people you don't love, and that my cynicism is driving you to despair. But tell me honestly, if I was a boy, your twenty-year-old son, who had been at the Front and had led an independent life, would you be so horrified if he'd been sleeping with women he liked? I don't mean with prostitutes he bought, or little girls he seduced, because I agree that is shabby but women he liked, and who liked him too. Would that horrify you so much? Admit it, it wouldn't, would it? So why are you in such despair about what you see as my immorality? I assure you, I'm exactly the same person, I'm perfectly well aware of my obligations and my responsibilities to the party.

'But I don't understand what the party, the revolution, the devastation of the country, the White Guard, and everything else you've been talking about have to do with the fact that I sleep with Andrei and with someone else at the same time I couldn't have a baby, I know that. It would be terribly wrong at this time, when there are so many political problems. I'm well aware of that, and at the moment I certainly don't intend to be a mother. But as for everything else . . .'

'But what about me, Zhenya?' cried Olga Sergeevna. 'Did you never consider how *I* might react to your relationship with Andrei?'

'But how can it make any difference to you?' Zhenya objected. 'It was you who wanted us to be close, you were so pleased we were friends. Where are the boundaries? Why is it all right for us to do things together, enjoy ourselves together, but not sleep together? It's not as if we've taken anything from you – Andrei still worships you as he always did, I haven't robbed you of one iota of his love for you, What does it matter to you? It's all the same to you, you never have time for that sort of thing anyway.

'Besides Mother, do you really want to tie Andrei to your apron strings so he can't have a life of his own without you knowing about it? That would be a terribly possessive attitude. It must be Grandmother's bourgeois upbringing coming out in you! You're being so unfair! In your day you lived your own life, why shouldn't Andrei now?'

What upset and angered Olga Sergeevna most of all was that neither her daughter nor her husband had shown any signs of remorse, they just saw it as natural, simple and not worth discussing. It was only with the greatest condescension to her, as someone who didn't really understand things, that Andrei and Zhenya laboriously made a few remarks about how sorry they were that things had worked out like this, and regretted making life unpleasant for her.

But she had been painfully aware that neither Zhenya nor her gentle sincere Andrei truly considered themselves to be in the wrong. Both constantly repeated variations on the theme that nothing had changed, and that she was viewing the thing needlessly as a tragedy. Nobody, they assured her, wanted to cause her pain or unhappiness, but if it really upset her so much they would agree to call it a day, though they couldn't imagine what difference it would make.

Plunged in a chaos of ideas and emotions, Olga Sergeevna had decided to ask for my advice and for some clarification of the matter. Was it nothing more than wanton promiscuity, unchecked by moral standards? Or was it some new phenomenon created by the new life?

Was this the new morality? We discussed these questions at great length.

'What I find most painful,' said Olga Sergeevna, wearily leaning on her shapely arm in a gesture which reminded me of Maria Stepanovna, 'is that they're so totally cold and rational, like two old people with no emotions left. I could understand if Zhenya loved Andrei and he loved her, and even if it did make me unhappy (because I love Andrei very much, you know) I wouldn't have this unpleasant taste in my mouth, this feeling of physical nausea. To put it bluntly, I feel very hostile towards Andrei and Zhenya – I can understand how they could have treated me so unscrupulously, with so little regard for my feelings. It's shaken my faith as to whether these two people are capable of loving at all. They both keep telling me that they love me, but what do they mean by love when they cause me so much unhappiness and inflict it so casually, without qualms or remorse. I really think they must be emotionally deficient in some way. I don't understand either of them.

'Once I couldn't help reproaching Zhenya, and she just retorted; "Well, didn't you conceal your relationship with my father from his wife? Didn't you lie too?" But surely that's the point – there's an enormous difference there that Zhenya can't or won't understand. First of all, I never loved M's wife, she was a total stranger to me. I never had deep feelings for her and I only spared her the truth for humane reasons. Secondly, I loved M, loved him passionately, no less than his wife did, if not more. Our feelings gave us both equal rights over him, and my justification then was the power of my love for him and the suffering he caused me.

'But in this case there's nothing – no love, no suffering, no remorse, nothing. Only an icy self-confidence and an insistence on their right to seize happiness however and wherever they find it. That's what I find so dreadful, the fact that they seem to lack any warmth or kindness or the most rudimentary sensitivity to others! And they call themselves communists!'

I couldn't help laughing at this illogical conclusion. Olga Sergeevna smiled shamefacedly, admitting that it did not really follow from her previous accusations.

When at last we said goodbye, we agreed that I should see Zhenya in a day or so.

It was two days later in the morning, that Zhenya came to see me – she worked in her district all day and in the evenings. She was a slender girl, very tall, with a lively face and a small head that reminded me of her grandmother's. She looked rather pale and had dark circles under her eyes. Her hand when I shook it was cold and damp; she had obviously not yet recovered from her operation. She had a simple direct manner, and started to speak at once.

'I expect the main thing that surprises you is that I sleep with men just because I like them, before I've had time to fall in love with them. But don't you see, you need *leisure* to fall in love – I've read enough novels to know how much time and energy it takes to fall in love and I don't have it! At the moment we've got a enormous load of work on our hands – when have we ever had any spare time these last few years? We're constantly in a rush, our heads are always full of other things.

'Of course, you have days when you're less busy and then you suddenly realize you like someone. But as for falling in love, there's no time for it! As soon as you grow fond of each other he's called to the Front or shoved off to some other town. Or else you have so much work to do that you forget all about him. That's why you cherish the moments when you *can* be together, and you both enjoy it. It doesn't commit you to anything, the only thing I'm always afraid of is catching venereal disease. But if you look someone straight in the eye and ask him whether he's got it or not, he'll never lie. There was a man who liked me very much, I think he even loved me, and when I asked him it was terribly hard for him to admit it and I could see how upset he was. But in the end we didn't sleep together. He knew I'd never have forgiven him if we had.'

Zhenya had lovely wide-open eyes, and she gave an impression of utter directness and honesty.

'But tell me, comrade Zhenya,' I said. 'If you can tell me that, how is it you didn't tell your mother everything immediately? Why did you conceal your relationship with Andrei from her all those months?'

'Well, I didn't think it concerned her. If I'd fallen in love with Andrei and he loved me, then of course I would have told her about it, and I would probably have gone out of her life. I'd hate to do anything to make her unhappy. But it wasn't as if there was anything that could have robbed her of Andrei's affections. Why doesn't she understand that! If it hadn't been me it would have been somebody else. She can't tie Andrei to her apron or prevent him getting involved with other women, can she? I can't understand her!

'She's not upset by the fact that I'm friends with Andrei, that he talks to me more than to her, that he's closer to me emotionally. But as far as she's concerned, the fact that I slept with him means I'm taking him away from her. Mother has no time to sleep with him – it's true, she hasn't time! Anyway, Andrei is nearer my age than Mother's, we share the same tastes, the whole thing's so natural . . .'

'But maybe without really being aware of it you actually have fallen in love with Andrei?' I interrupted her.

Zhenya shook her head. 'I don't know what you mean by love, but my feelings for him aren't anything like what I understand love to be. If you love a person, then you want to be together all the time, you want to sacrifice everything for his sake, you think about him, you worry about him. But if you suggested I set up permanently with Andrei, I'd say thanks a lot, but no. Oh, he's a pleasant person, and it's nice to be with him because he's so frail and so cheerful about it, as Mother probably told you. But I get bored if I have to spend too much time with him, and then I prefer Abrasha. Not that I love him either, I never did, although Abrasha did have some sort of hold over me. I used to be at his beck and call and there was nothing I could do about it!'

Zhenya frowned and thought a bit. Then she brightened again. 'The thing that upsets Mother so much is that I don't love any of them and she sees it as "immoral" and abnormal for someone of my age to be sleeping with men I don't love. But I think Mother is wrong, and that things are much simpler and better this way. I remember how when I was a child, Mother was always rushing between Konstantin and my father, eating her heart out and tormenting herself. Everyone suffered, Konstantin and my grandmother too. Why, even now I can hear my grandmother's voice ordering my mother to decide. "Stop being a coward," she used to say, "You must make your choice and come to a decision."

'But Mother was unable to decide. She loved both of them and they both loved her. They were all unhappy and made one another so wretched that they eventually started hating each other, and finally parted as enemies.

'As for me, I don't part with anyone as an enemy – when I stop liking them it's over, and that's all there is to it. Whenever someone starts being jealous I always remember how wretched Mother was and how jealous Konstantin and my father were of each other, and I tell myself that I wouldn't go through that for anything. I don't belong to anybody, they'll just have to accept that!'

'But do you really mean to say you've never loved anyone, and don't love anyone now?' I asked her. 'Quite apart from anything else, I doubt whether your definition of love is terribly plausible. It sounds as if you've got it out of books!'

'What makes you think I don't love anyone?' said Zhenya in honest amazement. 'What I said was that I didn't feel love for the men I slept with. I certainly didn't say I didn't love anyone . . .'

'Would you mind if I asked who you do love, then?' I said.

'Who do I love? Why, my mother, more than anyone else in the whole world. There's nobody like Mother – in some ways she's more important to me than Lenin! She's completely special, and I couldn't exist without her. Her happiness means more to me than anything else . . .'

'And yet you've put paid to your mother's happiness and almost broken her heart. How do you reconcile that with what you've just said?'

'Look,' replied Zhenya thoughtfully, 'if I'd thought for a moment that Mother would take it this way and it would make her so miserable, I expect – no, I'm *sure* – I would never have done it. But I really imagined she was above that sort of thing, and that she saw things the same way as Andrei and I did and wouldn't pay any attention to it. Now I realize how wrong I was, I feel terribly sad, much sadder than she realizes . . .'

For the first time during our conversation the tears welled up in Zhenya's eyes. Embarrassed, she wiped them away with the tips of her fingers, trying not to let me see them.

'I would give my life for Mother, and those aren't empty

words, that's how I feel about her. She can tell you how much I suffered when we thought she had typhus. But do you know what I find so painful now? I'm very, very sad for Mother, and furious with myself for being so foolish and for being unable to guess that the whole thing would affect her like this. I can't think of anything now that I wouldn't give for it not to have happened. But despite all this, deep down I still feel Mother is wrong and Andrei and I are right. There must be some other interpretation which will make it clear and simple and stop everyone being unhappy. Then we'll all be able to continue as friends and no one will despise anyone.

'You see, however deeply I love Mother, I feel for the first time in my life that she is terribly wrong, and that . . . That's what's so painful for me! I'd always considered Mother to be infallible, and now that's been shaken and I've lost my faith that she's above everybody and understands everything. It's dreadfully painful – I don't want to stop loving or trusting her How could I believe in other people if I did that? You can't imagine how unhappy this has made me, and not for the reasons that my mother thinks either. It's so sad . . .'

Zhenya no longer tried to conceal the large tears that ran down her cheeks and fell onto her frayed black skirt.

We talked about how best to resolve the situation. Zhenya had already decided to move into a hostel with some of her girl friends, and would be going there in a few days' time. She was only anxious as to how her mother and Andrei would cope without her there, for the whole tedious business of seeing to the provisions rested on her.

'I'm sure Mother won't eat properly,' she said. 'If someone isn't there to take care of her and push food at her she'll go the whole day without eating. And Andrei's just as bad. I can't imagine how they're going to manage without me, they're both as helpless as children. Of course I can call on them and do everything I can, but it won't be the same. I'm busy too, you know. Everything is much simpler when you all live together.'

She sighed, and went on talking about her mother and Andrei in a sober, maternal voice, as though she was dealing with children.

When it was time to say goodbye, I said, 'I'm so glad that I shall be able to reassure your mother about everything, and tell her how much you love her. What upset her particularly was the idea that you were incapable of strong, healthy emotions, and that you were too rational about things.'

Zhenya smiled. 'Well, she can rest easy about that. I'm sure I'll get myself into some stupid scrape again because of men! I'm not her daughter and my grandmother's grand-daughter for nothing. Anyway, there are people I love now, I love very much, other people besides Mother. There's Lenin, for instance – don't smile, I mean it! I love him far more than all the men I like and have slept with. I'm always beside myself for days whenever I know I'm going to see him and hear him talk – I'd give my life for him!

'And there's Comrade Gerasim, do you know him? He's our district secretary. Now there's a man for you! I love him too, I truly love him and even if he's not always correct I'll always submit to him because I know his intentions are good. Do you remember when there was that scandal about him last year? I didn't sleep for nights. What a fight we put up for him! I mobilized the entire district to support him. Yes, I love Gerasim,' Zhenya concluded with conviction, as if trying to vindicate herself and her feelings.

'Well, I must be running off. We've some urgent work to finish and now I've been elected secretary of our cell' (she said this with pride), 'there's even more work. Oh, how good life would be if only Mother could understand and accept things.' She sighed again, a deep childish sigh.

'I'll get in touch with Mother. Please, do try to convince her that Andrei is all hers. I need him about as much as I need this table here! Do you think she'll understand and go on loving me? I'm terrified of losing her love – I couldn't live without Mother, without her love. It's awful that this is affecting her work too. Say what you like, I never want to fall in love like Mother did! How would you ever find time to work?'

On this note Zhenya disappeared out of the door. I remained sitting where I was, wondering who was right, whose view would be taken up by the new generation, this emerging class grappling with new ideas and feelings.

Behind the door I could hear Zhenya's youthful laugh and her cheerful voice, saying 'Well, friends, I'll see you this evening! You mustn't delay me now, I'm late as it is, we have so much work to do!'

Sisters

She came to see me, as many women do, for advice and moral support. I had already met her in passing at delegates' conferences. She had a lovely face, with melancholy, observant eyes.

'I've come to you because I've nowhere to go,' she said. 'I've been without a roof over my head for three weeks, I've no money, nothing to live on. You must find me a job, otherwise there's nothing for me but the streets!'

'But how has this happened?' I asked. 'You used to work, didn't you? Surely you had a job? Did you get the sack?'

'Yes, I used to work in a despatch office, but I was sacked over two months ago. It was because of my baby. She was ill you see, which meant I had to miss work. I managed to avoid the sack three times, but finally in August I lost my job. Two weeks later my baby died, but they wouldn't take me back.'

She hung her head, concealing tears. 'But why did they sack you?' I asked her. 'Wasn't your work up to scratch?'

'Oh no, it wasn't that, I'm a good worker. They just thought I had no reason to work since my husband makes a good living. He's working at the moment for a government trust company. He's got an important job, he's an executive.'

'So why did you say you have no money and no roof over your head? Have you separated?'

'No, we haven't officially separated. I've just left him and haven't gone back. I'm not going back either, whatever happens!'

Now she could no longer hold back her tears. 'I'm so sorry! I haven't cried once all this time, I just couldn't, but now . . . When you meet someone who's sympathetic it's more difficult not to . . . If I tell you what happened, then you'll understand.'

She had met her husband in 1917, at the height of the revolution. He was a typesetter and she was working in the despatch office of a large publishing-house. They were both supporters of the Bolsheviks. Both were committed to the same passionate faith, the same desire to overthrow the power of the exploiters and to build a new and just world. They shared a love of books and were eager to educate themselves. They were caught up in the whirlwind of revolution.

In those October days, at their posts and in the heat of battle, amid the thunder of bullets, they had opened up their hearts to each other. There had been no time to formalize their liaison, and they each continued to live their own lives, meeting irregularly in the intervals between work. But these meetings had been full of joy and happiness, for in those days they had been true friends. Within a year she was expecting a baby. They registered their marriage and started living together. Her baby didn't take her away from work for long, and she set up a crèche in the district. Work was more important than family now. Her husband grumbled occasionally, with reason too, for she did neglect the housework. But he was never at home either. When she was elected as a delegate to a conference he was very proud of her.

'I hope you won't sulk when your lunch is cold!' she said.

'Who cares about lunch! So long as it's not your love for me that grows cold! I'm proud of you – everyone will see you up there with those people!'

They both joked about it, and it seemed nothing could destroy their love for each other. They were not just man and wife but true friends, both working for the same goal with no care for themselves, concerned only with their work. The baby was a source of great happiness to them too, and was healthy and lively.

But at some point all this changed. Perhaps it was when her husband was taken on at the trust company. At first they were overjoyed, even though life was tough for them. Then suddenly the crêche closed down, and she was at her wits' end as to what to do with the baby while she was working. Her husband took pride in the fact that he could now support his family properly, and suggested she stop work. But she was reluctant to do this – she enjoyed talking to her friends at work, and she enjoyed the work too. Besides, she was far too independent to give it up; she had been earning her living since she left school, after all.

So she decided to stay at work. At first there was no problem with this; things seemed in some ways easier. They moved into a new flat with two rooms and a kitchen, and a girl came in to look after the baby. Local political work took her out of the house even more than before, and her husband was also very busy, virtually only coming home to sleep.

On one occasion he had to go away on a business trip for the company, and spent three months away with some Nepmen. The minute he returned she sensed something about him that grated on her; he seemed like a stranger to her. He didn't listen to her stories and barely looked at her. He had taken to wearing stylish clothes and even used perfume. He no longer spent any more time than he had to at home.

That was the beginning of everything. He had never before been a drinking man, not even during holidays. But in the old days of the revolution, rushed off their feet, it would never have occurred to either of them to drink. Now this changed.

The first occasion when he came home drunk she worried more for him than for herself; she thought it would damage his reputation. Next morning she remonstrated with him, but he sat drinking his tea in silence. Then without a word in reply, he left the house. She was miserable, but comforted herself with the thought that he was probably too ashamed to discuss it.

Three days later he came home drunk again. She was now very distressed. Perhaps she would have to accompany him on his evening jaunts in future. It was an unpleasant prospect. He was a sweet man, but this was disgusting! Next morning she was anxious to have a talk with him, but no sooner did she start speaking than he turned on her with a look of loathing. She felt shattered. The words froze on her lips. He saw her as his enemy!

He began increasingly to come home drunk. One day she could endure it no longer, and decided to stay at home and confront him. She waited until he was sober, and started appealing to him, saying everything she had been bottling up – that they couldn't live like this, they couldn't be friends if the only thing they shared was the same bed. She poured out her feelings about his drunkenness, she warned him, threatened him and tried to shame him. She cried . . .

He heard her out, and began trying to justify himself. She didn't understand, he said. He was obliged to keep company with Nepmen, it was expected of him, there was no other way to do business. Then, after thinking for a moment, he told her that this life wasn't to his liking either. He begged her not to distress herself, and admitted that she was right.

When it was time for him to leave for work, he came up to her, held her head and looked into her eyes, kissing her the way he always used to.

Her mind at rest, she went happily to work. But before the week was out he again came home drunk. On this occasion when she tried to protest, he banged the table saying, 'It's none of your business! Everyone lives like this! If you don't like it, nobody's keeping you here!'

So saying he left the house, and all that day she felt as if a stone lay on her heart. Had he really stopped loving her? Should she leave him? That evening, however, he came home unexpectedly early. He was sober, apologetic and humble. They spent the whole evening talking, and once more relations between them became easier. She came to understand how difficult it was to exercise restraint in the sort of company he kept. Those people threw their money around, and it was very awkward to let them outdo him. He told her about the Nepmen, about their wives and their women, about how they did business and how difficult it was to detect the real proletarians among those sharks. You always had to be on your guard with them, he said.

She was very depressed by what he told her, more depressed than she had been in the whole course of the revolution. It was at this point that she discovered she was to be made redundant. Her anxieties were now very serious. But when she told her husband he was unperturbed; saying it might even be for the best. She could spend more time at home and attend properly to the housework. 'The flat looks like nothing on earth,' he said. 'We couldn't entertain respectable guests here.'

Amazed by his attitude, she began to protest, but he merely said, 'It's your affair, I'm not standing in your way. You can work if you want to.' And out he went.

She was very disturbed that her husband had so misunderstood her and had apparently taken offence, but she nevertheless decided to stand up for herself. She went to see her comrades at work and argued with them that they should give her her job back. They were finally persuaded to keep her on for the time being. But as soon as she'd settled that problem, her daughter fell ill.

'One night I was sitting with my sick baby feeling dreadfully lonely when the doorbell rang,' she said. 'I went to open it, assuming it would be my husband, glad that he was back and that I'd be able to share my unhappiness with him – at least if he was sober! But when I opened the door, I couldn't believe my eyes. Who was this creature with him? A young woman with rouge on her cheeks, evidently rather drunk.

' "Now be a nice wife and let me in," he said. "I've brought a girlfriend round. Don't take offence. I'm no worse than anyone else! We're going to have some fun and you're not to interfere!" '

'I realized how drunk he was – he could barely stand upright – but my knees were trembling. I let them into the dining-room, where my husband usually spent the night on the sofa, and I went straight back to my daughter.

'I locked myself in and sat there, stunned with misery. I didn't really feel angry with him – what can you expect from someone who's so drunk? – I just felt terribly hurt. What was more, I could hear everything that was going on in the next room. If I hadn't had to attend to my baby I would have blocked my ears to it. Fortunately they soon quietened down – they were drunk enough as it was. In the early hours of the morning I heard my husband take the woman to the door, then he went back to sleep. As for me, I didn't go to bed at all, just sat there thinking.

'That evening my husband once again came home earlier than usual. We hadn't seen each other all day, and I greeted him coldly, and avoided looking at him. He began to sort through his papers. Neither of us said a word, but I saw him looking at me. Let him, I thought. Most likely he'll pretend to be sorry and ask me to forgive him, so he can go on doing the same thing. I'm not taking any more, I thought, I'm going to leave him!

'How my heart was aching! I had once loved him, and there was no point pretending that I didn't love him still. But now it was all over. I felt as though he had died – or worse. At least my feelings for him would have survived if he had died . . .

'When he saw me putting on my coat and getting ready to leave, he exploded with rage. He grabbed my arm with such force that he bruised it, and tore off my coat, hurling it to the floor.

' "Why have you suddenly taken it into your head to throw a fit of hysterics? Where do you think you're going? What do you want of me? You'll never find another husband like me! I feed you, dress you, you want for nothing – don't you dare criticize me! I have to live this way if I'm to do business!" '

Love of Worker Bees

'He talked on and on. There was no stopping him; it was as if the dam had burst and he wouldn't let me get in a word edgewise. At one moment he would be shouting, venting his rage on me, then on himself; the next he would be justifying himself, arguing as though his life depended on it. I saw before me a man in torment, and I became so wretched for him that I forgot how unhappy I was. I tried to soothe him and reassure him that things weren't so bad. I told him the Nepmen were to blame, not him . . .

'That evening, we made up again, but I still felt very bitter when he said I shouldn't be angry with him. How could I have made demands on him when he was so drunk, he asked? I begged him not to drink any more. "It's not your bringing home a prostitute that I mind, it's the way you got yourself into such a horrible state," I said. He promised to behave more carefully and to avoid his old companions, but I still felt resentful. It's true you shouldn't make demands of someone who's drunk, and maybe he really didn't remember anything that happened, but from that day something nagged at my heart.

'I felt tormented by the thought that if he loved me as he had done in the days of the revolution, he would never have gone looking for other women. I remembered how in those days one of my friends had pursued him – she was prettier than me, but he never so much as glanced at her! Why couldn't he tell me openly if he no longer loved me? Once I tried to say this to him but he lost his temper, shouting that I was bothering him with my female inanities when he was up to his eyes in work, and that he didn't give a damn for women, including me! Then he left the house, leaving me more depressed than ever.

'Then the possibility of losing my job came up again. My little girl had been ill all this time, and I'd been missing work. I pleaded with them again, and eventually they agreed to defer my dismissal for the time being. I don't really know what I was hoping for, I just kept stalling. Now more than ever, I was terrified of becoming dependent on my husband. Life with him was increasingly difficult, we were becoming strangers. We lived in the same flat and yet we knew nothing about the other's life. He did occasionally look in on our little girl, and I gave up my political work to spend more time with her. During this period my husband drank less and always came home sober, but he totally ignored me. We slept apart – I would spend nights with my daughter while he slept on the sofa. Every so often he would come to me during the night, but there was no pleasure in it and it only made things more difficult afterwards, because I would feel all the old unhappiness with one more anxiety added to it. He would hold me in his arms, but he never asked me how I was feeling or anything about my life at all.

'So that was how we lived, both going our own ways, neither of us asking questions of the other. He had his anxieties, and I had mine – and it stayed that way. Then the final blow struck – our little girl died. A few days earlier I got the sack.

'I thought that now we shared the same grief my husband might start thinking a little more about me. But not a bit of it! Even this tragedy didn't bring us closer. He didn't even go to his own daughter's funeral – he had to go to an urgent meeting instead. From then on I stayed at home, unemployed and unpaid.

'Of course, there was plenty to be done in the district. But as for making a living, that was more difficult. In any case, it would have been tactless for me to demand paid work with so many unemployed people around; everybody knew that my husband was an executive and highly placed. How could I ask for a salary? It made me very unhappy to be supported by my husband, especially at that time, but there was nothing I could do about it. I just endured it, hoping and waiting for something to happen.

'How foolish we women are! You see, I realized that all my husband's old feelings for me had gone, and that I felt more bitterness and resentment than love for him. But I kept thinking

it would pass! I imagined he might love me again, and everything would be all right. And so I waited, waking up every
morning in hope, hurrying home after working in the district just
in case my husband had come home early, alone. But if he was at
home, he might just as well not have been; he didn't pay any
attention to me at all, and would busy himself with his work.
Either that, or his Nepmen friends would come round. Yet, I still
went on hoping and waiting! That is, until the last incident . . .
After that I left him for good, and I haven't been back.

'It was about midnight, and I'd just got back from a meeting. I
wanted some tea and I put on the samovar. My husband wasn't
back yet, and I wasn't really expecting him. Then I heard the
front door open – that meant he'd come back (he had his own
door key so as not to wake me when he came home). I was
attending to the samovar when I remembered that an important
parcel had come for him and was lying in my room. Leaving the
samovar, I took it in to him. When I saw him, I felt exactly as I
had on the other occasion – I just couldn't grasp who this woman
with him could be. There was my husband and beside him a tall
slender woman. They both turned to face me, and when my
husband's eyes met mine I saw immediately that he was sober.
That made it even more unbearable, so unbearable that I felt like
screaming out loud.

'The woman looked very upset. Somehow I managed to put
the parcel on the table calmly, saying "Here's an urgent parcel
for you", and then left the room. But as soon as I was on my own
I began to tremble all over. I was afraid they would hear me in
the next room, so I lay down on the bed and covered my head
with a blanket, doing my best to hear, feel and know nothing.
But thoughts kept crowding into my head, tormenting
thoughts . . .

'I could hear them whispering. They didn't sleep. The woman's
voice was louder than my husband's, and she seemed to be
berating him. Maybe she was his girlfriend, I thought, and he had

deceived her and not told her he was married. Maybe at that very moment he was renouncing me!

'I went through agony. I had been bitter, certainly, that time he'd been drunk and had brought home a prostitute, but it hadn't caused me anything like the same misery. Now I realized once and for all that he didn't love me! He didn't even love me as a sister or a friend – if he had, he would have spared me this! And what sort of women were they anyway! Street girls, prostitutes! This girl must be one. Only a woman like that would come home with him for the night! All of a sudden I was overcome with such violent rage that I was prepared to throw her out of the house with my bare hands.

'I went on torturing myself in this way until dawn, and didn't close my eyes once. It was quiet in the next room. Then suddenly I heard cautious footsteps in the corridor. It sounded as if someone was stealing out of the room, and I knew it must be her. I heard her open the kitchen door. What could she want in there? I waited and listened. Everything was quiet, so I sprang up and went into the kitchen. There she was, sitting on a stool near the window, her head bent, crying bitterly. Her beautiful long hair covered her like a shroud. She looked up at me with such grief in her eyes that I became afraid. I went to her, and she got up to speak to me.

' "I'm so sorry I came to your house," she said. "I never knew he wasn't alone. Oh, this is so hard for me . . ."

'I didn't understand. She couldn't be a prostitute, I thought, she must be his girlfriend. I don't know what made me speak, but I blurted out "Do you love him?"

'She gazed at me in amazement. "We met for the first time yesterday. He promised to pay well. I don't care who it is now, so long as they pay . . ."

'I don't remember how we got started, but soon she was telling me all about herself. Three months earlier she had been made redundant; she had sold everything, done without food and a

248

roof over her head for a while. She had been very distressed because she could no longer send money to her old mother, who had written to tell her she was dying of hunger. Two weeks ago she had gone on the streets, where she had immediately struck lucky. She had made a good friend, and now she had clothes and food, and could send her mother money too.

'As she talked, she was wringing her hands. "I've got a certificate, you know, I had a good education. I'm still very young, – I'm only nineteen. I don't want to end up on the garbage-heap like this!" '

'You may not believe this, but as I listened I was overwhelmed with feelings of pity for her. Then it suddenly dawned on me that if I hadn't had a husband, I would have been in the same position as her, with no job and nowhere to live! The previous night, lying on my bed, I had been in such agony, I was seething with rage about her. Now my rage turned against my husband. How dare he exploit this woman's desperation! And him a conscientious, highly placed worker! Instead of trying to help an unemployed friend, he had bought her body for his own pleasure! This struck me as so vile that I immediately realized I couldn't go on living with such a man.

'She talked to me a great deal more, and then together we lit the stove and made coffee. My husband was still asleep. She hurriedly got ready to leave.

' "Did he pay you?" I asked her.

'She blushed, insisting that she wouldn't dream of accepting any money after everything we had said to each other. She couldn't do it. I realized she was anxious to leave before my husband woke, and I didn't try to stop her.

'It may seem strange to you, but I was sad when she had to go. She was such a young creature, so unhappy and alone. I got dressed and accompanied her out. We walked together for a while, and then we sat down in a square and began talking again. I told her my problems. I still had my redundancy pay which I'd saved, and which I begged her to accept. For a long time she refused to take it, and only accepted on condition that I promised to come to her if ever I was in need. And that was how we parted, as sisters.

'My old feelings for my husband had finally died. There was no resentment, no pain now. It was as though I'd buried him. When I got home he tried to make excuses for what had happened. I didn't contradict him. I didn't cry, I didn't reproach him. Next day I moved in with a friend. I've been looking for work for three weeks now, but I don't expect anything to turn up.

'A few days ago I realized that it was becoming inconvenient for my friend to have me staying there, so I went to see the girl my husband had brought home. It turned out that she had left the previous day to go into hospital, and so I began roaming around, without work, money or anywhere to sleep. It seems as though I might well suffer the same fate as her . . .'

In my companion's eyes I saw so many questions and doubts – doubts about life itself. They expressed the horror, the misery and the anguish of women without work and without a home, facing the cruel enemy of unemployment. It was the expression of a woman on her own, challenging an outmoded way of life . . . After she had left, the look haunted me. It demanded an answer from us, it demanded action, work, struggle . . .

A Great Love

A Great Love

1

It all happened far away and long ago in the distant past, long before the world had experienced the bloody horrors of the First World War or the mighty upheavals of the Bolshevik revolution. It happened in the years of the savage Tsarist reaction which followed the revolution of 1905, and the story concerns a group of revolutionaries living in exile in France. Since then a new world has dawned in Russia, but we may see elements of the story repeating themselves in our lives, and perhaps by learning something about the characters here we may learn something about ourselves too . . .

It was seven months since she had seen him. Seven months ago they had parted, and both had decided the parting would be for ever.

'It's all over now,' they'd agreed, 'this is the end.' And he had buried his head on her shoulder, closed his eyes and confessed to her how unbearable it was and how defeated he felt. His face had seemed so touchingly childlike, so thin, and so infinitely precious.

'You see, the moment the doctor diagnosed her illness as a heart condition' (he was talking about his wife), 'I felt like a criminal, a butcher. I knew I couldn't go on doing this to her. Her life's been hard enough as it is – I couldn't bear to think I was adding to her troubles. I suppose I feel I must do all I can to see she stays reasonably healthy – can you understand that, Natasha dear? And then I thought about the children – how could I lie to them? Why, Sasha's old enough now to understand everything; nothing escapes those clever eyes of his. I think it's important for the children to feel their father is there when they need him.'

'Do you really think it will be so easy to forget the past and all we've meant to each other?' Natasha had ventured to ask (she was, as always, considering his needs first). 'Will you be able to forget how close we've been, the way we understand every look and word, everything we've done together. How can you go back to your family? Won't you feel dreadfully lonely?'

'Yes, of course I shall, unspeakably lonely. Life will be grim and depressing and I shall be wretched,' he clasped her tighter, 'but what else can we do?'

Then restlessly, as if trying to banish these dark premonitions from his mind, he began to cover her body with kisses, embracing her with an intensity which both excited and frightened her, and left her feeling afterwards that she no longer understood him. At such a time, feeling such pain at the prospect of losing him, she longed for the comfort of his caresses and she hadn't resisted him. Yet his caresses that night had been painful, excessive, and later she felt somehow insulted by them, abused.

It was pouring with rain the next morning, the day they had to part. Her train was leaving earlier than his, and she left him lying asleep. As she collected her things and packed her bag she moved around the room mechanically, her mind a blank, all feelings frozen, locked up deep inside her. It was strange to see him still sleeping there, calm and untroubled, in the bed they had shared.

She finished her packing, put on her hat and adjusted her veil, slung her travelling bag over her shoulder and went over to sit beside him on the edge of the bed. He started up, suddenly wide awake. 'Not leaving already, are you?' Her silent response was to stroke his forehead and hair, as if he were a sick child she was trying to comfort.

'Why d'you have to rush off at this hour of the morning? There's no earthly reason why you should leave now. There's an evening train you can catch. Won't you stay with me until then?' But as Natasha knew all too well that he had been spoilt by the love and rivalry of two women, and now he thought he could always get his way. At any other time this spontaneous habit he had of changing plans, this desire to be with her a little longer – if only for one more hour – would have filled her with joy. But on that cold wet morning of their final parting she was amazed he could be so capricious and demanding.

'You know quite well why I'm hurrying. If I leave this evening I shall miss the opening session of our party congress.'

'Oh, come now! It won't be a tragedy if you're a little late! They'll manage very nicely without you, you know.' Moving closer to her he started to nibble her ear and then, with mounting passion, to kiss her neck. But she didn't respond. His words had stung her and she thought of all the other occasions when he had referred so disparagingly to her work for the party – *their* party; she wondered if he would ever understand that it was only her commitment to her political work that gave her the strength to endure their separation for good.

So she had left to catch the train which was to carry her away from him for ever. Gazing through the film of rain on the compartment window at the unfamiliar scenery flashing past her she tried to shake off the anxiety which had settled in her heart, throbbing dully like a toothache. The contemptuous way he'd referred to her work, that remark of his that her party comrades would 'manage very nicely without her' had over-shadowed the pain of parting from him. Why, he attached absolutely no importance to her work and all the energy she put into it! As far as he saw it her work was expendable!

It was only as dusk was falling and the compartment emptied

that she began to cry about him; for those wonderful intelligent eyes of his which she would never see again, for the childish grin which so often lit up the stern face of a man who was, after all, an *authority*, a figure of power in the revolutionary circles in which they both moved.

When parting, they had both solemnly sworn to break all contact: there were to be no letters, no attempts to meet. When Natasha said 'Never, never forget that I shall be somewhere on this earth, and that if you should ever need me . . .' she didn't have to finish; he understood her and was grateful. Nevertheless, when the moment came to leave she was unable to believe it was really happening, just as we can never believe it when someone we love is about to die.

It wasn't their first attempt to end things. But invariably on those previous occasions, before three weeks were up she would receive a telegram from him, an abject letter, some sort of message in which he'd beg her to take him back, tell her how much he loved her, missed her, longed for her. And then of course his political work suffered without her, for he knew nobody else with whom he could talk so freely and at such length about his ideas; he might want to talk about the thesis of some party document he was thinking about, or sometimes it was a particular political campaign he felt an urgent need to discuss with her. In fact on quite a few occasions after these solemn partings she would receive a letter from him out of the blue which contained not one single reference to her, but merely described whatever agonising intellectual problems he happened to be struggling with at the time. It was like the continuation of some political argument. It was only at the very end of these letters that he would make his usual appeal for another meeting; he needed her, he'd say – and of course that was true.

After this last 'final parting' of theirs, however, day followed day, week followed week, and still there was no word, no telegram from him.

Natasha had gone straight back to work after leaving him. At first she had been able to think of little but her own aching loneliness, and had struggled with feelings of uselessness and indifference to the work that had been so important to her. But she became absorbed in it again soon enough. She re-established contact with her party comrades, all of them committed to the same values, and before long she was so happy to be working with her friends that sometimes she would suddenly realise she hadn't thought about him all day. She forgot to miss him – and she didn't know whether to feel pleased or sad.

It was only after some particularly nerve-racking day at work, returning late at night to her small solitary room, that she would lock the door behind her and feel the familiar pangs of longing. At moments like these, physically exhausted to the point of collapse, she would miss him desperately again, and seizing her pen she would pour out her feelings to him: 'Dearest Senechka, I love you so much still! Why did you abandon me? I'm lonely and miserable and afraid without you – don't you know that? Why did you go away when you could have stayed with me? We could have been just friends – you could still have cared more for her than you cared for me, given her everything, your tenderness and your caresses, but couldn't you have kept just a little warmth in your heart for me . . . ?'

Natasha never sent these letters, but it gave her some relief to pour out her feelings to him once in a while. She had to let off steam sometimes. While she was writing them, she would manage to convince herself it was external factors that prevented him from being with her: if they were in the same town, if they hadn't parted for ever, she would tell herself, of course he would give her the warmth, understanding and sympathy she needed from him. At these moments Natasha would forget the reality of their relationship, the number of times when even with him beside her she had felt alone and unloved. She would forget too what she knew in less troubled times to be true: that she must take responsibility for her own life, that she must stand alone and be strong.

She would forget the strain she so often felt when she was with him, a strain so exhausting that she would often breathe a secret sigh of relief when he had gone and she could return to her own thoughts and moods. All these things Natasha would forget, and she would feel only how sad and isolated her life was without him.

'I feel like a widow,' she had written once. 'I wander around the places we used to visit when we were together – all those places where we used to work, where we felt so much together. Do you remember those days, when we seemed like one person, with one heart, one mind? Do you remember how strangely close we felt the moment we met, and how that closeness grew gradually into passion? Now I often regret that it did, because it spelt the end of our friendship. How happy we were before – our friendship had wings! If we'd stayed friends you'd never have left me, Senya . . .'

But then there would be times when she could hardly believe there had ever been any intimacy between them, moments of overwhelming misery when an endless series of buried insults would surface and haunt her. At such times their past happiness seemed a fraud. She tormented herself with questions she couldn't answer: 'Did he ever love me? If so, does love mean the same thing to him as it does to me? If he did love me, how could he have rejected me like that? Couldn't he see how much he was hurting me? I don't think there ever was any *real* understanding between us – that closeness of ours was just something I dreamed up. I wanted it to be true so I thought I could make it true. To think of the energy and time I wasted on something completely unreal!'

And she would grow beside herself with rage, recalling bitterly how her work for the party had suffered in the years she had been with him. She thought of all the times she had delegated important matters to other people so as to be free for him, all the times she missed crucial meetings, all the times she was late. It was hardly surprising that her former reputation as an efficient party worker had suffered over the years. More than once her comrades had occasion to rebuke her for her slipshod work. She blamed him retrospectively for the accumulated bitterness and rage she felt at such times.

2

In the small room in which she lived alone, among her piles of books and papers, was his photograph. It was an old one, which he'd given her soon after they first met at a literary dinner-party. Although she had always been one of his supporters and had written a series of pamphlets to popularise his theories, they had hitherto known each other only by name.

She had arrived at the party with the man she was close to at the time. 'Guess who's here today,' he said shortly after they got there. 'It's your beloved Semyon Semyonovich.'

Her face lit up. 'Really? Oh do point him out to me, please! I'd so like to meet him!' She was childlike in her excitement.

'What's all the fuss? I fear you'll be sadly disappointed when you do see him; he's not much to look at, I shouldn't like to think what he's like as a man.' Her friend was clearly nettled and was trying to cool her enthusiasm. Natasha shrugged her shoulders in exasperation.

'Oh how stupid you are, talking about him like that!'

'Well, if you're really so keen to meet him, I'll introduce you.' And he went off, leaving her behind. She was smiling, and trembling a little too, for she was pleased and also suddenly nervous of seeing in the flesh someone she'd thought so much about, and perhaps even getting to know him. She saw how he winced when her friend dragged him off to meet her, and the funny eccentric way he behaved endeared him to her at once;

Semyon Semyonovich, of all people, was shy! After that she always thought of him as a charmer, a clumsy, comical child of a man who for some reason she found irresistibly touching. She loved to remember that time when they first met, and the two weeks that spring when their friendship began and quickly deepened.

The air they breathed was sweet, charged with the promise of new and unexplored joys – oh, in those days she hadn't known the meaning of loneliness! She overflowed with a new vitality, discovered in herself new strengths, overcame every obstacle in her life and work – in short she came to believe in herself. Of course there was the odd anxious moment too, and times when she was unhappy and frustrated, but the two of them were so exuberant when they were together that she felt protected against life's difficulties. Seeing him enhanced everything she did, and made her feel irrepressibly happy in those two wonderful weeks. It was as if nothing could daunt her. Her whole life lay before her and she saw herself boldly striding up a steep mountain path which beckoned her to go up, higher and higher.

'How *can* you live such a solitary life?' her friends (most of them women) asked in amazement. (This was after, uncharacteristically abruptly, she had broken off all contact with the other man.) 'Don't you feel the need for a family life – at least some person you're close to, somebody to live with and keep you company?'

She always laughed at this. No, she would say, she didn't feel at all sad to be living alone – far from it: she was happy to be single again. Her wings were no longer tied, and she was free. She had her work, she had a full life, she needed nothing more. Yes, she assured these friends, she had an extraordinary life, a wonderful life. She was surrounded by close friends and people she loved – she couldn't imagine what they meant when they talked of her 'living alone'.

What her friends didn't realise was that when she talked of the

people she loved she was thinking of him. And since his family –
his wife Anyuta and his children – were an inseparable part of
him, she loved them too. She wasn't too bothered by Anyuta's
irritatingly conventional 'femininity', or her blank incomp-
rehension of Natasha's life as a single woman. For even though
Anyuta's petty bourgeois pronouncements occasionally grated
on Natasha's ears, she was for all her faults a kind and generous
woman who always greeted Natasha warmly. She adored her
husband too, worshipped the ground he walked on – that too she
had in common with Natasha. And of course he was so brilliant,
so good, so loving – how could anyone fail to love him?

Anyuta often teased Natasha when they first met, and she
loved to show off what a wonderful family life they had. 'Really
my dear, I can't help feeling sorry for you,' she'd say, 'all alone,
with no husband and nobody to support you through life. Of
course, not every woman is lucky enough to find a husband like
my Senya, I'll grant you, and of course marriage isn't all roses
and smiles. But still, when you've lived with someone for twelve
years – and I'll tell you something, my Senya and I have been
together all that time and can you imagine, we still behave as
though we're on our honeymoon! – then I feel sorry for you
unmarried women. I think it must be wretched to be on your own
all the time, with nobody to care for you and nobody to look
after. Just think dear, Senya is still in love with me! You don't
believe me? Well listen to this: I know people don't usually
mention such things, but I know what a liberated soul you are
. . .' And some intimate detail of Semyon Semyonovich's marital
behaviour would follow, to prove to Natasha how much in love
with his wife he was.

These intimate revelations always embarrassed Natasha
acutely, and she would cut them short. She felt a sense of
revulsion and anger, not only with Anyuta but with Semyon
Semyonovich himself, and the sickening image of the 'good
husband' would obscure for a while the intelligent face of the

friend she loved. She would wait a while and try to forget Anyuta's anecdotes before visiting their house again; sometimes it seemed to her that these things were said only to exasperate her – sometimes she even imagined Anyuta must be making them up.

But these irritations were never more serious than pinpricks on the surface of her life, and could always be soothed away by the joy of their developing intimacy. This intimacy, born of shared political work, opened up a new world to them; it illuminated the hours Natasha spent alone in her little room, it transformed her life.

Then passion came, sweeping them off their feet with a suddenness that took their breath away. Natasha lost her head completely and fell deeply in love.

Before this, she had always been considered 'experienced' in affairs of the heart, and liked to believe that time had taught her good sense. Laughingly she would assure herself that she would never again get passionately involved with someone – she had suffered enough. She no longer wanted the crises, the traumas, the struggles, the sufferings and misunderstandings of love, she wanted friendship and understanding instead. She wanted the responsibility and commitment of political work, she wanted to collaborate with people she trusted on something important. That, at any rate, was what Natasha *thought* she wanted – until life decided otherwise for her.

3

They had arranged to travel together to a political meeting in another town, and got as far as buying two tickets for a crowded third-class compartment a few days before, when Anyuta suddenly started pleading with him not to leave her. She produced one reason after another why he should stay, and Semyon Semyonovich was beginning to waver. The day before they were due to leave, Natasha rushed round to their house to find out whether or not he would be going, and found him still undecided.

'I know I should go,' he said; 'If I don't, they'll certainly find some way to exploit the situation and knock our resolution on the head.' ('They' were the opposing faction.) 'But I don't see how I possibly can. Vityusha's running a high fever, Anyuta's rushed off her feet – in all conscience I can't leave her here to cope on her own. I know, why don't you pop in here tomorrow morning before the train leaves – it's on your way to the station – and then we'll see what can be done?'

The next day Natasha called round (his house wasn't in fact on her way to the station) to be met by a sour look from Anyuta and a guilty glance from a harassed Semyon Semyonovich. He couldn't possibly go, he said; but he urged Natasha that it was of the utmost importance that she attend the meeting. 'I know if I don't go there'll be hell to pay. If they defeat our resolution – and they almost certainly will – I'll never forgive myself. But Vityusha has a fever and poor Anyuta's at her wits' end. It's absolutely maddening, and I don't see why I should be made to miss important meetings like this . . .'

'Well, it's no tragedy, we'll try to manage without you and put up a fight – we'll defend that resolution of ours, you'll see!' Natasha consoled him, little suspecting the true cause of his agitation.

So she left on her own for the station. Secretly she couldn't help feeling relieved, for now she could consider calmly all the points contained in their resolution, and draw up a series of arguments in its defence. It was a bitterly cold day, and to keep herself warm she paced up and down the frosty platform, her hands deep in her muff, her head full of ideas. She was in a cheerful mood, elated by the prospect of fighting to win and then returning to him with the good news.

'Natalya Alexandrovna, Natalya Alexandrovna!' She swung

263

round. 'It's me: here I am – I made it!' Semyon Semyonovich stood there, breathless and triumphant. 'Well, I made my escape – what a time I had of it! It's a pity about Anyuta of course, but . . .' Then the train drew in and interrupted him, and with a familiarity and a confidence in his rights that seemed to her entirely natural, he took her arm. Their compartment was crowded and they had to sit very close. Time and again their eyes met, and there was something so searching, so unambiguous, about the way he gazed at her from behind his gold-rimmed spectacles, that Natasha grew agitated. When his hand brushed against hers as though by accident, she felt it tremble, and soon he had communicated his agitation to her. Talking became impossible. They spoke only with their eyes, now seeking, now avoiding each other. She felt the current that passed between them and through her, the sweet, tormenting current of desire. The train drew in to a large station.

They got off for a breath of air: the cold air hit them, fresh and aromatic. The grimy city was far away. They both sighed with relief, as though awakening from some weird and beautiful dream, and gulping down great lungfuls of air, they began to chatter and laugh again. 'Oh how beautiful it is here! Look, hoar-frost – Ah, what wonderful air . . . !' They felt so easy together now, their friendship seemed so good, so uncomplicated.

Neither of them felt like returning to their compartment, but as the train was about to move off they reluctantly got in again – and once again Cupid took aim. The train was even stuffier than before, and they were sitting very close together when Semyon Semyonovich reached for Natasha's hand. This time she did not take it away.

Inarticulately, incoherently, his voice breaking with emotion, he started to tell her about Anyuta and how jealous and unhappy she was. It was quite clear to her that by talking about Anyuta he was actually trying to talk about his love for Natasha. For Anyuta, he said, he had never felt anything but pity and compassion. He had married her because she needed him so much, and now, having lived with her for twelve years, he felt totally estranged from her. He was more and more locked up in his own thoughts and had become increasingly solitary. That was before he met Natasha – when she came into his life she had changed everything. Now he had forgotten what loneliness was. Every day was bright and happy now, for Natasha had unlocked his heart. He needed her. His love for her was like nothing he had ever experienced before, surpassing all limits of joy and pain. He had been in love with her for a long, long time, without ever daring to hope that she might also love him. Falling in love with her had left him as dizzy and helpless as a boy – it was like calf love! He was terribly jealous too, jealous of the man she had been close to before meeting him, the man who had introduced them at the party; he had been overjoyed when they ended their relationship. He had loved her for years, he said, loved her hopelessly, tenderly . . .

Natasha was stunned. She felt delighted, terrified and extremely confused. Was this her gentle intellectual friend, whose face was now transformed by passion? No, this was a new Semyon Semyonovich whom she did not know, this man leaning towards her, gazing at her and telling her that he couldn't live without her. This wasn't the dear Semyon Semyonovich she knew, the man with the childish grin. And what about his family, what about Anyuta and the children? He could never leave them. For a moment a vision of future tragedy flashed across her mind.

'What can we do, Natalya Alexandrovna?' He was in torment, and she felt overwhelmed by tenderness for him.

'How can you ask?' She addressed him now in the intimate 'you' form. 'I can't think of anything I want more than to be your friend, as if you haven't already given me so much happiness!'

'Oh my darling Natasha.' And oblivious to the staring people sharing their compartment he put his arms around her and kissed her on the forehead. 'Being with you is beautiful: you make me so happy.'

She gazed back at him. Her lips were smiling but her eyes were filled with tears. 'It's only because I'm happy,' she whispered, and he clung to her even tighter, murmuring 'My dearest Natasha, my darling.'

When the train finally arrived at their destination they stepped off, drunk with joy. They were met at the station by friends who led them off to their hotel, and from there to the first session of the conference. It all went very well. They were both in the best of spirits and enjoyed their evening immensely. It wasn't until much later that night that their friends walked them back to the hotel. They took their time to say goodnight. There was more laughing and joking. Natasha loved everyone that night, – even people she usually disagreed with politically seemed wonderfully good and lovable. She felt drunk with happiness and wanted this day never to end so that she could go on laughing with her friends for ever. Moments like these never came twice. Today it was all laughter and joy. Tomorrow, well, tomorrow would bring its own problems.

She was right, of course. It was the final day of the conference, and what with all the excitement, the hard work and three nights without sleep, she was beginning to get a little careless about her secretarial duties. Who could blame her for lacking the stamina to concentrate fully, listen carefully to what was being said, and accurately report everyone's speeches (which, like most speeches at most meetings, were inordinately long). Towards the end of the session the delegates decided that the minutes should be read out. It turned out that Natasha had slipped up in recording the speech of someone from the opposing faction, and had slightly misrepresented his views. All hell broke loose from the opposition; they were convinced this was some kind of dirty trick intended to discredit them. Natasha was distraught.

And then, as if this wasn't bad enough, Senya, her beloved Senya, stood up and launched into a fierce tirade against her. The thinking behind it was clear enough: he wanted the opposition delegates to think this was some little personal 'dirty trick' of Natasha's, rather than something engineered by their faction as a whole. But she could hardly believe her ears when he suggested that she wasn't really suited to the job.

The meeting ended. A large crowd of people walked back to the hotel, shouting and arguing, but Natasha was fighting back the tears. When at last they were alone together she threw herself into his arms, and, safe at last in his embrace, she burst out sobbing. Senya would understand, she knew that; there'd be no need to explain. Of *course* he would be feeling uneasy about what he had done, betraying her like that, even if it was 'for the good of the cause.' Shouldn't he have defended her instead, he'd be thinking? She wanted to tell him she understood what he was feeling, but also that the interests of their faction outweighed all such personal feelings of the moment. Just as long as he made *some* little gesture to show he was sorry for insulting her pride. She couldn't bear her comrades to think that a minor mistake caused only by tiredness was some awful plot she'd cooked up single-handed.

'You understand what I'm feeling, don't you, Senya?'

'Of course I do, my poor little love, and I'm sorry. I know how painful it is for you to leave me – but what's to be done?'

She stopped crying and stared at him, scarcely able to believe her ears.

'Don't you think it's hard for me too?' he continued, gently stroking her head. 'Do you think I feel it any less painfully than you do? But come now dear, it's not as if we're saying goodbye for ever. You must come and see me when we get back – you will, won't you, or Anyuta might suspect something . . . Ah, please don't cry any more my darling. All day I've longed to be alone with you like this. Won't you kiss me, Natasha . . . ?'

Was this the right moment to tell him the reason for her tears? How could she explain now, when he had so totally failed to understand? He saw she was unhappy, yet he could only imagine it was because they were about to part. Two large tears coursed down her cheeks and he kissed them away. 'Don't cry now, poor darling. We *will* see each other again, yes we will, many, many times . . .'

They travelled home in the train with their friends, and when they arrived they parted formally at the station. They might have been two strangers.

4

Looking back now, she understood better why she had cried at the moment of their first parting. At first he had almost persuaded her that it was the sorrow of their separation, but now she knew better – she knew that the cause of her tears was the first affront to her soul and her pride. By now, several years later, many, many humiliations and insults had bothered her and bruised her poor spirit. And to think it was her Senechka who had done this to her! Didn't he realise that endless subtle wounds can break a person's heart? That a damaged heart becomes incapable of love? That her love for him was ebbing away?

In the seven months they had been apart, Natasha had been reviewing things, trying to get a clearer perspective on their relationship, and coming gradually to accept that their happiness was poisoned. Nothing remained of the hours of happiness and the passion of their love-making, nothing except grief and bitter memories. Senya, she now realised, had failed to hear what she was telling him. She had stood before him, so vulnerable and eager to offer herself, to give herself to him body and soul – and he had neither seen nor heard her. He had merely possessed her as a woman, then left her feeling even more alone than before, arms outstretched to him. He knew nothing about her. He hadn't even *wanted* to know her!

Of course life had dealt him more than his fair share of blows, with his unbearable domestic situation, his constant financial crises and the setbacks he suffered in his extremely demanding work. His family life must be intolerable: he lived surrounded by an atmosphere of jealousy and suspicion which suffocated him and hampered his writing. Yes, it was true, his life was one long worry.

'Anyuta very nearly poisoned herself today' – it wasn't uncommon for their meetings to be prefaced by some such macabre remark. 'If I hadn't rushed in just in time she'd have been at the morphine. Oh Natasha, what's the answer to this ghastly mess? Tell me what to do . . .' Then he would bury his face in his hands and Natasha would kneel on the floor and stroke his head tenderly, as though he were a sick child she was trying to comfort. His sufferings always moved her.

At first Anyuta's suicide attempts had horrified her, but soon they became such a regular occurrence that she began almost to take them for granted. She certainly never blamed Anyuta, and these acts of frenzied desperation always aroused her deep pity. But it was always for him that she really suffered. *Why* must Anyuta take up so much of his precious time and fill his life with one petty anxiety after another? Why couldn't she see how important his party work was? Why couldn't she understand that every ounce of his strength had to be devoted to his work? Natasha understood this of course, which was why she was always so self-effacing, why she never brought her worries to him, why she never told him when she was unhappy, and why he never realised that she too suffered sometimes. All Natasha brought to him was the tenderest love and the greatest admiration for his work; all she wanted was to stand between him and the world, to relieve him of his worries, help him bear his cross.

'Ah, how strong you are,' he would sigh sometimes, 'and how

unlike Anyuta. You can build your own life and stand alone in the world – she could never survive without me.' And Natasha would smile at him, like a mother. She could never allow herself to be weak with him, she knew that, for she not only had her own problems to cope with but his as well; she had to bear the entire psychological burden for both of them. She was his support, his consolation, his ray of hope, his one and only joy – yes, she must always bring him joy, for with Anyuta it was nothing but gloom, tears and endless anxieties; with her it must be a perpetual holiday, fun and laughter all the time.

There were times when something would go wrong with this scheme of things, and then she felt revolted by the role she had chosen to play. Why in God's name did he always have to feel so wretchedly sorry for Anyuta? Could he not feel a little sorry for *her* once in a while? As if she didn't have enough struggles and worries in *her* life! Sometimes she had vast amounts of responsible and complex work to do, and she would worry herself sick. Hers wasn't an easy life – all her other friends in the party understood this and sympathised, so why couldn't Senya?

'I'm absolutely exhausted today, Senya dear,' she had said once, determined to make him listen to her and see her not merely as his lover but as a woman with a life of her own and problems to deal with. 'You know this resolution the other lot are putting through – they've been giving me hell about it these last few days, I've no idea what to do.'

'Oh I wouldn't trouble yourself over that,' he replied. 'It's all so trivial – they're trivial people anyway, aren't they? I'd rather talked about *us* instead. Lord knows, we've enough problems. Anyuta's been ill again, the doctor said she must rest, so that means we'll have to get a nanny to live in. But there's the money – you know the state of our finances. Then, oh Natasha, I see Anyuta wasting away before my eyes, and I think of everything she's given me and the children, how she never grudged us anything, and I feel like a self-centred swine who's good for nothing and no one . . .'

When life seemed such purgatory for her lover, Natasha's own problems receded into insignificance and she found it impossible to discuss them with him. There were times, although it must be said these were not frequent, when it would come home to him quite forcefully that she was always the giver in the relationship, and he was never anything but the taker.

'I know this is one long headache for you, Natasha,' he said once. 'I'm an egotistical brute, I know that, I don't give you half the love you deserve. Sooner or later you'll have had enough. You'll leave me and then I shall go to pieces. I treat you so badly. Yet you can't imagine how much I love you and how much you mean to me.'

'But I *do* know, Senechka, indeed I do. Otherwise how d'you imagine that I could tolerate the situation and go on with it?'

'I'm the best friend you ever had, Natasha my love, I want you to believe that – do you believe me? Sometimes I have the feeling I'm not getting through to you; sometimes when we're together there's a part of you which I sense is somewhere far away from me, and I wonder if we're growing apart. You often won't tell me what's on your mind and I find that terribly hurtful. You know I want us always to share everything – it's more important to me than anything else that we should be close . . .'

'Oh Senechka, that makes me very happy; so it *is* important to you – I'd thought it was just me who felt that way. Sometimes I feel I'm not the woman you need. It's a chilling thought and it terrifies me! But I don't want you to love me just as a *woman*, Senechka. Do you understand what I'm trying to say?'

'Now Natasha, don't be silly . . .'

'Yes, you're right, I have felt distant from you recently. I don't know why, and I don't want it to be like that. I want us to be able to tell each other everything.'

'Well, why don't you tell me everything?' He was watching her suspiciously; 'Do you have something you want to tell me? You've been hiding something from me, haven't you?'

'No, not really . . . well, yes, I suppose I haven't been completely open with you – and yes, I do have something on my mind which has been worrying me but I wasn't able to tell you about it.'

'And what is that?'

'You see, although . . . Anyway . . . Look, you know Anton Ivanovich? He's been visiting me a lot recently. He comes to my room and sits and sits, sometimes for hours at a time. And he looks at me in a way I don't like, you know, he *eyes* me. I hate it, but how can I tell him to get out and slam the door in his face? We have to work together! And then I suppose I feel sorry for him too, because I know how lonely he is . . .'

'Well Natasha, you baffle me sometimes – now I've heard everything! What in God's name has work to do with it? And as for pitying the fellow, I'm afraid I find that bizarre! He sits there for hours, gazing and sighing – he's obviously hopelessly besotted with you – and all you can say is "I feel sorry for him . . . !" If a man looks at you in a way you find offensive, just tell him to go and there's an end to it. If you *like* this man pursuing you though, then that's different . . .'

'Oh Senechka, don't be obtuse!' Natasha was angry, but she couldn't help laughing all the same. How could he be jealous! There was only one man in her life and she worshipped him, as he knew quite well, and the most beautiful man in the world would never entice her away from her darling, round-shouldered intellectual Semyon Semyonovich, for no one in the world could compare with him, his wonderful candour and his brilliant, beautiful mind.

Of course his jealousy was maddening, but then, as Natasha kept assuring herself, he was naive about a lot of things. Sometimes she could laugh it off, but at other times it outraged and saddened her. There'd been that time when they went to a concert together for instance, and for some reason he got it in his head to be jealous of the violinist. He sulked all the way home, and it wasn't until they talked it over at length that she finally managed to persuade him that she was a free person and could do as she liked. Then there'd been a similar scene once after she had a chat and a laugh with a tram conductor . . .

She teased him gently about it, although she had to be careful to choose the right moment. 'What's the matter with you! Do you seriously imagine I can't look at another man without falling in love with him!'

And of course he would grin, look abashed, and kiss the tips of her fingers. But Natasha knew that although she might for the moment have soothed his jealousy, he would never forget she had had lovers before him. For she was a woman with a 'past', and she would always have to answer to him for that. 'You remember you told me you'd been in love with that other fellow, you know, the one with dark eyes? How much did you love him? Did you love him a lot? More than me? Tell me, Natasha!' This was how his interrogations would start.

'But of course I did! Much, much more than you! . . . Really, Senechka dear, if I *had* loved him so much how d'you think I could have stopped seeing him so easily? You *know* my feelings for you, and yet you still refuse to accept that it's you I love, Senechka. You're a very clever man, but you know you can be very silly sometimes.'

'I know, I know, I just can't help thinking about all those other men of yours and the way they must have wooed and pursued you and said beautiful things to you – *I* could never be like that.'

'But that's what makes me love you, silly! That's why you're so precious to me, and why I find you so attractive – because you're *not* like that.'

'Oh, so you find me attractive, eh?' he would mumble de-lightedly, and Natasha would kneel on the floor and enumerate one by one all the qualities which made her love him so much.

Yet his jealousy made her feel resentful and unsure of herself: although she couldn't have said how or why, she felt constantly undermined by him. Even before they were lovers, he had always been quick to attack the men she'd been with before, passionately denouncing this one for making her unhappy, that one for mistrusting her. Then, when she fretted and blamed herself for her reckless past, he would have just the right words with which to console her. She would sob hopelessly as she recalled all she had suffered from previous lovers, and he would protect her like a true friend.

But it had been a long time since she had been able to talk so openly to him. In the days before they were lovers, she been able to confide in him as she would in a woman friend, and sometimes had even laughingly addressed him as a woman. But her 'Senka', as she called him then, was now a mere echo of the past. After seven months away from him, it seemed to Natasha that there had been two utterly different people – Semyon Semyonovich, the friend and colleague she'd so trusted in those early days, and Senya, her lover.

There was one aspect of their relationship which Natasha only began to make sense of after they had parted and she had begun to relive and analyse the past. It was with a sense of amazed outrage that she realised that not only had Senya failed to be sensitive to her feelings, he had actually never recognised her sexual needs as a woman. For all his sensitivity in other matters, his tenderness, his compassion for Anyuta, his natural childlike goodness, which people so often exploited, he could nonetheless be sexually very crude with her. No man had ever insulted her as he had insulted her – even though she realised that he probably did so unintentionally – which was why she knew she ought to forgive him.

Yet the sense of outrage she had felt during their first night together in the hotel lived on in her, refusing to be forgotten or buried. It was after their friends had left them at the hotel, and they had gone upstairs to their separate bedrooms. Alone at last, Natasha stood in the middle of her room, her heart racing with joy. He loved her! This man she'd always worshipped actually loved her! Her happiness knew no bounds. She moved about the room slowly, getting undressed and preparing for bed. Suddenly there was a knock at the door – but before she even had time to reply, Semyon Semyonovich had bounded in, locking the door behind him. Natasha stood rooted to the spot, toothbrush in hand, her mouth full of toothpaste.

'How funny you look!' he burst out laughing, 'just like a little boy!' And completely oblivious to her agitation, he seized her in his arms and kissed her. 'You smell of peppermint' he murmured.

'Please wait, let me go, I must rinse out my mouth first . . .' What could she say? She felt ridiculous but she had a mouth full of toothpaste. She struggled to get away from him, but he was already devouring her toothpaste-smeared lips, her neck and her bare shoulders, smothering her with hungry, insistent kisses – so that her principal memory of that first night they spent together was of the peppermint toothpaste grating on her teeth and the desperate urgency of his embraces. She couldn't respond fully to him for it was all too strange and awkward, too fumbling . . .

Yet afterwards, when he had fallen asleep exhausted with his head on her shoulder, she felt overwhelmed by a new kind of love for him, and tenderly, almost humbly, she had lightly brushed his high domed forehead with her lips. It was not the physical pleasure of lovemaking she experienced with him, or the wonderful lassitude which follows passion, but a new feeling of dazzling joy which quite overwhelmed her. This feeling of reverence must be something like pagan people experienced when worshipping *their* idols. But it was not reverence he wanted from her – he wanted her passion, he wanted her to love him as a man, for she was the first woman for whom he had ever felt such passionate desire.

5

Sometimes, in the long months after they said goodbye, Natasha would ask herself whether their love affair had really only brought her suffering and disappointment, whether she wasn't losing sight of the moments of joy. For these had been many; there had been breathtaking joy, surpassing anything she had previously experienced.

She remembered the first summer, spent beside a lake in the South of France. There was something almost theatrical about the lush vegetation there. The evenings were hot and sultry. He was living with his family in a house beside the lake, and she was staying with her young brother in a hotel up the mountain. At that time they were still observing the 'proprieties' ('for Anyuta's sake', he said), and Natasha would regularly visit his family.

That summer had been just like the time before their affair began, when it had still been a pleasure to visit his house and feel welcome as a guest. And there, in the rich and fertile country-side, far removed from her work and her commitments at home, Natasha found it perfectly easy to talk to Anyuta.

That summer Natasha and Senya relived the spring-time of their love-affair. They saw a great deal of each other, but invariably in the company of others, which lent a special secret enchantment to their meetings. It intensified their desire for each other and filled each new day with the sweet torment of anticipation. When they met they would seize moments when nobody was looking to touch hands. Their perpetual closeness aroused desires impossible to fulfil, so instead there were linger-ing glances more eloquent than words, half-smiles, remarks they alone understood. And then they talked long into the night about politics and their work – and how good *that* was too. They even had political arguments, just like two party comrades.

She would never forget the magical nights on the balcony of his house, gazing out at the lights of the distant village and the moon shining on the lake. They were oblivious to Anyuta or anyone else coming out on to the balcony; nothing mattered to them now. Everyone else existed outside this private world of theirs. They were aware only of each other and the spell of the burning, semi-tropical summer nights. Settling back in her wicker chair and closing her eyes, she felt an overwhelming sense of his closeness to her. She had only to stretch out her hand – but no, she dared not. The more she desired to touch him, the more agitated she would become, and the more she could sense that he too longed to touch her and was leaning towards her. She would open her eyes and see him secretly smiling at her in the moonlight. And then she would laugh, with a happiness too great for words. They would sit up until midnight, talking, arguing, falling silent, talking again – and the joy of those moments, the anticipation of new joys to come, would make her tremble.

At last, stretching, she would stand up. 'Time for me to go,' she would say, sighing with sadness and extreme happiness. Leaving him, she would step inside to say goodnight to everyone. 'We'll see you home!' they'd clamour, and a crowd of people would set off with her to her hotel, up the mountain path which was milky-white in the moonlight. He would be there, walking beside her. Every so often she would brush against his shoulder and these fleeting contacts were as exquisite to her as any caress. When they reached her hotel at last, they would all stand around the wicket-gate saying goodnight to each other, and again he would press her hand with a special intensity; again those secret eloquent smiles.

She remembered the strains of the popular song 'Hayawatha' and the sounds of laughter which greeted her from the hotel where the young people danced every night. Through the branches of the trees in the garden she could see the wide open french-windows and the dancers inside, their young faces radiant with excitement, flashing past in their bright clothes to the urgent beat of 'Hayawatha'. She saw the sweet childish face of her young brother in his best collar and tie, looking wildly happy. He was in love with a snub-nosed young thing with knowing eyes and hair plaited and tied up in an elaborate bow. She was extremely pretty and she knew it – she knew too that half the boys in the room were after her, but Natasha's brother was too happy to care, for he was in love.

Natasha stood for a long time in the garden below the window, looking but not wanting to go in, for her heart was too full and she wanted to be alone. The night was so magical that she longed for wings to fly, up to the stars which were calling to her. Or down the mountain path to this house, to fling herself into his arms . . . foolish thoughts! Her desires were as inconsequential as scraps of paper, distracting her and beguiling her so she could make sense of nothing. She inhaled deeply, drawing in the dense night smell of the tropical flowers. The young couples whirled past the brightly lit windows of the hotel, now merging, now separating, and the familiar exultant chorus of 'Hayawatha' sounded again and again in her ears.

A brief, vivid summer, distant as a dream.

Was that the last time – perhaps even the only time – they had been really happy together? Surely not – why, they'd often been breathtakingly happy together! Yet she could only frown as she tried to recall the good things, and her frown deepened as she remembered the hours of worry and all the painful things she had gone through with him. Then she brightened. Yes, there had been a time when it was good!

It was the following spring. She had rented a room (it had once been a child's nursery) in a large mansion out of town, and there, screened from the world by a dense wall of fragrant acacias, she had written the last chapters of her most ambitious book, writing feverishly, without a break, to the point of forgetting everything and everyone else. Now she no longer whiled away the hours waiting for his sudden flying visits, for she was completely carried away by her work, and she was working fast too. When a telegram did come from him she was just off to a meeting with a box of books under her arm, and when he arrived her cheeks were burning and she had that distracted look common to writers.

Then she had been happy! Was it love, or was it the joy of writing? She couldn't say. At the time it was all so exciting that such questions didn't occur to her. She existed in every fibre of her being, living from moment to moment with the pure uncorrupted happiness of childhood. She remembered vividly those warm spring nights when she would get out of bed and fling open the windows, and the scent of the acacias wafted into the bedroom and the moonlight filtered through the foliage on to the table which was still laid with the remains of their supper. It seemed wrong that sleep should intervene and cut short this extraordinary happiness . . .

One hot night, shortly before he was due to return, remained particularly clearly in her memory. On that night, half drunk with the sweet scent of the acacias, Natasha felt she had reached the pinnacle of human aspiration; this happiness was what gave life its meaning. Leaning out of the window, she reached out for a feathery branch of acacia, picked it and buried her nose in it. 'How beautiful, how beautiful!' she murmured, laughing and stretching. She longed to wake Senya up, to tell him how much she loved him and how happy she was. Suddenly he woke with a start.

'Natasha, where are you?'

'Here, Senechka darling. It's such a wonderful night, look at these flowers, smell them!' She leaned over him.

'Ah, but that's the smell of you – sweet and sensual'. His lips touched her fingers and Natasha felt her heart tremble and soar.

No, her love had brought her much more than unremitting misery – how could she have forgotten that exquisite joy, so fragile, in a world of its own? How could she bear the thought of never seeing him again?

279

6

Work had been building up over the past weeks to the point where it now required all of Natasha's time and imagination to cope with it. The party was at a turning-point and much was at stake. As always at these times of crisis, party members worked together especially closely; meetings were charged with new energy and a new spirit of determination, which soon infused Natasha. Her old *joie de vivre* gradually returned, and she began to enjoy life once more. She felt she was a necessary part of something larger than herself, something she helped to keep alive, and, more important, her friends and colleagues began to treat her with new warmth, and she knew she was appreciated. Slowly her reserve melted, and her laughter would often be heard in the dingy little flat they used for secret party meetings.

'Our Natasha Alexandrovna *is* cheerful nowadays,' her friends observed, grinning. 'She must have fallen in love, I suppose,' Vanya, her closest friend, said briskly, not raising his head from her paperwork. 'Well, *are* you in love, Natalya Alexandrovna?'

'Me? In love? Who would *I* be in love with? Surely not you, Vanechka! After all, you're the only man I ever see around here . . .'

'Aha! Shakespeare said it all about women! No Natasha my friend, you can't fool me, I'm not as blind as you think; I know everything that's going on around here!' Tossing back his long untidy hair, Vanechka glared mockingly at her from behind his glasses. He always made Natasha laugh and she loved to tease him, for she had a specially soft spot for him; she fancied she saw in Vanechka, with his gold-rimmed glasses and his shambling walk, something of Semyon Semyonovich.

It was late and she was exhausted when she finally hurried back home one night. Her back ached, her cheeks burned, her throat was parched, but her mind was at peace, for they had concluded the first and most difficult part of their work, and she knew things would be easier from now on. She dragged herself up the stairs to her room. All she wanted at that moment was to put on her dressing-gown, and sit down with a cup of hot tea and the latest issue of a magazine which had published a much-discussed article by one of the leading party theoreticians. It was at times like these, after a long day at work, when she felt thankful to be free, a single woman with the 'moral right', as she put it, to spend her evenings exactly as she liked. If Senya was here she would spend the evening rushing around for him, possibly preparing something for him to eat, possibly arriving home only to dash off immediately to another meeting with him at the other end of town. Tonight it would be just tea and biscuits, a read of her magazine, and then bed. What heaven! And what a blissful, long-forgotten feeling it was, this joy of being alive!

'I don't suppose anyone came for me did they, Darya Ivanovna?' she called to the landlady, as she always did, when she passed her room.

'Let me see . . . This morning some fellow delivered a book for you, and later the telegraph boy come . . .'

'With a telegram?'

'Yes, he left it in your room.'

She tried to ignore the sudden stab of anxiety she felt – it was sure to be something about work . . .

There in her room, lying on her writing desk beside the returned book, was the telegram, and beside it a grey square envelope addressed to her in handwriting which was so familiar to her and yet at that moment, utterly unexpected and unsettling. Her hands and legs were shaking so badly that she was forced to sit down; her muff slipped off her knees, scattering her purse and all her money and papers over the floor. For a while she stared at the telegram and the letter, incapable of deciding which to open first. Then finally she ripped open the telegram:

'Leaving 28th for G'ville. Await you there. Wire me. Will meet you. Semyon.'

The telegram slipped from her shaking hands and her arms dropped to her sides. On her face was an expression of panic. A year ago, this telegram would have made her dance about the room like a young girl, breathless with joy. She would have kissed the telegram and laughed with happiness. 'Senechka my darling, I'll be seeing you soon . . . !' She would have counted the days until the 28th, and lived only for their reunion.

Now she no longer felt like this – how could she, when for seven months she'd not heard a single word from him? What did he care about her? She might have fallen ill, or died of a broken heart. What did he know of her life? He knew nothing of her new political responsibilities and the sacrifices she had made for her work over the past seven months. He obviously couldn't care less – and yet now, as though nothing had changed, as though he had forgotten that seven months ago he'd sent her packing, he had the gall to say 'come back Natasha . . .!'

She could visualise him so clearly, and herself beside him. And she had the feeling she had so often before – that he was somehow deaf and blind to her, that he only saw her in profile, never head-on as a whole person, as she really was. Yes, that was it, she was a silhouette whose contours he had drawn himself, for that was all he was interested in seeing of her. And now this telegram – one more stab in the heart, one more insult. No, this time she wouldn't weaken, she wouldn't be caught out. She had had enough, she told herself, tossing her head with that proud gesture so characteristic of her, which had prompted friends to nickname her 'your highness.'

She reached for her pen. She had to reply, to tell him no, a thousand times no. But where was she going to write to him? At his house? Out of the question. Anyuta would have hysterics if she saw the letter. To some address in G'ville? Equally out of the question since he would only be arriving there on the 28th, and if his only reason in going there was to see her, what a blow that would be for poor dear Senechka. He'd break down and cry like a child. No, she had better discover first why he was going to G'ville, and then decide what to do. She snatched up the envelope, tore it open, and began to read.

And as she read, her irritation slowly melted away, her sense of outrage left her, and all the old buried feelings of joy crept up on her. Soon waves of love and an almost maternal tenderness for her Senechka had washed away all her rage – for he had never before written to her so lovingly.

He had mourned for her, longed constantly to see her again, blamed himself a thousand times. He had grasped desperately at any piece of news about her, however trivial, and in this way had tried to feel that he hadn't completely lost touch with her. He *knew* about her work and how hard it was, he *knew* about all her new responsibilities; he just hoped it was keeping her busy enough to take her mind off him. He only wanted her happiness. As for him, there wasn't a day when he hadn't longed for her, and now he could bear it no more. 'My feelings for you are far, far stronger than anything my reason might tell me,' he wrote, 'and now I can't struggle against my feelings any longer. I need you.'

His relationship with Anyuta was no better; on the contrary, he was becoming increasingly irritable with her, life at home was hell, and he had fallen behind with his work. It was just the other day that this exciting new theory had occurred to him, which he was very anxious to tell Natasha about. Wouldn't it be good if they could discuss it together?

He wanted to follow up the idea properly, but for this he badly needed new material. And so it had occurred to him that he might visit a certain well-known professor who lived at G'ville. This professor had offered to put the contents of his library at Senya's disposal, and he was planning to stay there at least one and-a-half months, perhaps two. Wasn't this a heaven-sent opportunity for them to meet? She *would* come, wouldn't she? Of course she would have to make sure nobody knew where she was going, or (for Anyuta's sake) with whom, but he knew she was the soul of discretion in these matters.

There was a PS: as he had no money in the bank, could she possibly supply the wherewithal for both of them? Natasha sighed. There was nothing unusual in this request; it was always assumed that she was richer than he was – indeed, right from the beginning of their love affair it had been her money that financed their assignations. She certainly couldn't have been accused of fleecing his family with her expensive tastes!

Senya, like so many bohemians, especially of the Russian intellectual variety, ran his money affairs extremely casually, with the result that his family finances were in a state of perpetual crisis. There might occasionally be a little cash in hand but it was never enough to cover the numerous petty debts they accumulated. Natasha, on the other hand, earned an adequate salary from her writing, as well as receiving a small regular allowance from her family. 'I'm the man in this relation-ship,' she used to smile ironically. 'I have to bear all the financial responsibility for it.'

On this occasion, however, she was dismayed by Senya's brisk injunction to supply the cash for their meeting. It was all very well for him to say that, but since she had just had to subsidise a political campaign with her allowance and had only left herself enough for her food and rent, her own resources had run very low. How could she possibly get together what was needed? The journey alone would cost heaven knows how much. But she was no longer hesitating about whether or not she would join Senya; that had been decided for her beyond any doubt as she read his letter. Now the only question was how to surmount all these petty obstacles and get hold of the money.

She began to jot down a few figures – she was no stranger to such calculations. The train journey would cost at least three hundred rubles, she reckoned, and counting up her cash she discovered she had just enough to cover it. But how was she going to lay hands on the rest? She thought of the pawnshop. There was her watch – but she would get nothing but a few sous for that. Then there was her fur collar – but no, that would fetch nothing at all. There was her family of course, she could write to them – but she rejected this idea immediately: it would be too appalling if instead of sending her the money they merely sent her a reproachful little lecture.

'Oh, if only Senya wasn't so peculiar, behaving as though I were some kind of millionaire! I suppose he never wondered *how* I might acquire this vast sum of money – and so quickly too . . .' Resentment began to stir in her, and soon she was feeling thoroughly irritable. He never once considered *her* difficulties, particularly when they involved money. He really was a child . . .

She softened at once. 'Yes, he is a child, which is one reason I love him so much. All intellectuals have this naivety about practical matters, that's what makes them irresistible. Most of the time he's not living in the real world at all.'

Natasha sat up until the small hours doing her sums and trying to get things straight in her mind. But the more she thought, the less she was able to work out a solution. 'How can I possibly *not* go and see him because of something so stupid as money? But *where* am I going to find it . . . ?' The questions revolved endlessly in her mind and went on tormenting her when she eventually climbed into bed. She lay there tossing and turning sleeplessly all night.

Then new, more serious anxieties began to loom. Her work. How could she possibly delegate all the responsibilities she had taken on? Part of her knew of course that since it was all running smoothly at the moment it should be feasible to find someone to replace her for the weeks she'd be away. She deserved a holiday. Yet it was easier said than done. And how would her friends react when she told them she was going off somewhere? She couldn't bear to think of the sarcastic comments and sidelong glances with which some of them would greet the announcement – it would make her miserable for days. There was one particular man – he had rather a bad limp – who'd never liked her. He always called her 'Lady Natasha' behind her back, it was only in the past few weeks that he had begun to treat her with a little more respect. She hated to think what his response would be. He'd certainly take a very dim view of this sudden, mysterious, and evidently clandestine journey, and would consider it – quite rightly, really, – as one more proof of the frivolity he despised in her. 'What did I tell you?' – she could imagine him limping from one end of the office to the other, announcing to the others in that grating voice of his – 'Lady Natasha's nothing but a dilettante!'

But she wasn't going to think about such things any more. She wanted only to set off for G'ville. The idea of letting Senya down – and herself too – appalled her, for she felt if she didn't meet him this time she would lose him forever. And this time the loss would be final. 'Oh no, I couldn't bear it,' she groaned, 'not that torture a second time. I'd rather die than face it again.'

The following morning she arrived at the office earlier than usual, looking haggard and distracted, her eyes red from sleeplessness and weeping. Vanechka was there alone, dragging on a cigarette and marking up the daily newspapers with a pencil. 'Hello there, your highness,' he called out to her without raising his eyes. (He was sprawling rather elegantly on a high stool).

'Good morning, Vanechka.' He detected immediately the misery in her voice and peered more closely at her over his spectacles.

'What's wrong with you this morning? Feeling blue?'

'Please don't ask me about it, Vanechka,' Natasha waved her arm. Life seemed so full of cruel irony and everything seemed so wretchedly wrong that she was over-sensitive even to Vanechka's humorous concern.

'Well, well,' he said in amazement. 'So there is something the matter – I'd never have believed it of you. So what are you moping about? Come on, you might as well tell me.'

He pushed his papers away as if he meant business, and avoiding her look so as not to embarrass her, he settled himself to listen as solemnly as if this were the confessional. Natasha needed to talk, and readily embarked on her long and incoherent story. She had to go away, she told him, 'on family business', but she was being held up by lack of money, and if she didn't go it would be a terrible disaster. 'It's life or death – yes, someone might die!' she cried and, no longer shy of Vanechka now, she began to sob.

Now Vanechka had seen Natasha preoccupied with her work and he had seen her when she was offended and angry, but he had never seen her cry. He could hardly believe it. Crying, he felt, was for idiots and children. 'Well, stop blubbering about it!' he shouted as soon as he had recovered from his amazement. 'Tears won't get you the money. More to the point, tell me how much you need. Is it a lot?'

'Yes it is rather, Vanechka, it's three hundred rubles I need.'

'You must be joking – that's a tidy sum, you won't find that lining the pockets of people like us! You must be budgeting for a few luxuries I'd say, your highness. I hope you're not flinging it around – you'll be begging on the streets soon if you go on wasting money like that!'

'Oh but it's not for me. You see, something just cropped up Vanechka, something very urgent. Yesterday I got a telegram – you can't imagine how important it is for me to leave. If I don't lay hands on that wretched three hundred . . . Well a person's life is at stake, I can't say more than that – two lives, even.'

'Ah, now I'm beginning to understand; you have to bail someone out, is that it?' Vanechka's face cleared.

'Yes . . . in a way, yes.'

'Well, why didn't you say so then, instead of inventing some story about relatives in Moscow or St Petersburg or wherever, not saying whether it was for a week or for good? Why not just tell me It was some conspiratorial affair which was none of my business, but you needed my help? I wouldn't have asked questions, I'm not over-inquisitive. I'm not wet behind the ears either. If you don't want to talk about it I won't ask, but I want to help if I can!'

Natasha didn't dare contradict Vanechka's interpretation of her dilemma, however awkward the deception made her feel, for he was already considering various ways he might get hold of the money for her, and she was terrified that if she even hinted at the truth she might lose his sympathy. Was it such a crime to deceive Vanechka like this? It was only a loan, after all, and Natasha was always as punctilious as a Prussian in repaying her debts, everyone knew that. An article of hers was already at the printers; she could let the royalties stand surety for the sum.

'Let's forget these financial transactions for now,' said Vanechka, 'and try instead to think who might be sitting on the pot of gold. There's that old fellow who's sympathetic to us, you know who I mean – he's got a fair bit of capital. But of course he may not feel like obliging just now.'

'Of course I know who you mean, Vanechka dear, and yes do please try him. It would be much easier for you to ask him than for me. But you can tell him the money's for me and that I'll vouch for it. Look, why don't I write a receipt for you to take to him?'

'But you're nowhere near getting the money, and you're already begging him to take a receipt for it! There's no sense in rushing things, though I can see you've got quite a head for business . . . Oh lord, I've been chatting away and completely forgot to make that phone-call. It's all your fault your highness, distracting honest workers from the path of duty.'

Two days later Vanechka triumphantly handed Natasha an envelope. 'Here you are, you're in luck – I did it!'

A Great Love

'Vanechka, you're an absolute dear!' Natasha delightedly leant forward to kiss him, but he stopped her. 'Steady on with the kissing and "Vanechka dears", and take your receipt. He's a tight-fisted old chap, he moaned and groaned about times being hard, and the fact that he'd just given away a lot to someone else and he needed it for himself. Anyway, I only had to mention it was you and that did the trick at once. Then I produced the receipt, and the old fellow softened up completely . . . Why are you tucking the envelope away without counting the money? You never know, I might have cheated you and taken a hundred for myself.'

'And I wouldn't mind, that's the honest trust!'

'So why did you ask for three hundred if you could have managed with two? Or are you planning to splash out that third hundred on a new fur coat? You should be ashamed of yourself your highness. Strikes me there's something suspicious going on. Who's this person you're bailing out, I'd like to know? Unless, of course you're really slipping off to a christening-party or something, in which case you can count me out as a friend!'

Natasha laughed and squeezed his hand. 'I don't know how to thank you Vanechka, you've saved my life. From now on I shall always think of you as my guardian angel!'

'Hah, and you'll make the sign of the cross and bow down before me when we meet?'

'Now don't be stupid, Vanechka.'

'What *I* think is stupid,' Vanechka retorted, pausing in the doorway, 'is to call someone your guardian angel. Just think what you're saying! If you're so grateful, why not send me a postcard from wherever it is you're going?' Natasha blushed. 'All right, all right,' he said quickly, sensing her embarrassment, 'I won't give you away, cross my heart. When I get your card I won't tell a soul where it was posted from – I'll carry the secret with me to the grave. I'd just like to hear from you. If you really trust me you'll write to me, if you don't I'll know our friendship's

289

not up to much.' Looking at her sternly, Vanechka pulled his fur cap over his ears, and disappeared through the door.

7

The journey to G'ville seemed endless, and by evening, after several hours in the train, Natasha was almost beside herself with nervousness, one moment in a frenzy of joy, the next full of gloomy apprehension. Over and over again she imagined their meeting and felt supremely happy, then the thought of the intervening hours on the train dampened her high spirits and soon anticipation would turn to anxiety. What if he didn't meet her at the station? And if he did, what if she missed him on the crowded platform? If he didn't meet her she'd have to wait for him until morning, and pass an endless night in some hotel – and that would be unendurable . . .

At last the train slowed down and she could see the lights of G'ville station through the window. Natasha's heart was thumping so wildly she was convinced her fellow-passengers could hear. She was frozen to her seat in a fever of anxiety, and sat there shaking, unable to make her numb fingers get the window open. When at last she did, she learned out, her body tense. Was he there? 'Oh lord, please make him be there; please make him meet me,' Natasha whispered, for although she put no faith in prayer, it ease her mind to repeat the familiar childhood words. How crowded the platform was, what a lot of people! However would he see her? Then yes, it was him, she was sure of it! Her legs nearly gave way under her and her heart thumped even louder. But now it was for joy – everything was going to be all right!

For hours Natasha had sat in the train picturing the moment when she and Senya would meet. She had imagined them rushing towards each other, oblivious to the crowds and the fear of being recognised; she had imagined them falling into each other's arms, kissing and embracing; she had imagined tears of joy. But things didn't happen that way.

Jumping on to the platform, she stumbled and fell, dropping her umbrella and handbag. She bent to gather up her scattered possessions. The next thing she knew, Senya was beside her. Before even greeting her he stooped down to pick up her umbrella. It was only then that he stretched out his hand to her, by which time she was so distraught she could only shake it, silently, as she might do with a complete stranger. 'Let's be off then, Natasha. I'm afraid there are a lot of people here – we don't want to bump into someone we know, do we? I think I'd better walk ahead to the hotel; you just follow me.' So saying, Senya walked away, stepping out briskly along the platform towards the exit, looking as though he had nothing to do with her.

Half-stunned, still hardly able to grasp that the long-imagined reunion had taken such a bizarre turn, Natasha trailed behind, trying not to lose him from sight.

As it was, she managed to get only fleeting glimpses of him, and then he seemed strangely different – maybe it was just that he had put on weight, or his beard had grown. He'd always had this fear that they might bump into an old acquaintance when they were out together, that was nothing new to her. (She vividly remembered being with him in a remote little town where it was inconceivable that they would meet anyone who might know them, but where he had nevertheless insisted that they follow each other in this strange Indian file.) But today she found Senya's persecution mania exasperating. 'Why, he didn't even say hello properly!' she fumed. 'And after all those months! He could have said just one word, or asked me one question about myself . . .'

They crossed a broad deserted square lit by flickering lamps and she followed him as he made for a hotel, a very ordinary sort of a place with a doorman in braided uniform standing outside. Inside, a messenger-boy with shiny buttons took her bags and led them to the lift. And here at last Semyon Semyonovich moved towards her and reached for her hand. 'Well, what d'you think of it?' he murmured. Natasha, with an instinct born of habitual discretion, drew back and indicated the messenger-boy beside them. 'Oh don't you worry about that!' Senya laughed. 'I told them I was waiting for my wife, you see, so I've booked us into a double room. We can move to another hotel later, but this one'll do nicely for the time being, I think. You see how experienced I'm getting at this!' He grinned slyly at her over the tops of his spectacles, and Natasha smiled back; but it was a small unhappy smile. On her way to meet him her cheeks had been flushed, and she had radiated such joy that the other passengers couldn't help looking at her. Now the fire in her eyes had gone and she felt confused, bewildered and tired. This wasn't the Senya she knew – this man in the lift beside her seemed like someone else, someone she had never met before.

The boy with the buttons led them out of the lift and along the corridor to their room. He flung the door open to reveal a bare, anonymous, rather shabby double room, indistinguishable from any hotel room anywhere in the world. Leaving them standing there, he went back for their bags; then, after taking his time bidding his guests goodnight, he finally took his leave of them.

Senya was in an exceptionally lively mood. He'd been so longing to see her, he said, he was so excited and happy. 'But now let's have a good look at you – why, you *are* thin! Or are you just tired from the journey?' He put his arms around her. She was standing facing him with her arms thrown back, struggling to remove her hat; a pin was caught in her veil and she could not get it out. 'Let me go a moment, Senechka dear,' she said. 'I must take off my hat.' But Senya merely clasped her to him even tighter. 'My darling Natasha,' he whispered, kissing her; 'How I love you, how I've longed to see you – I've wanted you so . . .'

By this time Natasha had abandoned the struggle to remove her hat and was lying across the double bed. She felt awkward and uncomfortable. Lying there underneath him, his hot breath burning her face, her hat dragging at her hair and the pins digging into her scalp, she suddenly felt once more, and quite terrifyingly, that he was a complete stranger to her. That unique and powerful joy which had given wings to her journey here broken into a thousand pieces, crushed by rough and brutally hasty embraces.

'Kiss me, Natasha, don't turn away from me. Don't you love me any more, dear?' She couldn't speak. Her only response was to clasp his dear head and smile at him. There were tears in her eyes. For all he knew they were tears of happiness, but she was past caring what he thought now. She knew that she was crying from the depths of her soul, crying for one more dream destroyed, one more insult, one more wound to her heart.

Later that night while he slept, exhausted and at peace, Natasha sat up beside him in the bed, gazing into the darkness and trying to make sense of her feelings. 'I suppose in his own funny way he does love someone – although that someone isn't me. Maybe he loves Anyuta, or maybe he loves things as he would like them to be, rather than as they really are. And to think it was for him that I left work, ran up massive debts, rushed here, there and everywhere organising this trip, one moment out of my mind with joy, the next moment worried sick about the whole thing – to think it was he who gave me something to live for, and believe in, and look forward to . . . What a fool I've been, what a fool . . . !'

Senya's embraces that night had been uncontrollable, violent – how could she ever have thought of him as a real friend when he so evidently had no sensitivity towards her at all, and when his interest in her was so crudely sexual? Why had she come? Waves of despair swept over her, and she was overwhelmed by a sense of hopelessness so boundless that she could do nothing but sob. She had never felt so alone at home, thousands of miles from him, as she did now, sitting in the bed beside him, violated, abandoned, desperate. At home she could dream and hope; here her dreams had been shattered.

Natasha got up next morning with a strange sense of apathy, her feelings numb. Senya, on the other hand, was in an excellent mood. 'Well now, Natasha, tell me everything you've been doing since we last saw each other,' he said as they sat drinking their morning coffee beside the unmade bed which made their shabby hotel room seem particularly horrible to Natasha. 'Come on, tell me who you've been seeing and all the latest news about our comrades.' But at that moment Natasha had no desire to tell him anything ever again. Yesterday – ah yesterday! – with the train steaming into G'ville, she had imagined herself telling him all her news, an endless succession of stories about what she had been doing. She'd pictured them both so clearly, talking the night away until dawn – she had even tried conscientiously to recall the particularly important details of her recent life for him. She had decided, too, to confess all her misgivings about their relationship, to try and express some of the resentment she felt for him. Then (for he would of course be very upset by her criticisms) she would stroke his head to show him she forgave him and understood him, and slowly the old harmony between them would be re-established.

And only when words were no longer adequate would they discover the ultimate expression of their feelings in sexual passion, that bright burning force which was so beautiful, which encompassed the colours of her dreams.

But now, after that soulless reunion at the station and their banal night of love together, Natasha had no desire to tell him anything, and her responses were listless and reluctant. He began to look anxious. 'My dear, you don't appear to be in very good spirits today,' he ventured at last, peering into her face.

'I didn't get enough sleep, that's all. I'm worn out.'

'You poor thing – one night in bed together and I've worn you out. What are we going to do with you?' He laughed, evidently very pleased with himself, and reached out for the slice of bread and honey which Natasha had prepared for him. She raised her eyebrows with displeasure, and was about to deliver herself of some uncharacteristically snappish remark when there was a knock at the door.

'Who's there?' called Senya, hurrying to open it. It was a telegram, addressed to the town's poste restante and redirected to the hotel, and it was from Anyuta. Kokochka had the measles; Anyuta was desperate, rushed off her feet. 'So this is it,' said Senya with a sigh that seemed to fill the room. To Natasha he looked as vulnerable as a child, standing there dismayed, his head bowed, his legs planted wide apart. Suddenly something changed in her: all her old tender feelings welled up and washed over the pain and anger of the past hours. Yes, now at last she could see before her the man she had always loved – and still did love – her poor troubled Senya whom she found so touching, so vulnerable.

Natasha leapt up from her chair to his side, clasping his head and kissing him again and again, as though she had only this moment seen him and recognised him. 'Why Natasha dear . . .' he murmured, confused by such tempestuous tenderness. 'Hold on a moment, there that's better. Now first we've got to decide how to sort this wretched business out – oh lord, what's to be done about Anyuta and Koko?' He flung out his arms in a gesture of helplessness, and Natasha caught his hands in hers, covering them with kisses and murmuring, 'Oh my darling Senya, d'you know I feel as if I've, only just come, only just recognised you after so long, so long without you? Oh Senya, the whole world looks up to you, then a little thing like this happens and you're defeated! I thought I'd lost you forever, you mean everything to me, Senya. How happy I am to have found you again . . . !'

8

Since Senya felt it would be awkward to hide out any longer in their first hotel they moved the next day to another, a large, genteel, formal place. Natasha arrived first, announced herself under a false name and was shown two rooms a respectable distance from each other along the same corridor. She selected the brighter, more spacious room for Senya, since he had to work, and took for herself the other, a little kennel of a place. But while waiting for him to arrive she shifted the sofa, arranged her books and ran out for some flowers, so that her kennel was soon almost habitable.

He entered her room unexpectedly – he never knocked, always burst in like this – while Natasha was sitting at her desk writing the postcard she had promised to send Vanechka. 'Ah, here you are,' he said, 'I had such a job finding you. They've mixed up these damned room numbers, so 57 comes after 85. I've been traipsing up and down the corridor – never mind. You *have* made it nice and comfortable in here, you clever thing . . . God, I'm exhausted, I had to take a long walk around the town to kill time before coming here,' he sprawled comfortably on the sofa. 'I've not had a moment to sit down. Now what time is it? Aha, six already, well, time for me to go off to the professor's.'

'What, today? Surely it can wait till tomorrow?'

'No no, I'm afraid it can't. You see, Anyuta may have written to tell them I left home on the twenty-eighth.'

'Well, what if she did? Why can't you tell her the truth, that you didn't visit the professor straight away? There's no reason why she should leap to the conclusion that you're with me – as far as she's concerned I'm out of your life now.'

'Ah, but that's not the point, is it? You *know* what Anyuta's like – if I don't go I shall be constantly worrying in case something gets back to her. No, whether you like it or not my dear, I'm going to have to show my face there today.' It was useless to argue. Natasha felt that his determination to keep Anyuta in ignorance virtually amounted to mania, but she refrained from saying so.

'So what have you been up to while I've been out?' he asked. 'Writing?'

'That's right.'

'A letter, eh?'

Now Natasha knew she wasn't supposed to mail letters directly from G'ville – she was under strict orders not to – but was meant instead to send them by a circuitous route via a woman friend of hers who acted as an intermediary. She felt embarrassed, for the postcard lying on her table addressed to Vanechka bore not only a view of G'ville but a message in her own hand which made some reference to the town.

'So who are you writing to?' Natasha was by now very flustered, and this provoked Senya to lean across the table, trying to spy out the address on the card. Natasha tried to conceal her embarrassment with a little laugh, and covered the card with both hands. 'I'm not telling you and I'm not showing you – it's my secret and there's an end to it!'

'Well, if it's a secret we'll soon get it out of you – now give me that card at once! You won't? Being difficult? You'll make me take it by force, will you?' They started to struggle – playfully at first, for both were equally anxious to make it seem a game. But there was nothing playful about the grim expression on their faces.

'What's happening, Natasha? This is something new, you've never hidden letters from me before.'

'Why shouldn't I? I don't want you reading my letters! It's none of your business who I write to . . . Let *go* – how *dare* you be so violent with me . . . ?'

He finally managed to part her fingers and wrench the postcard out of her hands.

'Don't you dare read that! It's despicable of you!' Natasha

screamed at him in a rare fit of fury, and in a flash she snatched it from him, tore it into tiny pieces and threw them into the waste-paper basket under her table.

'Natasha!'

They glared at each other like two enemies waiting to attack. Natasha was breathless, her cheeks burned with rage. 'I despise you – how dare you attack me like that, how dare you be so violent . . . ? You have no right to read my letters . . .' Her trembling lips kept repeating the same words over and over again: 'Despicable . . . attacking me . . . how dare you . . . ?'

'Oh Natasha, Natasha, what are you saying? So it *is* true then!' groaned Senya, covering his face with his hands and collapsing on to the sofa. He had never failed to melt Natasha's heart when he looked so helpless; now she was too baffled to feel pity for him: 'Can *what* be true? What are you talking about?'

'No, you don't need to tell me – you've found someone else, some other man you've fallen in love with, I know . . .'

'You know nothing of the sort – you've taken leave of your senses, Senya! Whatever gave you such a ridiculous idea?'

'Well I didn't want to tell you this, but recently I received two anonymous letters with details about you and some man . . .'

'Which you believed? Well, now I've heard everything!'

'No I didn't believe them, I burnt them right away and put them out of my mind. But now, well I'm not so sure. I don't know what to make of your behaviour just now Natasha, confused and embarrassed, then suddenly losing your temper with me like that – you've never spoken to me that way before – so that's why I felt it might be true you'd been seeing another man . . . Oh no, I couldn't bear it . . . Why did you come then? Why have you been deceiving me? The least you can do is tell me the truth, stop driving me out of my mind.'

'So you think I'm lying to you? Look Senya, I have no idea what you're talking about, but I wish you could hear yourself sometimes so you'd realise how silly you sound. What reason do you imagine I'd have for deceiving you? What would be the point of saying things I didn't mean? Why should I want to do that to you? Tell me!'

'Pity perhaps, I don't know . . .'

'Pity? For you?'

'Yes – you're a good person Natasha, generous . . .' Deep lines of grief etched themselves on his face, and he seemed so weighed down by suffering that before she knew what she was doing she was on the floor beside him, kissing his hands. 'Dearest Senya, why do you think all these things and make yourself suffer so much? How can I make you understand, it's *you* I love, *you're* the only man I could ever want!' She clung to him.

He resisted her kisses half-heartedly, still fearful that by responding he might be condoning some frightful deception. 'So what about that letter then?' he muttered, his eyes still smouldering with suspicion.

'You won't give up will you, stupid! Look, if you're really that bothered why not take it out of the basket and read it – go on, read it!' She ran to the table, dragged out the basket, tipped it upside down and shook it. Fragments of postcard fluttered to the floor, and while they squatted on their heels piecing them together Natasha quickly told Senya about her financial negotiations and Vanechka's help. Senya knew Vanechka of course, and knew he couldn't possibly be a rival for Natasha's love, and the jocular contents of her card soon put paid to all his suspicions.

'But you frightened me badly Natasha dear, making such a ludicrous performance out of the whole business,' he still sounded vexed with her. 'What got into you?'

'I suppose I was afraid you'd be angry with me for writing from here. But I felt I *had* to write to Vanechka since he asked me to, and he did us both such an enormous favour. I know Vanechka – he'd rather die than give away a secret.'

'Yes I see that now, of course. But I think it's extremely

imprudent of you to write to anyone from here. What if the card had been intercepted and someone got their hands on it before Vanechka? And what does he think you're up to anyway?'

'Who cares? It doesn't bother me I suppose he must realise I'm involved in some great romance and he'd like to know who the man is – but he knows it's none of his business.'

'I wouldn't be so sure. He's bound to put two and two together, see the coincidence, make the connection – sooner or later he'll discover I was in G'ville too. Before we know it there'll be a lot of rumours flying around . . .' His tone was becoming more and more peremptory. 'No, you can do whatever you like when you're at home, but please, I beg you, don't write to anyone from here, not even your dear Vanechka.'

'Well if you find the whole idea of my writing to people so unpleasant, then I won't,' she replied drily.

He regarded her closely. 'Still sulking, eh Natasha? Upset about being ordered around?' He hugged her. 'What's to become of you women, tell me that – getting into trouble all the time! All right, I admit at first I didn't understand what was going on, but now I see it all . . .' Natasha tossed her head in that defiant gesture of hers he knew so well. 'Ah now, don't be annoyed with me, I was only joking. Now that terrible worry's off me I feel so happy and I'm not angry with you anymore. Let's be friends again darling, you can't imagine how terrified I was – I thought I was going to lose you, and if I had . . . I don't think I could live without you.' He put his arms around her and clasped her head to his chest. 'I've never been so happy as I am with you, Natasha; I could stay with you forever and never think of the time . . . Oh my god!' He jumped up, clasping his head. 'The professor – I completely forgot! It's seven o'clock already. I must leave at once, Natasha – goodbye darling, see you later . . . !' He was out of the door in a flash.

Slowly, deep in thought, Natasha gathered up the scraps of postcard and threw them once more in the basket. She felt enormously tired. She longed to go home. An anguished thought was taking shape in her mind: they were strangers, complete strangers to each other.

9

It was much later that evening when Senya returned to the hotel. He entered Natasha's room in an exhilarated mood, bubbling over with the ideas he had brought from his discussion with the professor, who worked in the same academic field as he did.

'It's splendid! I've finally met someone I can talk to without translating everything into simple language – now there's a real intellectual for you, someone who has his own original responses to every question and forces you to clarify your position. Of course he made me realise what a vast number of issues there are to be worked out – I shall have to be more rigorous in my analysis and pursue a great many more questions, but it was all tremendously pleasing! Oh you can't imagine how starved I've been of real intellectual stimulation. I suppose it was only after talking to him that I realised how much I really need an intelligent friend to discuss my ideas with systematically, and encourage me in my work . . .'

He chatted on for several minutes in this vein, and was so naively pleased with himself that it never occurred to him that his remarks might evoke a less than sympathetic response from Natasha. Not for one moment did he realise that every word pierced her like a needle. So apparently she wasn't the 'intelligent friend' he so badly needed to provide him with 'intellectual stimulation'. So she had been completely wrong all these years when she imagined she was encouraging him to develop his ideas and helping him with his work.

'Might I enquire,' she interrupted caustically, '*what* the professor said to you that was so amazingly intelligent that he even cast doubts on the correctness of your position?' She could

301

hardly have been more provocative, yet it made little impression on Senya, who merely replied that he didn't feel up to repeating the discussion for her benefit at the moment, but that he would gladly do so tomorrow. But Natasha wasn't letting him off so lightly, and questioned him closely, persisting with unusual tenacity in eliciting answers from him. He only had to hint that the professor wasn't in total agreement with one of his opinions, and she would defend it as if her life depended on it – as though this were the cause of her anxiety.

Little did Senya know Natasha's true feelings. If she had allowed him a glimpse into her mind then, he would have seen to his amazement that for the first time in all the years he had known her she was jealous. Natasha, who hadn't once been jealous of Anyuta, and even when their love affair was at its most passionate had genuinely shared all his fears over Anyuta's last pregnancy and confinement, yes, Natasha was now suffering the pangs of a blind and tormenting jealousy over some old professor whom she had never even met. This man, it seemed to her, had effortlessly replaced her in Senya's life, making her superfluous precisely in those areas in which she had always believed she was so necessary to him.

Senya continued to summarise the professor's arguments for her, but in a bored and careless manner, as though they couldn't possibly be of any interest to her and he was merely repeating them to satisfy her idle curiosity. Natasha meanwhile continued to take malicious pleasure in pouncing on every one of the professor's illogicalities and non-sequiturs, pointing them out to him with increasing vehemence. But Senya wouldn't be drawn. 'If you'd grasped his entire argument you'd understand what I've been saying more clearly and realise it's more complicated than that,' he countered in an airy tone which she found particularly exasperation, and then added insult to injury with a yawn: 'Anyway I'm tired, time to turn in now. Sleep well, Natasha.'

'But you can't go to bed yet – I mean, I thought we'd sit and talk a while longer. I haven't seen you all day . . .'

'Talk But my dear d'you realise it's way past midnight? No, let's wait till tomorrow, then we can have a really good long chat together. I haven't been sleeping at all well lately, and tomorrow I must start work first thing, I arranged to visit the library with the professor. I really must get some rest.'

'Yes. *We* must get some rest, mustn't we?' At that moment she found the way he always emphasised his needs and disregarded hers quite intolerable. They kissed perfunctorily, as she imagined two long-married people must kiss, and Senya turned to walk out of the room, stopping at the door to remark, 'Well Natasha, I think it was a brilliant idea of mine to come to G'ville – I've had a tremendously pleasant day. Do sleep well, won't you dear, and see you in the morning.' He nodded amiably and closed the door behind him.

Natasha slammed the bolt and slumped down on the bed.

She'd spent the entire day on her own. Hours of loneliness had intensified the doubts and depressions of the previous night – now he had gone without having begun to talk to her properly, and all he could say as he went off to bed was what a marvellous day he'd had! What an insulting way to treat her, his friend and lover, his companion in work and his comrade in struggle; he had never behaved with such blatant bad manners before. She would never forgive him.

She thought back to the days when he had listened to her ideas and valued them, and of the confidence she derived from knowing this. It was he who had given her the strength to overcome all the setbacks and unfriendly criticisms at work, and to soldier on with her political tasks. He had believed in her, he had valued her intellect and her ideas, and nothing else had mattered to her. But what if he had merely beguiled her into thinking he was taking her seriously, just because she was 'his woman', his property. She shivered. How would he respond if she called him an ugly fatface? In the same emotionally detached manner in which he had spoken to her today probably. She felt a new and quite savage rage, closer to hatred than anger.

'I shall go to him at once, tell him what I think of him, tell him everything, and tomorrow I'll go straight back home to my friends. This is no life here – it's nothing but aggravation and anxiety and I'm sick of it! I don't even love him any more – I hate him . . .' Natasha strode to the door. But the moment she turned the handle she paused, as she pictured herself struggling to explain her feelings to him, foolishly attempting to elicit his sympathy and understanding . . . With a sense of helpless anger she sank back on the bed.

They were divided now by a wall which no words could break down. Indeed, it seemed the more they tried to communicate with each other through it the more impenetrable it became, and she knew that any words they might hurl at each other in anger would stick, deepening the silence which already cut them off from each other. She was deluded to imagine she could explain how unhappy and humiliated he made her feel. Why bother? He wouldn't listen. She might as well keep her mouth shut, bury her resentment. To hell with it, why should she explain, when she could simply announce, without any fussing or psychologising, that she had to leave? She could tell him she had urgent work to do, it couldn't be helped, she would just have to go, let him stay with his professor! She would feel miserably lonely, but better that than being hurt and humiliated all the time.

Natasha began to take off her clothes, pulling irritably at the tapes on her underwear, for all she wanted now was to lie down, sleep, and not think about anything. She was exhausted. But the tapes seemed to have their own mindlessly malignant purpose in defeating her, and knotted themselves more tightly as she struggled with them. 'Damn you!' she shouted, for to be mocked by mere objects, after all she had suffered, was more than she could endure. 'I'll just rip you off then!'

She flung off her clothes, leaving them in a crumpled heap on the floor, hurriedly brushed out her long hair and plaited it into two braids which she tied with white ribbons. It was only as she was putting on her dressing-gown and was about to get into bed that the sadness welled up afresh inside her. Senya had always loved her with her hair in plaits, and the dressing-gown carried all sorts of tender memories; he used to tell her it was more attractive than any of her dresses, and he loved to wrap her up in its soft folds while he embraced her. How could she leave him before he had even seen her in it? And how could she leave him when she felt so angry with him? She paced slowly about her little room, absent-mindedly tidying things away.

It seemed absurd that she should be in her room in this state of turmoil while he was only a few steps away. Wouldn't the natural thing be to go in and see him, pour out her grievances and then give him a big hug, showing that she forgave him for hurting her feelings so badly that day? And if he didn't understand why she was so angry with him, she must at least try to explain, and without losing her temper either. Yes, she *would* try to make him understand her and listen to what she was saying. If she didn't have it out with him, she would never get to sleep that night. What was their love worth if they concealed their most important feelings from each other? If she didn't speak to him how would she ever banish the monster of hatred and anger gnawing at her heart?

Gathering the folds of her dressing-gown, she opened the door a crack, glanced up and down the corridor to make sure nobody was around, and quickly went out. Her slippered feet sank into the deep pile of the red carpet. The corridor seemed endless. 64, 66, 68 – yes, 68, that was his room, those were his boots outside the door. She hesitated a moment. What if he were asleep? It was over an hour since they had said goodnight. But stronger feelings than these finally impelled her to turn the handle of his door – the longing to see him again and caress his dear head, the desire to melt the icy rage in her heart and to banish the feelings of uncertainty she had all day. The door squeaked as it opened, the light from the corridor shone into Senya's face, and he awoke with a start: 'Who's there? What is it?' Without his glasses he was too short-sighted to recognise her immediately.

'It's me dear, Natasha.' She closed the door softly behind her and went over to his bed where she knelt on the floor beside him.

'Aha, Natasha, fancy *you* coming in like this!' There was more than a hint of complacency in his greeting, which cut her to the quick.

'I've come because I've been feeling very bad, Senya, very bitter and angry and lonely . . .'

'Oh I *am* sorry about that – well, you mustn't let it get you down. Afraid of sleeping alone, are you? Well, don't then! I'm always here. Ah, and I see you've come to seduce me in that lovely gown of yours, you wonderful, fascinating woman . . .' He put his arms around her, trying to draw her on to the bed beside him. She resisted at first, responding halfheartedly to his kisses, then at last twisted her face away from his. 'Wait a bit Senya, please not yet. I've got other things on my mind now, that's why I came in to see you. I wanted to lie in your arms for a while and get warm, and then talk.'

'Oh that's all you want, eh? I don't know, you women baffle me sometimes, you really do, with your excuses and justifications. First it's this you want, then it's something else completely . . . You look all innocent, as though you never had a sinful thought in your life, as if it were men who were always leading you on. But it was you who came to my bedroom and woke me up. Now look at you – one minute it's hugs and kisses, next you're telling me to keep my hands off . . . Ah what is it, Natasha? Have I hurt your feelings? I was only joking! I'm *glad* you came, honestly I am. Oh my darling, my own sweet Natasha. Look at you, you came in to get warm and you're sitting on the floor – your feet must be like ice. Come to me, my love.'

Natasha's abandoned dressing-gown gleamed white against the dark hotel carpet.

'Well I don't think there's anything more to be said now. I need to sleep,' he interrupted her a little later. As far as he was concerned that was the end of it, and he was feeling far too relaxed and contented to pay attention to Natasha's determined efforts to bring a few psychological insights to bear on the situation. 'Look, I'm sure we can sort this out tomorrow – you seem to forget I have to go to the library in the morning. I shan't be able to work if my head's not fresh.' Why, he was practically rebuking her! He turned his face to the wall and wrapped himself more tightly in the blanket, while Natasha lay on her back, her hands clasped behind her head, thinking. At last she was beginning to understand the bitterness which so often took hold of her at these times, although this didn't make it any easier to bear the devastatingly abrupt way his attitude to her changed after they made love. Afterwards, he was like a different person, remote and unloving, whereas with her it was completely the opposite, passionate and joyful lovemaking always swept her away on a tide of tender emotions to the point where she felt they became one person.

Now she gazed despondently at the back of his head. How sweet that dear familiar head was to her, for all that she felt so crushed and downcast. She kissed it gently and then, very carefully, got out of the bed. 'Sleep well, Senechka, I think we'd sleep better in our own beds. Will you kiss me before I go?' she whispered, leaning over him.

'What's up, Natasha?' he murmured, half-asleep. 'Surely that's enough kisses for one night – why you're insatiable, woman! Are you ill?'

Natasha recoiled in horror. His words struck her like blows across the face. How could he so misinterpret her feelings, so fail to understand her unsatisfied desire for warmth and tenderness!

So, with nothing but a cold and lonely longing, she was to leave his room feeling more cheated, more numb, than when she had gone in.

Slowly, deep in thought, Natasha put on her dressing-gown and set off once more down the endless corridor with its awful red carpet. At the corner was a little table at which the night-porter sat dozing. As she passed him, he woke and eyed her brazenly, muttering something under his breath. She didn't hear what he said but it was undoubtedly obscene. She hunched her shoulders and made her way back to her room.

10

Natasha's stay in G'ville was rapidly turning into a kind of voluntary incarceration. In the early days of their love affair she had found it exciting to wait like a captive for Senya to arrive at their secret hiding-place. She called him her 'pasha', and referred to herself as the 'odalisk of the harem', the special attraction of this game being the complete break it made with the frantic bustle of her life at home. When she met Senya she became invisible to the world of politics and people, and she loved surrendering her name and identity when she went incognito to meet him. Nor did she have to worry about her friends in the party, who were generally most understanding about her tendency to disappear frequently at short notice. Some thought she was fulfilling family obligations, others simply assumed she had been summoned to carry out party work in another town. Up until now the break with everyday life had always been a welcome rest.

But this time in G'ville she found her role as 'odalisk of the harem' irksome and irritating. She couldn't walk down the street in case she met someone she knew. She couldn't even sit for an hour in the hotel dining-room in case Senya dashed back and, not finding her in her room, went straight off again. For Natasha the time hung heavy, empty and dull. The days dragged aimlessly by, and she had little to do but wait.

Senya, on the other hand, was anxious not to waste a minute of his time in G'ville. He was totally absorbed in his work, and even more obsessively absorbed – or so it seemed to Natasha – in the professor, with whose large and hospitable family he began to spend more and more of his time. Even when they were drinking their coffee together in the morning he was constantly glancing at his watch, anxious that he might be late. He invariably dined at the professor's house and whiled away most of his evenings there too, so that soon he could only spare the odd moment here and there for Natasha, when he would dash over to see her under the pretext of important letters to be written or material to be collected. He was always exceptionally lively during these brief snatched encounters with her, lounging on the sofa as he chatted away about this and that, recounting various anecdotes about the professor and his work.

On one occasion he let her make him some tea, and she improvised a feast for both of them with Gervaise cheese, fruit and jam. She listened to him carefully as she bustled about preparing it, not wanting to miss a word he was saying. Naturally it delighted her that he was happy and everything was going well for him. Nevertheless an evil worm was at work in her. It was rare now that he told her anything about his work. And he was less forthcoming these days with stories about the professor too, though Natasha was past caring about that. Her antipathy towards 'that old archive rat', ran deep, and she found it incomprehensible that Senya should consider him brilliant merely because he was so erudite. How could he be so naive?

'I don't understand you, Senya!' she burst out as she was pouring tea. 'You open your mind to him in this infantile fashion, you tell him all the ideas you've been working on and haven't fully thought through. Next thing you know he'll be making use of them, filling them out with that erudition of his and presenting them as his own, while you're still sweating it out and trying to finish your book.' She spoke calmly to make sure that her words went home and hurt him, as she intended them to.

'Really Natasha, what silly things you say. Quite frankly, you sometimes remind me of Anyuta. Have you ever heard of colleagues and friends in the same line of academic work stealing ideas from each other?'

'I certainly have! Surely you're not trying to tell me it doesn't happen – I can think of countless cases! If you think it doesn't, you're being foolish and naive!'

Senya continued to protest, but Natasha knew she had kindled a spark of suspicion in his mind, and this gave her some small malicious satisfaction. But after he left she felt what a mean thing she had done to him, and could only wonder at what was at the root of her desire to denigrate the professor in his eyes. What else but jealousy! She finally began to understand something of what Anyuta must have been feeling, and what made her act so hysterically. She felt disgusted with herself and longed to make amends, but realised with sickening clarity that what had been said couldn't be unsaid. 'God, how vile of me, there's no end to the damage I might have done . . .' And from that day she responded particularly appreciatively to Senya's lyrical praise of the professor and his family, hoping that by talking enthusiastically about the professor's qualities she might drive out the worm of distrust she had implanted in Senya's mind.

But her resentment was still very much alive. Each morning she got up with high hopes of Senya devoting the whole day to her – well not the whole day perhaps, maybe just a few peaceful hours in which they could be together and talk about their feelings. But as one day followed another, it became clear that the time would not be found. In the brief moments when they did meet during the day they hugged and kissed. There was much laughing and joking over tea, and at night they fell into each other's arms and embraced passionately. But somehow they never managed to find time to talk. Natasha tried to do some work on a pamphlet for which she had a deadline, but found the whole project daunting and made little progress with it. She might put a few thoughts together in the course of a day, but when she looked her writing over next day it never seemed satisfactory, and her style seemed laboured and lifeless. She was surprised and hurt, too, that Senya did not once ask her how her work was going.

They were killing time. Precious time was trickling through their fingers, wasted on trivial, futile things . . .

11

One day a large bundle of business and personal letters arrived at the hotel for Natasha, forwarded to her by a roundabout route. The letters related to party business, and contained some shocking news about two of her comrades who had 'fallen ill' (in party code this meant that they had been arrested). Their 'illness', it was feared, might well be prolonged, and would certainly have serious consequences for everyone associated with them. Natasha was deeply upset, and especially upset to be kicking her heels in G'ville in this crisis. What was she doing here anyway? Was it for his sake or hers that she was staying on? She neither knew nor cared. She knew she could never leave him with so much coldness in her heart, and that it would do her no good to go before expressing at least some of her resentment. She would only suffer afterwards. No, she really must speak to him. Today she would try to find the words to describe something of what she felt. The problem was that she didn't know what there was to describe. But she was determined to break down the barrier separating them, so she could leave calm in the knowledge that there was still some friendship and understanding between them. She waited with mounting impatience for him to return.

That day of all days, Senya was extremely late back. When he did eventually return, some time after midnight, it was straight from a large dinner-party given in his honour at the professor's house, and he was very drunk and merry. 'They fed and watered us until we burst!' he announced, oblivious to Natasha's glowering look. 'I'm afraid I've had one too many. Never mind, it'll pass. So what about you, my love? Been bored?' He nuzzled her cheek and kissed her ear.

'Please Senya, not now.' She extricated herself from his arms. 'I want to tell you about some letters I got this morning: Katerina Petrovna and Nikanor have both been arrested.'

'I don't believe it, god, how frightful!'

'I'm so sad for both of them – what a ghastly mess, what a tragedy . . .' Before she could stop herself she had collapsed in tears. She was sobbing more for herself than for her friends, but these distinctions were becoming increasingly blurred. Her emotions were in chaos, life was a dismal burden and the future seemed to hold out nothing but a long chain of humiliations and misfortunes. What had been the purpose of that brave new course on which she and the others had launched the party? What had possessed her to leave them, when her place was with them?

'Come Natasha dear, stop crying. You can't let something like this upset you so much.' He spoke wearily, reproachfully, as if he had had more than he could endure of women's tears. 'You never know, there may be something we can do.'

'Like what, for instance? But anyway, it's not that I'm crying for, it's everything about this wasted life of ours which is nothing but misery and pain.'

'Yes, but you know as well as I do the risks we run when we do political work. Now when I was working underground in the Volga region . . .' Senya assumed that Natasha was lamenting the hardship of party work and felt that the best way to distract her was by recounting some of the dangers from his own

312

revolutionary past. But Natasha had already heard these stories
of arrest, exile and escape, and listened with only half an ear. Her
mind was too full of the misgivings and anxieties she was
determined to talk to him about.

'. . . So what I'm saying is, we've always run these risks and
had to cope with crises,' he concluded, 'yet look at me – I'm still
alive, aren't I? And I haven't lost the ability to fall deeply in love
with a very beautiful woman, eh Natasha? Are you listening to
me, Natasha?'

'Yes, yes, I'm listening Senya, I just have other things on my
mind. There's something I want to tell you. I've decided to go
back tomorrow. I can't sit around here and do nothing any
longer . . .'

'But that's the most ridiculous thing I've ever heard! This is the
very time you *shouldn't* go back. You're sure to put your foot in
it and end up in trouble yourself, I shall do my damndest to see
you don't return. Please Natasha, be sensible, let the dust settle
before you go. They don't need you, not at the moment anyway.
They'll manage perfectly well without you.'

Natasha hotly contradicted him and they began to argue. It
was more important to her than almost anything else that Senya
should recognise the value of her political work, especially now
that she was about to leave him. But he kept stubbornly
repeating how childish and ridiculous she was being. 'As if they
can't find other people to do your work while you're here!
Believe me, anyone could do that work – as well or better than
you!'

He wouldn't listen to her. She actually quoted, word for word,
her friends' urgent requests for her to return, but these he
dismissed. 'Yes, and who is that writing? Maria Mikhailovna?
I might have known! Why she's nothing but a hysterical woman
who's always moaning about something. Now I'd understand
how you were feeling if it was Dontsov – he knows his stuff, that
would mean something. But Maria Mikhailovna, who gives a

damn what *she* thinks? I wouldn't worry about her, if I were you.'

Natasha felt unable to defend herself against these hurtful words. She had to admit she was disappointed it wasn't Dontsov (the man with the limp) who was urging her to return. That would have proved beyond doubt that her friends needed her and valued her work, and then, oh then she would have flown straight back to them, without another thought. All right, she was offended that Dontsov hadn't been among those begging her to return, she admitted that. But why couldn't Senya be a little more sympathetic, why did he have to rub things in? Why did he invariably fail to listen to her or understand what was going on in her mind? Did he mean to hurt her?

She said goodnight to him coldly, hoping that he might notice and respond in some way. But he was apparently oblivious to her icy manner. He retired to his room and left Natasha alone, assailed by a deep and all too familiar fear of her solitude – a fear mainly of her own unstated and unacknowledged grievances. Come what may, they would have to break this awful silence and have it out. Either he'd understand what she was talking about, or it would be the end of their relationship. Anything would be better than this silence which starved the spirit. She opened her door and hurried towards his room. 'Thank god I only have to be here until tomorrow – I couldn't endure another long pointless day in this place,' she thought.

As she reached his door she paused and put her ear to the keyhole. She could hear nothing. Senya must be sleeping. He always fell asleep the moment his head touched the pillow. She turned the door handle a little, then released it. Suddenly she could imagine the sleepy expression on his face as she opened the door, and she flushed with shame as she imagined what he say to her. 'Aha, so you've come again! What am I going to do with you? I'm tired, can't you get that into your head? Whatever will I do tomorrow if my head isn't fresh . . . ?'

'No, please no,' she whispered, 'I couldn't bear that again.' She ran back down the corridor to her room. The night porter was puzzled and fascinated. The lady had obviously changed her mind. 'Must've quarrelled, I suppose,' he muttered grinning, as she passed him.

12

Senya left the hotel first thing in the morning and didn't look in once to see her during the day, something he had never done before. By evening she was getting worried. She lost count of the times she opened the door of her room to listen and peer out into the empty, dimly lit corridor. Once the silence was broken by the sound of someone clearing his throat; a man's footsteps turned into the corridor and her heart leapt. But it wasn't him.

By three in the morning she was almost demented with anxiety, convinced that he must have had an accident. He'd never stayed out so late before. She kept hoping he had got back and gone straight to bed without coming in to see her. Again and again she set off down the corridor to his room, found it empty and retraced her steps. The night-porter, more fascinated than ever, eyed her and smirked. But such irritations were as nothing compared to her anxieties about Senya.

He could at least have telephoned to tell her what was happening. He might have lost track of the time while he was talking to the professor and decided to spend the night there, but she could hardly believe he would completely forget about her – that would be unforgivable. He must know how worried she would be. He would never do such a thing to Anyuta. The hours passed, her fantasies of what might have happened grew, and soon she was nearly beside herself with worry. She tried to rest, yet no sooner had she stretched herself out on the bed than she would leap up to open the door. But still the same dreary silence. There was never a soul to be seen in that ill-lit corridor with the loathsome red carpet – if it hadn't been for the carpet she'd be able to hear his footsteps from far away.

Someone coughed a few doors away, someone snored sweetly – then there was silence again, broken only by the clock on the tower opposite striking four-thirty. Her vigil was becoming unbearable. She longed for morning. Her only hope now was that he had spent the night at the professor's. She could picture him running back to her shamefaced in the morning, making a lot of silly excuses like a naughty child. 'But how could I have telephoned?' he would say. 'The professor would have guessed everything.' He'd stand there, looking ashamed of himself and waiting for her to tell him off, and she'd smile at him in her usual mild manner, and stroke back his untidy forelock to kiss his brow. 'You don't have to explain Senya, I understand,' she'd say, and he would sigh with relief; 'You're so good to me, Natasha . . .' Then they would both feel cheerful again, and her fears would seem foolish . . .

'I'm just on edge,' She tried now to reassure herself. 'There's no reason to assume anything terrible has happened. I can get some sleep while I'm waiting. I won't lock the door.' So she forced herself to lie down and managed to doze for a while. But even as she dozed she was perpetually listening for his footsteps. There was a faint rustle outside: in an instant she had leapt out of bed, her heart thumping wildly. But no, it was only the couple in the room next door brushing against the adjoining wall. She heard some people exchanging words with the hall porter, and once again she was wide awake.

Soon it was nine o'clock, and a dull grey morning light crept through the blinds into her room. Unable to stay in bed a moment longer, she got up and dressed with deliberate slowness, still intensely alert to every sound. She opened the door into the corridor one more time, but now that the lights had been switched off it looked even more desolate. Again and again she peered out, though part of her knew she was being ridiculous. She just kept hoping that at any minute the dear familiar figure in the battered cap would appear round the bend in the corridor. This night had proved to her just how precious her Senya was to her!

She reproached herself for all her grievances, and bitterly regretted the unkind things she had thought about him, the times she had hurt his feelings. Now she longed only for him to come back so she could know he was safe and well.

Of course he might have returned after she had gone to bed! The moment this happy thought flashed into her mind she ran down the corridor, her hair streaming down her back, comb in hand. Several people had to step out of her way as she rushed past, and she brushed against the woman washing the floor, splashing water on to the carpet as she did so. She stopped to apologise profusely. The woman grumbled and moved her bucket.

Senya's room was empty, his bed unslept in. Nonplussed, Natasha sank down on it to wait for him. She felt closer to him sitting there surrounded by his things – his familiar old trousers and waistcoat . . .

She realised now what must have happened. Anyuta had arrived in G'ville unexpectedly, and Senya was out of his mind with worry lest the two of them should accidentally meet. If this was so, Natasha ought to leave town. But then she did want to be of some comfort to Senya – or at least to let him know she was leaving so he wouldn't worry about bringing Anyuta to the hotel. It occurred to her that she might phone the professor, then she realised Anyuta might well be there. Anyway, she had been strictly forbidden to use the telephone. But what if Senya was at this moment on his way to the hotel with Anyuta? Galvanised by the thought, she leapt off the bed, swiftly scrutinised the room for any evidence of her presence, then poked her head out of the door to make sure the corridor was empty before hurrying back to her room.

The clock struck ten. The clock struck eleven, twelve, one . . . By now Natasha had long ceased to wait or listen, and had abandoned all hope of ever seeing him again. He might have been arrested. He might have had an accident (he was so short-sighted it was quite possible he'd been run over and seriously hurt). He might be dead. Of course, he *might* be alive and well somewhere – but if he was, surely he'd have found some way of getting a brief message to her and putting her mind at rest? This endless silence must mean something deeply and irreparably terrible had happened to him.

Natasha slumped in a chair with her eyes closed, for the daylight irritated them unbearably. In the long hours of the night she had longed for the day, but now she longed for darkness to come again. In the dark it had at least been possible to hope. Now all hope was gone. Maybe he was in hospital and nobody knew where he was, maybe he was calling for her. If he hadn't come back by three that afternoon (this was the time he generally called in at the hotel to see her), she would phone the professor and damn the consequences. She felt much better after making this decision, and began to move about the room tidying things away.

Just when she had finally persuaded herself to stop waiting for him, there was a loud rap at the door.

'Come in!' she called out, freezing with sudden apprehension. A young messenger-boy handed her a letter. She seized it from him, struggled with the envelope and tore out a letter from Senya.

'I'm afraid something most unpleasant and unexpected has happened to me. Last night, shortly after dinner, I began to experience the most excruciating stomach pains, and I was soon feeling so ill that I had to go to bed. My temperature shot up and they called the doctor, who feared it might be appendicitis. By then the pain was indescribable and I had to have two morphine injections.

'Today, thank heavens, I'm feeling a lot better. The doctor's just been, and he says I'll pull through and there won't be any need to operate. My temperature's lower but still above normal. I'm in a great deal of pain, but at least it's bearable now. I just need complete peace and quiet and a good rest.

'I hope you won't worry too much about me. I must say it could hardly have happened in a better place, here with the professor and his family. D'you know, they stayed up all night looking after me!

'I've told them I met this Russian family, old friends of mine, in the hotel, and that I wanted to ask them to choose a few books to send me. That was the excuse I gave them for writing to you. Do you think you could send me whatever comes to hand? I don't feel up to reading just now, so it really doesn't matter what. But one thing I beg of you: please don't under any circumstances phone or write to me here. I kiss your hands.

Senya.'

Poor, poor Senechka . . .

The little messenger-boy, who had been quietly waiting while she read this letter through, was becoming impatient. 'Will there be any reply then?' he asked.

'A reply? Oh yes, of course. Would you mind sitting down for a moment while I sort out some books for you to take back?'

She hurried off to his room, too numb to grasp anything but the fact that she must find some books for him but not write to him. Yet how she yearned to write just one line to let him know how much she had worried about him, how much she loved him. She hoped he wasn't too anxious about her. Everything seemed bearable now she knew he was alive. But despite her relief she was trembling so much she could hardly get her fingers to make the books into a parcel. Just a little note in the parcel! She was almost demented with frustration at being denied this small pleasure. She knew as well as he did that she couldn't though –

they'd only see it and ask him all sorts of embarrassing questions, and poor dear Senya, who was such a bad liar, would be sure to betray his confusion. She had no wish to put him through that. She handed the books to the messenger-boy, who went off at once leaving her alone once more in her tiny single room.

Her morning coffee, still undrunk, stood on the little table by the sofa. The melancholy which had settled within her was as sour and cold as those muddy dregs, a depression compounded of her worst fears and regrets.

The danger wasn't over yet. The doctor's words were of small consolation to her when she thought of Senya, writhing in agony. How could she complain of her own misery in the face of pain, fever, morphine? This was real suffering, making her own pale by comparison, and obliterating all her worries of the past few days.

13

Two days passed; three nights filled with hours of anxious solitary reflection and exhausting dreams from which she was invariably jolted awake with the same question on her lips: 'Senya, Where are you? What are you doing?' Once she dreamed she heard his voice, and woke up terrified that it might be some kind of omen. She ran downstairs several times a day to the hotel porter in the hope of finding a letter or a telephone message for her, or perhaps just a little note delivered by the messenger-boy. Behind her back the hotel servants whispered and sniggered among themselves: to her face they respectfully enquired whether the monsieur was reserving the room or had left for good.

Naturally he'd reserved it, she told them; it was simply that monsieur was ill, and it was more convenient for him to stay with friends. She found it irritating to have to go into all this – why should she be obliged to justify herself in this way when all she cared about was how Senya was? There was no longer any doubt in her mind that he had taken a turn for the worse. He must be very ill indeed not to have found some way of getting in touch with her. She longed only to know he was alive.

Long listless hours dragged by and by the third day she was beginning to feel desperate. She would imagine that hours had gone by, only to realise that the clock hand had moved one minute. She was incapable of doing any work, and unable to leave the building in case there was a message for her. Towards the evening of that day she felt she hadn't the strength to endure any more. The prospect of another night on her own terrified her. She no longer cared about the consequences – she would get the porter to cable the professor and find out how Senya was.

Trembling with fear, she rang the bell for room-service. What if her message got garbled? What if Anyuta was there? An endless series of dreadful possibilities flashed through her mind.

'*Que deésire madame?*' The porter arrived promptly in response to her call, but she felt this was calculated to startle and confuse her. At that moment her mind was a blank and she had no idea what to do next. She merely asked him for some tea. The porter enquired whether she wanted lemon or milk, flashed his little white napkin and was off. She paced listlessly around the room, groaning and wringing her hands, her aching head filled with ghastly images. The tea arrived, the clock struck nine, and her last hope for some message from Senya faded. She rang a second time, more decisively now. But this time the porter took his time in coming. When he arrived he stood looking bored and shuffling his feet. Little did he know what a struggle it was for her to appear calm! She asked him if he would kindly make a phone call for her, and told him as clearly as she could the questions she wanted him to ask. 'You don't have to mention it's a woman asking,' she added hastily. 'Just say it's his Russian friends who are worried about him and would like some news.'

'I understand perfectly, madame,' the porter said suavely, and hurried off bearing a scrap of paper with his instructions.

'I hope to god he doesn't get it wrong and say it's a woman asking him to make the call!' This was all that seemed important to her as she waited in a fever of agitation for him to return. She prayed that everything would go smoothly and nothing would happen to distress Senya. She stopped pacing about the room and sat down on the edge of the sofa. Her heart seemed to be beating in her throat; she had difficulty swallowing; she was as tense as a violin string. Any second now she would know the worst.

Five minutes, seven minutes, ten minutes dragged by – how unbearably long he was taking, why hadn't he come back yet? He must have some message so terrible that he couldn't bring himself to tell her. The thought made her practically faint from fear. An icy shiver gripped her. She knew that in an hour, by which time she would know all, she would look back with longing at this tortured respite. At least some hope was still alive and warm within her.

There was a knock at the door. 'Come in!' she managed to call out. The porter stood in the doorway and she fixed beseeching eyes on him. But he was in no hurry to deliver his message – the way his napkin was arranged on his arm was not to his liking, and his first concern was to put it straight. At last, he spoke: 'I am told to inform you that the monsieur thanks his Russian friends' (he smirked beneath his little moustache) 'for their concern. He is feeling very much better today. He has taken a walk around his room and is about to retire to sleep.'

Natasha sat motionless and silent.

'That is the end of the message. Will there be anything else, madame?'

'No thank you, nothing else.'

Whisking his white napkin he went off. How funny, she'd thought that if the porter had brought back hopeful news, some ray of light, however feeble, she would burst into tears of joy. An hour ago she would have endured anything just to know that he was well. Now she stood stock-still in the middle of the room in a state of shock. She no longer understood anything. Certainly she no longer understood Senya. Tormented and distraught, she was cut to the quick by feelings of bitterness that were new to her. Senya, who was afraid of inflicting the slightest pain on Anyuta, had made not the slightest move to end her torment. Dear gentle Senya indeed! How dare he behave like this, how dare he pretend he still loved her? She tossed her head, as though Senya were in the room to see her. She would never, never forget the insulting way he had treated her.

14

Natasha slept soundly that night and awoke refreshed, untroubled and determined to put last night's misery behind her. There was little point in being sad now the danger was over and Senya was alive and on the way to recovery. Any day now she would be seeing him again, and then she would tell him plainly what a terrible thing it was to treat love so carelessly. She would explain to him that if you stretched a person's heart-strings too far, love would die.

This was the first morning since her arrival that Natasha enjoyed her coffee. She smiled warmly at the chambermaid who brought it, and who stayed to tell her what a wonderful spring day it was and how madame must be sure to go out for a walk. If only she was free like madame, sighed the girl, she'd be walking outside from morning to night.

Natasha read through some papers, and for the first time in many days felt able to attend to them with the seriousness they demanded. She felt ashamed to have fallen so behind with her correspondence. In no time she had a large bundle of letters written, and no sooner had she cleared these out of the way than the urge came upon her to do some work on her pamphlet which had lain virtually untouched in her drawer. Now, for the first time in G'ville, she was able to write with her customary fluency. The right words, clear and precise, presented themselves at once to her mind and poured from her pen, arranging themselves in a neat logical chain of ideas. Before she knew it the whole day had passed and it was getting dark. She had finished the first chapter.

She stretched blissfully, and felt remarkably happy and clear-headed. She had made a start on the pamphlet, and she didn't have to worry about Senya any more or wait for the phone to ring. He was probably having the time of his life at the professor's house! He obviously had no time to think about Natasha. Sad, really. But she quickly shook away the thought, for after the stress of the last few days the muscles of her soul needed some relaxation. What she wanted now was to escape from this ridiculous imprisoned existence, and make for some cheerful place where she would be surrounded by people and movement and light. She decided to drop off some letters at the post-office and go on from there to a brightly lit café where she could sit and drink a cup of hot chocolate. She had just put on her hat and veil when the door opened and, without so much as a knock, Semyon Semyonovich burst in.

'Senya!' she gasped, more in amazement than joy, 'what are *you* doing here?'

'I'm exhausted, Natasha, this illness has taken it out of me. But I had to drag myself over here to see you, even though the doctor urged me to wait till tomorrow. You see I just couldn't wait that long . . .'

'But you must lie down at once Senya – oh how thin you are, how ill you look, your eyes are so hollow . . . Whatever made you come here, darling?'

'I was getting restless, Natasha, I had so much on my mind . . .'

'Now let me get you a pillow and I'll take your boots off for you. You lie here and I'll put this blanket over you. Would you like some tea perhaps? With lemon or milk? I'll ring and order it for you . . .' Natasha hoped that if she busied herself like this she might conceal the sad fact that there was none of that dizzy joy she had expected to feel when she saw him. She had pictured this moment so many times, imagined herself rushing into his arms to hug him and kiss his hands . . . Now she hadn't the slightest desire to do so. Senya had come back at the most inopportune moment, and had completely destroyed the calm abandon she had been feeling.

'Please don't put yourself out on my account, Natasha dear. Why don't you sit down here beside me instead of rushing about? Oh, I've missed you so much . . . Whatever are you doing with your hat on? About to sneak out? Might I ask where? You've been gadding about while I was ill? Well madam, I hope you've preserved your incognito in the process.' The rebuke beneath this clumsy joke was badly concealed.

'No this is the first time Senya, I swear! I haven't so much as poked my nose out of doors all this time. But now I really ought to because these letters have piled up. I was just off to the post-office to mail them by special delivery.'

'But isn't that rather rash, especially now, when Anyuta might arrive at any moment? And why did you phone the professor's house when I specifically asked you not to? I never realised my wishes meant so little to you. All the time I've been ill I haven't had a moment's peace, worrying that you'd phone, and when you did I knew I'd have to drag myself out of bed and get over here, even if it killed me. Why, for all I knew, you might have decided to visit . . .'

'Wait a moment,' Natasha's voice trembled with rage. 'Tell me, is that the only reason you come to see me today? Because you were afraid I might visit the professor's house?'

'No, of course it's not the only reason,' he said, seeing how deeply angry she was. 'I missed you, Natasha, surely I don't have to tell you that.'

'Hah, you missed me! What a joke!' He had never heard her

laugh like that before and it disturbed him. You missed me after you'd devised the cruellest way of torturing me . . .'

'Stop Natasha, what on earth's wrong with you? Why, that could have been Anyuta speaking just now. Do you realise what you're saying? Surely you're not blaming me for being ill? *How* did I torture you Natasha, tell me, what have I done? I don't understand, I didn't mean to hurt you . . . Oh Natasha, I love you so much – maybe Anyuta's right and I only hurt the people I love most, Anyuta, you . . . Oh god, how hard it is . . .'

He buried his face in his hands and looked so grief-stricken and vulnerable that her heart went out to him. 'Oh Senechka, forgive me, I don't know what possessed me to say that. I've been at the end of my tether these past few days, terrified you might die, with nothing to do here but brood and imagine the worst. And I do love you, do you hear me, Simeon?' This was her special name for him. He looked up at once with that bright untroubled smile of his and Natasha, kneeling on the floor before him, kissed his head. 'Let me kiss your hands. Senya, oh how I've dreamed of seeing you again – d'you know, I dreamt the first thing I'd do would be to kiss your hands!'

'You're a sweet thing, Natasha – but how you frightened me with that weird laugh of yours just now. Poor dear, I know your nerves are on edge, like mine. What a hard life it is . . . But what are you doing, squeezing me so tight?'

'I feel so happy now that you're here, *all* of you – you know what I mean, don't you?'

'Indeed I do darling, but I'm afraid I'm still very weak and I get excited when you hold me so tight. You know, the doctor said my illness was probably nervous in origin, and that all I need now is plenty of rest. Please don't be offended if I ask you to move away a little.'

Natasha got up and moved away, turning her face so he shouldn't see the hurt in her eyes. All she longed for was some physical warmth from him, some human contact. How could he have misinterpreted her desires like this? She poured tea for him and he lit a cigarette, lay back on the sofa and launched into a long discourse on the professor's family and how affectionately they had looked after him. He told her too how anxious he had been, afraid that she would come to the house and how frustrated at being unable to communicate with her.

At this she raised her eyebrows. 'But you might have sent me a note, some little message after I'd sent you those books. Surely you could have thought something up . . .'

'But you know what a hopeless liar I am, and then I *did* drag myself here to see you as soon as I was strong enough.'

As they drank their tea Natasha told him about the letters she had received, and about the latest developments in the party. Much of the news was depressing, for the political heat was on now. But there was much that was encouraging too, various exciting new developments. Senya and Natasha were soon deep in political discussion, going over all the possible tactics suggested by their friends, drawing up resolutions, outlining their next campaign, and trying to anticipate the opposition's next move – the situation would surely precipitate new conflicts. Suddenly party work seemed exciting again, and they both found themselves longing to get back to it.

'Oh lord!' Senya broke off. 'It's all play and no work here. With you time flies and I forget everything that's going on in the outside world. I promised I'd be home, the professor's home I mean, by half-past seven, and look, it's already eight. I hope they're not worrying about me, they might run over here to find out what's happening.'

'You're leaving? You're spending the night there?'

'Yes, I'm afraid they won't hear of me staying at the hotel. I must collect my things and dash back now. But Natasha, I want to say one thing to you before I go.' She knew something unpleasant was to follow, from the way he avoided her eyes. 'I want to put it to you that you might like to visit the town of B'ère.'

'But why should I want to visit that place?'

'Well, apparently it is a fascinating old town, full of ancient buildings, you know how much you love that sort of thing,' he said, pleading with her as one might coax a child to take medicine.

'I don't understand what you're saying.'

'Oh never mind, I can see you don't want to go.' He glanced guiltily at her. 'Look, the fact is that with you here I can't relax for a moment. I had to write to Anyuta when I was ill, and, well, you know Anyuta. For all I know she may turn up here at any moment. That's why I think it would be much less fraught for us all.'

Natasha bowed her head and two large tears dropped into her still undrunk tea. 'Ah, my poor sweet girl,' Senya stroked her hair. 'I know how hard it is for you to leave me.' He spoke tenderly, but at that moment his compassion sounded patronising.

'But why should I leave for B'ère? I might as well go straight home instead.' Natasha's tears had dried. She looked at him calmly and somewhat distantly.

'But you don't understand, I wasn't asking you to leave for good, just for a little while, for the next few days. You see, there's a holiday here at the end of the week and the library will be closed, and I've already dropped a few hints about the possibility of my visiting B'ère, told the professor I wanted to see the town and so on. If you go now, I'll follow in a few days and meet you there.'

'No, that's too ridiculous for words. If I'm in your way here I should go home.'

'But how could you think such a thing! You're not in my way! It's only because of Anyuta that I'm suggesting this. Imagine her coming here and making trouble – that's why I'm so anxious at the moment.' He grew more confident, convinced by his own arguments. 'Anyway we shan't be seeing much of each other as it is, because I agreed to leave the hotel for the professor's house today. If you go to B'ère we'll only have to wait till Friday, then we'll be able to spend time together and relax, without work or the professor to distract us. Doesn't that appeal to you?'

'But you're forgetting something. I have to be back by Tuesday at the latest.'

'Well why don't we see how it goes between now and then? If everything still seems quiet at your end surely you can snatch a day or two more. I think it's important for us to have a few uninterrupted, restful days together – I'll feel quite different when I know that neither the professor nor anyone else is around. At the moment I'm constantly on edge – why, at this very moment they might be on their way to look for me.'

'All right then, I'll think about it and we can talk about it tomorrow,' conceded Natasha grudgingly.

'No no, tomorrow's no good, you must leave today, without fail! I've already checked the trains and written them down somewhere . . . now wait a moment, let me find them for you,' he scanned his notebook shortsightedly. 'Yes, here we are. If you get the 10.30 train tonight you'll be there in just an hour-and-a-half. Isn't that convenient? That's the fast train, you'll catch it without any problem. Now don't look so miserable Natasha, or I'll think I've done something terrible to hurt you. I'm sad too that we have to part like this, but I remind myself that it won't be long till we see each other again. When you get there, book a double room, tell them you're waiting for your husband and send me a telegram signed with the usual initials, care of the post office here, to tell me which hotel you're at.' He clearly felt this would be some sort of consolation for her. 'Now be a dear and help me with my packing will you? I must be off. And oh yes, will you settle up with the hotel? You know how bad I am at that sort of thing. D'you need some cash? Because if you do, the professor's offered me some . . . Please don't look so wretched Natasha, I can't bear it.'

'Don't worry about me Senya, I'll get over it. Now lie down here while I go and pack your things. No, I'll do it, you mustn't tire yourself, you're not well. That's it, you just lie down.' Natasha ran off.

She was strapping up his hold-all when he crept in stealthily, making her start. 'Whatever are you doing here, Senechka? You should be lying down. Look, I've finished your packing.'

'I was so worried,' he cast a troubled look at her. 'I was afraid you might be sitting in here on your own and crying. I do love you Natasha, very, very much.' He said this so solemnly that she couldn't help smiling. But her feelings were numb, her mind a blank. She didn't know whether he really loved her or not, or what love meant to him anyway. And what did it mean for her, apart from pain, humiliation, worry . . . ?

'Come and get dressed Senechka, otherwise you'll be late for dinner at the professor's. You wouldn't want Mrs Professor to tell you off, would you?'

'Ah come now, you wouldn't be jealous of her, would you? She's an old lady!'

Natasha smiled again. 'You know Senechka you're so childish sometimes, you funny man. It's amazing the things you don't understand! Anyway, the main thing is for you to look after yourself and make sure you don't fall ill again. I've put your manuscript in its file and the books are here. Goodbye now, Senechka.' They embraced.

'You kissed me so coldly then,' he looked sadly at her, 'as though your heart wasn't in it.'

'I'm just behaving like a virtuous little wife; I wouldn't want to seduce you, after all,' Natasha laughed. Then she hurried off to call a porter to carry Senya's bags downstairs. 'We must order a car to take you there so you don't wear yourself out.'

In the corridor Senya embraced her impulsively and whispered in her ear: 'Please don't be angry with me, my dear, you're the woman I love. You can't imagine how much I need you. Believe me, all this is only because I'm afraid Anyuta may come.'

When they reached the turn in the corridor he stopped and gazed silently at her, shaking his head as though he longed to tell her something and explain himself to her. But she merely laughed and flapped the ends of her scarf in his face: 'Now don't go falling in love with the professor's wife, and come and see me soon!' At this he grinned at her, visibly relaxed. The next moment he was striding purposefully off down the corridor. Natasha bowed her head pensively and retraced her steps along the all too horribly familiar carpet to her room.

15

B'ère was indeed a beautiful old town. Its quiet, ancient streets and ornately decorated churches attracted quite a number of tourists, so that when Natasha arrived she had no difficulty in finding herself a comfortable room in a cheap hotel. She loved the room immediately. It was furnished simply in a modern uncluttered style, without the usual dust-traps of heavy carpets and velvet curtains, and had a pleasantly soothing effect on her.

More important, as she discovered the moment she woke up next morning, it was flooded with sunlight. The view from the window, unlike the dark roofs and the small courtyard at G'ville, was on to a broad, quiet square lined with old houses in which countless generations had lived and died. She got up, raised the blind and smiled at the warm spring sun with a sense of joy. She felt cheerful and energetic. Everything pleased her: the comfortable bed, the capacious wash-stand, and most of all the view. She flung open the window and a soft breeze, fragrant with sweet spring flowers, caressed her face. A chorus of birds rose from the garden below.

'How wonderful life is! And to think how anxious I was! What was it all for?'

She started eagerly on her work, and from the moment she sat down it went easily and quickly, without any sense of strain. She wrote all day and when evening came she was sorry to tear herself away, for she felt she could have written all night too. But she wanted to see the lovely old town, so she wandered out to gaze at B'ère's dreaming towers, domes and lacey cathedrals. She delighted in her new-found freedom like a schoolgirl on holiday. She was happy. She smiled as she walked along the quiet streets, ordered supper in a cheap workers' café and caught the last beams of the hot spring sun, and she smiled when, with a feeling of mild and pleasant exhaustion after a hard day's work, she eventually got into bed.

On Friday she called in at the post office to collect her letters. To her surprise there was one from Semyon Semyonovich. What on earth could he be writing to her about? Could he be ill again? Could it be that he wasn't coming after all?

She was in no hurry to open it, and put it with the others in her leather shoulder-bag. Then she walked through the town until she came to a little square where the birds were singing cheerful spring songs to each other, and delicate pink almond and apricot blossoms were beginning to appear between the dark fleshy leaves of the evergreens. She sat down on a bench and opened her letters one by one. The first was from her party friends. They had been anxious about her and urged her to return, or at least to get in touch. The tempo was quickening, party workers must be at their posts.

'I *shall* go back, the sooner the better, to my friends, my work, my commitments . . .' She would leave, whatever Senya might say in his letter. In fact it might be better if he didn't come at all, so she could leave first thing next morning.

She opened his envelope, secretly hoping he would say he wasn't coming. But no. The moment she left he had poured out his feelings in a long and loving letter in which he blamed himself bitterly, told her again and again how much he loved

332

her, and assured her he couldn't live without her. 'Your reproachful eyes have haunted me since you left,' he wrote. 'I feel
like a criminal and a murderer, treating you like that. You can't
imagine how precious you are to me Natasha, more precious
than I can tell you. Without you the sun would set forever on my
life and the world would be a cold and empty place . . .'

At any other time this letter would have made her heart race
and filled her with almost unbearable happiness. Once she would
have covered her face with her hands and repeated his words
over and over again, beside herself with joy. But that was in the
past. Now she just smiled, a small, patronising smile. 'It's too
late,' she thought bitterly, 'now it's too late.' He was counting the
hours before he saw her again, he wrote in a postscript. But
Natasha was still unmoved. His words didn't touch her. It might
have been the letter of a stranger. She stuffed it into her bag and
hurriedly started reading the others.

One contained a few brief remarks about Vanechka and his
party activities, and she realised guiltily that she still hadn't sent
him that postcard. Dear Vanechka, she thought as she wandered
away from the square, what a good friend he had always been to
her. She went into a shop, picked out a postcard with a nice
picture and pencilled a lighthearted message on the back. She
would be seeing him in a few days, she wrote. She was terribly
bored and longed to see them all again, even Dontsov. She knew
it was true. She was longing see all her friends again.

On her way back to the hotel she suddenly visualised that
terrible hotel at G'ville, the endless corridor, the repulsive carpet,
the porter dozing at his table – and herself in her dressing-gown,
her hair tied in white ribbons, hesitating at Semyon Semyonovich's door, wrestling with her emotions. Standing there like a
petitioner. Oh, how loathsome and humiliating it had been! She
tried to put it out of her mind.

A telegram was waiting for her at the hotel: 'I'll be there at
1.30 a.m. Meet me!'

'My husband is coming today,' she informed the porter tonelessly and went back to her room. She wanted to make use of these last precious hours of freedom to finish her pamphlet – and most of all to enjoy being on her own.

16

When Natasha arrived at the station half an hour before the train was due, she saw a message scrawled in chalk on a blackboard announcing that one of the night trains would be late. The porter did not know which one it was, but her question caught the attention of a passing man who raised his hat politely and told her a rainstorm had washed away the line, and that the train she was waiting for would be forty-five minutes late. As far as he knew there were no casualties. Natasha glanced at him. He was tall, with a small square-cut beard and dark, lively eyes. He seemed most sympathetic.

He went on talking. His mother, whom he was meeting, was also travelling on that train. He hadn't seen her for two months and it was too long. He would like his mother to live with him permanently, that would be a tremendous joy. 'The only love I can truly respect is a mother's love,' he said, 'because it's the only unselfish love.' He was expansive, like a lot of southerners. 'And might I ask who madame is waiting for? A friend? Or maybe her husband?'

'Yes, my husband,' she replied, not thinking, then blushed.

'And has madame been married long?'

'That depends when you start counting.'

'From before you go up the aisle, naturally – after that, well it's legal but so what? You see, I have my own ideas about this. I'm afraid most women wouldn't agree with me, but as far as I'm concerned there's *pas de difference* whether a woman living with a man is married to him or not. In fact, I think living with someone you're not married to imposes more chains than any legal marriage. I'm not talking about casual affairs of course, I'm talking about important relationships. I think a woman must feel eternally dissatisfied as a man's mistress, so she makes moral demands of him and is resentful. First it's one thing, then another . . . Yes, I've passed through that school of experience myself, feeling more and more trapped and dependent on your own suffering – I could tell you a few interesting things about that! Are you German by any chance, madame?'

'No I'm Russian, and a writer too, so you needn't worry, you can say anything you like to me! Nothing shocks me.'

'Ah, a writer,' he tipped his hat. 'I respect a woman who has a profession. My mother was a teacher, you know . . . But then of course none of that makes any difference in love – people are still bound to each other by the same emotional chains, don't you agree? No, I don't believe there can ever be any truth or honesty between a man and a woman. It's just one long mutual lie, an endless pose, a mask, lying for the sake of the other person's peace of mind, lying out of fear, lying because you don't know any better and because that's the only thing you know how to do. Do married people (I mean legally married or in long relationships) ever have time to be on their own, as single men and women do? Do they ever speak their true feelings to each other? Act on their real desires and needs and moods? Realise what may be the best in themselves? No, it's a game, a mask, a pose and a lie, that's all there is to it!'

He spoke with passion, and Natasha understood him perfectly, adding some observations of her own and citing examples to back up what he said. 'C'est ça, ç'est ça!' he nodded enthusiastically as Natasha equally vehemently poured out to this stranger everything she had been thinking and suffering these past months. He listened attentively, looking gravely into her face as she talked, occasionally finishing her thought for her with an apt word.

Natasha was the first to realise that the hands of the clock were creeping up to the time when the train was due. Neither of them had noticed how the hour had flown as they strolled up and down the dingy station platform, deep in conversation.

'I am so glad, madame, that fate has granted me this happy meeting with you. I shan't be so immodest as to ask your name, but I should like to tell you in all honesty that I've never before met a young woman of such maturity – I say young because it's generally amongst older people that I find such fellow-spirits. Older women don't talk about these things of course, but there's not much they don't know. Take my mother, a remarkable woman. I'm proud to be able to buy her everything she needs at the end of her life. What money I have, madame, I've made with my own hands. I'm a wine merchant now but I started off as an errand-boy in the cellars, and worked my way up. My mother was a teacher, and there were eight of us children, all boys. I was Mother's youngest – we never knew our father. Now I'm waiting for her as impatiently as a lover!'

People swarmed on to the platform as the train drew in. Natasha held out her hand to the man. He tipped his hat again and leaned forward to kiss her hand, then thought better of it. Their eyes met. Natasha blushed and withdrew quickly into the crowd. The train ground to a halt, filling the station with a thick cloud of smoke.

Then Semyon Semyonovich was by her side, hugging her. 'Natasha! How are you? Tired of waiting I expect – but how fresh you look, pink and lovely as a schoolgirl! You must be exhausted, I know I am. This past hour I've been so impatient I could hardly restrain myself from leaping out of the window and racing down the track all the way here!'

Abandoning his habitual caution, he embraced Natasha and kissed her passionately on the lips. Then he took her arm and led her to the exit, beaming as he recounted how he'd outwitted the professor and given him the slip. 'And now at last, my darling we can be together, and rest and talk and celebrate our twelfth honeymoon.' He squeezed her arm. 'I'm so happy to see you again. Natasha, so happy.' She smiled at him, observing him as calmly and coolly as she might observe an innocent child. How strangely remote he seemed to her – never before had she felt this way about him.

At the exit they almost bumped into Natasha's new acquaintance, attentively escorting a white-haired old lady by the arm. Natasha pretended not to notice him, knowing that if she greeted him she would only provoke a lot of unnecessary questions and explanations, tedious suspicions and justifications. But she hated this deception. She knew that by staying silent she was courting her own slavery to another's moods. She had had enough.

In the car on the way to the hotel Semyon Semyonovich drew her closer to him and sought her lips. 'You can't imagine how much I've missed you Natasha, and how empty and alone I felt without you. When I saw you looking so unhappy I hated myself and I knew at once what a stupid thing it was to send you away. It was very wrong of me and I'm terribly sorry now. I was being over-anxious – you know how on edge people can be when they've been ill, don't you? Do you believe me, will you ever forgive me?'

'Yes, of course, Senechka.'

'And you're not still angry with me? I can't help feeling you're not very happy to see me. Please Natasha, you must tell me,' he gazed beseechingly into her face. 'Perhaps you no longer love me?' He was almost whispering, as though the terrifying idea had formed itself into words before he had had time to think.

'No I don't, I don't love you at all, so there!' Natasha said with a forced little laugh, trying to break the awkwardness between them. But the joke rang hollow in her ears. Semyon Semyonovich sighed and leaned back in a deep brooding silence. Certainly Natasha felt sorry for him, but it was no longer with that sharp, burning compassion compounded of tenderness and respect which she had always felt for him in the past. Now she was simply sorry for him as she would feel sorry for any friend in trouble.

Eventually she managed to cheer him up by telling him about all the letters from their mutual friends, and soon he was taking a lively interest in the latest news. By the time they reached the hotel they were like two colleagues talking over their day's work.

17

The next morning they got up late, and the sun had already left the bedroom when Natasha raised the blind and opened the window. 'Look how lovely it is Senya, spring's here!'

'Yes, it's absolutely lovely, what a little paradise you have here!' He came over to the window, put his arm round her shoulder and hugged her. They stood silently together looking out, deep in thought. Natasha felt more at peace than she had done for a long time. It was as if she were somewhere else, observing from a distance. She was beginning to feel a calm and tender sympathy for this dear and extraordinary man who now seemed so remote from her.

The previous night she had responded to his embraces with this same detachment and with none of her usual responsive passion. 'You oughtn't to tire yourself out Senya, you'll only fall ill again. Why don't I tell you what I've seen here instead?' she had urged, trying to distract his attention.

For the first time in their relationship it was *she* who set the mood, treating him rather as one might treat a much younger friend. Before that, she had always faithfully echoed his moods; now he was following hers without even realising it. He was happy that she appeared so much more contented; and more importantly, she wasn't embarking on long psychological discussions, as he had feared she would. He began to feel quite carefree, and wished that things between them could always be as easy as this.

He had been worrying a lot recently about Natasha's evident unhappiness, although this was something he sensed rather than consciously acknowledged. He didn't understand what its origins were or what he was supposed to do about it, and the more he tried to understand her the worse it became and the more stupid he felt. It had been like this in the past with Anyuta, and now it was happening more and more frequently with Natasha too. The fault, he felt, must lie with him and his inability to relate sexually to women. A few of his friends were Don Juans, and recently he had begun to envy them, had even tried to discover the secrets of their success.

But now, in B'ere, he felt at last as though he and Natasha were on firm ground, and the thought that they had 'found each other again', as she would have put it, filled him with joy. They laughed and joked as they had their breakfast. Semyon Semyonovich enjoyed his rolls and coffee, and laughingly assured Natasha that she made a perfect hostess. He was on top of the world. For Natasha it was like entertaining an old acquaintance.

'I'd love to stay a bit longer,' he was saying, 'but unfortunately the library opens again on Tuesday and the professor has invited a colleague of his to show me round the archives. Theoretically I'm free till Tuesday but that means I should really be back by Monday . . .'

'Monday, oh that's excellent.'

'Well I don't think it's excellent at all!'

'I do Senya, because I'm dying to get back – I can't bear sitting around here doing nothing when they're waiting for me at home. This way I'll be able to get back to them by Monday.'

'Why, what nonsense! Why should they be waiting for you? You know they can cope perfectly well on their own. One day more or less is neither here nor there, I don't see why we should be in such a rush to leave here.'

'But how *can* you say that in this political climate?'

'Our friends exaggerate, as you well know.'

Natasha said nothing. Even now he was putting his own needs first. In all the years she had known him he hadn't once offered to sacrifice his time for her, even when she'd entreated him to do so. No, if Anyuta was waiting, then he had to go; that was an iron law, and there'd never been any getting around it. That she too might be in a hurry to return, and that for her every extra day spent here was a wasted one was something he couldn't understand.

'Do you remember, Senya?' she began slowly, thinking aloud, 'the time two years ago when we met in that little town in the north?'

'Yes of course I do. Why?'

'And do you remember how I had a sudden attack of angina? I had a high temperature, I didn't know a soul in the town, it was a horrible hotel . . . D'you remember I asked you to spend an extra day with me so I wouldn't have to lie there alone in a strange and uncomfortable hotel? I said to you then: "Just one day, Senechka, that's all I'm asking! What will one day matter to Anyuta when she has you all the rest of the time?" I'd never begged you for anything you know, but I was begging you then. But you left all the same, and I stayed there, sick, alone and delirious . . .'

'But why are you bringing all this up now, Natasha?' He looked terribly hurt and worried.

'Because when we're discussing *your* arrangements you have no difficulty in understanding that one day might be important, but when we're discussing mine you take absolutely no account of my needs. I find that a strange kind of equality, I must say.' Natasha spoke calmly and unusually coolly.

'How can you say I take no account of your needs, Natasha? You're quite wrong my dear, and you know it. Tell me, have I ever forced you to do anything you didn't want to do? If I *have*

been doing something wrong, it's unintentional and unconscious. I assure you. I want there to be complete equality between
us!'

'Well, let's not go into that now, I expect you're right. Anyway, it's not important any more. I'm sorry I spoke.' She tried to
change the subject, but Senya responded absent-mindedly and
paced the room deep in thought. Then suddenly his face brightened and he beamed, with that generous childlike smile which
Natasha had always loved so much. Peering slyly at her over the
rims of his glasses, he said, 'I'm going to have a shave now, then
afterwards how about wandering around the town together for a
bit?' Going up to her, he gazed tenderly at her, kissed her eyes
and hands, then, looking somewhat embarrased, disappeared
through the door.

Natasha was baffled. 'Hurry up, it'll be dark soon!' she called
out after him.

He was back again in no time. 'That was a quick shave,' she
said. His mysterious air made her laugh, for he reminded her of a
child with a secret. 'Come on now, tell me what you've done!'

'Guess!'

'Get on with you, how can I guess? Tell me, Senechka!' She
gave him a playful push.

'I sent a telegram to the professor, so there!' He stuck out his
tongue at her.

'Saying what, for god's sake?'

'Saying I'm not going back until Friday, that's what!'

'Senya!'

He had expected Natasha to throw herself at him and hug him
to suffocation in a transport of joy and gratitude. But she didn't;
she stood with her hands at her sides and an expression on her
face not of joy but of something quite different, an expression
which closely resembled rage.

'I see. So without consulting me or even asking how I felt
about it, you sent a telegram postponing your departure. How

could you do such a thing, Senya? How could you take a decision like that on your own . . . ?'

'Natasha, what's the matter with you?'

'I told you Tuesday! You knew perfectly well that I couldn't go back later than Tuesday!'

'But I only did it because you were so upset when I told you. I had to go back on Monday night. I did it for you Natasha, to show you I *do* care about your feelings, I *do* value you, more than my work, more than anything else in the world . . . I thought you'd be pleased . . .'

He looked so crestfallen that Natasha felt she must try to make him understand how she felt. But she checked the impulse. Why bother, when their spirits were no longer in harmony and they had stopped listening to each other? After all, Senechka had wanted to do something, anything, to make her happy, and she realised what an enormous concession it was for him to have deferred his departure.

Once Natasha would have been in seventh heaven at such evidence of his love for her. Now she was painfully aware that it was too late.

She decided to deflect the incident. She would avoid any discussion of her feelings, for she wanted things to be as easy as possible between them. So she calculated how long her journey back would take, then mildly pointed out that there wasn't enough money for them to stay a day longer than Wednesday. Besides, she added, wouldn't it seem suspicious to the professor if he stayed on? And what if Anyuta turned up unannounced in G'ville?

As she spelt out these possibilities, she felt like a wise mother with years of experience of her child's psychology. She didn't once discuss what *she* wanted, she talked as if she was in no hurry to leave, she even thanked him for trying to put her happiness first and offering to stay with her for a few more days. Gradually as she spoke she saw him relax, and when an hour later they stepped out of the hotel to walk arm in arm through the peaceful streets of the old town, she knew he was feeling quite tranquil, elated even.

To her he might have been a sympathetic relative whom she was showing around town, someone with whom she felt happy, not at all bored, someone who is an agreeable but by no means indispensable part of one's life.

18

'Do you know, Natasha?' Semyon Semyonovich said, closing his suitcase (he was leaving before her), 'I think these have been the happiest days I can remember for many years.'

'Really?'

'I had the impression you felt like that too. True, you seemed a little strange sometimes, distant and a bit cold, but as soon as I *listened* to you, as you put it, and tried to be more sensitive to your needs, all your coldness melted. Am I right? It's a long time since I've seen you looking so cheerful and laughing such a lot. I shall be able to feel almost good about leaving you . . .' He stopped, pondered a moment, and then, in an uncharacteristic gesture, knelt down before her and buried his head in her lap.

'Senya dear, what is it?'

'I sometimes get these strange feelings, Natasha – I'm terrified of losing you. I tell myself I'm being stupid, but I can't help it. I feel like a little boy who's afraid his mother might abandon him in the woods. We're not getting on very well, are we, Natasha? D'you think we're becoming strangers to each other? Tell me Natasha, I must know: do you still love me?'

He gazed at her with anguished eyes, but once again she avoided his question with a laugh. 'This psychologising and self-questioning isn't like you, I'm afraid you must have picked it up from me, my foolish Senya!'

'You're right, we've reversed roles,' he said quietly, gently stroking her hands. 'This is very hard for me, Natasha. In a way everything's as it used to be, yet at the same time I sense something different, terrifying. I'm afraid, Natasha.'

Natasha's heart missed a beat. Could it be that now of all times, when everything was over, he was learning something and was beginning to understand her needs, needs which she herself might have been afraid to acknowledge? 'We've gone through too much together over the years ever to become strangers, Senya. I feel far too much for you to stop loving you. But at the moment I see you like a younger brother who I know and love deeply, but in a different way.' She stroked that clever head which for so long she had loved to distraction.

'Goodbye, sweet head . . .' A spasm of sadness brought a lump to her throat, and she could no longer check her tears. She sobbed, not for the living Senya she was parting from, but for the end of a dream, the passing of their love and the memory of the joys and anxieties they had gone through together. Her tears helped her to accept that this was the end. Semyon Semyonovich was consoled by them. 'There, nothing's changed,' he hugged her, 'we can go on as we were before . . .' He picked her up and carried her to the bed.

Natasha stood on the station platform in her hat and veil, her travelling bag slung across her shoulder. Semyon Semyonovich stood on the steps of the train which was about to leave. 'So you go north and I go south, who knows when we'll meet again? Not for some time, I suppose – these trips cost quite a bit, don't they? But I feel we're only alive when we're together, don't you feel that too? And this time was especially good, wasn't it Natasha?' He was pleading with her to agree with him.

'Yes, it's a heavenly, poetic place, I shall leave with lots of new ideas – which I've stolen from you, I need hardly say!' She often flattered him in this way.

'Don't try currying favour with me, you've a perfectly good head of your own! You'll write to me, won't you Natasha?'

'Of course I will.'

'I'm already dreaming of the next time we meet . . .'

'Just a minute, I want to check with you whether this is right,' Natasha interrupted him in a deliberately businesslike manner to run over the main outlines of a resolution they had agreed she would put to the others. The doors were being slammed shut now.

'Goodbye then Natasha, don't be miserable,' he stepped out on to the platform to embrace her once more. 'I have so much to thank you for . . .'

'For what, Senechka?'

'Everything, my darling. Give me your hand, there, you must go now. The train's leaving. Write to me, sweetheart.' He hung out of the window as the train slowly moved off, waved his shabby cap at her, then put it on. Natasha had always found this old cap of his so touching; now she couldn't help noticing how its floppy brim drooped over his face. The train was disappearing into the darkness and the people on the platform were crowding towards the exit, but Natasha didn't move. She didn't peer anxiously after the train, as once she would have done. She just felt very peaceful – a little sad perhaps, but not painfully unhappy. She knew that this time they had parted for good, and that if they ever met again it would be as acquaintances. Of course it was possible that some time in the future, political work might throw them together again. But that would be a meeting of two party comrades, nothing more. The great love which had made her heart beat all these years, which she thought would never fade, had gone forever. It was dead, extinguished, and nothing, no tenderness, no prayers, not even understanding, could reawaken it. It was too late.

By the time Natasha's train arrived she was no longer thinking about the end of her great love affair with Semyon Semyonovich. She took her seat and at once began to sort through her papers and letters, throwing some away, putting some aside for future reference, replying to others. Now she belonged body and soul to her work. Long, long ago she had experienced a great love, but that love had ebbed away. Semyon Semyonovich, in his heedless, male stupidity, had destroyed it. So learn from this, all you men who have made women suffer through your blindness, and know that if you injure a woman's heart you will kill her love for you!

Thirty-Two Pages

1

Workshops and factories flashed past, their windows gleaming bright spots in the night, then a row of identical workers' houses, then more houses, the army barracks, and at last the shake and rumble of the railway bridge. As the train finally came to a halt, the station-lamps cast their brightness into the murky autumn darkness and lit up her compartment. Footsteps shuffled along the grey platform; the wind danced around the lights, whistling into the dark expanse of field beyond the factory wall. She glanced around to check that she had left nothing behind, then buttoned up her jacket, stepped on to the platform and headed for the exit.

Before her stretched an endless empty street lined with buildings, twenty or thirty little houses indistinguishable from one another. There were no lights in the windows, for by now most of the workers in the little factory settlement were asleep. The street-lamps flickered. There was no sound.

But as she walked on down the street intermittent sounds, muffled by the distance, reached her ears and she recognised the familiar din of the night shift. A dog barked nearby, a shrill nervous bark which made her start. Then she smiled. 'Stop that, stupid dog – it's *me* who's scared!'

She quickened her step and suddenly things didn't seem so

bad. She was probably worrying needlessly, forcing herself to make a lot of irrelevant decisions. Why should she make any decisions at all?

Nobody else made such heavy weather of life – why couldn't she be like other people? Why not simply drop her research and her precious scientific theories. Wash her hands of the whole thing, give it up, move in with him in this little town, stop living for her work and live for love?

It was out of the question. How could she even contemplate giving up her work, which had so preoccupied her all these months? She sighed and tossed her head, trying to shake off the nagging anxieties which beset her.

She had reached the end of the street. On the corner was a teashop. It was locked now, its shutters were closed, the lamp over the doorway was switched off. Could it really be that late, she wondered, stepping under the street-lamp to glance at her watch. Yes, it was a quarter past two. She'd have to find some way of passing the time until three, when the night shift ended.

She turned off the road and cut across a piece of wasteland, making for the grey windowless walls of some great unfinished building, and stumbled on to an unmade gravel track. She was beginning to feel very tired.

She turned the corner of the building, and for a moment she was blinded. Towering over her, flooded with light, panting, clanking and clamouring, stood the factory. One whole wall was crimson with the brightly-lit windows of eight workshops. Outside the locked factory gates it was silent and deserted, but inside, behind that dazzling wall of windows, there was a completely different life, one of endless, strenuous work. She could picture the hundreds of figures in their blue work-shirts moving about their business with measured concentration, their eyes fixed on the work in hand; she imagined conveyor-belts rolling, wheels turning, great hammers falling, sharpened steel hissing, hot filings shattering the air with sparks. And she pictured him in there, among those hundreds of figures in their identical blue.

Where exactly would he be? Probably somewhere between the fifth and sixth windows. Would she recognise him if he were suddenly to come out? She dismissed the thought. How silly. Of course she would. One movement of his hand, the way he turned his head – she'd know him anywhere, she knew him so well that he was a part of her, that was why she loved him. What was the expression on his face at this moment, she wondered? Concentration, like the other workers? Or perhaps sadness?

The wall of light cleared before her eyes and suddenly she could see everything inside the workshop as clearly as if she had walked through the door. She saw the wheels, the belts and the hammers, and the blue figures moving methodically about their business – and she saw him. His face was pinched, and his eyes – what lay behind those eyes? Was he suffering? Did he know why she had come today, did he sense that she had finally come to a decision after much anguish and conflict, and that she too was suffering?

Maybe. But why couldn't she stop thinking only of *his* unhappiness? What about her own aching sadness, this spectre of the loneliness which was staring her in the face? And . . . ah, now she was drowning in the sweet tenderness of her feelings for him . . . !

No, her resolve mustn't weaken. She mustn't look in through the window. Forget him working on the machines in there. Ignore the pain in his eyes. Shake off the chains of love and make her own life. No looking back.

She started walking again. That was the way to do it – pursue her own goal in life alone, with no one to stop her or divert her along the way. Walk on as she was walking now, through the darkness, knowing there was a light ahead, knowing there was always her work. It would be hard, she knew that. It was hard now, with her feet sinking into the gravel at every step, her arms laden with books and shopping-bags, the hem of her skirt flapping about her ankles. But what did all that matter in the end? God knows, it was hard to be alone. But in return she would have her freedom, she would belong once more to the scientific work she loved, and her life would be free of misunderstandings, pain and arguments. She would no longer be hurt by his failure to listen to her or value the work she loved. Was it possible to *love* and *not* suffer? She didn't know. But why shouldn't she try instead to *live*, and not love him so desperately any more? She no longer really cared whether or not he listened to her or understood her.

For so long she had lived for the times when they were together, longing only to see him, convincing herself over and over again that he really did love her. But what had happened to her work in all this time? Nothing! Despite the fact that it was so well planned and original, she had made absolutely no progress with it over the past months! She recalled all the times she had woken up in the morning, her brain burning with the knowledge that in the past five months she had written no more than thirty-two pages, had collected no new material, and hadn't once visited her old professor, her supervisor and inspiration.

Work steadily and do a bit each day, that had been his advice to her. Instead of which she had done nothing but wait, worry and live only to see her beloved, counting the minutes between meetings, and returning from her visits drained and distraught, her head empty and her heart full of grief – yes, she could admit it now, grief. And anger that another day had been wasted and still she had written only thirty-two pages.

What if she really was incapable of achieving anything, as he kept telling her she was? Other people managed to get things done in spite of their problems, why couldn't she? Perhaps this was something all women shared, this conflict between love and work.

These and many other doubts had grown within her over the past weeks, tormenting her, tearing her apart. Terrified of being alone, she had longed for him to be with her to help her forget her fears, and she had telephoned the factory office.

'Hello, has the lunch break started yet? . . . It has? Could you ask Pyotr Mikhailovich to come to the phone please? . . . Darling, is that you? . . . When can we meet? . . . You can't get away today? . . . Why not, too busy? . . . I'll come and see you then. I'm feeling so wretched without you . . .'

She had immediately set off on the train to see him. Her heart would leap for joy and she would fling herself into his arms the moment she saw him, then she would try to tell him how miserable she was that her work had ground to a halt. Yet she knew that the more she struggled to explain herself to him, the less she managed to communicate across the chasm that was separating them. He seemed incapable of listening to her.

So what? he'd say. Stop making a fuss and get on with it – it'll sort itself out. Why didn't she bring her work and move in with him? That way she wouldn't have to waste time travelling to and fro. She needed the library? She could still visit her precious library. Just like a woman, worrying about nothing . . . And so on and so forth. She knew how it would go.

And she knew that later, when they had made love and she was lying in his arms, something would tug at her heart, and she would grow tense. They'd be lying so close together, yet she would feel terribly alone and distant from him in a desert of desperation and loneliness, trapped in feelings she hadn't the words to describe. And they would freeze her heart.

As she imagined their meeting, and how at once again he would fail to understand her, she could only think this was somehow because *she* was hurting *him*. And she knew that soon she would be feeling sorry for him (for he was much younger than her in many ways). Altogether it would be better if she held her tongue when she saw him, and thought more about her work than about him. She had had enough!

Now she had decided to put all her energy into her work, she would no longer have to suffer his insults and hide her resentment. Time wouldn't hang heavy on her hands any more, for she would no longer be sacrificing her life, her tenderness, to him. No more counting the hours or killing time, for she would be living alone again, on her own terms. The first thing she must do when she got back was to visit her professor and collect some material. From then on it would be work, work and more work. It wasn't too late – her life was ahead of her! She could still enrich science with her ideas, make her small contribution to the new Russia. All it needed was a mighty effort of will – and that meant banishing for a while all thoughts of love and marriage. Her mind was made up, and she knew it must be right, for life suddenly seemed much easier. Her decision even brought with it a kind of happiness. Come what may, she must stick to it. She quickened her step, and soon the factory lights were behind her.

The fresh autumn wind fanned her face and teased the ends of her scarf as she set off across the vast reaped field to the residential part of the town where her lover lived. She shivered with apprehension as she plunged across the field. She was now enveloped by darkness and chilled to the bone.

For a moment she glanced back regretfully, longing to retrace her steps towards the bright factory she had left behind . . . Perish the thought! How could she be so craven! How could she dream of going back there, just to wait by the gates until the night shift ended! How childish to be afraid of the dark at her age!

To her right was a sharp slope with a clump of trees at the bottom. What was that rustling sound down there? It must be the wind, she told herself, but it frightened her. What was that, crawling out of the bushes – some person or thing . . . ? Now she was beside herself with fear. There was no point in shouting for help, no one would hear. She could see the factory lights blazing.

He was there, so near, but he'd never hear her cries through the
din of the machinery. She must walk on quickly and stop
dithering on the slope, shivering and frightened to death.

'You're a coward and you're afraid of the dark. You thought
you'd manage on your own? Living alone as an "independent
woman"? There's no such thing! You sweet little thing, you're a
woman at heart, and you know it . . .' That's what he'd say to her
with that easy laugh of his, and for once she thought he might be
right.

She walked on briskly. She mustn't waste time thinking about
her fear of the dark; she must think about how she was going to
tell him. How would she broach it? And when? Today, yes today,
the moment they met, the moment he got back to his room after
work. But was that the best time? He'd be worn out and she'd feel
so close to him, so excited to see him again.

'Aha, so my runaway housewife has paid me a visit!' he'd say,
'I've missed you, my love – why didn't you come before? Come
on now, confess, tell me what you've been up to. But before you
do . . .' And then her heart would submit so tenderly, and
shivering with delight she would press her body to his and close
her eyes . . . No, today was quite the wrong time to tell him.
Tomorrow would be much better, tomorrow morning.

As she skirted the hill a gust of wind lashed her face, tearing at
her hat and stirring the fallen leaves. What a dark and desolate
place this was! She turned, heading for the houses, and soon the
windows of the factory were mere faint patches of light and the
din faded. Far ahead she could make out the lights of the
workers' living quarters where his flat was – one small room
and a kitchen – but how far she still had to go!

Her legs ached, her arms were weighed down with parcels and
bags, and she was chilled through. She cursed the wind, and
shrank from the dark bushes which rocked and stretched their
gnarled arms out to her. Once again there was that ominous
rustling among the leaves, and she froze. Suddenly the wind had

become some other nameless force; this was the terror she had experienced so often in childhood when, alone for the night in her dark nursery, she would feel 'them' – those fearful, incomprehensible yet lifelike creatures – creeping out of the corners.

It's probably a passer-by, she told herself firmly, or a dog.

The path was narrow, and she kept stumbling. Burdock clung to her skirt. At that moment she would give anything to be with people – surrounded by the lights and bustle of town. What had possessed her to come here at night? Why couldn't she have been more patient? What difference did one day make – why did it have to be today? She had been ridiculously over-anxious, unable to focus on anything but her own desperate need to finish with him and lead her own life. She could imagine herself so clearly in her new life, in the room she loved, among her books and manuscripts, sitting by the lamp at her writing desk, and hearing . . .

She stopped dead in her tracks. What was that muffled silvery peal, like a church bell. Where was it coming from? Then she relaxed. Of course, it was the sound of the railway signal borne on the wind. How stupid of her. She started off again, determined to hurry, but her skirt flapped about her legs and hampered her every step. She lifted her legs higher to lengthen her stride. Her back tingled and she had the sickening sensation that someone was following her and was about to seize hold of her from behind.

She swung round. There was nobody. Silence. The air was light and damp, smelling of earth and old leaves. She took several deep breaths. By now the factory lights had disappeared completely.

The wind started up again, but now it was a mysterious night wind, quite unlike the winds of daytime Whipping and whirling, swirling and surging, this wind had sovereign power over the night. It chased long spectral shadows. She couldn't see them, but she knew they were there. They were very close too, for couldn't she hear them rustling and stirring, couldn't she sense them retreating and approaching, brushing her as they passed?

She was unspeakably frightened now. There! She felt them again. Yet she could see nothing but the night, thick and stifling. Her leaden feet moved as in a dream. She wanted to shout, but the sound of her own voice terrified her. She wanted to run, but she felt too weak. She wanted to break free of the dark and escape to a place where there were people and lights – to run, run . . . !

Heavy black wings flapped around her head, and she was surrounded by something hooting and puffing cold breath in her face. Behind her and all about her now the elongated spectres whirled, touching her, grasping her. Her head would burst – she could endure no more. Air, she needed air. Fiery red and blue circles whirled and leapt before her eyes. A heavy bell boomed and trembled in her ears, flooding the earth with its sound. Gasping for breath, she rushed forward, and crashed unconscious to the ground . . .

2

'Tell me what happened, What have you been up to? Fighting again? Did someone scare you out there? Did you hurt yourself? Have you sprained your ankle? Tell me why you're crying – are you hurt? Tell me, don't be upset, please stop crying!'

'I'm all right honestly, I'm just happy you're here.'

'Well I should hope I *would* be, silly. Now won't you tell me how you ended up half dead in a field? I'm walking home from work, and suddenly I hear this sound in the distance, more of a squeak than a sob. There's someone being strangled over there, I thought, or maybe it's a suicide or a robbery. So anyway I run to the spot, and what do I see but this person huddled on the path, surrounded by a pile of parcels. You tell me the rest. Tell me who frightened you – I'm still in the dark.'

'Nothing happened. I'm sorry but it's true, nothing happened. I was just being stupid and suddenly felt afraid of the dark, so I began to run. I thought my heart was going to burst, my head was spinning, and I tripped and fell. I'm all right now you're here – oh how good you are to me, I love you so much – much, much more than you can imagine. I'd never leave you, you know that, don't you? Not for anything in the world.'

'Stop being so silly – have I ever asked you to leave? Oh dear, now you're crying again, I only wanted to comfort you. Put your head on my shoulder, that's right, I let me warm your hands – they're like blocks of ice. You just relax now and tell me what happened in the field. Please, I must know, were you attacked?' He peered at her. He was clearly losing patience, becoming confused and suspicious.

'But I keep telling you – no one hurt me, nothing happened, I just . . .'

'Oh come on, how d'you expect me to believe that? I saw you sprawled semi-conscious at dead of night, alone in the middle of a field, with your bags scattered around you, your skirt torn to shreds . . .'

'All right then, I'll tell you. I'd made up my mind to come and see you immediately and not wait until morning, that was why I was walking to your room in the middle of the night. I'd spent yesterday steeling myself to do it, I wanted to try and tell you everything. I can't go on like this. You don't love me as a friend or as a comrade, or even just another human being – you love me only as a woman. You can't grasp the fact that I need to work. I need . . . No, I can't bear it any longer.'

'I'm sorry, I don't understand.' He spoke coolly, withdrawing slightly from her. 'Perhaps you could tell me what it is you can't bear any longer?'

'I can't bear us to go on living like this, making each other miserable, arguing all the time, never understanding what the other's trying to say . . . When I think of all the energy we've wasted, all the times I've arrived back from your place feeling exhausted and drained and unable to put two thoughts together. D'you realise that in five months I've written only thirty-two pages of my thesis? When Vera Samsonovna wrote the other day to tell me hers was at the typesetters I thought of mine . . . I'll never be allowed to stay on the course if I don't finish it this year, and then that'll be goodbye to all my dreams, goodbye to my future in science . . .'

'Who's standing in your way then?' His voice remained cool.

'That's not the point. The point is that since we've been together I've spent every moment feeling torn between you and my work – it's not as if I haven't tried to tell you, you just don't understand, in fact I think you deliberately refuse to understand. And now I don't think I can take any more. It would be easy if I didn't love you so much . . .'

'Oh cut it out. You know I hate meaningless words; it makes no sense to say you love me. When two people are in love, they want to live together, spend time together, that's how we non-scientists understand the word. To you it apparently means the opposite. But I've given up trying to understand what you want. You spend day after day at your place in town, leaving me here alone with nothing to do but work – it's not as though I don't have any work of my own, you know, lots of it. I don't talk about it but I could do with some support from you. But that's by the way, I'm not complaining. I'd hate to stand in your way if you've made up your mind to be a scientist. What more is there to say?'

'But I want you to try to understand me, darling! It's only because of my work that I can't live here with you.'

'Well let's talk about this work of yours. Will you please tell me why living with me makes it impossible? I spend ten hours a day at the factory – you can hardly complain that I'm around the house all day getting under your feet. Why can't you work at my place?'

'But I have tried to explain to you. I have to go to lectures and

to the lab. I need my books and the library. I can't work in a
camp. I tried, you know.' Gloomily she shook her head. 'I tried to
make a go of it here with you; it was the damned housework and
cooking that made it impossible.'

'I should think so too! Why should a lady scientist do housework!'

'Stop, or you'll make me angry. I feel so tired, so fed up.'

'And what about me? *You're* fed up – don't you think I'm fed
up? D'you think I have an easy time with you, having to fall in
with *your* wishes all the time?'

'So why in god's name are we dragging on with it?' she
shouted at him in a sudden frenzy of range. 'I came to see you
today because I wanted to say that to you, to tell you I can't go
on. My energy's draining away, there's no pleasure left in it for
you or for me; we're just torturing each other. Let's end it, now!
I'm going to leave you . . . !'

'Leave me then, lead your own life! Why did you come here?
What d'you want from me? Did you think I'd throw myself at
your feet blubbering and beseeching you to stay? Think on! I
don't go in for that kind of behaviour!'

'That's a horrible way to talk, stop it!'

'Horrible eh? You think you're so superior? I suppose you
think . . .'

'I don't think anything. I don't want to either at the moment –
I only want you to leave me alone.'

'I'm not touching you!'

Dawn was glimmering through the window and the oil lamp
was burning low. They sat in a brooding, angry silence, alone
with their thoughts.

'All the same,' he resumed more gently, 'I would like to know
what happened to you out there last night, and about that
"decision" of yours – there must be some connection.' Once
again she saw the suspicion in his eyes as he glanced at her.

'Please can't we change the subject – I've told you. My nerves are shot. I haven't been sleeping. I keep racking my brains for a solution.'

'Yes?'

'Why are you looking at me like that, as if you didn't believe me?'

'Well after seeing you lying there, tears pouring down your face, bags and parcels scattered about you on the ground, you must admit it's a bit hard for me to believe you. Won't you tell me what happened? All right, I know it's over between us, but I still care about you. If something's happened. Well, there are tramps prowling about those fields. Believe me, I won't think the worse of you, please stop lying and tell me as a friend what happened.'

'What are you suggesting? How *dare* you? Why do you refuse to understand?'

She was becoming more and more inarticulate and agitated. 'What sort of a friend are you? You have no respect or sympathy for me. Why do you leap to conclusions? Why is that always in your mind? Of course, that's it! Now I understand why I have to leave you – because when you talk down to me in that insulting way I want to run and run, far away from you, just like I tried to run away from the ghosts last night. I can't imagine why I love you still . . .'

Immediately the words were out he softened. 'Do you mean that? Do you really love me still?'

'But why else d'you think I'd be so miserable? These past few days I've never been so miserable in my life. Twenty times I made up my mind to leave you, twenty times I thought better of it. One moment I felt I couldn't live without you, next moment I'd think of my work and your attitudes . . .'

'My attitudes to what?'

'Oh you know, darling. You don't love me, no you don't, not how I understand it anyway.'

'I don't know what you mean' he said airily, visibly relieved.

359

'But let's not bother about that now. What bothers me, you silly thing, is your strange behaviour. I know you keep trying to convince me you're going to be a scientist and you're as good as a man, but despite all that research of yours you seem a bit lacking in common sense. Frankly you surprise me sometimes. You say you love me, yet in the same breath you say you want to leave me – what am I to make of that? Don't you think you must be a little soft in the head to come out with that? Now madam, look at me with your lovely eyes,' he took her hand, 'and tell me what you're thinking about. Go on, give us a nice smile. So you still love me, do you? What am I to do with you? I don't know – an intelligent, independent woman afraid of the dark! However did you get in such a panic? And to think you were going to leave me! All I want is to protect you and look after you. I suppose you knew deep down you couldn't go through with it. Why don't you snuggle closer and give me a big hug – I know you love me, of course you do. Honestly I can't think what this argument has been about, unless you want to torment me for some reason, and yourself too. On second thoughts, perhaps you just need to be treated more like a woman – I'm going to put my foot down and *forbid* you to leave me; I won't let you go, and that's the end of it! Why don't we go to your place tomorrow and collect your books, then you can move in with me – isn't that a great idea? We'll start all over again and everything will be fine, you'll see . . . Why are you staring at me with those great big terrified eyes of yours?'

'Not terrified.'

'What then?'

'They're just thinking their own thoughts.'

'Can I ask what about?'

'No point in talking about it really, not now anyway.'

'If that's how you feel,' he sighed. 'But I'll never be able to make you out . . . Look it's almost light, you must be exhausted, we've been talking for hours . . . Tell me what you're thinking?'

'Nothing I can put into words, please stop asking,' she stroked his head tenderly. 'Please don't be anxious. You're sweet, you know that.' She wanted so much to ease his pain – he might have been her child, for he was as tough, unthinking and resourceful as a child, and he certainly loved her in his own way. Why not try to work things out with him, stay here for a while, postpone her decision?

'Well then, tomorrow afternoon we'll go and fetch your books. We can put up some shelves for them here, then you'll be mistress of this house. How about it?'

'Yes, how about it?' But the idea filled her with gloom. Her books . . . Why, this would mean moving out of her room for good! And what about her thesis? What about the professor? What about the library? It would mean goodbye to her work and all hopes of finishing it by January. No she must escape, find some excuse to go to town alone. Fast. Tomorrow. First thing . . .

'Why are you looking so wretched? Why are there tears in your eyes again? Tell me.'

'I'm crying because I love you still, I love you so much . . . !'

Conversation Piece

The man flung open the compartment door at Berlin's Frie-
drichstrasse Station and stood aside for the woman as she
stepped out. Everything about him – his confident, knowing
look, his sensual lips – radiated youthful energy. Unlike her. She
was thin and fragile, with untidy dark hair which hung in a long
fringe over her anxiously raised eyebrows. Her tired face showed
the shadows of experience.

'To think if we hadn't happened to meet like this you'd have
slipped off without saying goodbye to me! You must be the
greatest fool I ever met – I can hardly credit it!' His snappish tone
was in contrast with the expression in his eyes, which told a very
different story. 'To think of all the letters you wrote, telling me
how passionately you missed me, how you couldn't live a
moment longer without me! And then you run off like that,
without a word! Why, even common logic should have told
you . . .'

'I did miss you, yes indeed I did, you know that, but won't you
try to see my side . . . ?'

'Why should I? You listen to me. You're putting yourself and
me through hell, and the reason is, you're a fool. All that rubbish
about being a "free woman" or whatever you call it – a "single
woman", is it? It sounds damn silly to me. Be your own boss, is
that what you want, eh? Lucky you, is all I can say. As well as
that legally wedded husband you get down on bended knee to
every day – that's what husbands are for, aren't they? – you have

me. What d'you want of me? How am I any less of a husband than he is? Tell me that!'

'Now you're the one who's being stupid, Kotinka. Please try to understand. You see, for ten years he and I have worked together. Emotionally, intellectually, in every way we've been so united. You must see how precious that is to me.'

'All right, there's nothing wrong with that I suppose – it's just your enslavement to him I can't stomach. Look at you, a "free woman", preaching and writing about woman's emancipation, then you get down on your knees saying "forgive me Vanechka darling, I've wronged you, I promise never to be unfaithful again".'

'Must you always joke about it?'

'I don't see what else I can do. I suppose I could wring my hands and go into a frenzy of jealousy over you and your precious "feelings". But no, I thought, better not get too worked up – it's my nature to be easygoing. So tell me, what is this ideal couple, linked by all their deep spiritual affinities, going to do next – or shouldn't I ask? I suppose you'll return to him and beg him to take you back. Then, ever so magnanimously, he'll accept you, you'll write more books together, everything will go back to how it was before, and you'll be his grateful servant for ever more. Ah well, you'll just have to trample on all the "guilty dreams" you had about me, over which you used to sigh so poetically in your letters. You'll have to put me out of your mind, won't you? You wouldn't want to recognise me if we bumped upto again. You'll have to forget those evenings we spent walking in the Tiergarten, not to mention my "deadly kisses". And . . .'

'Stop it Kotya, stop being so cruel!'

'Ah, so *I'm* being cruel now! It's *you* who are leaving me, remember? It's *you* who decided you couldn't bear to sacrifice *his* peace of mind for this young lad who seems to have some deadly hold over you and only knows about loving and kissing. It's you who are leaving me – so don't you call *me* cruel, right? Its not logical!'

He tried to maintain this insouciant tone, but his nervousness was nonetheless evident. She sat slumped on the station bench, her head bowed. He stood beside her. Both were silent a moment.

'Kotya?' She looked up, pleading with him.

'Yes?' His eyes met hers.

'Can't you understand – it's difficult for me too.'

'So what d'you expect me to do – feel sorry for you? Be your ever-sympathetic and faithful follower? No thanks. I did that before, and I'm not doing it again, understand? I can't think why you don't leave him if he's making you so unhappy. Go on, be brave, do it! You're an independent woman, you're free, you don't need him. Think how *we've* loved each other, ever since that first night, think how good it's always been, think how you'd melt in my arms this very moment if . . . Oh, cut the hypocrisy my darling foolish woman, start making your own life again. Why are you doing this to us? What's the point of inflicting all this punishment and suffering on us both? Oh yes, a moment ago I might have been laughing, but how do you imagine I'm feeling inside? How can I bear to let you leave me? Please, stay with me tonight. Hold me one last time as you promised you would. Stay with me tonight – then decide. If you choose to go back to him then, that's your funeral. But now come with me – I've waited for you so long. Morning, noon and night I've waited. The flowers won't bloom until you love me again, come with me now. Please. It's not much to ask when you're taking away everything I have . . .'

'But Kotya, how *can* I? How could I look him in the eyes when I got back? How could I live with myself? I hate myself, I hate everything!'

'Now everyone's watching you cry – and you an independent woman too! I believe now what you told me the first night we met. You said, "you're quite wrong about me, you know". Do you remember? "I'm really the most ordinary woman you could imagine, with all kinds of silly prejudices, and your ways don't attract me in the slightest." Aha, you do remember! And d'you remember how I replied? Yes, you obviously do, because you're grinning all over your face. Well, if you insist on crying in public, I shall employ a time-honoured remedy right here in front of everyone, and you'll only have yourself to blame. Oh, so you won't, you coward!'

'No, I won't,' she said firmly. 'I'm not going to compromise myself for you, because you're not worth it! I don't care enough about you. Look, there's the Charlottenburg train. Come on, quick, let's catch it before it leaves. No more talk now, that can wait – we can talk afterwards, after we've said goodbye each other, for ever . . .'

The two figures disappeared into the crowd.

Afterword
Sheila Rowbotham

In these moving love stories Kollontai pursues themes from her non-fiction writing – particularly those from *Communism and the Family* and *The New Morality and the Working Class*. She was concerned with the complicated connections between personal life and political ideas, and was convinced that relations between the sexes must be freed from the restraints imposed by women's economic dependence on men.

Yet she tried always to examine the gap between the official surface of things and the actuality within – and would not rest content with the easy formula that changes in the mode of production and the external structures of work relations under communism would automatically create a new freedom and equality between the sexes.

Though completely opposed to those feminists who thought there could be women's emancipation within capitalism, she also fought continually inside the Bolshevik party against the kind of complacency which failed to take sexual relations and the positive creation of a new culture of daily life seriously. She wanted complete equality between the sexes, realizing that this necessitated big changes in the structure of the family, the organization of domestic work and the economic position of women.

Convinced of the need for all these changes, she also indicates

in her non-fiction writing that she hoped for an inner transformation – for a 'new eros under communism', a love which
extended throughout humanity. Kollontai is more optimistic
about emotional love between her women characters than
passionate sexual love between men and women. Indeed, the
conflict between passion and freedom appears in her writing
almost as a natural tension. And in addition Kollontai realized
that there was more than the ideal future to consider; there was
the immediate – and difficult – present. The past haunted this
present, and the peculiar circumstances of 'socialism in one
country'. Civil war, scarcity and reconstruction restricted the
emergence of the new culture of which she conceived.

Kollontai shows how the state of the Soviet economy in the
New Economic Policy period helped maintain old-style relationships between men and women. Free unions became a cover for
male irresponsibility, and women were left with the children.
Communal housing turned into overcrowded barracks. The
material problems facing the country fed the conservatism of
the vast majority of women – for them, new freedom also meant
insecurity, and perhaps better the devil you knew . . . It is clear
in these stories how much Kollontai felt it necessary to struggle
against this conservatism.

Her characters experience conflict between their desire to
create new forms of personal relationships and the need to
subordinate their personal feelings to the revolutionary cause.
The grandmother in 'Three Generations' believes in 'the great
love' and defies convention to follow her ideal, with painful
consequences. Her daughter Olga Sergeevna appears on the
surface quite removed from the inner turmoils of physical
passion – a responsible, competent party cadre: the reality is,
however, quite different. Vasilisa Malygina sees changes in
living as a form of learning; political education is not just a
matter of new ideas, but of creating a culture of everyday life.
She struggles with a recalcitrant co-operative household, and

against being overwhelmed by sexual longing for her husband. These sexual feelings conflict with her dislike of her role of the passive, director's wife, and with her political beliefs; and she finally breaks with her love, deciding to bring up her child 'in true communist fashion'. Vladimir, her husband, on the other hand, falls easily into a traditional bourgeois pattern of masculinity. He is, in the final resort, ready to accept the divisions of wife and mistress, respecting one, desiring the other, one belonging to his public world, the other the object of his passion. His desire for Vasilisa is diminished by his unease with her political principles, by which he feels criticized, and this affects their whole relationship. Absorbed in his work, he is also able to cut himself off from his feelings.

At the time all these stories were written, sexuality was a subject of great controversy in many countries. The conservative elements saw the feminist movements, easier divorce, freer relationships between the sexes as part of a process of disintegration; for liberals these events represented an evolution towards progress. Marxists frequently dismissed sexuality as peripheral, seeing it as subject simply to changes in the external structures of social relations.

Kollontai was conscious always of a more complex dialectic. In her stories she describes economic and social circumstances *and* inner patterns of feelings. She was aware of an unevenness in the relation between new social forms and sexual passion – an unevenness which bore the weight of centuries of oppression. Here Kollontai is straining towards an alternative culture of communism, which would transform all human relationships. Though the context for such a culture has completely changed, and we face a very different political situation, the problems that Alexandra Kollontai so intensely describes persist. If the setting and some of the assumptions seem strange to us, the stories still have an immediate relevance.

Glossary

Names Russians have a first ('Christian') name, a patronymic and a surname. The customary mode of address is first name plus patronymic, thus, Vasilisa Dementevna, Maria Semenovna. There are more intimate abbreviations of first names which have subtly affectionate, patronizing or friendly overtones. So for instance Vasilisa becomes Vasya, Vasyuk, and Vladimir becomes Volodya, Volodka, Volodechka, Volya.

Meals The main meal, lunch, at this period was usually eaten between 3.00 and 5.00 in the afternoon. There would be a light meal before going to bed.

Name days In the atheist Soviet Union people nevertheless still celebrated their saints' days.

Names, events, groups before and after the Revolution are listed chronologically.

BEFORE THE REVOLUTION

Emancipation of the serfs After the Crimean War, the return of demobilized soldiers to the impoverished countryside exacerbated thousands of peasants' revolts, which finally forced Alexander II to emancipate the serfs in 1861.

Zemstvo Introduced after Emancipation as the elected provincial authority. Though without any real executive powers, it came under much police pressure at the end of the nineteenth century, as *zemstvo* liberals took up more radical positions. By 1905 it had already become officially representative of conservative public opinion.

Populism Populists (active around 1860–95) believed Russia could achieve revolution (bypassing capitalism) by strengthening the peasant commune, regarded as the embryo of socialism. Populists travelled to the countryside to learn from the peasants and to urge them to seize land.

Mobile libraries Used by Populists to take books to the peasants.

Socialist Revolutionaries (srs) various Populist groups joined together in the 1890s to form this party, which believed that the revolution would be achieved by the peasants rather than the urban workers. They carried out many terrorist attacks against local governors in the period 1901–5. In February 1917, the srs rose to high government positions, and after October 1917 they struggled against the Bolsheviks, splitting off from the pro-Bolshevik left sr group.

Union of Struggle for the Liberation of the Working Class Underground illegal Marxist organization founded in St Petersburg in 1895 by Lenin and Martov with the aim of training factory workers, theoretically and practically, to prepare them for their role as the nucleus of a new centralized revolutionary party.

The 'Reaction' These stories mention two periods when revolutionary activities provoked extreme reactionary measures against the entire Russian population – after the assassination of Alexander II in 1881, and the period following the 1905 revolution.

Suyatopolk-Mirsky Minister of the Interior from 1904. It was thought his liberal reputation would ensure a period of reforms, but it was he who was responsible for ordering soldiers to shoot

down workers in St Petersburg in the peaceful demonstration on
9 January 1905.

Bolsheviks and Mensheviks. The Russian Social Democratic party
split decisively into two groups in 1903. Lenin and the Bolsheviks
as they called themselves, wanted a small party of dedicated
revolutionaries, while Martov and the Mensheviks wanted a party
open to all who accepted its programme and was willing to obey its
leadership. The February 1917 revolution was largely set off by
Mensheviks while Lenin was in exile, and between February and
October 1917 the antagonism between them was at its most acute.
It was when (thanks largely to Trotsky) the Military Revolutionary
Committee of the Petrograd Soviet joined the Bolsheviks that
soldiers were able to seize power for the Bolsheviks on 25 October
1917, and installed the new government.

Soviets Emerged in the 1905 revolution as councils elected by
strike committees to co-ordinate and supervise their demands.
The first and most important soviet was the St Petersburg one,
but soviets rapidly spread throughout all the major towns of
Russia. Trotsky, who was close to the Mensheviks in the 1905
period, led the St Petersburg soviet, in which members of the
various socialist parties predominated. By February 1917, soviets
in all towns were knows as 'soviets of the workers' and 'soldiers'
deputies'. The creation of the new Petrograd soviet and the
assumption of power by the Provisional government happened
within days of each other and inaugurated a period of dual
power, in which the soviet constantly undermined the latter's
authority, especially in the army.

When Lenin returned to Russia in April 1917 demanding 'All
Power to the Soviets', he meant the Bolsheviks in the soviets, as
well as the soviets themselves as a rudimentary form of self-
management. Since then, Bolsheviks and soviets have often
been referred to interchangeably.

By September 1917, the Bolsheviks already had a majority in

various soviets, including Petrograd, and could use the Military Revolutionary Committee of the Petrograd soviet as the co-ordinating centre of the October revolution. By the early 1920s the soviets had evolved into local one-party bodies of the Bolsheviks, and Stalin was later to describe them as 'transmission belts from the party to the masses'.

Duma The State Duma was set up after the 1905 revolution by the Tsar as a weak parliamentary body for discussing legislation. The peasantry was heavily represented, and there were a few members of the urban working-class. Nevertheless, the Social Democrats were able to use the Duma as a forum for criticizing the government.

Provisional Government; February revolution February 1917 the Tsar decreed the dissolution of the Duma, at which the Duma's Provisional Committee was set up with the intention of reforming rather than abolishing the monarchy. After negotiations with the (largely Menshevik) Petrograd Soviet, the Provisional Committee announced the formation of a new Provisional government, and the Tsar was forced to abdicate.

'Liberationist position' ie a member of the Union of Liberation, a liberal landowning organization working within the Duma for a programme of universal suffrage and a variety of social reforms. In October 1905 it was assimilated into the Constitutional Democratic party.

Eduard Bernstein The German Social Democrat economist who attacked Marxism's economic foundations, arguing that the path of reform and steady economic pressure from the trade unions would achieve more for the working class than a proletarian revolution.

'Defensist position' The Mensheviks were divided in their attitude to the First World War. One group, the Defensists, took the

patriotic line of most of the European social democrat parties in supporting the war, while the Internationalists, like the Bolsheviks, saw the war as the prelude to the coming international revolution.

AFTER THE REVOLUTION

'October Days' The days in October 1917 when the Bolsheviks took power.

Civil War Many anti-Bolshevik groups joined forces to fight the authority of the new government. A White Army was formed out of these groups, to fight the powerful Red Army created in 1918 by Trotsky, and under his leadership. The Bolshevik government was under constant threat from the fighting, which continued from 1918 until 1921 when the Western armies propping up the White forces were eventually withdrawn.

Industrial Front The economic crisis created by the civil war necessitated the organization of workers into labour armies and the militarization of labour.

New Economic Policy (NEP, hence nepman and nepwoman) Introduced by Lenin at the 10th party Congress in 1921, after the Bolshevik civil war victory. The economic and political alliance of the proletariat (urban working class) and the peasantry, threatened during the civil war by economic pressures and grain requisitions, was to be safeguarded by granting peasants relatively free use of the land and its products. NEP's main aim was to 'increase at all costs the quantity of output', to expand large-scale industry, and thus provide the economic basis for the dictatorship of the proletariat. Although the 'commanding heights' of the economy remained under state control, private enterprise was selectively authorized and so was born the 'nepman'.

'One-man' management of industry; was the manner in which many party members described this selective private control of the economy.

'Nepman' These were the new managers, directors, 'red' merchants all of whom prospered under the new economy. Many bourgeois industrialists and technical specialists who had flourished before the revolution had considerable control over small enterprises under the NEP.

'Nepwomen' These were the wives of nepmen, or women who kept company with these men. (The term is, needless to say, a derogatory one.)

Trust companies Small private enterprises were encouraged under the NEP to combine into units called trusts, whose fixed capital was in state hands.

Syndicates Trusts could combine into larger groups called syndicates.

Red Guards Armed Bolshevik detachments before the revolution, encouraged and funded by the Bolsheviks during the Provisional government.

Co-operatives Established after the emancipation of the serfs, they accompanied the growth of numerous small business enterprises. Co-operatives set up direct channels to the sources of supply, and many of them became rich and politically powerful after the revolution.

GPU September 1917 saw the establishment of the 'Cheka', the Commission for the Struggle against Sabotage and the Counter-revolution. In 1922 it was replaced by the Government Political Administration (GPU), the political police force. Today it comes under the KGB.

Central Committee of the Bolshevik party Elected by party congresses as the executive arm of the party, instructed by the party rules to direct the whole work of the party in the intervals between congresses. Under Lenin, the Central Committee was an important decision-making body.

party membership Because the Bolsheviks initially defined themselves by their illegal underground activities, there was little fear that the party would attract unsuitable opportunist members. For most people, the dangers and difficulties of membership in the civil war period did not provide much incentive to join, although as early as 1919 the open-door policy was threatening the party with an influx of careerists. Recruitment constantly alternated with 'sifting out', and party membership fluctuated. It was, however, in the 20s, a predominantly male party (only $7\frac{1}{2}$ per cent of its members were women in 1922, most of them politically inexperienced and without formal education).

Apropos of Vladimir's threatened expulsion in 'Vasilisa Malygina', it is interesting to note that of the members expelled in the early 30s, most were expelled for political 'passivity', about a quarter for 'bourgeois life style', drunkenness or careerism, and a small number for bribery and corruption.

Komsomol The youth organization of the party. Its initially loose connection with Bolsheviks strengthened in 1919; the Komsomol reached its peak of activity in the civil war, but membership dropped sharply after 1921.

Central Control Commission Set up by the party Central Committee to direct the party purges (which hadn't yet acquired the sinister connotations they had under Stalin).

House of Motherhood Kollontai wanted to see buildings all over Russia where women could go and learn about birth control, child-birth and child care.

Prostitutes Prostitution was legal in Tsarist Russia, and prostitutes had to carry 'yellow tickets' instead of passports, and work in registered houses. Prostitution decreased sharply after the revolution only to rise again with the rise in women's unemployment under the NEP.

The 'New Morality' The ambiguous connotations of this phrase reveal much both of people's optimism and their fears about the way in which their private sexual lives suddenly became so public after the revolution. It was used optimistically by those who welcomed the benefits of the humane marriage laws and divorce legislation, and the legalizing of abortion. It was used derisively by many people in the party for whom it meant free love and frivolous promiscuity. It is significant that, in 'Vasilisa Malygina', the fact that Vasilisa's marriage to Vladimir was a common-law one was considered unimportant.

Lightning Source UK Ltd.
Milton Keynes UK
UKOW04f1007081117
312356UK00001B/15/P